Praise for the novels of Frank Anthony Polito

"This former 1980s band fag declares *Band Fags!* totally wicked awesome."

—Josh Kilmer-Purcell,
The Fabulous Beekman Boys

"*Band Fags!* is like the gay teen flick John Hughes never got around to making..."

—Dennis Hensley,
author of *Misadventures in the (213)*

"The book jacket alone is enough to make anyone who loves a man in a white uniform with red trim quiver with glee..."

—Charlotte Abbott,
The Advocate

"Polito captures perfectly the acne and the angst of teen boys..."

—Richard Labonté,
Book Marks

"*Drama Queers!* is the 1980s version of *High School Musical*— only with characters who are a bit more overtly gay."

—*Philly Gay News*

"*Lost in the '90s* is a humorous and touching coming-of-age novel filled with modern day and past pop culture that may appeal, not only to teens and young adults, but also their parents... [5 stars]"

—*IndieReader*

Books by Frank Anthony Polito

BAND FAGS!

DRAMA QUEERS!

LOST IN THE '90s

T♦H♦E
SPIRIT OF
DETROIT

♦

FRANK ANTHONY POLITO

WOODWARD AVENUE BOOKS
Detroit

For information contact Woodward Avenue Books:
 WoodwardAvenueBooks@gmail.com

Grateful acknowledgment is made for permission to use the following:

"Star is Mine." Copyright © 1990 by Missy Gibson. From *A Ride on the Swinging Gate* by Strange Bedfellows.

First Trade Paperback Printing, September 2013

ISBN-13: 978-0-6157-1510-0
ISBN-10: 0-6157-1510-9

13 14 15 16 17 ◆ 10 9 8 7 6 5 4 3 2 1

DEDICATED TO
MY FELLOW DETROITERS

You've got the spirit, tell 'em you're from Detroit
C'mon let's hear it, tell 'em you're from Detroit
We're a team that's home town, there's no town like Motown
Stand up and tell 'em you're from Detroit!

—WXYZ-TV jingle

T◆H◆E
SPIRIT OF
DETROIT

1

WALKING ON BROKEN GLASS

◆   ◆   ◆

At the end of the summer, I had dinner with my dad the Detroit cop, whom I hadn't seen since up and abandoning him on Memorial Day to go and live an hour away in Ann Arbor. I'd spent the good part of the past three months in love with, and in the same apartment as, a handsome, egotistical second-year University of Michigan med student, whose existence my Baptist father knew nothing of—other than the fact that we'd been (quote-unquote) good friends during high school, sharing the spotlight in two different theatrical productions. But Richie Tyler and I had broken up, for the second time in twice as many years, and it appeared that I was once again without a place to call home. Dad and I both knew that our mutual breaking of bread that Monday evening in late August could only mean one thing.

"So you'd like your old room back, son?" He referred to the ten-by-twelve space as mine, but there were two others just like it on the second floor of the boarding house Dad owned, over near 9 Mile and Van Dyke in south Warren.

"If it's still available." I watched as he extracted the pointy wooden toothpicks, with their colored crinkly cellophane flags, from the middle of his Slim Jim before accidentally injuring himself mid-bite. I don't know why I felt so nervous. The man was my father after all, not just some landlord I was hoping to impress so he'd rent me a room for a hundred bucks a month.

Still, I drank more coffee than I did eat my sandwich, the bacon on my turkey club gone cold and limp. Dad rambled on and I listened, waiting for the dreaded reason as to why I was no longer welcome.

"You're a grown man. I can't take care of you anymore."

I felt for sure his hesitancy to have me residing under his roof would have something to do with my being a homosexual, a secret I'd been hiding from him for as long as I could recall, and one I'd hoped would remain unspoken until long after the man's weary bones were at last laid to rest.

Dad asked me what my plans were for the coming fall and, in a flash of confident calculation, I said more or less: It's the start of a new semester, and I'm waiting in the wings of a thousand seat theatre, where I will soon be temporarily blinded as I step out onto the stage before the illuminated footlights. Dressed in an ornate costume of only the finest material, I will play my designated part, speaking my dialogue with a clear and vibrant voice, taking care not to over articulate while projecting far enough so the patrons in the upper balcony will enjoy the performance as much as those in the orchestra. Around me, a cast of characters will support my creative endeavor. Following countless hours of meticulous preparation, the moment will arrive when we unleash unto the world our artistic undertaking, compelling a thousand pairs of hands to clap together in thunderous applause. After graciously taking our bows and returning to our humble, human existences, we will gather together at the local tavern and reward ourselves for a job well done by drinking ourselves into oblivion.

"I'm going back to school to study Theatre," I said in actuality. "Down at Wayne State."

Dad told me I was being impractical, and that he hoped my infantile dreams of becoming a *dramat* had long ago ended, after I'd failed to impress the Powers That Be at The Juilliard School in New York City. But something in his eyes said he understood that I needed to do this, and he wouldn't attempt to stop me, though he did have one final, pressing thought.

"Just how do you expect to pay for tuition?"

To quote the Bard of Avon, William Shakespeare, "That *is* the question!"

When I looked into transferring the few credits I'd accrued over the two years I'd spent attending Oakland Community College, right out of high school, one of the benefits I discovered about enrolling at Wayne State was that most of its thirty thousand-plus students commuted to the urban university on a daily basis from the outlying Detroit suburbs. With my dad's house being located less than ten miles to the north, all I'd have to do is hop on I-75 and make my way south each morning. I could easily be to school in twenty minutes, give or take, depending on traffic and/or road construction which, in Michigan, seemed a perpetual process.

I moved out of Richie's apartment on the 29th of August, taking with me all my Pet Shop Boys, Erasure, and Madonna CDs, along with the collection of play scripts I'd accumulated over the years I'd spent as a Drama Queer. At some point toward the end of the sexless and conversation-less finale of *Bradley Loves Richie*, I informed him that, as an aspiring actor, I was supposed to be the self-absorbed individual. I later told my friends I'd lived with a narcissist, and also that I'd found being a doctor's wife overrated.

After making the Pomp and Circumcision march across the football field just over four years prior, leaving Richie Tyler to fend for himself during his junior and senior years at Hazel Park High, I should've resigned myself to the fact that our fling was simply what it was: something we'd started when we were both still kids. Once I finally turned eighteen that September 4th, thus becoming a legal adult, Richie and I could no longer legally be together the way we'd been before, i.e., *intimately*.

Running into Richie last December down at The Gas Station while he was home on Christmas break was probably the biggest mistake I'd made since allowing my former friend

Bobby Russell to talk me into getting high and fooling around with him on a regular basis back when we were both still in junior high. In retrospect, I now realize I should've never allowed myself to allow Richie to follow me out back into the back alley serving as the bar's parking lot, or to follow me back to my father's place and up the back steps to the tiny room I'd been living in since politely being asked to leave my mother's home three years before by her homophobic (and eventual ex) husband, Albert.

The last weeks of my last summer leading up to my once again becoming a college co-ed flew by in a whirlwind of activity, sadly not of the social variety. Because my epiphany to return to the world of higher education had struck me so suddenly, I had to practically beg the registrars of my former educational institutions to provide me with my permanent records so I could complete the necessary paperwork to complete my enrollment down at WSU.

Founded in 1868, Wayne State was a public research university consisting of thirteen schools and colleges offering more than four hundred major areas of studies. The main campus encompassed over two hundred acres, comprised of education and research buildings, right in the heart of the Motor City. The first component of modern day Wayne State University was established as the Detroit Medical College. Old Main Hall, built in 1896 as Central High School, later began adding college classes in 1913, evolving into the Detroit Junior College in 1917, the four-year degree granting College of the City of Detroit in 1923, and more recently, the College of Liberal Arts and Sciences. In 1933, the Detroit Board of Education organized the six colleges it ran—education, engineering, liberal arts, medical, pharmacy, and a graduate school—into one united university. In January 1934, that institution was officially called Wayne University, taking its title from the county in which it was located, named for US Army general and statesman Anthony Wayne, who served during the Revolutionary War and later died of complications from gout during a return trip to Pennsylvania from a military post in Detroit.

Wayne University continued to grow, adding the Law School in 1927, the School of Social Work in 1935, and the School of Business Administration in 1946. Wayne University was christened Wayne *State* University in 1956, and the school became a constitutionally established university by an adopted amendment to the Michigan Constitution in 1959. In 1973, the College of Lifelong Learning was created, and in 1985, the College of Urban, Labor and Metropolitan Affairs along with the School of Fine and Performing Arts.

So one afternoon, on the day before September began, I strolled through the infamous (and once riotous) Cass Corridor, rounding the corner onto West Hancock in search of number 95. Down the block, a half-dozen Roman columns held up the façade of the historic Hilberry, home to Wayne State's graduate Acting Company. Walking past the wall of windows outside the Theatre Production Center, I looked into them at my reflection: my khaki pants, my button-down Oxford, my mess of Simply Red hair. Then I felt guilty for calling Richie conceited, and I glanced away.

There was hardly anyone in the building, the school year not officially under way until the following morning. I stepped into the lobby, my loafers clicking loudly against the polished tile. To my right, a narrow hallway led down to what appeared to be the costume shop, on the left. On the cinder block wall opposite, there loomed a large bulletin board, decorated by a collection of pinned-up announcements. I took a closer glance at the assortment of casting notices, rehearsal schedule call times, and costume fitting sign-up sheets. According to one colorful flyer, auditions were being held that very evening for the Bonstelle Theatre's season opener: a production of the vaudeville musical *Chicago* by Kander and Ebb, the creative team behind the 1970s Broadway classic *Cabaret.*

As if a door to another dimension had been unlocked and

opened, the hallway unexpectedly erupted into a tunnel of wind. The callboard sprang to life, its leaves of paper rustling in the blustery breeze. I glanced over my shoulder to see a Greek god of a guy appear through the building's front double doors. Well-muscled beneath his silk shirt and pressed dress slacks, his dark features complimented the Italian leather shoes he wore on what had to be a pair of size twelve feet. He reminded me of a more massive version of a boy I'd gone to high school with by the name of Joey Palladino, the first love of my best friend, Jack Paterno.

We looked at each other for a few seconds, then I made my way toward where the tall guy was standing, intentionally averting my eyes so he wouldn't get the impression I was staring, even though I totally had been. When I passed him by, ascending the carpeted staircase to my academic advisor's office on the second floor, I heard him utter a single, solitary word in a rich, resonate voice that rumbled right through me.

"*Hello.*"

I was positive.

Unfortunately Dr. Gill, my advisor, wasn't available to advise me on that particular afternoon. His assistant, Jennifer, wasn't of much assistance either. I thanked her and returned to the lower level, this time stopping to marvel at a black-and-white photo mounted on the wall above the staircase: a 1960s production shot from *A Funny Thing Happened on the Way to the Forum,* featuring a bald actor I immediately recognized as Jeffrey Tambor, the neighbor on the short-lived *Three's Company* spin-off *The Ropers.*

Hoping for another run in with Prince Charming, I found my wish unfulfilled the moment my feet hit the lobby floor. The stud was nowhere to be seen. I decided to take another peek at the callboard, as I should probably have made it a point to attend that evening's audition, no matter how unprepared I might have been to put myself out there. This was the sole purpose for my paying close to a thousand dollars per semester in order to gain additional stage experience and build up my résumé, so that one day—in the not-too-distant future—I could burn up the neon lights of Broadway.

When I stepped back up to the board, with the intent of committing the audition details to memory, I found myself joined by an attractive young woman who looked as if she'd just stepped out of the pages of a *Vogue Paris* fashion spread. A slinky, dark-colored dress clung to the beautiful brunette's slender body. The strap of a vintage, vinyl purse containing an actual working clock crossed her heart, bisecting a set of rather buxom breasts. From her lobes hung an assortment of small silver hoops, totaling a dozen between the two ears. She smelled slightly of ammonia, an indicator that Raven Black was not her hair's natural shade.

"Anything interesting?" she asked seductively.

We discussed the impending audition, and she unequivocally encouraged me to add my signature to the sign-up sheet.

"The problem is," I lamented after complying, "I don't have anything to sing."

"That's easy enough," she insisted. "Walk your cute little behind down to the DPL and find yourself some sheet music."

"DPL?" I said, intentionally overlooking the fact that she'd just commented on the condition of my posterior.

"Detroit Public Library. What's the matter? You're not from around here?"

"No, I'm new."

She consulted her clock-purse. "It's not even four. You've got a good three hours before auditions. Would you like me to come with you?"

"That's okay."

"I'm not doing anything else. I'll just end up sitting around worrying myself to death. I dread auditioning! It's the worst part of being an actress."

I agreed completely. Then I asked her to point me toward the library, and we went on our separate ways, vowing to see each other again later that evening.

• • •

It wasn't until 1910, when the great American library philan-
thropist of the early 20th century, Andrew Carnegie, donated
funds that Detroiters decided to build a large central library.
The second biggest system in Michigan, the Detroit Public
Library was composed of a Main Library on Woodward Avenue, home of the DPL administration offices, and another
twenty-three branches across the city. The Main Library,
listed on the National Register of Historic Places, was located adjacent to Wayne State University and across from the
Detroit Institute of Arts. Designed by Cass Gilbert, known
for his designs of the United States Supreme Court Building in Washington, DC, the Minnesota State Capital, and
the Woolworth Building in New York City, the three-floor,
early Italian Renaissance-style building was constructed out
of Vermont marble and serpentine Italian marble trim.

Gilbert's son, Cass Gilbert Jr., partnered with Francis J.
Keally to design the library's additional wings added in 1963.
The north and south wings opened on June 23rd of that year,
adding a significant amount of space to the overall structure.
The wings were connected along the rear of the original edi-
fice and a new entrance created on Cass Avenue. Above this
entry was a mosaic by American painter Millard Sheets called
The River of Knowledge. As part of the addition, a triptych
was added to the west wall of Adam Strohm Hall on the third
floor entitled *Man's Mobility.* The mural by local artist John
Stephens Coppin portrays a history of transportation and
compliments a tryparch on the opposite wall depicting Detroit's own early history, completed in 1921 by Gari
Melchers.

It was on this floor that I found myself frantically scour-
ing the stacks of the Music, Art, and Literature collection in
a desperate search for the sheet music to a familiar song I
could sing for my impending audition. Overwhelmed by such
an extensive selection, I finally settled on the titular tune
from the aforementioned *Cabaret,* which happened to be the

name of the cabin I'd spent the longest two weeks of my life living in as a 12-year-old, the first time I'd attended Blue Lake Fine Arts Camp the summer after 7th grade.

When I completed the check-out process at the circulation desk, after filling out the requisite forms to obtain my official DPL library card, it was just after five o'clock. With a habitual "Thank God!" I walked over to one of the glass doors that looked out onto Cass. Across the avenue, the steel-framed Prentis Building stood tall and strong, dutifully protecting the eastern edge of the Wayne State campus. A creation of Minoru Yamasaki, the Twin Towers architect, who died in Bloomfield Hills in 1986, the buff-colored marble façade appeared a smoky brown through the tinted glass. At the far end of the horseshoe-shaped driveway running the length of the rear of the library, I noticed a flashing light. Through the turnstile I passed, my music books held firm against one hip, and went outside to investigate.

I stood leaning on one of the four red pillars that held up the back of the building, feeling the humidity and smoking a tasty cigarette. Then came the familiar loud crack of voices on a police radio. Instinctively I searched around for my father. The Wayne State area was part of Dad's regular beat and part of the reason he'd been so wary about my attending school there. Back in the late '70s, he'd gotten his degree in Phys. Ed. from WSU before returning to the force after being unable to find work as a gym teacher, and he was well aware of the on-campus crime stats. Again I noticed the flash of lights off to the right. Little clusters of onlookers congregated, trying to determine whether what they were witnessing was worth the wasting of their time.

Center stage stood a young black boy, dressed in colors akin to the African flag, hunched over the hood of a Detroit Police car, one arm twisted behind his back by a burly, mustached officer who, thankfully, was not my father. Nearby, another cop—more muscular and more handsome than the first—with tree trunk legs and a thick torso, tore forcefully through a black nylon backpack. His meaty forearms flexed and his biceps bulged as he dug inside, determined to unearth whatever evidence he'd hoped to use against the alleged perpetrator, who promptly swore at the other police officer holding him hostage.

"Asshole! Y' ain't got nothin' on me. Lemme the fuck go!" He was thin yet fit, and he wriggled like a fish trying to free itself from a fisherman's hook.

I stole a second glimpse of the second, more attractive officer. He had dark hair, cropped close on the sides so the white of his scalp showed, with a brown-eyed, turned upnosed, nondescript hillbilly face; the kind I'd seen often on the Hazeltucky boys I'd fantasized about daily during puberty. I wondered if he knew my dad from the force. The first cop had gotten his handcuffs out and was busy slapping them tightly around the black boy's skinny wrists. He couldn't have been more than twenty, and the beaded braids he wore were almost identical to the woman who'd helped me with my scheduling earlier that afternoon at the Student Center.

"You call this nothing?" the sexier officer accused, holding up a clear plastic baggie that, I'm guessing, contained some kind of illegal substance.

"Crack," someone in the crowd assumed.

"Busted," added another.

It was over. The African-American boy was escorted into the back of the squad car by his captor, and he and my hot cop boyfriend hopped into the front seat, disappearing from my life forever in a squeal of rubber and a wail of sirens.

"One more Motor City shakedown," said a voice at my side.

It was Raven Black.

"Hey," I said. "Good old McGruff the Crime Dog takes another bite outta crime." We moved down the walkway together, away from the dispersing crowd. "What are you doing here?"

I worried that maybe she'd intentionally followed me to the library when I'd explicitly told her she shouldn't bother.

"I had some time to kill," she answered innocently. "Before auditions. Did you find anything?"

I held up my music book with its hard blue binding, the title of the particular show printed in white capital lettering along the well-worn spine.

"'Life is a cabaret, old chum,'" she sang sweetly, as if she'd approved whole-heartedly of my selection. "Great musical! Wouldn't I make the best Sally Bowles? I keep telling Pia we *must* do it before I graduate."

Not knowing who this Pia person was, I admired her confidence and concurred that she would indeed make a splendid Sally, glancing down at her fingernails to see if by chance she'd painted them emerald green. She had not; they were crimson red to coordinate with her lipstick color. For the first time, I noticed how pale her skin was, almost powder-white and amplified even more so by the dark mass of hair framing her angular face.

"Did you see that back there?" I said in reference to the turn of events we'd both just taken in.

"Did I!" she exclaimed. "I kept wondering what I could do to get that cop with the buzz cut to manhandle me."

Intentionally ignoring her innuendo, I asked, "Do you get that a lot down here?"

"Drug dealers? Oh, sure. This is Detroit. Where the weak are killed and eaten."

Even the first time I'd heard Rain DuBois utter this phrase, I got the distinct impression she was a dramatic woman. There was a *femme fatale* sort of quality in her tone as she pronounced it, as if she'd assumed the surname of the classic Tennessee Williams character, not the one handed down by her daddy, Mr. DuBois, who no doubt proudly proclaimed himself *Doo-boys*.

Reaching out for a shake, I said, "I'm Bradley, by the way."

She regarded me with the rapt horror of a Southern Belle greeting a gentleman caller who'd failed to bring her flowers. "You must never, *ever* offer a lady your hand. It's perfectly impolite."

I had no idea. Nor did I get the notion her people hailed from anywhere near the Mason-Dixon, the way my mother's had down in Alabama.

She offered me hers, replying, "Rain. As in 'soon it's gonna...' You know, *The Fantasticks?*"

I'd heard of it but not seen it. Still, I nodded and smiled. "Of course."

"Wouldn't I make the best Luisa?" she beamed. "I keep telling Pia we *must* do it before I graduate."

At Cass, Rain started left, her head turned toward me on her right, her bare shoulder lingering slightly behind her, like she was expecting me to automatically follow. Her fragile ankles teetered on her four-inch fuck-me pumps as she stood tapping an exposed toe against the uneven pavement.

"Which way are you going?" she inquired.

"I'm not sure," I said. There was still an hour and a half until auditions began at seven, and I really needed to grab a bite to eat before I fainted from a lack of sustenance.

"We could go back to my apartment," she offered, "and visit." With a manicured hand, she gave my upper arm a suggestive squeeze. Sensing my apprehension, she added, "Or we could grab a drink and chat, until it's time to head down to the Bonstelle. The Circa is just up the block."

"Do they serve food?"

"I think so. I don't eat much."

One look at her and it was obvious. The girl couldn't have weighed more than one hundred and ten pounds, soaking wet.

"Um..."

I had to choose between dining with a flirt, who surprisingly seemed to be blatantly flirting with me, and driving back to my dad's, where I had absolutely no groceries and would almost immediately have to turn back around in order to make it downtown for my audition on time. The gas tank in my car, I remembered, was almost on E, and I couldn't afford to refill it until after my next payday, which was still over four days away.

"I'd hate to waste your time," I said, allowing her an out.

"Please! We might as well get to know each other," she said, batting her bright blue eyes. "We're going to be spending a lot of time together once we both get cast in this show."

"I guess I could go for a glass of wine," I concluded.

"There you go!" she cried, the cat about to eat the canary.

Why I didn't just tell her up front that I'm gay, I'm not certain. Something about the way she looked at me, the way she drank me in, made me eager to accept her offer and see where this adventure might take us. I had no intention of leading her on, but... The expression she wore at that precise moment was one I'd seen on many a guy before but never on a girl—at least not one as attractive as Rain DuBois.

And so, with an anxious shrug, I went to have dinner with a woman.

2

RAIN

◆　　　　　　　　　◆　　　　　　　　　◆

She grew up in Rochester, the only daughter of a General Motors executive and a woman who sold cosmetics at J.L. Hudson's before losing her life to cancer at age forty. From early on, Rain DuBois knew that she wanted nothing more than to be a performer. When her cousins would come over for holiday visits, she'd force them to put on play-shows for their parents, grandparents, aunts and uncles. At seven, she wrote, directed, and starred in a backyard production of *Alice in Wonderland,* adapted from the original Lewis Carroll.

In her youth, she attended the prestigious Interlochen Summer Arts Camp, appearing in significant roles ranging from Annie in *Annie* to Annie in *Annie Get Your Gun.* The first, she had the fortune to play Detroit's own Fisher Theatre as understudy when the third National Tour hit town in the early '8os. Her high school years she spent at Mercy, a Catholic college preparatory school for young women, located in suburban Farmington Hills, where she continued to perform in the annual Fall Play, a joint venture with brother school University of Detroit Jesuit. Each December, from the time she was twelve until she enrolled at Wayne State at eighteen, she appeared in the Michigan Ballet Theatre's *The Nutcracker,* beginning as a sugar plum fairy and working her way up to the female lead of Clara. In the spring, she would focus on honing her skills by studying with a private acting coach from the Attic Theatre and, occasionally, auditioning for local film and industrial video projects.

Sixty minutes and several glasses of cheap Merlot later, I

found myself still picking at a plate of cold French fries, wondering if the fog inside my brain would burn off before it came time for me to sing my sixteen bars. As predicted, Rain hadn't eaten a bite, preferring to chain-smoke clove cigarettes and chatter away. She filled me in on the details of her life, which I found fascinating, though I couldn't help but wonder why someone so theatrically accomplished, not to mention financially well-off, had settled on a state college like Wayne, known for its fairly inexpensive education—and also its lack of carding on the part of the waitresses who served its students at its campus bars and restaurants. But, ever wanting to be civil, I held my tongue and didn't call into conversation this burning question. Instead I listened intently as Rain DuBois knocked back three of the five glasses of wine that we'd ordered against my better judgment. Not only did we both have an important appointment coming up, the Circa 1890 didn't strike me as the kind of establishment known for their fine dining or choice beverage selection.

The bar itself sat on the east side of Cass Avenue, one long block north of the DPL, on the corner of Ferry, facing what was called the Ferry Mall, a walkway that led, I would later learn, past the Alumni House and Law School and over to Anthony Wayne Drive on the opposite side of the modest campus. Simply marked SALOON in big black letters and sandwiched between a RESTAURANT and the WAYNE PARTY STORE, both identified in the same non-descript style, what made the Circa and its surrounding environs so noteworthy wasn't their step-back-in-time-to-the-1960s design and décor, it was the puffy white awning that arched outward from each building and down to the sidewalk, calling to mind the marshmallow-like rings of *Bibendum*, better known as the Michelin Man.

"So what about you?" Coming up for a breath, Rain lapped at the last red drop lolling about the bottom of her wine glass.

"What about me what?" I asked, knowing it was my turn

to talk, something I'd been dreading since first sitting down to dine with Ms. DuBois. Or would she no doubt prefer *Miss*?

"I've told you more than I'm sure you ever wanted to know. Your turn."

"Where should I start?"

"What about, where are you from? Where did you go to high school? How old are you?"

"Where am I from now?" I asked, stalling while I got my story together. "Or where did I grow up?"

"Either," she answered. "Both."

When I chose to begin my life anew as a Wayne State student, I also decided it was time for a personal makeover—and not just a physical transformation. While I wouldn't go as drastic as giving myself a new name, I did decide to kiss Bradley-Dayton-formerly-of-Ferndale-now-living-in-White-Trash-Warren goodbye, in exchange for something a tad more glamorous and upwardly mobile.

"You're from Birmingham?" asked Rain, sounding super impressed once the requested (and completely fabricated) information started spewing forth. "Do you know Brad Woodward?"

"Not sure," I answered cautiously, my head spinning from the alcohol stemming through my bloodstream. "Who's Brad Woodward?"

"He's an actor in The Department." By which she meant the WSU Theatre Department, I assumed. "He's from Birmingham... Or is it Bloomfield Hills? I always confuse the two. Where did you say you went to high school?"

I hadn't.

My choice was Seaholm or Groves. I knew nothing of either, other than the fact that the former faced Hazel Park each season in football, as the two schools were in the same athletic league, the SMA. I picked the lesser of two evils.

"Seaholm," I said, "Class of '90."

I prayed this Brad Woodward person wouldn't have been

a classmate of mine had I actually graduated from the school the way I was pretending I had, having just shaved two years off my real age.

"Maybe you don't know him then?" Rain said. "He went to Country Day."

This was the top-rated private college preparatory school located in Beverly Hills, just outside of Birmingham, which meant this Brad Woodward person was not only a smarty-pants, he came from *beaucoup* bucks. As with Rain, I wondered what he was doing at Wayne State. Surely a person who'd attended Country Day could afford the tuition of a major university like Michigan. Especially when he hailed from one of Detroit's most prominent and historical families, which I was about to learn.

"Woodward as in Woodward *Avenue?*" So surprised was I that I almost spit out the post-dinner coffee I'd been drinking, in my desperate attempt to sober up, once Rain had revealed this juicy bit of information regarding our classmate.

"The very same," she said, sounding rather nonplussed. "His great-great-great grandfather, or something like that, was the original."

Augustus Brevoort Woodward, appointed the first Chief Justice of the Michigan Territory by President Thomas Jefferson, arrived in Detroit in June 1805 to find the city in ruins, the result of a devastating fire. At 31 years old, Woodward was a Freemason from Virginia. He stood six feet three inches tall, with a long, narrow face dominated by a prominent nose and a thick crop of dark black hair, his only outward appearance of vanity. Many believed him to be the prototype for Washington Irving's Ichabod Crane and have credited Woodward, along with Governor William Hull, with planning the once capital of the Michigan Territory.

Under Woodward, for the first time in history, attention shifted fully from Detroit's river to its roads. Woodward Avenue, originally called Court House Avenue, was popularly named for Woodward's efforts in the rebuilding of the city.

Woodward himself proposed a system of hexagonal street blocks, with the Grand Circus at its center, and wide avenues, alternatively two hundred feet and one hundred and twenty feet, emanating from circular plazas like spokes from the hub of a wheel. As the metropolis grew, these spokes would spread outward in all directions from the banks of the Detroit River. Most prominent were the six main avenues: Woodward, Michigan, Grand River, Gratiot, and Jefferson, together with Fort Street. Unfortunately, after only eleven years, the plan was abandoned, but not before some of its most significant elements had been implemented.

In his later life, Woodward focused his efforts on science and the establishment of a university in Michigan, based on the model for the one formed by his friend, Thomas Jefferson, in his native Virginia. Along with Reverend John Montieth and Father Gabriel Richard, Woodward drafted a charter for an institution he called the *Catholepistemiad* or the *University of Michigania*. On August 26, 1817, the Governor and Judges of the Michigan Territory signed the university act into law, and this institution became known as the University of Michigan.

"Can I get you's anything else?" Our waitress stopped by the table to check on us. She was a surly, middle-aged, typical Midwestern white woman with a nasally, typical Michigan accent. According to the red label on the brown plastic badge pinned over her left breast, her name was PAM. She reminded me of the women with whom I waited tables at Country Boy, the local twenty-four hour greasy spoon up in Hazel Park.

"I think we're good." I checked the time on my Swatch. It was close to six-thirty, and I certainly didn't want to be late for my very first Wayne State audition.

Pam tore off our bill from her pad, placed it facedown on the dirty table, and waddled away toward the kitchen. In Detroit, possibly more than anyplace else in our lovely country, a waitress doesn't give two shits.

I turned to Rain. "We should probably get going."

Her eyes fluttered heavily. Obviously she'd reached the threshold of her alcohol intake, and she looked as if she could fall asleep at any moment. She rummaged around inside her clock-purse and pulled out a twenty, slurring, "On me."

Only because I wanted to get the hell out of there, I didn't bother arguing. Leaving the money on the table, I helped Miss DuBois out of the booth, wrapping one bare arm around my shoulder.

"My hero," she murmured as I lifted her from the seat. She leaned her warm body against mine, allowing me to lead her to the front door.

Outside on the sidewalk, I stood breathing in the not-so-fresh air, wondering what my next move should be. There was no way Rain could possibly drive herself over to the theatre in her inebriated condition. Still, I asked, "Where's your car?"

She answered, "Thelma," her knees buckling beneath her.

"Who's Thelma?" I said, doing my best to hold her up.

It turned out that Thelma was a what—not a who. *The* Thelma to be exact.

Rain lived in an apartment on the first floor of an old building on Forest, in a quiet area of campus between Third Street and Second Avenues. Because we were running late on time, I suggested that we take my car, which was still parked in the structure over on Palmer, a mere block or so from where we were presently standing. Rain was eager to agree, and I all but carried her to my cream-colored '68 Plymouth Valiant, a gift presented to me by my dad once I'd finally gotten my driver's license at the age of seventeen, after several failed attempts at trying. Leave it to James Bradley Dayton to give me an automobile that's two years older than I was! I had no idea how I'd explain to my new, rich friend the reason I was driving such a piece of crap car. Hopefully she wouldn't be conscious enough to comprehend, and if she did comment, I'd already decided I would just lie some more and say that my Audi was in the shop.

I'd only been to the Bonstelle Theatre once before, back in high school. Our Drama teacher, Mr. Dell'Olio, took me and my fellow Drama Queers to see a production of *The Music Man* during senior year. All I really remembered about the experience was sitting in the upper balcony with my good friend Audrey Wojczek, who was unfortunately killed in a fatal car accident a few months later. Because we'd always shared the same taste in boys, both of us had thought the guy playing Tommy Djilas was a total babe. I had a vague memory of the theatre's location, just south of the Wayne State campus.

I started driving in that direction, until Rain's eyes rolled open and she turned toward me, mumbling from where she sat slumped in my front seat, "Sarah."

I stopped at the red light on the corner of West Warren and Woodward Avenue, next to an art supply store called U-Trecht. "Who's Sarah?"

"Roommate," Rain groggily replied. "Need to pick her up. Can't drive."

"She can't—?"

For a split second, I wondered what kind of person grows up in the *Motor* City and isn't able to operate an automobile? Other than my best friend Jack Paterno's mom, Dianne, who didn't start driving until her oldest son got his own license and they learned together, sharing a 1979 pea green Dodge Omni between them.

"She's blind."

Blind?

Surely I couldn't have heard Rain correctly. A blind actress auditioning for a musical... How crazy was that concept? I couldn't imagine the girl being able to sing and dance and act without falling off the stage into the orchestra pit. Still, I took the turn onto Woodward Avenue and another quick right at West Hancock.

On the left-hand side of the street, just before the Theatre

Production Center, I noticed a charming three-story Victorian-style home covered with creeping ivy and surrounded by a wrought iron fence. The rust-colored brick building featured a rounded turret on one side, topped off by a tiny pointed roof with a half-dozen tiny windows beneath. One level down, another trio of larger, rectangular panes peered out, complimented by a circular window that was framed by a spiral pattern of bricks, opposite. Just outside this particular porthole sat what appeared to be a small balcony that also served as a covering for the dwelling's front porch.

And who did I see precisely at that moment, appearing through the heavy wooden front door and sauntering through a lovely brick archway and down the stone front steps? None other than Prince Charming himself.

I almost crashed my car into a white Mercedes parked alongside the curb, trying to steal a peek at him. As I drove past, I quickly checked the reflection in my rearview mirror, just in time to see him hop into the luxury vehicle and pull away from in front of the Victorian apartment. Not only was he a handsome boy, he was rich to boot!

Finally we arrived at The Thelma. I glanced over at Rain, still asleep with her head against the passenger window. Her breathing had grown shallow, and she was snoring ever so slightly. I pulled up in front of the building, put the Valiant in park, and made sure to lock the doors before hopping out onto the street. Piece of crap car or not, we were still in Detroit.

Thankfully The Thelma was unmistakably marked, the words THE THELMA etched in large letters on a stone banner situated between the two center windows of the second floor. Blond-colored bricks adorned the façade. A small shingled awning spanned the length of the duplex, held up by a sextet of white pillars. Scurrying up the sidewalk, I paused at the sight of a pair of stone lions lounging sphinx-like along either side of the porch steps, protecting The Thelma's inhabitants from any unlawful intruders. I wasn't sure which unit Rain and her roommate specifically resided in, so I consulted the list of names printed on the mailboxes, finding exactly what I was searching for: DUBOIS/SCHWARTZ, handwritten in what appeared to be the penmanship of a 5-year-old. I pressed the corresponding buzzer and waited anxiously.

Within moments, the front door to one of the lower-level apartments partially opened, and a pair of emerald eyes peered out from behind the confines of a still-fastened protective chain. "Who is it?"

"Are you Sarah?"

"Yes... Who are you?" the woman asked warily.

"My name is Bradley Dayton. I'm a friend of Rain's."

"Rain! Where is she?"

"Waiting in the car. *My* car," I corrected. "We're here to pick you up for auditions."

Sarah sighed. "It's about time!" She slammed the front door and promptly re-opened it after removing the fastener. "Sorry," she apologized. "I don't mean to be a bitch. I was just getting worried about being late."

She stepped onto the porch, wearing a little jade dress draped in horizontal layers of flapper-style fringe. Her copper curls she'd decorated with a matching sequined headband. The entire ensemble was absolutely fabulous. She reminded me of someone I'd seen somewhere before, though I couldn't recall whom, and I instantly saw this girl playing the role of Roxie Hart, the cute redheaded chorine, in *Chicago.*

The one thing I did not see when I looked at Sarah Schwartz was a person with a visual impairment. Wielding a cumbersome guitar case, down the porch and up the sidewalk she strutted, missing not a single step. I kept wondering where her white cane and dark sunglasses were, and how she could possibly see where she was going without my assistance. Maybe I'd misheard Rain when she'd described her roommate as being blind?

"Nice car," Sarah said sincerely. I unlocked the back door,

held it open, and she crawled into the cluttered backseat.

"Just push that stuff on the floor," I told her, embarrassed at the mess of empty pop bottles, crumpled cigarette packs, and old copies of *Metra* magazine that I'd picked up at the gay bar over the last several months.

Sarah did as instructed, and I closed the door, shutting her and her instrument inside. As I fastened my seatbelt, after climbing up front, Rain's head rolled slowly from one side to the other. Clearly she was still asleep, and I worried at the thought of waking her.

"She had a bit to drink with dinner," I whispered over my shoulder to my second passenger.

Sarah shook her bobbed head, the explanation coming as no big surprise.

According to the *Production Handbook for Undergraduate Theatre Majors at Wayne State*, the actress and theatre manager, Jessie Bonstelle, was born Laura Justine on 11 November 1871 in Rochester, New York. Called Bonnie by her friends, she played the title role in *Camille* over two hundred times, in productions that toured from Canada to Michigan. Her favorite play was *Little Women*, which she adapted for Broadway to mild success. In 1910, and for fourteen summers thereafter, Jessie Bonstelle had the pleasure of bringing new plays and actors to Detroit's Garrick Theatre, located on Griswold, while managing its resident stock company.

In 1922, the congregation of the Temple Beth-El on Woodward Avenue would build a new home further north, allowing Miss Bonstelle to purchase the building and arrange for its conversion into a live theatre, the Bonstelle Playhouse. Work on the renovations at Temple Beth-El, the majority of funds coming from local Prohibition-era rum runners, was completed in 1925. Jessie lived on the theatre's third floor in a private apartment overlooking the stage, providing her own personal view of each performance. In 1928, with the support of Mayor Frank Murphy, Miss Bonstelle created the first non-profit professional theatre in the country known as the Detroit Civic Theatre, after organizing summer productions of Shakespeare's *A Midsummer Night's Dream* on Belle Isle, along with the Detroit Symphony Orchestra, in order to raise revenue. The perpetually near-bankrupt company would only continue to operate out of Jessie Bonstelle's sheer will.

In the early 1930s, MGM lured Jessie away from her home in Detroit and out to California, where she was hired to train new actors for the screen in Hollywood. While living in Los Angeles, she was diagnosed with inoperable breast cancer but did not reveal her illness to anyone until two days before her death on 14 November 1932. Legend has it that the body of Jessie Bonstelle was laid out on the stage of the Bonstelle Theatre costumed as Juliet Capulet. In 1956, under the guidance of Leonard Leone, then-Director of Theatre at Wayne State University, the Bonstelle became home to WSU's student theatre company. The 1173 seat Broadway-style house was listed on the National Register of Historic Places in 1982. Some believe that the spirit of Jessie Bonstelle still treads the boards of the theatre bearing her name.

By the time we arrived at our destination, Rain had finally awoken. She stretched and yawned as we pulled into one of the few empty spaces alongside the theatre.

"Rise and shine!" I sang sweetly, shutting off the car's engine before stepping out onto the warm blacktop. The late summer sun had started to set, casting long shadows across the length of the crowded parking lot.

A shiver of excitement shot through me as I stared up at the theatre's signature copper-colored dome, imagining what the inside must look like from a backstage vantage point—or better yet, an onstage one. It had been over four years since my last appearance in a theatrical production, one that had been regrettably overshadowed by Joey Palladino, the former love of my best friend Jack Paterno's life, usurping my role as Danny Zuko in my senior musical, *Grease*. After taking so much time off, I was itching to get back up in front of a live audience and do some acting, singing, and dancing. Fingers crossed I hadn't grown rusty.

While I stood waiting for Rain and Sarah to climb out of my car, I overheard a brief exchange of words between the women.

"I can't believe you dyed your hair," said Sarah, sounding somewhat disgusted.

"So?" Rain casually responded. "Julia Roberts dyed her hair when she auditioned for *Mystic Pizza*."

Sarah gave Rain a look. "Did she also go out and get drunk right beforehand?"

"I'm not drunk," Rain slurred, doing her best not to stumble. "Tell her, Bradley..." She leaned against the hood of my car for support. "I had a couple glasses of wine with dinner."

We both knew both of these statements were false, but I said nothing to contradict Rain's story.

"You know how nervous I get over these things," she added, off my silence.

"Well," Sarah said, "you're lucky your hair smells so bad. Maybe no one will notice your booze breath?" She turned on her heels and headed toward the stage door, guitar case in hand.

Rain looked at me again, this time rolling her eyes. "Welcome to the Bonstelle."

Inside, we came upon a sign-in sheet hanging on the left-hand wall of the dimly lit stairwell that, I assumed, led up to the dressing and makeup rooms. We each checked off our names on the list to indicate our arrival, and Sarah said nothing further with regards to Rain's present state of intoxication. I felt it best to mind my own beeswax, as my mother was wont to advise me and my three sisters, Janelle, Nina, and Brittany, while we were growing up. Sarah took an immediate right, disappearing into the dark through a heavy-curtained archway. Rain promptly followed, and I promptly followed Rain.

The main level of the Bonstelle consisted of twenty-five rows, lettered B through Z, with two side aisles separating the center section from the odd-numbered seats, house left, and the even-numbered, on house right. A large balcony hung from high above, covering the back portion of the auditorium, accommodating another fifteen rows of seats, lettered A-N, with two side aisles dividing off the odd- and even-numbered rows in the lower portion and three aisles in the upper. Another horizontal aisle ran the width of the balcony, separating these two sections.

From my seat in the second row of the side orchestra, I sat admiring the vast expanse of the proscenium arch and the capacity of the fly loft beyond. Backstage, I could see the pin rail with its corded ropes and envisioned the lot of scenery that would soon fly in and out. After lacking almost everything back at Hazel Park High, performing on the Bonstelle stage was sure to be the greatest experience of my theatrical life thus far.

"Listen up!" The brash voice of a young woman called out with conviction, waking me from my daydream.

Standing in the far aisle, beside a table crafted from a platform that had been placed across the center section of seats, she appeared around my age, early twenties, and was dressed in a style I often described as lesbianic. I didn't assume the girl was gay, but she sported an oversized Indigo Girls concert jersey, baggy corduroys, and clunky work boots. Over a mane of mousey hair, she wore a headset attached to a battery pack, clipped to a tool belt.

"We're about to get started with the singing portion of the auditions," the young woman told the group of a hundred or so student actors who had assembled in the Bonstelle that evening, all vying for one of about twenty available roles. "For those of you who don't know me, I'm Amelia Morganti."

"Amelia?" I heard Rain mutter. "Since when?" She leaned over and spoke softly in my ear. "As long as I've known her, it's always been Amy."

The self-proclaimed Amelia went on with her spiel. "I'm the production stage manager for *Chicago*. Here with me is the director, Will Bilson."

A good-looking guy in his early thirties, I'd guess, with shaggy brown hair and a dimpled smile, held up a hand and gestured at the group. "Hey, everybody," he said keeping it short and sweet.

Immediately I noticed the band of gold cutting off the circulation to his left ring finger and sighed. Not only was he hetero, he was locked by holy matrimony.

"And this is Pia Mullins," Amelia continued. "Our choreographer."

So this was the famous Pia whom Rain had kept referring to in our earlier conversation? Ms. Mullins was early middle-aged, maybe thirty-five or forty, and she had the body of a former ballerina. Her sandy brown hair was cut in a short pixie style, and her big eyes sparkled as she beamed at us brightly.

"Welcome, everyone. It's good to see you all back, safe and sound."

"We also have our musical director, Patrick Singer." Amelia plowed ahead, nodding toward a young man who appeared older than his years, sitting onstage at an upright piano near the proscenium.

"Patrick is a graduate student in the School of Music," Pia added for our benefit, "and we're happy to have him joining us for this production."

Patrick smiled shyly, appearing out of place, as if he'd been suddenly thrust into this position. But his face was friendly, with rosy, chubby cheeks that I wanted to reach out and pinch.

"I'm happy to be here," he said softly.

Back to business, Amelia asked, "Everybody signed in? All right, let's get started. First up..." She glanced at the clipboard she held firmly in her mannish hands. "We have Brad..."

The moment I heard my name, I panicked. My heart started pounding; my forehead began dripping with perspiration; my arms pits were instantly soaking wet. I totally wanted to slouch down and make myself disappear. I would've never signed up to be the first person to sing. Eager I was; stupid I was not.

"Woodward." Amelia craned her thick neck, scanning the cavernous room. "*Brad Woodward!*"

Breathing a sigh of relief, I sat up straight and tall in my seat, thankful for the much appreciated reprieve. I'd also grown curious to catch a glimpse of the mysterious Brad Woodward, heir to the Woodward Avenue dynasty. Especially after hearing so many fabulous things about him earlier over dinner.

Imagine my surprise when a deep baritone called out, "I'm here!"

And who did I see bounding through the door at the back of the theatre auditorium, a bundle of excited energy? None other than my Mercedes-driving Prince Charming.

3

DAMN I WISH I WAS YOUR LOVER

The first time I laid eyes on Brad Woodward, I knew we were destined to be together in some way, shape, or form. I wouldn't call it love, since the existence of such an emotion had been something I'd learned from an early age to no longer believe in, like Santa Claus, the Easter Bunny, and Tooth Fairy.

When Dad walked out on Mom, along with me and my three sisters, I pretty much gave up on thinking I would ever find someone to love who would love me back, like in the movies and on TV. Call me a cynic, but what else could a 12-year-old expect after his whole world had been turned upside down, all because his parents no longer cared for each other?

"Hello, I'm Brad Woodward," he said after taking to the stage with the utmost confidence and finding his light.

It was evident that everyone in the theatre already knew the guy, particularly *Chicago* director Will Bilson and his choreographer Pia Mullins, who both looked like they were going to bust a nut the second Brad Woodward opened his mouth. He was clearly the golden boy of the Bonstelle company.

"Hey, Brad," droned Will Bilson, acting like a total dude. "Thanks for coming by."

"No problem."

"How was your summer?" asked Pia, grinning from ear to

ear enthusiastically.

"Awesome!" answered Brad. "I did three shows in rep out at Utah Shakes."

Well, smell him! Working as a professional already. What the hell was he doing getting a degree in Theatre if he could find work as an actor without it? The proof was going to be in the proverbial pudding.

"Which shows did you do?" wondered Will.

"Let's see... Romeo in *Romeo and Juliet*," Brad totally bragged, while acting as if it was no big deal. "Sebastian in *Twelfth Night*..."

"Did you work with Doug on that?" Will asked, name dropping.

"I did."

"And what about the other show?"

"*West Side Story*. I played Tony."

Totally on the verge of wetting her panties, Pia cried, "How perfect!"

For his audition, he chose "Morning Glow" from *Pippin*, a song that didn't seem particularly fitting for a Kander and Ebb musical set in the 1920s. But again, it appeared that Brad Woodward could do no wrong. He could've gotten up and sang "The Star-Spangled Banner" and I'm sure he would've received a standing ovation and been offered the part of Billy Flynn on a silver platter.

As smitten as I found myself, I decided right then and there I was going to give him a run for his money. I wasn't about to allow the guy to steal my role out from under me, the way Joey Palladino and Richie Tyler had both done before, with Richie taking his turn my senior year when I'd been relegated to the supporting role of Bob Cratchit to his Ebenezer Scrooge in Dickens' *A Christmas Carol*.

"Very nice," Will Bilson gushed once Brad had sung his sixteen bars.

"Beautiful," added Pia, echoing the sentiment. "Always."

I knew it wasn't going to be easy to prove myself, being

the new boy in town. But I wasn't about to go down without a fight. Man, did I need a cigarette!

"Be sure to check the callboard in the morning," Will told Brad before releasing him.

"Dance auditions are tomorrow evening," Pia explained.

"Awesome!" Brad said. He stepped down from the stage and walked right past where I was sitting with Sarah and Rain.

"Good job," Sarah whispered, reaching out to squeeze Brad's big hand.

"Break a leg," he told her, continuing up the side aisle toward the back of the auditorium.

Amelia consulted the sign-in sheet attached to her clipboard. "Rain DuBois!"

Once again, Rain was sound asleep. I gave her shoulder a gentle nudge, and her azure eyes snapped opened. She looked around the theatre, clearly lost. "Am I up?"

Rain rose from her seat and wobbled her way down the aisle toward a small set of stairs that had been placed in front of the lip of the stage. I kept my fingers crossed she didn't trip, or worse yet, fall head first into the orchestra pit.

"Hello," I heard her say softly to Patrick the accompanist once she'd taken her place by his side.

"Do you have your sheet music?" he asked timidly.

Rain paused. "I'm sorry. I must've left it in my bag. Bradley," she cooed, "could you be a darling and grab my purse?"

Sitting in my spot two rows from where she was standing, I reached under the seat Rain had occupied and frantically felt around for the clock. I couldn't find it.

"Um..." I said, stalling. My cheeks flushed as I felt all eyes in the Bonstelle focus on me. "I think maybe you left it out in my car."

Rain sighed, shrugging her slender shoulders.

"Is there a problem?" Will Bilson asked from high on his director's horse, totally aggravated and annoyed.

"No problem," replied Rain. Her jaw tightened with noticeable tension. She wasn't about to become embarrassed in front of a room full of her peers by this Will Bilson person, whoever he happened to be to her.

"Have you been drinking?" Will blatantly accused.

Rain lied through her wine-stained teeth. "Of course not."

"You're obviously in no condition to be here—"

I snuck a peek at Sarah sitting beside me. She stared down at the floor, shaking her head in disdain.

"I'm perfectly fine, *William*," Rain insisted.

"Then go ahead and sing for us. What have you got?"

She stood in silence, her bright blue eyes twinkling beneath the stage lights, as if she might weep at any moment.

"Doesn't look like you're ready to me," said Will smugly.

I got the distinct impression they shared some past history, which I would definitely make it a point to ask Rain about the second I got the chance. Another quick take at Sarah confirmed my sneaking suspicion. Something was not right as rain with Rain DuBois and the handsome, thirty-something director.

"Rain, dear..." Pia piped up, saving the day. "When we take a break, why don't you go and get your music, okay? For now we'll move on to someone else. We can fit you back into the rotation once you're ready."

"Thank you, Pia," Rain replied, relieved. "That would be lovely."

"I like your new hair color, by the way," said Pia, acknowledging Rain's recent dye job.

"Aren't you sweet?" Rain carefully stepped down from the stage and returned to her seat between me and Sarah, who I couldn't help but notice refused to make eye contact with her roommate.

"Sarah Gibson!" Amelia called out. She checked her clipboard again, like she hadn't recognized the name she'd just read.

"That would be me," said Sarah, rising from her seat. She removed her guitar from its case and carefully marched up the precarious set of stairs leading to the stage.

"Are you okay, Sarah?" Pia rose to her feet, keeping a close eye on the girl's every move. "Do you need some help?"

"I'm fine, thanks," Sarah answered. "Haven't fallen off the stage yet," she added humorously.

Turning my attention toward the back of the theatre momentarily, I watched Brad Woodward remove a cigarette pack from his pants pocket, shake one out, and gingerly place the smoke between his lips. At any minute, he would probably step outside, allowing me the perfect opportunity to make my move and follow.

In the parking lot, I could conveniently bump into Brad and introduce myself to my future boyfriend. But I didn't want to be rude and miss out on Sarah's singing audition, so in my seat I stayed.

Onstage, Sarah smiled at Patrick the accompanist/musical director. "If you don't mind," she said amiably, holding up her instrument, "I'll play for myself."

"Not at all," said Patrick, gesturing for Sarah to have at it with pleasure.

"Um... Is there a stool somewhere?"

Down in the orchestra, Amelia leapt to her feet. "I'll get it!"

Assuming her stage managerly duties, she bounded up to the stage, arriving to assist Sarah in five seconds flat. I couldn't help but wonder if somebody had a little crush.

"Thanks," Sarah said, taking a seat as Amelia practically positioned the metal object beneath her butt.

"So it's Sarah Gibson now?" Will Bilson inquired, once Amelia had returned to her spot at the directors' table.

Sarah nodded, looking somewhat embarrassed at having to explain herself. "New year, new name."

"Well, I hope not a new you," Pia said, smiling.

"Oh, no... Still the same old Sarah." She gazed out over the audience, squinting ever so slightly.

"Are the lights bothering you?" asked Pia, sensing Sarah's

discomfort.

"You want me to turn them down?" Amelia eagerly inter-jected.

"I'm fine," Sarah said. "Really." She strummed the guitar strings softly, making sure the instrument was in tune. "Good evening, my name is Sarah Sch—*Gibson*," she chuck-led, still getting used to her new calling card. "My selection is 'I Don't Know How to Love Him' from *Jesus Christ Super-star*."

She sang with the voice of an angel. From the first note, I couldn't take my eyes (or ears) off her. The way she com-manded the stage, the amount of focus and concentration she put into performing the song, was like nothing I'd witnessed since Liza Larson, my Skid Row smoking buddy, who played the female lead in every musical I'd been in back at Hazel Park High.

"Very nice," said Will Bilson, complimenting Sarah once she'd concluded her song.

"Are you still singing with your band?" added Pia. "What's the name again?"

"Strange Bedfellows."

Impressed, Will said, "Shakespeare!" And to show off his academic smarts, he quoted, "'Misery acquaints a man with...'"

"Exactly," Sarah confirmed.

Down in the orchestra seats, Rain muttered, "Wouldn't I know?"

Maybe it was just me, but I could've sworn I saw her look back over her shoulder at Will Bilson when she said this.

After about an hour of listening to the other actor/singer/dancers singing their hearts out, my bottom was starting to kill me from sitting still for so long. A lot of other folks were also getting antsy, including the audition panel. Fifteen min-utes before, Sarah Schwartz/Gibson had disappeared, mum-bling something about needing to make a phone call.

Once a tall, leggy blond senior by the name of Wanda Freeman had finished her booming rendition of "Turn Back, O Man" from *Godspell*, Amelia Morganti stood up and announced that we'd be taking a ten minute break.

"When we return," she said, "Rain DuBois, you'll be up—again." Whatever adoration Amelia felt for Sarah was completely lost when it came to her roommate, Rain.

"Shit," Rain swore, struggling to her feet. "Bradley, would you go and fetch my purse for me, please? I'll be downstairs warming up."

Sprinting out to the parking lot, I found Rain's bag right where she'd left it on the floor of my front seat. After sneaking a quick smoke, I realized I could stand to partake of the facilities, so I dashed back inside the Bonstelle and down to the lower level restrooms in search of Miss DuBois.

"Knock-knock..." Poking my head around the corner of the ladies' lounge doorway, I prayed I wouldn't discover Rain doing anything but practicing her audition piece.

I'd always had a fear of women's bathrooms, most likely because when I was little, my mom would make me come in with her and my sisters whenever we were out shopping. Most of the time, no one even noticed since I was constantly being mistaken for a girl myself, I was so cute.

"Thank you!" cried Rain at the sight of the clock. She wrapped her arms around me wildly, as if I'd saved her from a fate worse than death, and proceeded to peck my cheeks with kisses, like we were a pair of Parisians.

I honestly didn't know how to react, or what I should say, other than "You're welcome," followed by "I really gotta pee."

Fortunately I found myself alone when I entered the men's room. Even after all my years, I was still terribly shy when it came to urinating in public.

I stepped up to one of the porcelain toilets, undid my fly, and was about to whip myself out when I heard a sound coming from behind one of the stall doors. I also smelled a strange scent, like the toxic burning of plastic, followed by a minty freshness reminiscent of Binaca breath spray. Instantly I froze, unable to begin the task of emptying my full bladder.

A sudden flush confirmed my suspicion that I wasn't solo like I'd originally thought. Not wanting to appear pathetic at not being able to take a piss in the presence of another person, I shook the non-existent dew from my willy-lily and tucked myself back inside my BVDs.

The stall door opened and whoever had been inside stepped out, the echo of wooden heels against the tile floor reverberating throughout the restroom.

"Hey..."

A familiar baritone paid me a greeting, and I turned to find Mr. Woodward Avenue standing behind me, hands deep in his pockets.

Up close he was even more gorgeous than when admired from a distance, with his dark brown hair, deep brown eyes, and olive skin. But with a last name like Woodward... What nationality was that?

Honestly I couldn't have cared less. Not when he was standing near enough for me to breathe in the aquatic fragrance of his Cool Water for Men by Davidoff cologne.

"Hey, yourself," I replied, hoping to sound more sexy than sarcastic, as we washed our hands side by side in the sinks.

We exchanged names, even though I was already well aware of his, and shook hands over the fact that we were both named Bradley.

"But they call me Brad," he said.

"They call me Bradley," I told him, intentionally trying to come off as cheeky this time.

Truth be told, I'd grown up being referred to as Brad by everyone I'd encountered, with the exception of my mother. It wasn't until I'd decided to embark on my full-time education at Wayne State that I also chose to live my life full-time as Bradley. And now that I was well on my way to becoming friends with Mr. Woodward, I figured it would help differentiate between us once we officially became a couple.

Neither outwardly acknowledged that we'd seen the other earlier that afternoon. Instead we headed back up to the theatre auditorium together. At the top of the stairs leading into the lobby, we passed by an old-fashioned telephone booth where Sarah sat inside, receiver to her ear. Because of the sound proof glass door, we weren't able to hear what she was saying (rather animatedly) to the person on the other end of the line.

"Columbus," mused Brad, a mischievous grin gracing his luscious lips. I wanted to bite them even more than I already had.

"Ohio?" I said, having no idea how the subject had been changed to States that Border Michigan.

"Columbus Howard," he clarified. "Sarah's beau."

"What kinda name is Columbus?" I said, surprised by such a unique moniker.

"Not a Jewish one," he answered, as if the fact had been a bone of contention that he and Sarah had discussed time and again.

"Is Sarah Jewish?"

"Sarah *Schwartz*—from Oak Park? Hello!"

I don't know why I seemed so shocked to learn that Sarah was of Hebrew descent. Growing up in Hazeltucky, one didn't often encounter anyone of the non-Gentile persuasion, unless maybe they were Arab or Asian. In fact, I pretty much had only met one other Jewish person up until that point: my 5th grade teacher, Mrs. Goldfeder, who'd come to Michigan from Long Island, New York. But it wasn't like she ever talked about being Jewish. She never made us sing Chanukah songs or anything like that in her classroom.

"Is that why Sarah changed her last name to Gibson?" I wondered.

"Uh-huh," Brad confirmed. "Dina told her it sounded too ethnic."

"Who's Dina?"

"Only the most awesome acting teacher ever," he stated emphatically. "Dina French. She went to the Hilberry."

I would later come to learn that this was a common expression among members of The Department. Grad school actors *went* to the Hilberry. But, for some reason, undergrads did not *go* to the Bonstelle.

"Yo, Schwartz!" Brad obnoxiously rapped on the glass door of the booth.

Sarah quickly opened the louver and peeked out. "I'll be done in a sec," she snapped, covering the phone.

"I'm just playing with you," Brad snickered. "Take your time... It's Brad, by the way."

"And Bradley," I added, giving a subtle wave.

Sarah's tone went from rock hard to soft serve. "Sorry, I couldn't see you guys through the door. I'm talking to Columbus."

"I figured as much." Brad turned to look at me, as if to say, *See? I told you.* Then back to Sarah he said, "Tell Colombo I said hey."

"I will," Sarah said, sealing herself back inside the booth.

Brad and I continued moving toward the auditorium. "How about you?" I asked.

"How about me what?"

I didn't want to be rude, but since we were on the subject... "What kinda name is Woodward?"

"It's my mother's maiden name," Brad answered, sounding annoyed that I'd asked such a silly question.

"Oh," I said. "What's your real name?"

"Woodward *is* my real name."

I was still confused. "So is it like your stage name?"

"No, it's my real name. I changed it. Legally. When I turned eighteen."

This was a minor detail that Rain had failed to mention. When she'd said that Brad was an ancestor of the original Woodward, she could've also informed me that the relation came on his mother's branch of the family tree.

"Do you mind if I ask why?" I said.

"As a matter of fact I do," said Brad before heading back inside the theatre.

I couldn't tell if he was joking or being genuine. Leave it to me to put my foot in my mouth and ruin the one chance I might have at getting laid anytime soon. This was providing that Brad Woodward did indeed bat for the pink team. From the way he'd been locking his eyes directly with mine as we spoke—something a straight guy wouldn't be caught dead doing—I got the impression that he totally did.

After we returned from break, as previously announced, Rain resumed her spot onstage, sheet music in hand, which she promptly proffered to Patrick the accompanist, and proceeded to sing her sixteen bars.

She rocked the Bonstelle house, I'm happy to report, bumping and grinding, belting out "All That Jazz," the *Chicago* theme first made famous by Chita Rivera. It was a bold choice to sing something from the actual show, I thought, but the director and choreographer both didn't seem to mind. I left the audition believing she'd nailed it, and the part of Velma Kelly was as good as hers.

As for me, I wasn't sure if I fared so well. By the time my name was finally called, I was totally over the sitting around factor. Guess that's what I got for waiting till the very last minute to sign up for an appointment. Next time I'd know better.

It was at least nine forty-five when I took to the stage and introduced my new (but not-so-fresh) face to the auditioners and what little remained of my new classmates.

Will Bilson seemed totally unimpressed with my rendition of "Cabaret" from *Cabaret.* Maybe because, in the course of close to three hours, he'd heard a dozen interpretations of the tune?

The most recent before mine had been sung by a short, svelte girl with a carrot-colored pageboy haircut, who put her own sardonic spin on the song by singing it with a slight trace of a German accent, à la Joel Grey from the movie version. Both the director and choreographer, and even the stoic stage manager, sat hanging on her every syllable, laughing out loud, smiling their ears off.

Her name, if I recalled correctly, was Ann Marie Tyson, and she totally reminded me of Velma from *Scooby-Doo*, so much so that I expected her to exclaim "jinkies!" at any minute.

Like with Brad Woodward, we were all told before departing to check the board over at 95 West Hancock tomorrow morning for a list of those actors who would be called back for the dance portion of the audition.

Outside in the parking lot, I noticed Ann Marie Tyson smoking a Marlboro Light, my brand of choice. I asked if I could bum one, even though I had an almost full pack in my possession. I was really just looking for a chance to chat with her. In those fast five minutes, I learned that she, too, was a junior in The Department, and she grew up in Troy, which was where my dad used to be a cop, I told her. I could tell by her appearance, the way her nose crinkled when she grinned, that she was totally a hoot and someone I wanted to become close friends with over the next two years.

4

DEEPER AND DEEPER

♦   ♦   ♦

They say a good college bar is hard to find. On the Wayne State campus, however, there certainly was no shortage of options when it came to quality watering holes. Within a mile radius we had the aforementioned Circa down on Cass near the DPL; Union Street, not located on a street called Union but on Woodward Avenue at Willis, slightly north of the Bonstelle; the Bronx on the corner of Second Avenue and Prentis, probably the closet place to knock 'em back after a hard day's classes; Tappers Ten Tavern on Anthony Wayne Drive; and finally, around the block from Tappers on the corner of Forest and Third Street, the aptly named Third Street Saloon, or as everyone in The Department called it, Third's.

This was where I'd found myself, sipping an ice cold Rolling Rock, after the singing portion of the *Chicago* auditions had come to a conclusion around 10:00 p.m.

As I sat admiring the dimly lit, windowless bar, with its smell of stale beer and something I'd heard one of the other patrons refer to as an *olive* burger, I remembered the way Ann Marie Tyson had come running up to me once I'd sung my song, gushing about what a great voice I had, and I thought maybe I didn't sound half bad after all. Perhaps I would indeed find my name listed on the callback sheet come tomorrow morning?

For the umpteenth time that evening, I glanced at my

Swatch, the plastic face informing me that it was way past my
bedtime. I wondered what the hell I was doing out so late,
and why I'd agreed to accompany Rain for "just one drink,"
after she earlier made me aware that she might have a problem when it came to alcohol consumption.

I felt the touch of a feminine hand on my shoulder.

"Miss me?" said Rain in a low, sexy voice, upon returning
from the restroom.

Only this time, she didn't assume her original place in the
seat opposite, as she had when we'd originally arrived. Instead she scooted into the booth beside me, acting as if she
thought we were inevitably going to snuggle. Or have sex.

Had I given her the wrong impression by accepting her
offer to go for a nightcap, à la *The Love Boat*? I'd only acqui-
esced because I thought others would be accompanying us,
like Sarah and, more importantly, Brad Woodward, who'd
totally left me hanging after our run in down in the Bonstelle
men's room. Had I offended him in some way, I wondered?
Here it was, not even the first day of school, and I'd already
gotten off to not such a great start.

When I'd showed up at Third's, I was unfortunately informed that Sarah had decided to bail, insisting she needed to
go home to work on memorizing her lines, in case she got
called back for a speaking role. She couldn't simply read them
cold off the page due to her visual disability, which I still
didn't quite comprehend.

Personally I would've bet money that Sarah didn't want to
spend time with Rain within the confines of a bar after what
had happened at auditions. But that was just a feeling I'd gotten from seeing their brief interaction out in the parking lot
beforehand.

As for Brad Woodward, it seemed by the way Rain acted
when I eventually asked about the boy's whereabouts that
she'd never even invited him to come for cocktails. This made
me wonder if the woman was indeed trying to get me alone,
so she could have me all to herself to do God only knows

what with.

She pretty much answered my question when a new tune started playing on the jukebox and she squealed with delight. "I love this song! Dance with me."

I didn't recognize the ballad, clearly from the early '80s, with its synth-driven rhythm that sounded like the beating of tom-tom drums. A smooth male voice soon cut in with the lyrics, something about a party being over and feeling so tired, till he sees "coming out of nowhere" what I presumed was a female.

As beckoning as the music was, I didn't feel the least bit like dancing. Not at midnight on a Monday that was technically Tuesday. I had my first day of class at a new school in the morning, and I was hoping to make a better impression than I had on the day prior.

"I really should go home," I decided, despite allowing Rain to take me by the arm and lead me onto the makeshift dance floor in a dark corner near the bathrooms.

"Just one dance," she insisted. "We don't have Costume Design in the morning until ten."

"Yes, but I have to drive back to—" I caught myself and quickly covered. "Birmingham." Hopefully Rain was intoxicated enough not to notice the slip.

One thing I'd learn over the years of being a habitual fibber was that if you're going to tell a lie, you'd better have a good memory.

I was forever forgetting whether it was my idea to resurrect TV mega-hunk Jon-Erik Hexum after he'd shot himself in the head or my best friend Jack Paterno's, or if we'd really held a séance in Jack's bedroom late one Devil's Night back in 1984 or not.

Holding my right hand loosely in hers, Rain twirled herself around before spinning inward and leaning her back against my chest. With my right arm wrapped around her waist, we slowly swayed to the beat.

"Don't you just adore this song?" she sighed as it played on.

"I don't think I know it," I shamefully confessed.

"Really? Roxy Music, 'Avalon.' It's off one of my all-time favorite make-out albums." With her free hand, she reached down and gently massaged my left thigh.

I pretended not to feel a thing, but it was my manhood that betrayed me when, miracle of miracles, it responded for the first time—ever—to a woman's touch. Never in my life had I even contemplated anything remotely sexual with a member of the opposite sex; and not since the one time when I French kissed Carrie Johnson at a Fun Night in 7th grade had I even touched a girl, let alone had relations with one.

Like the homosexual hero, Michael Tolliver, in Armistead Maupin's *Tales of the City*, I prided myself on being a perfect Kinsey Six; unlike my best friend Jack, who spent his formative years trying to fool himself into thinking he wasn't *like that*, our teenage code when we still couldn't bring ourselves to utter the word gay.

I made a mental note to self to remember this moment the next time I needed to perform a scene from a play in which I had to act the part of a straight man.

While the song continued with its sax solo, I continued going with the flow, spinning Rain around several times more, twirling her in and out, even dipping her dramatically.

The music finally faded, but she didn't let go of my hand. Instead she turned to face me, her lips mere inches from mine, causing me to put on the brakes—though not before Rain DuBois leaned forward and tenderly kissed me.

She tasted of clove cigarettes, slightly sweet but smoky. Her tongue felt foreign as it worked its way inside my mouth, like something I'd been forced to ingest against my will; *escargot*, perhaps?

I'm not saying it was gross kissing a girl. It just wasn't the least bit entrancing. And yet I still had a raging hard-on.

What the hell was wrong with me?

We came up for air and I looked closely at Rain. There was a faint flush in her cheeks, and her azure eyes appeared red and glassy. I could feel something. It fluttered around inside my belly like a lost butterfly that had flown indoors, totally freaked me out for a bit, and then disappeared.

"'You kiss by the book,'" she said, quoting Shakespeare. "Shall we take this party back to my place?"

"I don't think so," I answered, ashamed of myself for allowing the farce to go this far. "I'm gay, Rain. I like guys."

She smiled demurely. "If you're not interested, say so. There's no need to tell tall tales."

"Cross my heart," I confessed, suiting my action to the words like Hamlet.

"Maybe you just haven't met the right girl?" She cupped my crotch. I flinched. "Are you sure?" she asked, as though I'd passed or failed a test.

"We can still be friends, can't we?"

"Of course." She turned on her high heels and quickly crossed to the exit.

Outside on the deserted street, Rain fumbled for her purse. For the second instance that evening, I came to her rescue by retrieving the clock. This time she'd left it inside the bar, on the bench seat of the booth we'd been happily occupying only moments before. Now it felt as if a metaphoric wedge had been forced between us.

"You want me to walk you home?" I wondered.

She reached inside the bag, found the maroon and white pack of Djarum specials and tried lighting one.

I snapped open my silver Zippo, a gift from Richie Tyler on our first (and only) Sweetest Day, and held the flame aloft.

"Nonsense," she answered, exhaling a plume of gray up into the night sky. "I live three doors down."

I hadn't realized how close we were to her home. But there it was, The Thelma, just a hop, skip, and a jump beyond the Third's parking lot, past an empty alley, and then a few apartment buildings up the block.

"Are you sure?" This was Detroit after all. I knew a single woman shouldn't be wandering the streets alone after midnight. And yet, this wasn't what I was really asking with my question. "Is everything okay?" I said, by which I meant, was everything okay between us.

She smiled at me with a sad smirk, her eyes shiny in the light of the street lamp. "Silly boy," she said, shaking her dark head. "Why wouldn't it be?"

And with that, I watched Rain DuBois stagger away, disappearing into the darkness.

There was no possibility of my making it to class on time the next morning. I'd struggled with the idea of not going; of skipping altogether, but how would that have looked? Especially on the first day. *Better late than never.* My mother's sound advice echoed inside my mind as I sat idling in I-75 traffic just north of I-94, aka the Edsel Ford Freeway, named for the only child of Henry and Clara; a boy who'd been groomed to take over the family's automotive empire, only to die tragically of stomach cancer in 1943 at the age of forty-nine.

Off to the east, something caught my attention. A giant smokestack of sorts, it reminded me of one I would often see when I was little, near 12 Mile in Madison Heights, whenever we'd drive up John R with Mom on our way out to Oakland Mall. My sisters and I would sit in the backseat of our little tan K-car, staring out the back window, keeping our eyes peeled for what we'd affectionately christened The Cloud Maker.

That particular stack, I remembered, was made of reddish brown brick. It sat back from the road, maybe half a mile, adjacent to what was later the Red Oaks Golf Course. Or was it Red Run? I was always mixing up the two Reds.

The chimney before me at this instant was at least twice

as tall as the one from my childhood, if not taller. Maybe even three times the size? It was hard to tell, exactly, from where I sat parked in my car on the freeway.

The color of concrete, the cylindrical object shot up toward the sky like a cement cigar. Three smaller stacks, grouped together, sat atop the summit, from which a plume of gray-white smoke billowed forth. I'd probably seen this place (this factory?) a dozen different times on my travels to and from downtown, and yet I'd never stopped to consider its purpose until this precise moment.

As quickly as the flow of traffic had subsided, it once again resumed. I went on my way, proceeding full speed ahead in search of an available spot in the structure on Palmer.

Unfortunately all levels were full, except for the tippy top, where I had no problem parking, my poor Plymouth exposed to the elements. Before leaving Dad's, I'd heard Channel 4 meteorologist Chuck Gaidica warn that the temperature would be climbing to above normal that afternoon. When I returned to drive home later, the vinyl interior would surely be scorching, and I'd burn my bare thighs.

Technically it was still summer for another three weeks, so I probably shouldn't have been surprised, which is why I decided to throw caution to the wind and wear my favorite khaki-colored shorts, along with the dark green tee I'd gotten on sale at Express. I also didn't think it would hurt to be showing a little leg when I ran into a certain someone, as I knew I'd inevitably encounter Brad Woodward.

With a song in my heart, I turned off the car's engine and yanked the keys from the ignition. Tossing them into my book bag, I remembered I needed to call Jack and invite him and his new boyfriend to my birthday fête on Friday night. Not that I was excited about turning twenty-two—I mean *twenty*, thanks to the new fake age I'd recently adopted.

Twenty-two... God was I getting old!

I completely missed the beginning of the lecture, arriving even later than anticipated after not being able to locate the small design studio where Costuming I (THR 510) was being held, tucked away in a back corner of the Theatre Production Center, aka Ninety-Five.

"Come on in!" the woman standing at the board squawked as I tentatively stuck my head in the door. "Take a seat. We're just getting started."

I assumed she was the teacher, Marian Stockholm, but she didn't bother introducing herself. Instead she spoke to me as if we'd already met many a time. She appeared fortyish, with short brown hair that was flecked with specks of gray and cut in a blunt style, complete with bangs. She wore an aqua-and-white floral print dress with a wide belt wrapped around her hippy midsection. The garment's silhouette—and the woman, in general—reminded me of Barbara Billingsley of *Leave it to Beaver* fame. Yet this lady's demeanor was nothing like that of a 1950s housewife.

After almost every word, every sentence that she completed, a cackling laugh echoed off the walls of the windowless room, and I seriously expected her to drop an F-bomb or four before the hour was up. I totally loved her.

"*Bradley!*"

Hearing someone hiss my name, I turned to discover Rain DuBois perched at one of the drafting tables along the back wall, legs crossed, looking quite the sight. She sported a black leather mini-skirt, paired with a shiny white blouse worn beneath a dark silk blazer with serious Krystle Carrington, aka Linda Evans from *Dynasty,* shoulder pads. Fishnet stockings covered her shapely calves, and a pair of candy apple-colored pumps decorated her petit feet. Bright crimson coated her lips, as it had when I'd first made her acquaintance.

To Rain's right, an empty stool eagerly awaited my arrival. I hesitated, contemplating whether I wanted to further interrupt class by having to cross all the way to the other side.

Instead I chose to take a seat beside Sarah, who sat hunched over a composition book, black Sharpie in hand, at the table closest to where Marian Stockholm stood. Glancing down at Sarah's notes, I noticed her handwriting matched the child-like scrawl I'd seen printed on the mailbox outside her and Rain's apartment over at The Thelma.

Rain glared at me with her baby blues. Her jaw tensed, and I could totally tell she thought I was intentionally avoiding her. This wasn't the case—not exactly—and I promised myself that I'd fully explain the situation should she call into question my rude behavior.

At the sudden movement of me sliding onto the stool next to her, Sarah looked up, startled. Dressed more sensibly for school in jeans and a light summer sweater, she stared at me for a split second then smiled with warm recognition. "Oh, hey, Bradley."

"Hi," I said softly, focusing on the woman at the front of the room who waited to resume speaking.

"Now where were we?" said Marian to no one special.

"Magic garments," a resonant male voice replied.

There was no need to turn around in order to figure out who was sitting at the table directly behind me: none other than Brad Woodward.

It had only been a little over twelve hours since singing auditions had concluded when I, along with Rain DuBois, Sarah Schwartz, Brad Woodward, and a host of other Wayne State actor-types, crowded around the callboard in the downstairs hallway of 95 West Hancock to ogle surly stage manager, Amelia Morganti, as she posted the *Chicago* callback sheet and see if we had, as they said in showbiz, "made the cut."

Me, I couldn't bring myself to take a peek, an apprehension dating back to high school when I first started auditioning for shows. I dreaded the moment the cast list went up and had always been one to anxiously avoid it.

The first time I got a part in a play, I didn't even know it until two days later when Mr. Dell'Olio called to ask why I hadn't accepted by initialing next to my name, something that was standard practice in the world of the Theatre. Or at least it had been at Hazel Park High.

As Amelia slunk away, there were cries of excitement mixed with moans of disappointment as the mosh pit of bodies vied for position, all clamoring to get a closer look at the list, like lions in the Detroit Zoo at feeding time.

Brad Woodward, being one of the taller boys in The Department, towered well above most of the other Thespians. His reaction at seeing his own name listed among the actors up for leading roles was one of calm recognition. He closed his dark eyes, their long dark lashes brushing lightly against the lower lids. Opening them, he shook his head wildly and let out a whooping howl.

"Congratulations, Brad!" someone cheered, squeezing his baseball of a shoulder as he weaseled his way through the crowd and disappeared into the restroom.

It was Ann Marie Tyson, aka Velma from *Scooby-Doo*, not to be confused with Velma Kelly from *Chicago*.

The grin that stretched her chubby cheeks clearly indicated that she, too, had been called back for a significant part: Mama Morton, the corrupt Cook County prison matron. I found this an interesting choice and was super psyched for her. No doubt she was a talented performer, and I could just imagine her take on Mama's show stopping number, "When You're Good to Mama."

"Congrats, Ann Marie!" I said, giving her a hug.

Her face lit up, and she enveloped me in a sea of patchouli oil. "You, too!"

I did a double take, giving myself permission to peek at the list where, lo' and behold, my very name was included at the bottom, under the leading male role of Billy Flynn, famed Chicago lawyer, responsible for the exoneration of murderesses Velma Kelly and Roxie Hart; two roles that both Rain and Sarah were up for, respectively.

Of course I didn't expect to get the part. From what I could tell, Brad Woodward was the Tom Cruise of the Bonstelle acting company. I would've totally been pleased just to be part of the ensemble.

In the ecstasy of the moment, I'd almost forgotten something crucial: I had to work from five to eleven that evening.

"I don't know if I can make it tonight," I told the girls, though I didn't say why, lest they should ask questions. To tell my new friends I waited tables at a hick diner in a podunk town would've totally blown my new cover.

"You have to come to callbacks," Rain cried. Her brow furrowed, and her face contorted into a look of pure panic.

In the three-plus years I'd worked at Country Boy, never had I ever taken time off that I hadn't requested weeks in advance. If there was one thing instilled in me by my dad, it was a serious work ethic and the appreciation of a dollar.

Growing up dirt poor on the south side of Ferndale, just four blocks north of the Detroit border, made me realize that once I started making my own money, like my all-time favorite movie heroine, Scarlett O'Hara, "As God is my witness, I'll never go hungry again!" Still, I'd come to Wayne State to be an actor, not a waiter.

"I'll see if I can change my plans," I decided, making up my mind to do whatever it took to secure a spot on the *Chicago* cast list.

"I don't even know why they're bothering to hold callbacks," Sarah said. "It's gonna be you as Velma..." She looked directly at Rain, who seemed satisfied with her roommate's prediction. "And Brad as Billy Flynn. Sorry, Bradley."

"And you as Roxie, of course," Rain replied.

Sarah said, "From your lips to God's ears," sounding like the Jewish grandmother I imagined she'd grown up with.

"I'm just happy to get a callback," I insisted, because it was true.

Nobody at Wayne State knew me from Adam. To find myself up for a leading role in a mainstage show after my very first audition was an amazing accomplishment, and one of which I was rather proud. I couldn't wait to tell my parents.

"So should we head over to Old Main?" Sarah suggested, the crowd in the hallway at Ninety-Five starting to thin.

"I'm ready." Rain took hold of my arm. Surprisingly she acted as if nothing awkward had gone down at Third's last night when she kissed me or, as a result of her action, I told her I'm queer.

I looked around the empty corridor, not quite ready to depart. "Should we wait for Brad?" I wondered. "I think he went to the bathroom."

"He'll find his way across the street, I'm sure," said Rain. "He's a big boy."

Sarah snickered. "You would know."

"Don't remind me," Rain replied, repulsed.

Judging by the look she gave Sarah, I got the distinct impression that Rain DuBois and Brad Woodward (my Brad Woodward!) had slept together—at least once.

This was something I did not want to think about and, therefore, I switched back to my original subject. "I'd hate to just take off on him."

"Rain's right," said Sarah. "Dina gets totally heck-yeah if you're late for class."

"Seriously?" I asked, stalling.

Sarah nodded, saying, "One time I got to Two Forty-Five," the number of our classroom in Old Main, I would soon learn, "like two seconds after she already shut the door..."

"And what happened?"

"She wouldn't let me come in till the break."

"You're kidding?"

"She also wouldn't let me make up my scene," added Sarah. "My partner was totally pissed."

"I remember," said Rain, turning to me. "I was her scene partner. *Laundry and Bourbon.*"

"I don't know it," I confessed. "Sorry."

"Don't be," Rain told me. "It's not a very memorable play."

"Well, if I was *Rain*," Sarah said, "Dina would've totally let me in the room. She loves her."

"What can I say?" asked Rain innocently. "Everybody does."

"Especially Dina French," said Sarah.

A subtle hint of innuendo hung above this statement, but neither Sarah nor Rain would bother elaborating for my benefit.

5

IT'S A FINE DAY

♦   ♦   ♦

Upon arrival at Old Main, I will admit, I was a tad disappointed. Yes, the building was totally ancient, which made it totally awesome, but it was also the type of place one might describe as being a total pit. The ochre-colored brick was in dire need of sandblasting after years of dirty Detroit air had soiled and discolored its exterior. I almost tripped up the stairs in the dim front entryway that led into an even darker lobby, a single naked bulb providing the only bit of illumination. My classmates, Rain and Sarah, both acted as if it was no big deal paying good money to attend a university with one of the most reputable Theatre programs, and there wasn't even adequate lighting in the facility where they received ninety percent of their training. But who was I to complain? I felt lucky just to be studying at Wayne State.

"Should we take the elevator?" I asked, noticing the one inside, off to our left.

"If you want us to be late for sure," answered Rain sarcastically.

"It's the slowest elevator on campus," Sarah explained. "We always take the stairs."

Our footsteps echoed off the high arched ceilings as we hurried down the wide center hallway. On either side, a series of classrooms sat, each with heavy wooden doors, dark wooden floors, and small student desks placed before actual old-fashioned blackboards. Again, each room was scantily lit by a singular bare light bulb; maybe a pair at most. I now understood why they called the campus's central building *Old* Main. It looked like nothing had been updated or replaced since the Nixon administration, if not earlier.

The girls took a left through a set of double doors and huffed their way up two flights of steps, Sarah in clunky Doc Martens, and Rain in her dainty stilettos, until they reached the next floor. The women seemed quite used to this type of physical strain, actually, as they'd been doing it on a daily basis for the past four semesters. Me, I'd done more walking in the last day than I could remember since I started driving, with hiking the mile to and from the parking structure, now taking the stairs. Where I grew up, we got into our cars and drove a single block just to mail a letter. The Daytons were not a pedestrian people, nor were the citizens of Hazel Park and/or Ferndale for that matter. No wonder there was a growing obesity epidemic in the state of Michigan. Plus my habitual smoking didn't help with my lung capacity either. And yet I knew Rain DuBois to be a smoker, and she seemed just dandy.

"You coming, Bradley darling?" she asked, turning to gaze down on me from where she stood at the top landing.

"Oh, sure," I said. "If I don't die of heart failure."

"No rest for the wicked," Sarah said, quoting someone.

That person of authority would turn out to be our fearless Scene Study teacher, Dina French.

The woman was a god! The entire junior class of the Wayne State Theatre Department (me included, and I'd only just met her) found themselves completely enamored by the instructor. The minute she burst into our acting studio, like a damn breaking, I could tell she meant business. Dina flung open the door to Two Forty-Five, designer leather bag slung over one shoulder, decked out in a black leather mini-skirt, similar to the one Rain wore, also paired with fishnets and four-inch matching pumps. Like Rain, the rest of her ensemble consisted of a shiny white blouse, unbuttoned to show off a tasteful amount of cleavage, and a black silk suit jacket with serious shoulder pads. Even her skin resembled Rain's: snow white and powdered to perfection. Her full lips were also painted the brightest red. The only real difference between the two women was the shock of short black hair that adorned the top of Dina's head, and her heavily-mascaraed, chestnut brown eyes. They twinkled brightly as she greeted the student actors waiting with rapt attention for her arrival.

"Good morning, everybody!"

I could tell from the raspy quality of her voice that Dina was a pack a day smoker. I prayed that we would get along famously and vowed to do whatever I possibly could to impress her with my talents.

She strode across the worn wood floor with its strips of colored tape laid down over the years, mapping out the set pieces and scenery for one rehearsal or another. Dina plopped her black leather bag down onto a sturdy wooden table that had been set up for her use as a teacher's desk. I hadn't seen who'd done the deed, but I assumed it was the boy sitting eagerly beside it, hoping to be acknowledged by the master, Dina French herself.

She completely ignored him.

"What time is it?" she asked, pulling up the left sleeve of her suit jacket to reveal a chunky man's watch with a silver face and black leather band.

I noticed that the boy sitting beside Dina's desk wore a similar item about his wrist, in addition to gray acid wash jeans, a purple paisley shirt unbuttoned to the center of his baby smooth chest, and what Zack Rakoff, my high school classmate and fellow Drama Queer, would refer to as New Wave boots. I hadn't a doubt the guy was gay. Whether he knew it or not, only time would tell. Looking around the room, I caught sight of several other distinct Dina clones. A different boy sat with a similar black leather bag by his side. A second girl had the exact same short, spiky haircut, only hers wasn't quite as dark as dear Dina's.

The boy sitting beside Dina's desk flashed his same silver watch in a way that looked, to me, like he was trying to show it off for Dina's sake, hoping she would take note and sing his praises for his taste in time pieces.

"It's eleven-seventeen," he promptly replied, though it was perfectly clear to everyone else that the question had been rhetorical.

Dina turned her attention to the boy at last, eyes crinkling up at the corners, her plump cheeks dented by a duo of dimples. "Thank you, Sage."

I visibly blanched at the mention of his name.

"No problem," he blushed.

Something told me that Sage's parents were former hippies, and I decided he might be a good person to befriend, for when I needed a partner in crime to go out to the gay bars.

"And what time does this class start?" wondered Dina, addressing the room.

Rain shifted slightly and crossed her legs, deliberately for Dina's benefit. "Eleven-fifteen."

It totally worked.

Dina whipped her head around at the sound of Rain's voice. She gasped, dramatically placing a hand to her heart. "Rain? I almost didn't recognize you. What happened to your beautiful blond hair?"

"I colored it?" she said, confidence slowly fading. "For *Chicago* auditions last night. I got a callback for Velma Kelly."

Dina's lips twisted into an approving sneer. "So you did? Break a leg! And I love what you're wearing, darling."

"Thank you," said Rain, clearly flattered by the sought-after compliment.

"Sorry I'm late!" At that moment, Brad Woodward came barreling through the double doors. He'd obviously also taken the stairs, and yet he wasn't the least bit fatigued. On the contrary, he appeared totally pumped up and was practically bouncing off the walls.

"*Entrez*, Mr. Woodward," Dina said sternly, but with a smile. "If this were an audition and you walked in one second past your allotted time slot, what would happen?"

"They wouldn't see me," Brad answered, the dutiful disciple. "I know." He glided across the floor, moving to take one of the empty mismatched seats among his peers.

"Don't even bother getting comfortable," Dina told him. "You're up!"

Brad smiled sheepishly. "I am?" With that, he changed directions, mid-step, and literally skipped to the front of the room.

How someone could have so much energy at this time of morning, I couldn't comprehend. Maybe he was an early riser and had been up for hours, taking a jog or working out in the weight room at the Matthaei Athletic Center? Brad was certainly hopped up on something, and I hadn't seen him come into class with a cup of coffee or even a Big Gulp.

"Good morning," he said, instantly turning on the charm.

"Good morning," said Dina, one hip resting against the top of the table. "You're a bundle of nerves today. Too much caffeine?"

Brad grinned. "Not enough." He laughed, as did everyone else in the room.

I could tell that all the women—and even some of the men—were totally smitten with the guy. Even if it wasn't in a sexual way, he definitely had them eating out of the palm of his hot big hands.

Brad quickly shook out his limbs and tilted his chin to his chest, allowing his head to loll around on his shoulders in a circle as he warmed up his instrument. He wasn't dressed particularly well: faded jeans, a blue Yale sweatshirt that appeared to have been laundered several dozen times, and white canvas Chuck Taylor's. His hair wasn't even styled, and he hadn't bothered shaving. Yet he still looked totally hot.

God I hated him!

"Good morning," Brad repeated, doing his best to stand still and remain serious as he delivered his standard audition monologue introduction. "My name is Brad Woodward. My selection is Bernard from *Sexual Perversity in Chicago* by David Mamet."

The room fell silent. All ears focused on Brad Woodward's every word. Before our very eyes, he went from a rich, Preppy, 20-year-old kid to this totally sexy man, talking about picking up a chick at the Pancake House and banging her in a hotel room after buying her a pack of Viceroys. He even had the Chicago accent down perfectly, which made him even sexier. Maybe I'd been totally wrong about Brad being gay? Unless, of course, he was pulling another Rock Hudson and fooling us all.

I sat in my seat feeling like a total fraud because, sooner or later, I would have to get up in front of everybody and present my piece. I knew there was no way Larry the gay best friend from *Burn This*, ranting about going to a gay New Year's Eve party, would come off as anything but my being totally gay. As my mom liked to say, "You only get one chance to make a first impression." What would Dina French and the rest of my new classmates think of me (or my talent) if I came across as a flaming faggot? Surely that guy Sage would love it, but him, I wasn't hoping to impress.

I really should've given my monologue selection a little more consideration when I learned I'd need to present one on the first day of Acting. Instead I asked my best friend Jack to ask his new boyfriend Kirk, who also fancied himself an actor, for a suggestion. Kirk loaned me a copy of the script by Lanford Wilson, and I thoroughly enjoyed it on the first read. But I should've chosen one of Pale's speeches, the butch leading man played by John Malkovich on Broadway.

"Thank you."

I'd been so inside my head I failed to hear the final half of

Brad's monologue. At its conclusion, he took a seat on one of the torn pumpkin-colored, vinyl-covered chairs in the back of the classroom. Sarah reached up and gave him a high-five. Clearly they were good friends, despite his implied past relationship with Sarah's roommate, and I decided I could try pumping her for information on Brad once I'd gotten to know her better.

"Who'd like to go next?" Dina surveyed her students. A smattering of hands shot up, including Sage's, the girl with the Dina haircut, and the guy who carried the similar leather satchel. Of course none of these three acolytes did she cast her eyes upon. Instead she stared directly at yours truly. "You must be Bradley Dayton," Dina said sweetly. Obviously I was the only actor in the room whom she hadn't instructed before.

"Yes, ma'am," I replied politely, harkening back to my mother's Southern roots out of nowhere.

"Call me Dina," she insisted. "Are you ready to wow us?"

"I don't know about that," I answered humbly. "I'll try."

"Please do." With a flourish of her wrist, Dina presented me with the floor.

Standing in front of my classmates, I took in my surroundings. Behind me, a set of dirty windows looked out at a dirty alley-like alcove alongside the soot-covered brick building. Two dirty dumpsters overflowed with industrial strength garbage bags, and I could've sworn I also saw an industrial-sized rat scurrying off, carrying an entire bagel in its not-so-tiny mouth.

In the corner to my right, a spiral staircase made of wrought iron, with an intricately detailed handrail, wound its way upward, disappearing into a boarded up hole in the ceiling. It appeared as if the steps had once led to somewhere, another floor most likely. I remembered hearing that Old Main used to be a high school, that Two Forty-Five and the adjacent Hilberry rehearsal room had been part of the gymnasium, and that an old track still existed in the rafters above.

Like adjoining hotel suites, each studio could be accessed separately, or from one to the other through either a pair of double doors that had been built into an orange partition located on my left, or through a separate single entrance at the opposite end of the room, built into the same orange wall.

"Good morning," I said to Dina and to my classmates. A lump lodged in the depths of my throat, and I coughed twice, trying to clear away the clog caused by pure panic.

From her desktop perch, Dina beamed at me with her twinkling brown eyes. "Good morning."

"I'm Bradley Dayton. I'll be doing—"

"Stop," said Dina, abruptly interrupting me. "Start over, please."

"I'm Bradley Dayton. My monologue is from—"

"Stop," Dina ordered, yet again. "My name is Dina French," she demonstrated. "My selection is Hermione from *The Winters Tale* by William Shakespeare. Now you try it."

"My name is Bradley Dayton. My selection is Larry from *Burn This*," I said, voice quavering.

"And who, pray tell, is the playwright?"

My mind became a blank slate. For the life of me, I couldn't remember who wrote the damn play I'd only just recently read. I stood there feeling totally lame, the world slipping out from under me. I wanted nothing more than to crawl up the spiral staircase with the wrought iron rail and disappear into the boarded up ceiling.

"Lanford Wilson," said Dina, providing me with the answer. She turned toward the others in my class. "We must always give the playwright credit. Do you hear me? Without her—or him—we actors would have no words."

"I'm sorry," I said from my position in front of the firing squad. "I knew it when I came up here. Guess I'm just nervous." I laughed, hoping to have the same effect on the room as Brad Woodward had, but the silence was deafening. I could see Sarah sitting in the front row, head buried in her notebook, and Rain, in back, looking at me like I'd totally let her down.

"Don't be sorry," Dina insisted, "and don't be nervous. Be brilliant. As the great Goethe once said..." She paused dramatically, as if she were about to pluck an obscure object from the Theatrical ether. "'I wish the stage were as narrow as the wire of a tightrope dancer, so that no incompetent would dare step upon it.' Whenever you're ready, Bradley Dayton. Wow us."

If only it were that easy.

And so, with the stealth mind and body of a surgeon about to execute the most critical of operations, I mustered up my courage, my focus, and my will and opened my mouth to speak. The next two minutes whizzed by like a bullet, a high-speed train crossing the Japanese countryside, a Bavarian racecar traversing the *Autobahn*. By the time I finally finished, it felt as if I'd yet to begin.

On the break, I found a payphone in the Old Main lobby, shut myself inside, and called my boss up at Country Boy. She was a handsome woman, in her mid-thirties, with a gap-toothed grin that showed too much gum. A housewife and mother of five kids, she'd married her high school sweetheart and was still wed to the same man after almost two decades. She'd always been kind to me, and we got along well, telling each other crass jokes and gossiping about which waitress was carrying on with what dishwasher or busboy. It pained me deeply to have to lie to her, as it had with my new friends.

"Hey, Barb... It's Bradley. I don't think I can make it in tonight."

"Oh, no, hon!" she cried with concern. "You's ain't caught that flu bug what's been goin' around, did-ja? My oldest boy Mikey's been losin' it from both ends all week."

I feigned a cough, hoping it would aid in my acting the part of a sick person. "That must be it. I just threw up. I hope it's only a twenty-four hour virus."

"Bless your heart," said Barb. "I'll ask one of the girls if they can cover your shift. Feel better, hon! Okay?"

"I'll try."

The rest of Acting was spent with Dina giving us feedback on our audition monologues. She also provided suggestions as to what we should focus on for the rest of the semester, in terms of both our strengths and our weaknesses. Not in so many words, she advised that I choose some more masculine material, perhaps Stanley from *Street Car* or something by a playwright I'd never heard of before, David Rabe; either *Hurly Burly* or *In the Boom Boom Room*—but not the effeminate neighbor character. She said the exact same thing to that Sage guy, who gained a last name in the span of the two hours we'd spent together: Ang. I didn't think he was Asian in the least bit, but I could've been wrong.

Personally I thought Sarah gave the best performance when she got up to present her piece, a beautiful soliloquy from a seldom produced 1950s play called *The Ladies of the Corridor* by Dorothy Parker. I'd not known Ms. Parker to be anything but a poet and wasn't the least bit familiar with this heartbreaking drama about a group of women residing in a boarding hotel in Manhattan. The character that Sarah chose to take on was the middle-aged Mildred Tynan who, like a certain type of widowed lady living in NYC during the Eisenhower years, would spend her afternoons sitting alone at the front counter of Schraff's Drugs, getting falling down drunk. The transformation that this 20-year-old Jewish girl from Oak Park made the moment she spoke her first line totally blew my mind and took my breath away.

At one-fifteen, we broke for lunch. I was invited by Rain and Sarah to join them at Little Caesars in the Student Center, or as they called it, the Stupid Center. Reluctantly I accepted, after learning Brad Woodward would be heading home to take a catnap before our next class began.

"Are you sure you don't wanna come?" I asked, stopping

him from slipping out the side door of Old Main and down
the fire escape.

"Thanks for the invite," he declined. "I need to go home
and get some rest. I'm pooped all of a sudden."

I'd noticed his energy level start to fade after sitting in the
same chair for over an hour, listening to our classmates acting
up a storm. Most were exciting enough to hold our attention.
Rain, for one, gave an interesting take on Lady M from
Macbeth, playing her as a total sex kitten while she attempted to wash the "damn spot" from her hands.

Even Sage Ang made me laugh with his rendition of a
man giving a speech on how he no longer was a negative person after taking a personality workshop, from a comedy
called *Laughing Wild* by someone named Christopher Du-
rang. One thing I learned on that first day of class, to my disappointment, was that I didn't know a whole lot about the
goings on in the New York Theatre world, for someone who
aspired to be a part of it.

"Are you coming, Bradley?" Rain stood in the doorway of
Two Forty-Five, waiting impatiently for me to stop gabbing
with Mr. Golden Boy.

I was starting to get the feeling that she didn't want me
even looking at Brad Woodward, let alone speaking to him.
"Be right there," I told her. "Have a good nap," I said to Brad.
"See you in Theatre History?"

He grimaced. "I'm actually not taking that course."

"You're not?" I said, hoping I didn't sound too disappointed.

"No, I took it last year, to get it out of the way. I have a
private voice lesson with Francine Brockton at three."

"Who's Francine Brockton?"

"Only the most awesome opera diva in Detroit. She
teaches over in the Music Department."

"Really? I've always wanted to take private singing lessons," I lied. "Maybe you can hook me up with her?" Anything so we would have more in common.

"Maybe," he replied, a hesitation in his voice that made me think he didn't want the potential competition.

Well, too bad! I was there at Wayne State to become a star. As much as I had the hots for him, Brad Woodward wasn't about to stop me from succeeding in my mission.

6

MYSTERIOUS WAYS

◆　　　　　　　　　◆　　　　　　　　　◆

Try as I might to resist, it seemed I'd be spending the rest of my afternoon in the company of a woman who, I was beginning to realize, didn't comprehend the meaning of the word no. After lunch, I weighed the pros and cons of driving home to my dad's verses sticking around campus for another three hours.

"You're welcome to come by our place," Rain offered. "Until it's time for callbacks. Sarah won't mind."

"Not at all," Sarah answered the non-question. "Columbus isn't home. I'm just gonna sit in my room and go over my script."

"That's a good idea." Rain took me by the arm, leading me down the stone steps. "We can work on a Velma/Roxy/Billy scene, the three of us."

En route to The Thelma, we passed by an abandoned, burned out building, up the block from the prestigious, pillared Hilberry Theatre, facing the side of Old Main. In black scrawl, the words HOUSE YOUR HOMELESS had been spray painted across the brick façade. I found it hard to believe that, on the campus of a major state-owned university, such a relic was allowed to remain, a reminder of the gritty urban decay that had plagued the city of Detroit for over two decades.

Ten minutes later, Rain dug into her clock-purse in search of her keys. "Welcome to our love den," she said devilishly, as Sarah and I followed her inside.

Believe it or not, I caught myself staring at the back of Rain's skirt, totally checking out her rather shapely rear. Never in my life had I taken the time to admire a woman's figure. But there it was, right in front of me. How could I not notice?

"Make yourself comfortable," Sarah told me, turning on a tarnished brass floor lamp.

Outside, the sun had not yet begun setting, but the home into which we'd entered had been shut up like a tomb for much of the afternoon, giving it a funereal feel.

The living room was rather spacious for a student apartment, with mismatched secondhand pieces that looked as if they'd been stolen from the supply of rehearsal furniture in Two Forty-Five. A tan wingback chair with the faintest pink pinstripe sat against the left-hand wall. In the not-quite-center of the room, a gray upholstered sofa faced a portable TV set perched on a stand in front of the front windows. What could only be described as drapes hung from above, shiny and wrinkled, like something fresh from the 1960s.

The most ornate object in the room had to be the fireplace situated on the right-hand side, with its wood mantel and beveled mirror. It was both beautiful and tacky. On the mantle shelf, an array of half-empty booze bottles happily awaited the arrival of the next drunken brawl.

"I love this," I couldn't help remarking aloud.

"What's that?" asked Sarah, unaware of what I was looking at.

"This horse picture on the wall here," I clarified.

Beside the fireplace hung one of those wood-framed prints matted on cardboard that one would buy at someplace like Kmart or Kresge's. This particular piece of art work presented a nighttime scene, dark with heavy clouds, and two wild stallions galloping away from the threat of a distant storm.

"Oh, thanks," Sarah replied. "That's what I call it. The

Horse Picture."

"You do?"

She nodded sheepishly, as if she was ashamed to admit such a silly thing. "I got it from my grandma up in Bad Axe. It used to hang over the back of her living room couch."

"My grandma had a framed picture hanging over her couch, too," I said, happily surprised at the similarity in our childhood memories. Only Grandma Victor's showed a pastoral scene, with a babbling brook and cider mill and a ginger-headed boy she'd always say was me, out hunting pheasants with his salt-and-pepper speckled pointer.

"Is that right?" asked Sarah. "Where did you grow up?"

I hated myself for having to lie to her. Still, I said, "Birmingham. But my grandma lived in Highland Park," which was the total truth.

A city completely surrounded by Detroit, except for the small section of the southeast corner touching Hamtramck, the area that would become Highland Park started out as a small farming community, located on a large ridge at what is now Woodward Avenue and Highland, six miles north of downtown. In 1860, the settlement was given a post office under the name of Whitewood, and in 1889, finally became incorporated as a village using its present moniker.

In 1907, famed American automaker Henry Ford purchased one hundred and sixty acres of land between Woodward Avenue and Oakland Street, just north of Manchester Street, to build an automobile plant. Completed in 1909, the construction of the Highland Park Ford Plant dramatically increased the area's inhabitants in just a few short years, particularly after 1913 when Ford opened its first assembly line.

In 1925, American automotive industry executive Walter Chrysler founded the Chrysler Corporation, also in Highland Park, after purchasing the Brush-Maxwell plant located within the city limits. Chrysler Corp. eventually grew to a size of one hundred and fifty acres and became the site of the company's headquarters for the next seventy years. Ford Motor Company would wind down operations at its Highland Park plant in the late 1950s. In the last decades of the 20th century, the city experienced many of the same difficulties as neighboring Detroit, including an increase in street crime, accompanied by accelerated "white flight" that resulted after the infamous Detroit 12th Street Riot of 1967. Ford's last operation at the factory was discontinued in 1973. A year later, the entire property was sold to a private developer for general industrial usage. To the disdain of most of its citizens, the population of Highland Park became heavily black and impoverished by the 1980s.

Fortunately my mom was able to get out once she met and married my dad. After graduating in 1964 from the other HPHS—Highland Park High School—Laura Victor continued working in the tissues and pathology lab at Detroit Osteopathic Hospital, right near her home in HP, where she first became employed part-time at the tender age of Sweet Sixteen. In the winter of 1966, she met James Bradley Dayton, an officer on the Troy police force who, at the time, was attending night school down at Wayne State, pursuing a degree in Physical Education.

The pair became acquainted one evening, by chance, when Laura's car broke down alongside I-75 after she'd been out holiday shopping at Oakland Mall. Officer Dayton picked up Miss Victor in his squad car and offered to drive her home, all the way down to Highland Park. On the way, they got to talking, and the couple bonded over their mutual Baptist upbringing and shared love of bowling.

A whirlwind courtship soon followed, and the happy couple tied the knot in November 1967. Within months, Laura found herself pregnant with her first child. Jim insisted that his wife immediately quit her job to stay at home and be a proper mother. It wasn't that he didn't want Laura to work, but Jim worried his fellow officers would accuse him of not being able to provide for his family on his own accord. On

October 19, 1968, Janelle Lynn was welcomed into the world. A son, Bradley James, followed on September 4, 1970. Two more daughters came along within the next four years: Nina Renée on February 3, 1973 and Brittany Susan on April 29, 1974. The Daytons first resided in the suburb of Center Line, until 1979 when a fire ripped through their home, forcing Jim and Laura to move the family to nearby Ferndale, where they would live together (not always happily) for the next three years. In the winter of 1982, Jim and Laura separated, citing Irreconcilable Differences. An order of divorce was soon filed and granted the following spring.

Back in The Thelma...

Sarah stood beneath the doorway to the hall, holding a black three-ring binder. "I'm gonna go look at my Roxie lines a bit," she told Rain and me.

"Let us know when you're ready to rehearse," Rain replied. She stretched and yawned in a rather showy display, revealing a bit of her bare midriff. "I could stand to rest a spell. Bradley, care to join me?"

I wasn't sure if it was the tiny hangover I'd awoken with after last night's drinking binge, or the fact that I'd been going all day after not being a student for the past few years, but I was plum tuckered out.

"I can lay down here on the couch," I decided. "Just make sure you don't let me sleep too long."

"Nonsense!" Rain sang sweetly. "You'll do no such thing. The bed in my boudoir sleeps three." Linking her fingers in mine, she gently pulled me into the dark of the corridor.

"Pleasant dreams," Sarah said, shutting her door.

From the way she bid us goodbye, I got the faint impression that Rain hadn't told Sarah about my professed homosexuality, and that Sarah thought, perhaps, for the next hour Rain and I would be doing anything but resting.

I found her room unexpected and terrifying; crimson-colored and covered in lace and leather, both hard and soft, feminine yet masculine. In one corner, a dressmaker's dummy wore a black rubber bustier, like something out of Victoria's Secret—or perhaps naughty Noir in Royal Oak. Pinned-up posters papered the walls. But unlike the innocent portrait of Sarah's youth hanging in the front room, these were dark images of Alternative bands like Nine Inch Nails, The Cult, and Tool. I was horrified, in particular, by the black-and-white image of a hairy boar being stabbed in the belly by a bevy of silver forks, the word UNDERTOW shaved into its side. In total contrast to these stark images, a beaded rosary hung draped on the spindle of her antique vanity dressing table mirror. Along the table's surface, a vast collection of vials rested in a row, filled with womanly liquids of differing aromas.

I felt like a lamb being led to the slaughter. Never had I been in a bedroom belonging to any woman other than my three sisters, my lesbian friend from high school, Luanne Kowalski, or my dearly departed Audrey Wojczek at whose house I would sometimes spend the night, that's how platonic our relationship had been.

"Why don't you take a load off," Rain suggested before she stepped out to use the restroom.

I couldn't bring myself to sit down on her bed, so I stood admiring the books that lined the bookcase beside it. Among her collection I discovered *Le Petit Prince*, in both French and the English translation, a tattered paperback copy of *Interview with the Vampire*, *The Story of O*, and *Flowers in the Attic*. I'd read none of these novels, though I'd heard about the upcoming film version of the Anne Rice bestseller with River Phoenix slated to play the role of the interviewer. I had the biggest crush on him when I first saw *Stand By Me* back in junior high, and I loved his portrayal of a gay hustler in *My Own Private Idaho*. Too bad Keanu Reeves had to go and ruin most of the movie with his bad acting and accent from nowhere.

When she returned, Rain wore nothing but a black silk

robe, slim-hipped, her dark hair pulled back into a ponytail
held up by a pink scrunchie. She looked like someone from
another era, the wife of some 1940s mobster, off bootlegging
booze or shooting up somebody. For a brief moment, I felt
the thrill of what it must be like for a heterosexual male to
stand before a beautiful woman.

"You wear Poison," I stammered.

"Aren't you a smart man?" she said coyly.

"So does my sister, Janelle."

"Please don't tell me I remind you of your sister."

"No, you most definitely do not."

She grinned impishly. "I hope you're not bothered by my
changing. I can't sleep unless I'm practically nude beneath the
covers."

"Actually I'm the same way," I said, wishing I hadn't, but
it was true. I also needed to lie on my side with a pillow
propped between my knees, though this bit of personal information I managed to keep to myself.

"Feel free to undress, if it makes you more comfortable."
Rain sat down on the edge of the chenille bedspread. "I won't
bite," she promised, patting the spot beside her. "Unless you
want me to."

Without consciously knowing what I was doing, I
reached for the buckle on my belt. My shorts fell to the floor
in a heap around my ankles. Stepping out of the khakis, I
climbed into her bed, breathing in the spicy scent.

"Goodnight," I said, even though it was barely five o'clock
in the afternoon. I rolled over to face the wall, hoping to con-
ceal the uncontrollable swelling in my underwear.

For the callback, Pia led us upstairs to the Bonstelle Room.
The space was small, with a slick floor of polished blond
wood and a low ceiling, and was used for dance rehearsals
during mainstage musical productions and concession sales at
actual performances. Pia lined us up, boy-girl, and she taught
us a Charleston, set to the *Chicago* overture. Apparently this

move was a big one of sorts, as most productions never involved choreography at the very top. Usually the orchestra would just play and the curtain opened on Velma Kelly already in the night club setting, singing. But this was something Pia had been dying to replicate since first seeing the original on Broadway, on a very special occasion when Gwen Verdon was out sick and her last minute understudy was announced as none other than the legendary Ms. Liza Minnelli.

For the combination, I found myself paired not with Rain DuBois as I feared she might see to it, but with a petit blond sophomore, Hannah Weiss, who was a killer dancer with a killer bod to boot and the second Jewish person I'd met in a single week. Unfortunately Brad Woodward totally ended up beating me out for the male lead, Billy Flynn—as if there had ever been a doubt to his getting the part. I'd thought that maybe my Irish ancestral background, not to mention my auburn-colored curls, would serve me well in the auditioners' minds. But there was no way in hell that Brad Woodward was walking out without another star credit to add to his already lengthy résumé.

The good news was: I ended up getting cast as a member of the *Chicago* ensemble, which was perfectly fine by me considering I don't think my dance audition was quite up to par with some of the other performers. One in particular, a tall, lithe boy with long silky hair the color of toffee (and even longer limbs) was sure to be dancing on Broadway within the next decade, he was that amazing.

His name was Torrance Andrews, but Rain and Sarah simply referred to him as Rance. I had the feeling he might also be gay, but there was a shy innocence about him that made me wonder if he had any sexual preference whatsoever. Not that he wasn't worthy of someone's affection, male or female. Torrance was gorgeous! Just not my type. Still, I hoped we'd become lifelong friends, and one day we'd find ourselves sipping late night Long Islands in some New York

City go-go boy bar down in the East Village.

Thinking about it, I'd have bet donuts to dollars—thank you again, Mom, for the lovely turn of phrase—that every guy in the entire *Chicago* cast, with the exception of a couple, was of my same sexual persuasion. There was the man playing the Emcee, Leslie Wolf, who was intriguing in his own right since he was well into his mid-thirties and only a senior in college. The other, Brett Pearson, was also a senior and an excellent tapper with ankles of rubber. He seemed like a really nice guy from the little bit I'd talked to him over at the Bonstelle. With the exception of Max Wilson, whom I'd been friends with since 4th grade, I didn't have a lot of straight males in my immediate social circle, and I looked forward to getting to know these two better.

One casting bit of note: Sage Ang won the role of Mary Sunshine, the savvy newspaper reporter who follows the trials of both Roxie Hart and Velma Kelly and who, in most productions, was revealed to be a man by show's end. Based on Sage's singing audition the night before, I had no doubt he could pull it off. The guy had a falsetto to rival opera soprano, Renée Flemming. I was more interested in how he'd appear as a dame, and I berated myself for not thinking to audition for the part.

In high school, I competed in an amateur drag contest at a club called Gigi's, dressing up like Lynn-Holly Johnson, aka Lexie Winston from one of my all-time favorite movies, *Ice Castles.* Sadly I didn't win the fifty dollar first prize. But at least I had the balls to actually sing my song, "Through the Eyes of Love" by Melissa Manchester, while wearing a pair of actual ladies' ice skates. I didn't lip sync like the bitch who won, Honey from Chattanooga, with her stupid pet boa constrictor and her fake boobies!

The big *Chicago* scandal came with the casting of the women's roles. When the final list went up on the callboard in Ninety-Five on Friday morning, as per usual, we all gathered around waiting anxiously for Amelia Morganti to post the results. As expected, Ann Marie Tyson single-handedly stole the part of Matron Mama Morton. No surprise, Sarah Schwartz—make that Gibson—also got cast in one of the lead roles, but the poor visually impaired girl couldn't read her own name as printed on the list. The type was too small.

"What's it say?" Sarah asked obliviously. "Did I get Roxie?"

All around her, she heard everyone cheering and offering their honest good wishes—excluding her roommate.

"No, I'm sorry to say you did not," Rain replied. The expression on her face had fallen completely flat after realizing that her supposed best friend had been chosen to play the part she'd been openly coveting since the production had first been announced. "Congratulations, *Velma*."

"Oh, my God!" Even Sarah herself couldn't believe the upset. At callbacks, she'd never even read or sang for Velma Kelly. She'd been up onstage most of the night singing "Funny Honey" and "Roxie," two of Roxie Hart's big songs. Pia hadn't even bothered teaching her the choreography for "Cell Block Tango" because Roxie wasn't in the number.

Clearly there was some sort of a coup going on and, judging by the rage turning Rain's azure eyes green with envy, the girl wasn't having it. She wasn't about to pick a fight with Sarah in public, however. No, she would save her accusations for when the women were alone in the privacy of The Thelma.

I honestly didn't know what to say. I certainly wasn't about to get stuck in the middle of my two new friends, so I observed the right to remain silent.

We headed over to Old Main where we had Voice with a man named Stefan Hinckley. He'd started teaching us this special technique called Alexander that involved a process of lengthening and widening the body, and letting the neck be free, so that an actor could speak better when performing. We'd only had one class so far, on Wednesday morning. I hadn't a clue as to what I was doing really, but Stefan was cute in an elf-like sort of way, and it felt good to just lie on the floor of Three Hundred, aka the dance studio, and relax for a little while; so long as I didn't fall asleep and start snoring.

7

FRIDAY I'M IN LOVE

♦   ♦   ♦

A new gay-owned restaurant had recently opened up, and my good friend Miss Peter had been dying to check it out. At last I relented, promising we could go for dinner before heading down to Detroit to go dancing, though at my age, I wasn't even sure I had it in me. I'd been going out to the bars on a regular basis since I turned sixteen, and I was starting to tire of the scene.

As I'd figured (and feared), Royal Oak was a buzz of social activity, as per usual for a Friday night. Along with the arrival of quaint little boutiques like Cinderella's Attic and Incognito, the area had become totally trendy. But it was also beginning to attract the wrong kind of crowd. On the corner of Fourth Street and Lafayette, a wannabe Hard Rock known as the Metro Music Café had popped up a few years prior. Jack and Kirk had gone there on one of their first dates, and Jack conned me into checking it out, claiming how cool it was to see such Motown memorabilia as a framed gold record belonging to The Supremes or an electric guitar autographed by Joey Ramone. Big deal! It wasn't as if they had Madonna's wedding dress from when she sang "Like a Virgin" on the MTV Video Music Awards on display. One would think they would have, being that Ms. Ciccone was a famous native Detroiter.

Parking my car in the structure on Sixth Street, I was becoming an old pro at knowing on which level to find the best spot: always the top. With any luck, I'd lost five pounds after all the walking I'd done the past week. The night air was crisp and cool, and I took the opportunity to light myself a fresh cigarette and amble along slowly, "in the moment" as Dina French would say. I'd never been one to revel in the celebration of turning another year older, unlike Jack who'd thrown himself a bash on practically every birthday since I'd known him. There was always so much going on, with Labor Day and the start of school, and Mom had always spent what little pennies she'd managed to pinch on getting our school clothes out of lay-away. I couldn't expect her to also throw me a party or buy me a present. Plus a birthday was just another reminder of how much closer to death I was crawling. Who wanted to think about that? And yet I didn't feel a day older than I did on the first day of 7th grade when Jack and I first met.

To make a long story short...

Like all good little gay boys, Jack Paterno had found himself sitting with a group of girls in the Webb Junior High cafeteria at lunch. Ava Reese, Jack's rival for Student of the Year and later our high school drum major, had been going through a slam book she'd made, asking everybody at the table to answer the important questions she'd come up with: "Smurfs or Garfield?" "John Cougar or Rick Springfield?" "Calvins or Jordache?" Precisely at that instant, I waltzed up to the table where Ava sat on her throne, high and mighty, holding court and was all like, "Fuck those! I like Sergio Valentes better 'cause they make your ass look hot." At least that's the tale Jack had enjoyed telling over the past ten years. I seriously doubted I'd ever use such foul language in front of my female classmates.

Standing on the corner near an antique furniture store, I smoked my Marlboro Light. It was my birthday, and all I wanted to do was go and find Brad Woodward—or any gay boy for that matter—and get myself a great big, sloppy birthday kiss. I couldn't remember the last time I'd engaged in a remotely sexual act, let alone gotten laid; probably back in the late spring when Richie Tyler and I were still romantically linked. I really wanted to run far, far away and hook up with some random stranger. But I knew it wasn't possible, what with the whole AIDS epidemic getting worse with each passing day. I'd never been one to have promiscuous sex out of fear that I'd end up contracting some horrible disease, be it HIV or gonorrhea or, God forbid, crabs. Besides, I couldn't go off on some rampant sexual adventure even if I'd wanted to. I was obligated to attend my own birthday gathering.

"Isn't this place cute?" Miss Peter cried, once she and I had finally been seated with Jack and Kirk outside. She wasn't really a she. Miss Peter was a man, Peter Little. But I'd been referring to her as Miss Peter since our first meeting when I was a wee lad of seventeen. I also sometimes called her The Once-ler, after the character in Dr. Seuss's *The Lorax*; the one who's always sitting with its arm out the window, cigarette in hand.

Officially called Pronto! "608" after the street address etched into the glass above the front door, the place was cute indeed, with brightly painted primary-colored walls and matching table tops. As the story went, four friends—Jim Domanski, Tom and Joy Murray, and Bill Thomas—opened a small carryout deli and catering company in late December of 1991. Business was slow at first but eventually picked up speed once local food critic Molly Abraham wrote about the new dining establishment in her column, exactly one month after the initial opening. The wonderful food and delightful atmosphere had impressed Abraham, and the first weekend after her review ran, business tripled with customers lining up around the corner. In the spring of '92, the forty-seat patio was added, making it the largest of all the outdoor cafés in downtown Royal Oak.

"I don't know why we haven't been here before," Jack wondered.

"Beats me," said his better half, joining the conversation.

All around us, groups of other gay men were dining and drinking and having a gay old time. I could tell by the way Jack beamed when he looked about, and the way he lightly touched Kirk's arm as it rested on the table top, that it felt good for him to be a part of that gay camaraderie; to be (quote-unquote) out and about after so many years of living in a closet. Granted, Jack still hadn't told his family he was gay, but neither had I. Not officially. At least he'd finally found someone, and I hoped his relationship with Kirk would last well into the next century.

"I haven't been here either," I said, picking up a menu to peruse the list of specials. "But I'm all the way on the other side of town."

"Are you still living at your dad's?" Kirk asked me across the table.

I'd almost forgotten he'd been to my father's house before, on the first night he and Jack had spent together. Both guys were home on Christmas break from Michigan State but staying separately at each of their parents' places. They had nowhere they could go and be alone, so I agreed to loan them my room for the evening. Like Barbra Streisand in *Hello, Dolly!*, I prided myself in playing matchmaker whenever possible.

"I am," I said in answer to Kirk's question. I explained how I'd been down in Ann Arbor with my ex, but I'd returned after we'd broken up. "How about you?"

"I'm back with my folks in Center Line," said Kirk, "saving money to move to New York. Jack's gonna try his hand at playwriting, and I'm gonna be on Broadway, of course." There was a slight hint of sarcasm in his tone, but I had the feeling Kirk believed what he was saying, and I envied his confidence.

"I love New York!" Miss Peter gushed. "I've never been, but it's on my bucket list."

"You'll have to come visit us," Kirk offered.

"I'll be sure to take you up on that, Kurt," Miss Peter promised. None of us at the table had the heart to correct her. "Don't you live in Center Line, too, Opie?"

"No," I said, mortified that Miss Peter had referred to me by the nickname she'd given me on the night we'd first met; and in front of Jack and Kirk no less. "I used to live in Center Line, when I was like seven."

I'd lost track of the number of times I'd reminded Miss Peter of this fact over the course of our five-plus year friendship.

"You lived in Center Line?" Kirk asked, sounding stunned, even though I was positive we'd discussed this pertinent detail before. "On what street?"

Whether I'd wanted to or not, I was about to take a walk on Memory Lane. "We lived down from the Vern Haney's on Sterling."

"Kirk's family lives on Sterling!" cried Jack, like we were all gathered around some Las Vegas slot machine, and we'd just hit the jackpot.

Learning this made me feel the way I had upon discovering that Brad Woodward and I both shared the same first name. At first, the coincidence came as a bit of an unexpected surprise. To think that you'd resided for a time on the same stretch of land as someone you'd only recently met, but your paths had never crossed... It was really just another example of how the randomness of life can't really be so random; how we were all interconnected by some cosmic destiny, some divine intervention that brought us together at the precise moment we were meant to meet. I mean, what were the odds I'd be a gay kid growing up in a hick town like Hazel Park, and I'd befriend another gay kid who would wind up becoming my very best friend in the world?

The waiter arrived to take our orders. I went with the Pronto! pasta and a glass of Merlot, which made me think of

Rain. I'd only mentioned her briefly to Jack and had said nothing further with regards to how close we'd quickly become. I definitely hadn't uttered a word about the effect she'd started having on me down yonder in my nether regions. Brad Woodward, however, was a whole 'nother story, and I couldn't wait for the chance to introduce them.

Jack and Kirk both ordered burgers and a beer. Miss Peter asked for a salad "with the dressing on the side," something she'd been insisting on since first seeing *When Harry Met Sally* a few years back. I kept reminding her she was no Meg Ryan, but she just told me to eat shit and die.

Kirk and I spent the next few minutes going over the details of our growing up in the same city. It turned out that he'd gone to Saint Clement, the private parochial school, while I was at Miller, a public elementary. Eventually Kirk convinced his parents to allow him to attend Center Line Schools. But by the time he'd enrolled at Bush Junior High, my family had already moved to Ferndale.

We did discover that we had some of the same mutual friends: Lydia Zahn, Katie Cardellini, Stephen O'Donnell, Kelly LaPere, Diane Genia, Nissa Washburn, John Valente, Beth Westland, to name just a few.

"I did *Breakfast Club* with Lydia, Diane, and Beth, and *Snoopy* with Kelly," Kirk told me. "She was Peppermint Patty, and I played Snoopy."

"Of course you did," I said, trying not to sound too snotty, though I was beginning to think that Kirk Bailey and Brad Woodward needed to start comparing notes on what it was like to be such a Golden Boy.

"So how did you two kids meet?" Miss Peter asked Jack, sucking on her Merit Ultra Light. I could tell they'd both gotten bored listening to Kirk and me ramble on about our bygone Center Line days.

"They met at Michigan State, right?" I said to Jack, hoping to draw him back into the story.

"Let Jack talk," Miss Peter scolded in her Brenda Vaccaro

smoker's voice.

"We met at Michigan State," Jack confirmed. "We were in the same class."

"And what class was it?" asked Miss Peter, clinging to Jack's every word. "I didn't go to college. I wanna imagine I'm right there with you, sharing the experience. Leave out no detail." She took a big swig of her Captain Morgan and Diet Coke, her preferred beverage of choice.

"It was called Theatre Lab," Kirk chimed in. He and Jack had both been drinking Coronas with limes. They did this thing where they stuck their thumb over the bottle opening, turned it upside down and waited for the citrus wedge to drift upward before clinking the bottle bottoms together.

The moment Jack turned his bottle right-side up and removed his thumb, *cerveza* sprayed all over, shooting directly in Miss Peter's direction.

She cried, "Careful, the coif!" and shielded herself like a chrysalis in a cocoon. Luckily she wore her favorite black shawl wrapped around her shoulders (to "ward off a chill") which she used to cover her head, à la the Virgin Mary.

"Oh, my God! I'm so sorry," Jack apologized. He grabbed a fistful of napkins, leaned across the table and helped Miss Peter wipe herself off.

"That's okay," she droned dryly, "I haven't been shot in the face since like 1985." Safely out of harm's way she said, "Continue."

If there was one thing that Miss Peter was proud of, it was her hair. Sometimes she wore it up, all ratted like Robert Smith from The Cure. Other times I'd see her, she'd look totally different, with a long bang drooping down over her left eye or a prominent side part. In honor of my birthday, however, she chose a more masculine style similar to the way Jack had been wearing his hair for the past year or so, like those two totally cute guys on that TV show, *Beverly Hills, 90210*; sort of reminiscent to something out of the '50s, à la James

Dean, i.e., puffy in front, short around the sides and back, and with sideburns. Miss Peter had become a professional stylist after studying Cosmetology in high school twenty years before. She worked at one of the most high-end *salons* in all of Metro Detroit, Palazzolo, located right up the block from Pronto! on Washington.

"It was a class called Theatre Lab," Jack reiterated for Miss Peter's benefit after her hair emergency. "I was studying playwriting and Kirk was—"

"Is," Kirk interrupted.

"*Is* an actor," Jack corrected.

Miss Peter's perfectly shaped, caterpillar-like eyebrows inched up her well-exfoliated forehead. "Our boy Opie is an actor, too, you know?"

This was the last topic I felt like discussing on my birthday, of all evenings.

"He is?" asked Kirk, giving me a glance that indicated he was again surprised (but also intrigued) at our having something else in common.

"I told you that," Jack interjected. "I told you Brad starred in all the plays we did in high school. I mean, I didn't do them. I wasn't a Drama Queer, but..."

"That's awesome," Kirk said. "What parts did you play?"

I could've killed Jack for opening his big mouth. Now I would have to admit I hadn't played all the lead roles—just most of them.

"I really don't remember," I lied. "It was sooo long ago."

"Yes, you do," said Jack, sounding exactly like my mom. Whenever I would say something like, "Mom, I'm sick," so I could get out of going to school, Laura would be all like, "No, you're not," totally contradicting me.

"Kirk really doesn't care about my high school Thespian credits," I decided.

"Sure, I do," said Kirk. "I wouldn't ask if I didn't."

Pretending to jog my fading memory, I said, "Let's see... I played Seymour in *Little Shop*, Will Parker in *Oklahoma!*"

"You mean *Okla*-homo*!*," Jack interrupted, reminding me of the old joke we'd shared since we were sophomores and I auditioned for my first musical at HPHS.

"I played Curly in our production," Kirk informed us coolly. "Too bad my hair's not the least bit."

That was sure for certain. Kirk wasn't a bad looking guy, but his dark blond hair was bone straight, as my mom would say, and almost shoulder length; much longer that it had been the first time I'd met him last Christmas.

"You should've been Curly, huh, Opie?" said Miss Peter, laughing like a hyena before hacking up a lung. She crushed out her cigarette—and promptly lit another. "So what are you working on now, Kurt?"

God bless her!

Kirk smiled and replied, "I just started rehearsals for *Mass Appeal* out at Meadow Brook."

This bit of information suddenly caught my attention. Meadow Brook was a professional Equity theatre situated on the campus of Oakland University. Not to be confused with Oakland Community College. In fact, it was *the* theatre to work at in the Detroit area in terms of prestige and, more importantly, pay.

"How'd you get cast in a show at Meadow Brook?" I asked, attempting to express more curiosity than envy.

"I went to their general auditions right after I graduated from MSU last spring," Kirk nonchalantly answered. "I got a callback, and then they offered me the part. It's a really awesome play and a really awesome theatre."

"The Bonstelle is pretty awesome." I decided I wasn't about to allow this guy to continue making me feel inferior. While I'd never seen Kirk do a lick of performing, I knew that I, too, was a talented actor and that one day soon, my time for working on a professional level would also come.

"Brad goes to Wayne State," Jack said, forgetting I'd made it perfectly clear that part of my new collegiate identity involved calling me by my full first name.

"Wayne State's a good school," Kirk said, "from what I've heard. Are you in a show now?"

"I just got cast in *Chicago*," I said. "We start rehearsals on Monday. It's a musical."

"I know! It's one my favorites. We did it my junior year up at State. Are you Billy Flynn?"

"I'm in the ensemble... And I'm Billy Flynn's understudy."

"Isn't he the guy you were gushing about?" asked Jack, his ears perking up at my mention of Brad Woodward.

"He is," I sighed, wishing Brad was right there with us.

Miss Peter shook her head. "Don't even get him started," she warned. "On and on about this Billy Flynn babe. I keep telling Opie, just get the guy drunk and jump his bones."

Kirk smiled at me, knowingly. "That's what Jack did. Plied me with White Zinfandel." I noticed the color of his eyes, like two crystal pools, and of course I thought of Rain DuBois.

"Kirk played Billy Flynn," said Jack, embarrassed by his boyfriend's revelation, though I'd already heard the story of how Jack had managed to weasel his way into Kirk's life (and his bed) despite Kirk's dating a *woman* named Raquel at the time.

"Of course he did," I said.

"I saw the show," Jack added. "Kirk was awesome."

"Of course he was." I called over our waiter, desperately needing a refill on my Merlot. Something told me it was going to be a long birthday.

Two hours and several glasses of wine later, the waiter brought our bill, and we began settling up. The other guys insisted I put my money away, and I couldn't refuse their generosity. As I'd taken the other night off from work for the callback, I knew cash would be tight in the coming week. We paid the check and stepped out onto the sidewalk in front of the restaurant.

"Where to next?" Kirk asked, folding a stick of Double Mint into his mouth.

"That's up to Brad," answered Jack. "It's *his* birthday."

I glanced at the happy couple a moment and noticed how much they looked like twins. Not that their appearance was identical, but they both wore similar short-sleeve, button-down, polka-dotted shirts, blue jeans and black leather belts with big Santa Claus buckles, and clunky black leather shoes. A small silver hoop hung from each of their left earlobes. Jack Paterno had sure come a long way from the Preppy who cuffed his pants and popped the collars of his polo shirts.

"The only decent place on Friday nights is Menjo's," I declared from firsthand experience.

The thing about the gay scene in Detroit that always amazed me was how certain bars were only busy on certain nights. Fridays and Sundays, everybody frequented Menjo's on 6 Mile. Saturdays and Wednesdays, the crowds clamored into Backstreet, behind the Farmer Jack out on Joy Road. Monday drag nights were a tradition at Gigi's. Tuesdays were totally reserved for the wet Jockey shorts contest at The Gas Station, where I actually worked for a brief time back in high school, waiting tables and occasionally assisting the drag queen hostess, Lady Z. Zephyr. I'd help squeeze her into her swimsuit before she'd crawl into the kiddie pool to hose down the boys. At one point, I was sooo poor I'd considered entering the contest myself, but Miss Peter wouldn't allow it, as I was then still a minor.

"Sorry, Opie," Miss Peter apologized. "My old pussy is beat. I'm going to bed."

"It's only ten-thirty," Jack whined.

"At eleven, I turn into a big gay pumpkin."

"It's okay," I said. "I'm not really feeling it either."

"You can't go home," Kirk informed me. "Not on your birthday."

"I'm sorry, you guys. I've had a long week. Now I'm all

bloated from dinner. Can we take a rain check?"

"Sounds perfect," said Miss Peter. She reached into her man-bag and removed her car keys, attached to the Chippendales keychain I'd given her for her Big 3-0 a few years before. "Who's walking this old lady to her wheelchair?"

"I will," I told her. "Where are you guys parked?" I asked Jack.

"At a meter over by Jimi's."

"Who's Jimi?" said Miss Peter, making a face that looked like she'd smelled something foul.

"It's that dairy queen," answered Kirk, "across from the Methodist church, right around the corner."

"Must be why I don't know it," Miss Peter mused. "I can't go within ten feet of a holy place. I'll spontaneously combust. Goodnight, girls." She leaned in and gave Jack a kiss on the cheek. "Bring your cute boyfriend to see my new house sometime."

"New house?" asked Jack, taking care not to muss Miss Peter's hair as they hugged. "You're not still living in East Detroit?"

"You mean East*pointe*," snapped Miss Peter sarcastically. "And no, I'm not. Not since they got all hoity-toity."

The city where she'd lived since childhood had recently changed its name after residents approved a referendum, the intended desire being to remove any perceived association with neighboring Detroit, lying directly to the south. The new suffix had been chosen in order to associate the municipality with the nearby affluent communities of the Grosse Pointes. A few months prior, Miss Peter had come into some money when her only living relative, an aunt named Eleanor, had passed away, leaving her million dollar fortune to her only nephew. Having had enough of the pretentiousness that came with living in the newly appointed *pointe*, Miss Peter opted to make the move to an entirely different neighborhood.

"You should see Peter's new place," I told Jack, taking

care to not call Peter *Miss* in front of her—I mean *his*—face. "It's totally fabulous."

"He's right," Miss Peter agreed. "It totally is."

"It's a Frank Lloyd Wright house," I bragged for my own benefit, hoping to finally impress Jack's boyfriend.

"Awesome!" Kirk cried. "Where is there a Frank Lloyd Wright house in this area?

"Palmer Park."

"Palmer *Woods*," Miss Peter corrected. "Get it right, Opie. How many times I gotta tell you?"

We were totally blocking the sidewalk, but I hadn't realized we'd be continuing our conversation after we'd already said our goodbyes. I really just wanted to get into my car and drive back to Dad's. All the talk at dinner about Kirk and his budding professional acting career had really gotten me bummed.

"Shall we go?" I said to Miss Peter after thanking Jack and Kirk again for a lovely evening, even if I really hadn't enjoyed most of it.

"It was nice meeting you, Kurt," Miss Peter told Kirk, and she and I headed up the sidewalk.

As soon as I got in my car, I completely regretted my decision to send my friends on their merry way. I was 22 years old, not some middle-aged relic like Miss Peter who needed a full night's beauty rest. Only a little over an hour of my birthday remained, and I was bound and determined that if I wasn't going to have sex with somebody, I'd at least get myself a special birthday kiss—from a sexy, special guy.

8

I'M TOO SEXY

♦ ♦ ♦

Before I could change my mind, I headed west on Lincoln toward Woodward Avenue. Seeing the reflective white letters on the green metal street sign, of course, totally reminded me of Brad, the boy I hoped would give me my special birthday kiss before the stroke of midnight. Next thing I knew, I was Detroit-bound on I-75 with the radio blaring my new favorite Reba song. I contemplated, for all of two seconds, driving down to the Wayne State campus, but I convinced myself how crazy I'd look if I just showed up at Brad's front door and threw myself at him. Especially since I worried he wasn't actually gay, after overhearing Rain and Sarah's earlier discussion.

At 7 Mile, I exited the freeway and, against my better judgment, headed over to Dequindre, driving through a foreign neighborhood that sat a mile due south of Hazel Park. Growing up in the "Friendly City"—though I would defend myself if anybody accused me of doing so, stating proudly that I hailed from Ferndale—I had no idea that just six blocks away there existed this seedy, underground world of gay bars and nightclubs.

I hadn't been down to this particular part of Detroit in longer than I could remember. Not since the last time I'd hit the Malebox with my good friend Sean. Three years my senior, Sean had gone to high school on the eastside in Fraser, but he'd wised up and gotten the hell out of Motown back in the late '80s. Living with his longtime companion out in Anaheim, California, Sean would only come home to visit family each Christmas, which was the last time I'd run into him down at The Gas Station, the exact same night I'd made the mistake of leaving with Richie Tyler, resulting in my wasting eight months of my life with a boy who wound up breaking my heart a second time around.

When I met Sean back in the day, we were both employed at Oakland Mall. I used to go into Harmony House, where he worked, on my lunch break from the Gap next door, and we soon bonded over our mutual joy for The Judds. Sean had always reminded me of Nick Kamen, the British model and singer-songwriter from the Levi's "Launderette" commercial, circa 1985; the one where the totally hot guy strips down to his undies so that he can wash his stone-wash jeans in the washer. Kamen also hit the UK pop charts with his debut single "Each Time You Break My Heart," which was written and produced by my favorite Material Girl, Madonna, coincidentally enough.

Stopping at the red light, I double checked that my car doors were locked, safe and tight. In the distance, I could see my final destination, kitty-corner from the fluorescent-lit Church's Chicken, where an overweight African-American woman counted out crispy legs and thighs behind bullet-proof glass. It wasn't too late to turn back, I told myself. But my twenty-second birthday had almost come to a close, and I realized maybe I was indeed in the mood to experience some debauchery. It might have been all the wine I drank with dinner clouding my better judgment, though thankfully not impairing my ability to operate an automobile, but suddenly I felt the need for someone to notice me.

While I'd never been adventurous enough to frequent this particular club before, I'd heard tell that, for a few measly dollars, one could rather easily get themselves some attention; and I was hell bent on getting myself that special birthday kiss—even if I had to pay for it.

The light turned green. I lifted my foot off the brake pedal and forged ahead.

Dennis Bruce had the reputation for being a real queen. He was an attractive man, more pretty than handsome, recognized for his strawberry blond locks and the flashy gold jewelry he regularly wore. But despite his effeminate demeanor, when push came to shove (and the alcohol started flowing), Bruce could become one nasty son of a bitch. He had no qualms whatsoever about tossing a disorderly patron out the door on his ass or firing a bartender for refusing to pool his tips. Descended from one of Detroit's richest families, Bruce first opened the infamous Club Riviera as a disco in the mid-1970s. Under his ownership, The Riviera catered to a clientele of older, married men who turned out in search of discrete sexual encounters with much younger boys. This was how Bruce had met his longtime lover and eventual business partner, Salvatore Lombardi.

Rumored to be a member of the Detroit mafia, Big Sal was a made man with a wife and kid somewhere out in one of the wealthier suburbs. Because of his so-called underworld connections, the club soon became a den of drugs and sin. Lombardi was said to have certain members of the Detroit PD tucked away in his back pocket, resulting in no shortage of hustlers working the room, mixed in with a barrage of go-go boys chatting with the chummy clientele, clad in their skimpiest Fruit of the Looms. The strippers who appeared onstage nightly were said to have been part of a male prostitution ring, run jointly by both Bruce and Lombardi.

As gay history goes, in the spring of 1984, the couple had a major falling out. After almost an entire decade together, Bruce had grown tired of sharing his man. He presented Lombardi with an ultimatum: either leave the wife and kid and settle down permanently with Bruce, or Bruce threatened to have a little chat with Lombardi's little lady. Not one to be blackmailed, Lombardi called Bruce's bluff. But Bruce stuck to his guns and paid Mrs. Lombardi a personal visit, where he laid it all on the line, outing the woman's husband of fifteen years. When Lombardi returned home that evening, he found his beloved spouse lying facedown in the marble bathtub, her wrists slit and seeping blood. An autopsy would also reveal a slew of prescription drugs in the woman's system, predominately Methaqualone, or in layman's terms, Quaaludes.

Two nights later at The Riviera, Dennis Bruce encountered a pair of handsome strangers. The trio got to talking and a mutual attraction was acknowledged, at which point the newly single Bruce invited the gentlemen back to his Sherwood Forest mansion, just west of Palmer Park, for a little private party. As lore would have it, the men proceeded to tie Bruce up. But instead of the kinky *ménage* the bar owner had been expecting, the duo beat the 33-year-old man to a senseless, bloody pulp. When Dennis Bruce's dead body was later discovered, his signature strawberry blond curls had been cut off, and all his gold rings had gone missing—as did the fingers upon which he'd once worn them. Shortly thereafter, after laying his wife to rest in the White Chapel family plot, Sal Lombardi became the sole proprietor of Club Riviera.

On the rare occasion that I frequented the bars in this notoriously unsafe area, I'd take my chances, parking across the street in one of the cyclone fenced-in lots. Some burly black man was always standing by to guard your car, so long as you tipped him on your way home. Trying to cross 7 Mile was the challenge. One either ran the risk of getting shot—seriously—or having someone scream *faggot!* as they drove on by. But since I was flying solo (and always feared dying on my birthday), I decided to invest the two bucks and valet.

I'd like to think that one couldn't discern by my appearance alone that deep down I had a thing for dodgy male strippers. Growing up, I'd seen all the movies that touched

upon the taboo subject, however brief: *For Ladies Only* featuring Gregory Harris, *A Night in Heaven* starring Christopher Atkins, the scene from *Bachelor Party* with Nick the
Dick, aka Thomas the Gardener from *Young Lady Chatter-
ley II.* Not only did my infatuation focus on the hot-bodied,
half-naked men, there was something about the power one
must've felt in knowing these hunky guys would do anything
to get you to shove money down their drawers.

There was also a part of me that wondered what it must
feel like to be the one up onstage doing the stripping; to have
all eyes lusting after you; to make a shitload of cash for simply taking off your clothes. I seriously considered applying
for a job in a gay male strip joint, if the whole acting thing
didn't end up working out.

After giving over my car keys, I waltzed up to the windowless brick building on the warm late summer eve. A neon
pink awning spanned the length of the bar's exterior, and I
stood beneath the canopy, patiently waiting to be buzzed inside.

As I stepped through the glass door, the scent of stale beer
and cigarette smoke smacked me full-on. I smiled at the sil-
ver-haired Bea Arthur look-alike manning the electronic register. She was elegantly dressed in a pair of white polyester
pants with the crispest creases running up the front and a sequined leopard print blazer that twinkled beneath the disco
lights. She sat side saddle on a high stool, striking her best
1950s movie starlet pose, the toes of her taupe slingbacks
daintily touching the filthy tile floor. All the while, an Eve
120 dangled from her lower lip.

"Five dollars," she told me in a loud, deep voice, compet-
ing with the song-stylings of SNAP!'s "Rhythm is a Dancer"
blaring from the DJ booth. Maude accepted my money with
her bejeweled right hand while using the left to press the buttons on the cash machine with her red manicured nails.

Pausing a moment, I stopped to admire my surroundings.
A well-stocked bar lined the left-hand wall, at which a shirt-

less bartender mixed drinks. He'd obviously seen the movie *Cocktail*, deftly twirling the liquor bottles before he poured. Glassware, cleaned and polished, hung down from a gold-painted rack high above. On the wall opposite sat another bar, this one horseshoe-shaped, with yet another shirtless bartender planted behind. On top of this particular counter, three muscular men (two African-Americans and an Arab) gyrated to the beat of the music. Each adonis sported only a skimpy G-string and tan Timberlands. The guys didn't so much dance; there wasn't room. Instead they gingerly tip-toed about, doing their best to avoid stepping on the fingers of the spectators leaning against the bar, staring up in lustful admiration with their dollar bills ready. The trio of go-go guys couldn't have been much taller than me; otherwise they'd not have been able to stand in an upright position. As it was, two of the three had to keep his head tucked against his massive chest, so as to avoid hitting it against the low-hanging ceiling.

To the right of the horseshoe-shaped bar, a group of middle-aged, middle class men sipped cocktails and smoked cigarettes at small café tables. A heavy cloud hovered over the area, obscuring the row of red banquettes that lined the far wall. Whoever designed the place had been smart by covering the perimeter in mirrored tiles. They not only classed up the tiny club but gave it a sense of being grander than it actually was—at least in terms of square footage.

Due to the warm weather, I hadn't bothered wearing a jacket along with my Girbaud jeans and black T-shirt, so there was no need to visit the coat check. I crossed to the non-go-go boy bar and ordered a Bud Light. After all these years, I couldn't believe I'd taken to liking beer. When I'd first started drinking back in high school, about the only thing I could stomach was either Sloe Gin Fizz or Boone's Farm Strawberry Hill. I lit a cigarette and scanned the crowd for potential suitors. On the whole, it wasn't an attractive bunch. Most of the Club Riviera patrons appeared forty-plus, with receding hairlines, walrus mustaches, and pot bellies. In short, they looked a lot like my dad. From everything I'd read, the strippers were by far the hottest guys to ever step foot in the joint.

According to my Swatch, it was just a hair shy of eleven-thirty. I pictured Miss Peter at home sound asleep, curlers in her hair, an avocado mask covering her freshly moisturized *visage*. I wasn't sure where Jack and Kirk would wind up. They weren't big into the bar scene, at least not when it came to the ones in the bowels of Detroit, where the majority of the gay clubs could be found. They'd been spending a lot of time at this straight bar out in Pontiac called Industry. Despite having a serious boyfriend, Jack had a flirty thing going with the 28-year-old DJ, a studly dude named Tony, and he took advantage of having his drinks paid for whenever possible.

Speaking of studs... I couldn't help but wonder where Brad Woodward was spending his Friday night, and I berated myself for being too much of a coward to drive down to Wayne State and ring his door bell. There was nothing I could do but drink my beer and try to forget, all the while focusing my attention on finding someone worthy of kissing before the next thirty-three minutes ticked by.

"Want some company?"

After about two seconds, I was approached by one of the would-be hustlers. He was all of eighteen, if the kid was even that, a classic ectomorph with a slender, hairless torso, small, narrow shoulders and long, thin limbs. The bunny from *Bambi* thumpered its way across his flat, square chest. As a general rule, the twink-types did nothing for me, sexually speaking. It wasn't even like I was at the bar to hook up. I just wanted to get some innocent play—but only from a hot male stripper.

"I'm waiting for someone," I told the boy with the rabbit tattoo. "Sorry."

"I'm someone," he said, giving my bicep a playful squeeze. "Ooh, you must work out."

Not wanting to be rude, I craned my neck and peered aimlessly about. "Um..."

The entire bar went black.

"And now..." A booming voice broke through the thick fog that had begun filling the room from all four corners. "Put your hands together, boys, and get your dollars ready. Club Riviera is proud to welcome our favorite Friday night attraction..."

A blue spotlight came up on the far side of the horseshoe-shaped bar, where a real-live shower had been placed upon a small stage, completely encased in Plexiglas to impede the excessive flow of water.

"The one, the only..."

The new single by the British duo Right Said Fred started playing, the deep bass of the lead singer declaring that he was far too sexy for his love. The song may have been totally silly, but the two bald guys in the band were both totally gorgeous, and the more I heard the tune, the more it grew on me.

"*Sexy Sid!*"

Inside the see-through shower, a dark-skinned black man materialized, the muscled knots of his back turned to the audience. He slowly spun around to face front and began lathering up the mounds of his beefy pecs provocatively. Soap suds dripped down the crevice between his chiseled six pack, en route toward the bulge in his red *Baywatch* bathing suit.

"I'm sorry," I told my admirer. "I think I see my friend." And with that, I tore myself away, hoping to get a better view of the hunk of man-meat now prominently on display.

Never in my life had I watched another man bathing. Well, in junior high, I'd discretely spy on my swim coach, Mr. Grant, rinsing off naked after swim practice. But back then, I wasn't supposed to be gawking. At Club Riviera, voyeurism was strongly encouraged. By far the best move Sexy

Sid made was bending forward completely, offering his back-side to the hoard of horny men gathered before his shower-cage. Sliding his swim trunks to his ankles, he wore nothing beneath but the skimpiest black Speedo. After Sid stood erect, he turned toward us again—his mast at full sail. Sure, the thing was fully sheathed in spandex, but all could easily perceive the size of the porpoise swimming within his suit.

The music morphed from the band of British brothers to En Vogue's "My Lovin' (You're Never Gonna Get It)." Sexy Sid stepped out of the shower and started toweling himself off suggestively. Once dry, he began directing his act out to the audience. I managed to weasel through the crowd, up to the front of the stage, and could've easily reached out and touched Sexy Sid's trouser worm, as my mother would surely have called it. Only in Sid's case, the animal in question was more similar to a serpent. He was a big boy, no doubt about it—and in more ways than one! Minding my manners, I re-sisted giving into my carnal impulse. While I'd never been to a strip club before, I knew from all my TV and movie watch-ing that feeling the merchandise was strictly forbidden.

Out of nowhere, Sid pulled me up onstage. Surprisingly I discovered him to be what I liked to call SWB—Short With a Bod. But what he lacked in height, he more than made up for in size. And not just below the belt. Wrapping his wet towel around my torso, not only did Sid rub the bath cloth up and down my body, he rubbed himself all over me as well. At first, I felt embarrassed being on display. But when I looked out at the audience (all drunken, middle-aged men for the most part), cheering me on, it was as if I was performing a role in yet another theatrical production. This time, instead of being a nerdy plant shop assistant, or a cowpoke roaming the plains, or a 1950s greaser, I was the love slave to a sexy black stripper. Only my wish was *his* command, so long as I had my money ready.

After our onstage duet had ended, Sid paraded me to a musty

smelling storage closet in the back of the club, beyond the horseshoe-shaped bar and the toilets, known as The Champagne Room. Taking a quick detour, I stopped to grab another beer and check the time on my Swatch: eleven forty-six. I had less than a quarter of an hour to realize my birthday wish. The way things had been progressing, Sexy Sid looked like the lucky boy who would make my dream come true. I knew it would cost me, of course. Nothing worthwhile in life—particularly at a strip club—came without a price. Hopefully twenty bucks would cover it, because that was about all my wallet held, and I didn't think Sexy Sid took plastic for his services.

"So what it gonna be, homes?"

Even though I knew full well that the transaction between us was sorely professional, I didn't want it to transpire without significance.

"How are you?" I asked, intentionally not answering Sid's query. "You having a good night?"

"Even bett-a if'n you tell me what-choo want." He sounded like a total thug, fresh from the ghetto; the type of guy who if I'd run into him anywhere else, he'd have taken one look at me with his light brown eyes, called me fag, and totally kicked my ass.

I suspected he wasn't even gay himself. Sean had mentioned that most of the guys who stripped at The Riviera were straight. A lot of them had girlfriends and babies they had to help support. Or they were just looking to make some easy cash, though letting a gay guy touch your private parts (or vice-versa) didn't seem such a simple task.

"You wants-ta feel it?" asked Sid, grabbing his full basket.

My face flushed, and I could feel myself turning beet red. I took a big swig of my beer. "Sure, if it's okay."

"Costs ten fo' a cop."

I shook my head, cloudy and confused. "I'm not a cop. My dad is..."

"A cop," Sid repeated. "Cop-a feel, sees what I'm sayin'?"

I opened my wallet in search of the Alexander Hamilton that hid among the honest Abes and a few George Washingtons. Sid stuck out his meaty paw and accepted the ten dollar bill with the utmost delight.

"Don't be shy, boy," he ordered. "Reach out an' touch somebody."

I couldn't bring myself to do it. It was my birthday, and I was hanging out in the backroom of some sleazy gay strip bar, about to give myself a cheap thrill by tugging on the tool of a straight guy. If my mother knew where I was (or what I was doing), she would've been mortified. It was bad enough that her own former husband had thought me some sort of pervert, but there I was practically proving the bastard right.

"I should get going," I said softly. "Thanks for the dance. You can keep the ten dollars."

"Easy there, Red..." Sid reached out and gripped my wrist, forcibly keeping me in his manly company.

"It's my birthday," I admitted. "Well, for another five minutes."

Sid's plump lips parted, revealing a smile of perfectly straight, super bright teeth. "Happy birf-day! How old you be, boy?"

I answered, "Twenty-two," seeing no real reason to lie about my age to Sid. I wasn't down at Wayne State with my classmates, whose friendships had been built upon nothing but untruths.

He scoffed. "You still a youngin'."

"I don't feel like it."

"Talk-ta me when you turn twenty-five," Sid told me. With his big hand, he gave my curly head a tussle. "So what-choo want fo' yo' birf-day?"

Feeling totally stupid, I confessed, "I came here tonight hoping for a kiss."

"That's all you askin' fo'? Shit! Kiss on'y cost you twen'y."

I couldn't believe that to touch his privates I only had to

pay ten. For some people, kissing was seen as a more intimate behavior than anything sexual, I supposed. Again I reached into my wallet.

"Looks like I'm outta luck. I've only got ten dollars left."

Sid held up the bill I'd given him before. "You gots ten here. And ten there. Even a dummy like me knows how-ta count." He turned up his pink palm and rubbed his thick thumb and first two fingers together, an indicator I should fork over the rest of my cash.

Happily I surrendered the dirty pieces of paper. And so, for a mere twenty dollars, I received my special kiss—with one hundred and twenty seconds of my birthday left to spare.

9

CAN'T STOP THIS THING
WE STARTED

◆   ◆   ◆

Next morning, I slipped into my jeans, still smoky smelling
from the night before, pulled on my too-tight navy Blue Lake
Fine Arts Camp sweatshirt, and crept down to Dad's kitchen
to make myself a pot of coffee. While it brewed, I sat at the
table with the morning *Detroit News*. My paper of choice
had always been the *Free Press*. They featured a better Sunday comics section, with Charlie Brown and the Peanuts
gang smack dab on the front page above the fold. The phone
started ringing and, since technically it wasn't my house, I allowed the answering machine to take the call.

My father's high-pitched voice on the message playback
tickled me inside. He sounded like Winnie-the-Pooh ponder-
ing over a pot of honey. Dad didn't know the first thing
about rooting his voice down, something we'd started working on in Stefan's class that week. I couldn't believe I'd been
in college for only four days, so much had already happened.

The machine beeped.

"Good morning! This message is for Bradley..."

I jumped up from my chair and ripped the receiver from
the wall. "Hey, Rain. What's up?"

She said she was calling to wish me a belated happy birthday, though I don't know how she realized she'd missed the
big event, because I intentionally hadn't mentioned it to any-

body. I also wasn't aware how Rain had gotten my phone number. Then I remembered she performed work-study duties in the production office at Ninety-Five, where I'm sure the secretary, Fran Schreiber, kept a copy of my permanent record on file.

"Did you enjoy yourself last night?" she asked. "And why weren't Sarah and I invited along on your special evening?"

I explained how I'd had a nice dinner with some old friends—just us guys—conveniently leaving out the part where I wound up at a seedy gay strip club, kissing a hot, beefy black man in the dirty bird backroom. Thank God I ran out of money when I did! Who knows what else might have gone on had I been able to afford the fee?

"Well, we're going over to Canada, and you're coming," Rain informed me.

I poured myself a cup of coffee and just about burned my tongue, impatiently taking a sip. "What's in Canada?"

As kids, my sister, Janelle, and I begged Mom and Dad to take us to Niagara Falls for our family vacation. Both Jack and Max Wilson had cottages Up North. They'd spend every summer swimming and visiting tourist traps like Call of the Wild in Gaylord, Mystery Spot up in the UP, or Mackinac Island, where they filmed one of my favorite movies, *Somewhere in Time* with Jane Seymour and Christopher Reeves— I mean *Reeve*. Not the Daytons. Our parents couldn't even afford a weekend trip out to Cass Lake, that's how poor we were.

"A club," replied Rain.

"Oh. Why can't we just go out downtown?"

"Because," she said, as if the answer were totally obvious. "The drinking age in Canada is only nineteen. And we're going to get you good and liquored up in honor of your turning twenty, like us."

I'd heard tell of the existence of this alcohol consumption-related law, but it was one that I'd never taken advantage of.

I'd been drinking in gay bars since before I was even sixteen. Now that I was technically twenty-two, it didn't matter in which country I got my drink on. But I couldn't reveal this to Rain DuBois.

"Can't we just stay on campus and get drunk at Third's," I said, "or anywhere else? They never check ID."

"We *could*," said Rain. "But I really want to go dancing. There's this wonderful bar in Windsor, and they play the best music."

Now that I'd had half a cup of coffee, my brain had started to function properly. I remembered the reason I couldn't possibly go out that night even if I'd wanted to. I had to work the late shift up at Country Boy: 11:00 p.m. until 7:00 a.m. Of course I didn't want to mention it to Rain, out of fear that she might ask me where I worked, and I'd have to tell her yet another white lie. I also didn't want to insult my new friends by refusing Rain and Sarah's offer. Plus it was a Saturday night. I was in college, and I shouldn't have to miss out on the experience, all because of some stupid job I was eventually going to quit someday anyway.

"What time are we leaving?"

I hung up with Rain and immediately called Barb Foeman, my boss up at Country Boy, to tell her I wouldn't be able to work—again. I thought about saying I'd drank too much the night before when I went out for my birthday, but I decided that such an excuse would make me sound irresponsible. Instead I went with my earlier fib and said that my flu bug had come back to bite me on the behind.

Being a kind hearted soul, Barb wished me well, and I silently hoped she would forgive me for letting her down twice in one week.

More than one-quarter of all merchandise traded between the US and Canada crossed the Ambassador, a suspension bridge spanning a total length of 7,500 feet over the Detroit River, linking the Motor City to its international neighbor, Windsor, Ontario. Plans to connect the two countries were first conceived shortly after the conclusion of the Civil War. The increase of manufacturing output led to an increase in the volume of freight traversing the border. Railroads were the major means of transportation in those days, but train cars leaving Detroit had to be placed on ferries for the short trip to Canada and reassembled upon arrival. This procedure, though it continued for more than a century, was quite a costly endeavor. In 1903, the Detroit Board of Commerce formed the International Bridge Committee. But it wasn't until 1924 that Joseph A. Bower, a New York banker formerly of Detroit, was brought on board as the entrepreneur who would arrange financing for the Ambassador.

When completed in November 1929, the bridge boasted the longest suspended center span in the world at 1,850 feet and would retain the title until 1931 with the opening of the George Washington in New York City. In 1959, Bower retired as chairman of the Detroit International Bridge Committee. He went on to serve the firm until his death in 1977 at the age of ninety-six, at which point his family put their holdings in the Ambassador up for sale. Two years later, billionaire trucking magnet Manuel "Matty" Moroun, an American of Lebanese decent, purchased the bridge from Bowers' heirs, making Detroit-Windsor the only privately owned international border crossing between the United States and Canada.

"Citizenship?"

As we arrived on the opposite side of the river, Rain rolled down her window. "US," she told the handsome customs agent, batting her baby blues.

The dark-haired man reminded me of Ken Olin, aka Michael Steadman on *thirtysomething*. He tilted his head down to get a better look into our car. We'd taken Rain's 1972 Cadillac Fleetwood Eldorado, a high school graduation gift from her father, the GM executive, handpicked for the year his only daughter had made her appearance in this world. Compared to my ancient Valiant—whom I'd come to affectionately call Val—the luxury car was a classic, not to mention colossal. I don't know how the girl managed to navigate the boat of an automobile through the tiny back alley behind The Thelma, where she kept it parked, without scraping the Coronation Red paint.

"Citizenship?"

"US," Sarah said, punctually answering the customs man's query.

From my spot in the backseat, I noticed Sarah lower her gaze, as if she were silently praying the government official would accept her answer without further confrontation. Granted, I assumed she couldn't see the guy's expression, what with her visual impairment, but her demure behavior was a far cry from the confident persona I'd seen at *Chicago* auditions and in Dina French's class.

"Citizenship?" the customs official said to me next.

I told him that I, too, was United States born, though I felt like I'd been hooked up to a lie detector and was about to short circuit the machine. Being questioned by authority always made me anxious.

"And what's the purpose of your visit tonight?" the man asked Rain in the driver's seat, remaining all business-like.

"We're going to Changez. It's a club down on Wyandotte."

"Are you bringing anything illegal into the country?"

"Do whips and chains count?"

The agent grinned. "Not if they're yours."

We drove away, down and around the exit ramp, and I realized I'd been holding my breath. "Oh, my God!" I exclaimed, exhaling. "I can't believe you got away with that."

"She always does," Sarah said. "Meanwhile, I feel like they're gonna bust me for *something*. Every time we come over here."

"Oh, Sarah," Rain sighed. "You worry far too much."

At the red light on the next corner, Rain slowed the car to a stop. She'd turned the radio on, and we were listening to 89X, a relatively new Modern Rock station broadcast from right there in Windsor. I settled back in my seat and lit a cigarette, having no idea how far a drive we had to this Changez place. Outside, the small Canadian town appeared quaint and quiet, unlike the big American city we'd crossed over from on the opposite side of the river. I found it mind boggling (and absolutely thrilling) that within a matter of minutes, we'd entered a completely different country. Something compelled me to remain on my best behavior, as if I'd been appointed to represent my homeland on foreign soil.

"I'm sorry Columbus couldn't make it," I called out to Sarah in the passenger seat, my cigarette held tight between my teeth. A thin cloud of smoke circled about my curly head, and I rolled down my window to release it.

Sarah looked back at me over her shoulder. I noticed, for the first time, how much makeup she was wearing. Compared to the plain and simple girl she arrived at school as on a daily basis, tonight she resembled what my mother would call the Whore of Babylon.

"Yeah," Sarah said soberly. "I've been wanting you guys to meet. But he got this new job... They make him work late every Friday and Saturday night."

"What does he do anyway?" I inquired, realizing Sarah hadn't divulged many details about her absent boyfriend.

"He's a photographer," she proudly announced. "But right now he's working as a bouncer."

"Oh, really?" Immediately the physical image I'd fabricated in my mind's eye of Columbus Howard morphed itself into something more along the lines of burly. "Where does he work?"

Sarah hesitated a moment, averting her emerald eyes again. "Um... A place called Booby Trap."

"Booby Trap!" I burst out. "I used to—"

Now I was the one who wavered. I'd been on the verge of admitting I grew up just blocks from the silly-named strip club, back when we still lived on Wanda in Ferndale. Instead the impatient blare of someone honking their car horn stopped me from completely blowing my cover.

Rain glanced up in her rearview mirror. "What's the matter, mister?" she said aloud to the annoying old man.

He pulled his Buick up beside us and lowered his window before declaring, "In Canada, we turn right on red!" And with that, he drove completely around us, completing the turn onto Wyandotte Street, near the University of Windsor.

We were all so flummoxed by the bizarre circumstances that Sarah and I both forgot we'd been talking about her boyfriend working security at a trashy tittie bar.

The light went green and Rain drove on.

After parking her Caddy on a residential block behind the corner building, we got in line out front and waited for the doorman to check our IDs. From his appearance alone, I had a feeling once we entered I'd stick out like a bastard at a family reunion, to quote Doralee Rhodes, aka Dolly Parton from *9 to 5*. This guy outside Changez By Night, as the sign read, wore a black motorcycle jacket with silver zippers galore, a black undershirt, black jeans, and black Doc Martens. His hair was also black and slicked back, a large silver hoop hung from his left ear, and he had super long sideburns. Sure enough, inside it was pretty much the same. Every single guy (and girl) had on a leather of some sort, including both Rain and Sarah, and were dressed head to toe in varying shades of dark.

"You didn't tell me this was a biker bar," I joked.

"You look awesome," Sarah assured me, of my blue jeans and tan T-shirt. Thank God I'd opted for brown loafers over white tennis shoes!

We snagged an empty table off to the left, just beyond the bar area. The rather small dance floor was situated in the rear of the room, on the right of where we were sitting. The DJ booth and restrooms could be found at the opposite end, closer to the entrance. The whole scene reminded me of any other bar I'd ever been to, except at this one, the men weren't so cute, and there were lots and lots of ladies. Sure, the occasional fag hag could be spotted hanging out at Menjo's or The Gas Station. But here at Changez, the joint was full of women.

"Who wants a Blue Motorcycle?" Rain hung her leather coat on the back of her chair, allowing me a full glimpse of her chic ensemble: slim-fitting black cigarette pants, paired with a tight black tank top, sans brassiere.

"I'll have one!" cried Sarah. Her look was less attention grabbing: an old Henry Rollins concert tee, worn with cuffed jeans shorts—black denim, of course—and flats. She reached into her purse and pulled out some cash. "Is this a five?"

I confirmed her suspicion, noticing she'd arranged her bills in order of their monetary value. "What's a Blue Motorcycle?"

"You've never had a Blue Motorcycle?" said Rain, her azure eyes going wide with amazement. "Sarah, what's in it again? Vodka..."

"Vodka, 7UP, blue curaçao."

"What's blue curaçao?" I asked, not familiar with the exotic ingredient.

"No idea," Sarah said. "Some kinda liqueur. Turns your tongue blue."

"It's like candy," said Rain, relishing the drink's description. "You're having one."

The girls held onto our table while I headed up to the bar. Luckily it was still early so there wasn't too long a line. Of course I totally felt self-conscious standing there in my Gap wear with everybody else sporting their best army surplus.

"Can I get three Blue Motorcycles?" I hoped the young bartenderess knew what the hell I was ordering. Evidently she did because, in a matter of minutes, she set before me three skinny glasses full of what looked like fizzy Windex, each garnished with a Maraschino cherry.

"Twelve dollars Canadian," the woman droned, adjusting the plaid flannel worn tied in a knot around her petite waist.

I gave her exact change, a ten and two singles. She handed me back two big gold coins and a few copper pennies. Examining the larger pieces, I discovered they were Canadian dollars. On one side, a goose-like bird swam above the dates 1867-1992. On the other, three children gazed up at an impressive government-type building, pointing and waving a maple leaf flag. I'd forgotten about the fluctuating currency that came with visiting a foreign country and appreciated the fact. Leaving the two Loonies as a tip, I returned to Rain and Sarah at our table, where I toasted my female friends with my fresh cup of sparkling, electric blue antifreeze.

"Cheers!"

We clinked our trio of cocktails together and each took a generous sip. The drink tasted super sweet, like lemon-lime with just a hint of orange flavor. I knew I wouldn't have a problem sucking down several.

"Happy birthday, Bradley!" Rain proposed.

"Happy birthday," echoed Sarah.

"Thanks," I said, draining my glass dry.

Not even five seconds later, Rain let out a whooping "Well, shit!"

"What's up?" said Sarah with concern.

"Is something wrong with your beverage?" I asked. Mine had tasted terrific. I was well on the road to Drunkville and ready to order another round.

"No," Rain sighed, "my Motorcycle is perfectly lovely. Look..." She nodded toward the front entrance.

"Who is it?" Sarah wondered, unable to see the leather jacket-clad hunk entering the club.

Craning my neck, I peeked past the group of giggling girls at the table next to us, and who did I see? None other than Mr. Brad Woodward, fresh from the neighboring shores of the US of A and looking oh-so dreamy in a tight black T-shirt, black chinos, and boots.

He made a stop at the bar to order a beer and, through the smoky haze, I watched him blatantly flirting with the bar-maid. I couldn't believe the Grunge girl had caught his atten-tion. Not only was she a total blond bimbo, she was female! Again, maybe I'd been wrong about Brad being gay. He was hanging out on a Saturday night in a straight club in Win-dsor, Ontario, wasn't he?

"Brad!"

"Please don't call him over here," Rain begged, once he'd come within five feet of our table and Sarah could better make out his figure.

It was too late. Brad had already spotted us and was strut-ting his way over to where we were sitting.

"Hey, guys!" he said cheerfully, swigging his Molson Ice. The glass bottle from which Brad drank was dark brown, not green, the way it would've been back in Michigan. "What are you kids doing here?"

"It's Bradley's birthday," said Sarah.

"It *was*," I corrected. "Yesterday."

"Happy birthday!"

Before I knew what was happening, Brad bent down, wrapped his leathery arms around me, and squeezed. He held me tightly, and I breathed in his cool scent, burying my face in the folds of his warm neck.

"Have a seat," I said, once the awkward embrace had been broken.

Brad took the chair to my left, opposite Rain. Our imme-diate surroundings were filled with the sweet scent of cloves as Rain lit a cigarette—and blew the smoke right into Brad's face. If he noticed, he didn't let on. Instead he felt inside his coat pocket and pulled out his own pack, an unfamiliar brand I'd not seen before. The white and blue box reminded me of Parliaments, only it was flat and square and contained twenty-five "navy cut" cigarettes, as opposed to the standard American twenty. Brad placed one between his lips, and I reached for my Zippo, sparking it up. His brown eyes met my blue. As soon as the glow of his cherry popped, I nodded; something I'd been taught by my sister, Janelle, back in junior high when I'd first picked up her dirty habit.

"Are you smoking Players?" Sarah picked up Brad's box of cigarettes and held it close, examining the label.

Brad stared lovingly at the one he'd been sucking on. "Smooth Lights."

"Ooh! May I?" asked Sarah, excited.

Brad removed a Players from his pack, offered it to Sarah, and I lit it for her with my lighter.

Dragon-like, she exhaled a thick double stream of smoke through her nostrils. "The Canadians always do things so much better."

"They do?" I asked, unaware of this theory.

"Sure," answered Brad. "Better beer. Better cigarettes. Better TV shows."

I only knew of one television program made in Canada, called *Mr. Dressup*. When we were little, my sisters and I watched every morning at ten-thirty on CBC-Windsor, channel 9. Mr. Dressup was sort of like the Canadian Mr. Rogers. He was this jovial, fatherly figure, and he had this pair of puppet friends, a boy named Casey and a dog, Finnegan. Mom used to say I reminded her of Casey because he also had red hair. For the longest time, I thought Casey was a girl because of his high-pitched voice. Mr. Dressup was such an awesome guy. He was always telling stories, and cracking corny jokes, and singing songs like "Down by the Bay" and "Wheels of the Bus." He also had this giant red-orange Tickle Trunk from which he'd pull out an endless supply of costumes, and he'd *dress up* in them, putting on a show for Casey and Finnegan and all the little girls and boys out in TV Land, like me, Janelle, Nina, and Brittany.

"*You Can't Do That on Television*," Brad continued, rattling off his list of favorite Canadian-made programs. "*Kids in the Hall, Degrassi High, Super Dave.*"

"*Anne of Avonlea,*" added Sarah enthusiastically.

"Megan Follows played Juliet up at the Stratford Festival this summer," Brad said. "With Colm Feore as Mercutio."

"I love Colm Feore!" Sarah gushed with what sounded like lust. "Why didn't we road trip to see it?"

"I was out in Utah," answered Brad. "Remember?"

"Oh, right. Mr. Working Actor," Sarah joked.

Silently I sat in my seat listening to their back-and-forth banter, having no idea who—or what—they were talking about. I felt totally jealous of the obvious bond that had formed between Brad Woodward and Sarah Schwartz over the last two years. No matter how well I might get to know him in the future, nothing would make up for our lost past.

"Who's Colm Feore?" I said, finally choosing to inquire.

"Colm Feore is only *the* sexiest man alive," Rain revealed, taking the time to stop sulking and join the conversation.

"*Okay...*"

"He's an incredible Canadian actor," Brad explained, since Rain wasn't about to fill me in any more than she already had. "He comes to Wayne State every spring to work on Shakespeare with the juniors."

"And a few select sophomores," Sarah teased, eyeing Rain, who made no reply.

I took Sarah's comment to infer that Rain had had an illicit affair with Mr. Feore last semester. But again, it was none of my business who the woman slept with, be it Brad Woodward or any other man for that matter.

The next couple hours we spent sitting around drinking and listening to the music, which included a fair mix of '80s retro that left me yearning for my youth. The girls and I got up to boogie on the tiny tiled area while Brad kept guard back at the table. "I only dance onstage," he'd said stubbornly.

I dubbed a short chubby girl with a super short haircut,

whom I was pretty sure was a lesbian, Chubba. She stood by herself in a corner, bopping up and down in her too-tight Trashcan Sinatras T-shirt to some tune I later learned was called "Boy" by some band named Book of Love. At ten minutes till one, the DJ announced "Last call!" I hadn't realized that, to quote our old man friend from the earlier red light incident, "In Canada..." the bars close at 1:00 a.m., allowing all the drunken Americans sufficient time to hightail it back across the border and imbibe one last alcoholic beverage on their native soil before closing time at two o'clock.

The dance floor began to clear as Alphaville's "Forever Young" filled the bar with its melancholy melody. Rain reached out dramatically to take my hand. "Will you do me this honor, *monsieur*?"

Evidently "in Canada..." they ended the evening with one final slow song. Suddenly the pick-up bar transformed itself into a junior high dance, with couples pairing off one by one. Of course Rain DuBois couldn't allow herself to partake in something as simple as spinning round and round in circles, like all the other surrounding duos. She launched us into what might as well have been a completely choreographed routine—only we hadn't rehearsed it one bit. The entire *pas de deux* was totally improvised and, no doubt, resembled something out of *Dirty Dancing*.

The instant Rain started twirling in and out, intruding upon the dance space of everyone else, the floor pretty much finished clearing itself. Like lovers in a spotlight, Rain and I revolved about in perfect synchronicity, two bodies moving as one. I hadn't danced like that with a girl since my sister, Janelle, and I competed in the Webster Elementary *Gong Show* talent contest, where we performed to ELO's "I'm Alive" from the *Xanadu* original soundtrack, while wearing identical pink Sears "Braggin' Dragon" polo shirts and maroon polyester pants that Mom made for us herself on her Singer sewing machine. Total side bar: we received a perfect score of thirty and took home the first prize trophy. Although one of the judges, the school psychologist, criticized me for allowing Janelle (a girl) to lead, to which I replied, "She's taller."

As the slow song concluded, I dipped Rain back in a perfectly elegant ending pose. We held it a moment, an indicator that we'd indeed finished our display of talent. Then the ugly lights came on. The bar had totally emptied out. We gathered our belongings, and I lit one last cigarette for the walk to the car, before we headed out into the cool night.

Surprised I was relatively sober, I offered to drive Rain's Cadillac back to campus. She'd had more Blue Motorcycles than anyone could care to count. The last thing I wanted was for us to get pulled over on the Ambassador Bridge and Rain to be arrested for drunk driving. It was bad enough that when we'd crossed halfway over international waters, I caught a glimpse of her in the rearview mirror, head hanging out the window, heaving her guts out.

Thankfully Sarah had been there to hold Rain's hair back.

10

TELL IT LIKE IT T-I-IS

◆   ◆   ◆

Around one-thirty, I dropped off the girls at home and carefully parked Rain's car in its designated spot behind The Thelma. Brad offered to chauffeur me to mine, which I'd left in the mud lot on Prentis, the property of an elderly couple who lived across the street. They only charged a dollar to park during school hours, and it was a hell of a lot closer (and more convenient) than the structure I'd been using since classes had begun.

Climbing into Brad's Mercedes-Benz 420SEL, I noticed that same strange scent from the first night I'd met him down in the bathroom at the Bonstelle: burning plastic masked by mint.

"What is that smell?" I wondered, worried I'd seen Brad smoking what looked like a small pipe, before I'd gotten into the vehicle with him.

"Must be my air freshener," he insisted, tapping at the felt-covered pine tree dangling from the mirror.

I hoped he was telling the truth and not involved with illegal substances. I couldn't possibly date an addict. Alcohol abuse was one thing. Drugs were a whole 'nother story, and one I would not tolerate.

"This is me," I said, ashamed at the sight of my piece of crap car sitting all alone in the empty parking lot, beneath the harsh light of the streetlamp. "Thanks for the ride."

"Any time. It was good seeing you tonight," he said. "You've got some serious moves, boy. Don't waste them on

Rain DuBois."

I assured Brad that Rain and I were nothing but platonic pals, and he shouldn't worry.

Reaching to open the door with my right arm, he took hold of my left and turned me toward him, ever so gently, gazing into my eyes. And then, as the old song goes, he kissed me.

The minute we'd parked Brad's car in the well-lit lot next to his apartment building, the boy was all over me. With his massive, muscular body, he pinned me up against the passenger side window, our tongues locked tightly in a game of tonsil hockey.

I tried twisting myself, the better to support his two hundred pounds, and caught my foot against the gear shift. "Ouch!"

"Sorry," he said, still forging ahead.

We continued kissing, and I did my best to disregard the minty freshness of his mouth, covering up something that called to mind the taste of tin foil.

"Why don't we go upstairs?" I suggested. All we needed was for a cop to drive by and discover us making out in the not-so-dark. Especially if said officer ended up being my policeman father.

Brad kissed me one final time. "Sounds good," he agreed, grabbing my backside with his meaty paws. He grunted. "*Ungh!* I can't wait to fuck that ass."

This statement caught me completely off-guard.

I don't know why I found it surprising to discover, when it came to his preferred role in the game of gay love, Brad Woodward also deemed himself a dominant top. His outward appearance was certainly masculine enough. The first time I fooled around with Bobby Russell back in junior high, I had no choice in the matter. We would hang out together at Bobby's house, getting high, he'd get a hard-on, and I'd take care of it for him. Not once did he ever reciprocate. Then after Jack Paterno and I became (quote-unquote) involved during junior year, I'm ashamed to admit, he'd always assumed the passive position. Well, in Jack's case, he came off much more aggressive in taking advantage of me which, at the time, I didn't mind at all. It wasn't until we'd finish messing around that I'd feel guilty for enjoying myself. The entire affair almost put an unfortunate end to our friendship. Luckily we managed to survive it once the air had been cleared, and I realized Jack wasn't actually in love with me—he was just horny.

With Richie Tyler, my first real boyfriend, I once again found myself back in the driver's seat, so to speak. Maybe because he was younger and less experienced, but sexually there were certain things I enjoyed doing to the boy, and he enjoyed having done to him. And with Mr. Tyler, things were different than they'd been with either Bobby or Jack. By the time we finally got around to having actual sex, Richie and I had known each other almost an entire year. What we did together, physically, could only be described as making love. The idea of following Brad Woodward up to his place, with the expectation that I would be the one lying facedown biting my pillow, freaked me the fuck out—pardon my French.

Despite being almost two o'clock on a Sunday morning, the inside of the Victorian building smelled of Indian food cooking.

"Be quiet," Brad whispered as we entered the interior lobby with its high ceiling, low-hanging light fixture and full-length wall mirror, and we climbed the wide staircase leading to the second floor. "Welcome to Studio Four."

The apartment faced the street. A trio of large rectangular window panes peered out from the living/bedroom/kitchen onto a quiet West Hancock. Off to the right, the only other room was the bath, where I immediately asked to be excused.

"Don't take too long," Brad told me, grabbing his groin.

"I just need to freshen up," I said, shutting the door.

Standing in the fluorescence, I had no idea what to do next. Thankfully I'd already taken a shower earlier, though after all the dancing we'd done over in Canada, the scent I was emitting down yonder was anything but fresh. Turning on the tap, I hoisted my exposed bum onto the sink's edge and gave myself, what Mom liked to call, a whore's bath.

"All set?" asked Brad after I sheepishly returned, all clean and tidy.

A sweet and woody scent filled the air. He'd lit a couple vanilla candles; some sandalwood incense burned on the shelf of his bookcase. Our dark shadows danced playfully on the pale wall above the kitchenette, where a pile of dirty dishes and coffee cups cluttered the sink, long neglected. For someone who hailed from Bloomfield Hills, Brad's apartment was modest at best.

"Do you mind if I ask how much rent you pay for this place?" I said, curious.

"I don't," he answered. "Pay rent."

"You own it?"

"Just the studio, not the whole building." Brad embraced me and we kissed again, this time more slowly than we had outside in his car. Again, his huge hands worked their way south, palming my posterior. He gave my melons a firm squeeze, testing their ripeness. "Has anybody ever told you, you've got a great ass?"

I didn't want to lie. Richie used to love it. Personally I'd always thought my booty too big for the rest of my body.

"You ready?" asked Brad slyly.

"Sure," I lied.

"It's about time. I've wanted you since that first day in the lobby of Ninety-Five."

This made me smile. "I had a feeling you were a fag," I teased.

"I'm not a fag," he said. "I just like to fuck around with other guys sometimes." He must've been a good actor because he totally sounded serious. Judging by the speed with which he got me out of my clothes and into position, he certainly possessed experience in having sex with other men.

Fifteen, maybe twenty minutes after my arrival in Brad's studio, we lay naked, side by side, the slats of the wood futon protruding against our backs.

"Now," I said. "Right now. Or I'll never do it."

"Wait," said Brad, grinning. "You've never—with a guy?"

"No, I have. Just not like this."

In the past, I would've been the one holding the back of my partner's head, tugging and pulling at his hair. I would've been the one thrusting my hips, pounding hard against his bare behind. Never before had I been on the receiving end, at least not when it came to penetration.

What the hell was I going to do?

"We need some stuff," said Brad. "Hang on." He got up, the firm mounds of his buttocks bouncing as he headed into the bathroom.

I could hear the squeak of the medicine cabinet and Brad rummaging around inside. Lying nude on the rumpled sheets, I looked at the red glow of his alarm clock. It was almost 3:00 a.m., and I was well aware I had to wake up in approximately five hours. I wanted desperately to get this thing over with. I also wanted the night to never end. My lungs fought to keep up with my rapid intake of oxygen; my mind reeled at the notion of what was about to transpire. For the first time in my life, I was on the verge of getting fucked by a guy. And I wanted it bad!

The digits on the clock morphed; a loose frame on one of the front windows rattled. A minute later, a door slammed and Brad reappeared, brandishing a small bottle.

"Oob," I said, shamefully mocking an Asian store clerk who'd once sold me some Wet at a sex shop on Woodward Avenue and 6 Mile. Then I started giggling like a girl.

Brad's brow furrowed and his nostrils flared in confusion. "You're delirious," he decided, climbing back on top of me.

Never had a man made me feel so wonderfully small.

It hurt—a lot—and the lubricant was cold and sticky. But once we found our rhythm, once I was able to relax, and to trust and accept Brad wholly, I found that intercourse from this particular perspective felt just as satisfying as any other. I also appreciated that, for once, I hadn't been the one needing to wear a condom.

When I heard Brad's breathing build and his groans of pleasure grow quiet, I anticipated his imminent eruption. I didn't want him to stop; I begged him not to stop; and he tried his best. But the inevitable snap of latex sounded as Brad ripped off the thin layer of synthetic skin that had separated us. I collapsed into a heap, sans completion, and I began to cry. He held me tight, I stopped crying, and we were soon laughing about a noise he insisted I'd made in the heat of the moment. Our faces close together, his dark eyes grew wide, and he sat up suddenly then bent down toward me again.

"Are you okay?"

"Um, yes," I winced. "Who knew you were so well endowed?"

"No. You've got a nosebleed."

"I do?" Reaching up with a finger, sure enough, I felt a warm pool trickle from my left nostril, the tell-tale sign of my newly lost purity.

Despite asking him to move out of her house when she married a homophobe, Laura Victor-Dayton-Victor had made it a point that she wanted to maintain a healthy relationship with her only son. And because Bradley loved his mother unconditionally, diligently he woke up bright and early on the first day of each week, put on his best dress shirt and slacks, and drove the ten-plus miles over to his family church, Central Freewill Baptist in Royal Oak.

Even though I'd accepted my homosexuality at an early age, I refused to believe that my being gay made me a sinner, or that I could no longer call myself a Christian. This opinion I didn't discuss with my parents, however, and only my oldest sister, Janelle, knew anything about my true nature—and only because she once walked in on me and Richie Tyler totally making out in my bedroom. We weren't having sex, thank God! But I'll never forget the look on my sister's face when she caught her only brother in the heat of passion with another boy. She actually ended up being cool with the whole incident, though she begged me to please tell our mother, making claim to the fact that she'd already figured it out. But Mom wouldn't call anything into question as she was allowing me the time to personally confess my sins. Okay, Janelle hadn't worded it quite like that, but in my retelling of most stories, I tend to err on the overdramatic.

After services, as per tradition, Mom, the girls, and I would head out to Oakland Mall and have lunch at our favorite restaurant, Olga's Kitchen. I don't remember how this particular ritual first started. It was just something we'd been doing for as long as I could remember. Even when I'd temporarily relocated to Ann Arbor, I would still drive up on Sundays to meet my mother and sisters for our weekly gathering.

Of course, on this particular morning, all I kept thinking about during both the sermon and the salad was what happened the night before with Brad Woodward kissing me in his car, which led to our having relations in his studio. The even weirder thing was, after the fact, he got up to get me a Kleenex, making sure my nose was no longer a gushing geyser—and we simply got dressed. He told me to get home safely, and I departed his apartment without so much as a goodbye kiss.

I couldn't let Brad's odd behavior bother me or ruin my visit with Mom and the girls. It felt good spending time with my sisters, though I realized much to my denial, they'd all grown up into gorgeous young women. Janelle had been married for over four years, and her son, Teddy, had just turned three. Nina, bless her heart, was now nineteen. Her cerebral palsy still posing problems, she'd recently undergone surgery to have the shunt in her head replaced, and one side of her hair had been shaved. I told her she resembled Cyndi Lauper in her Airstream circa "Time After Time." She didn't buy it, nor do I think she knew who, exactly, I was talking about. Brittany looked even more beautiful (and like Mom) than ever. That June she'd graduated from Hazel Park High, and she'd just the week prior, like me, started college, taking classes at OCC the same way I had, in hopes of transferring her credits up to Central Michigan in two years. Neither Janelle nor Nina said a word, but I got the feeling they were both envious of my and Brittany's newfound status as co-eds.

Unable to finish the rest of my Olga's Original, the seasoned beef and lamb topped with onions, tomatoes, and Olga sauce sitting mixed together in a pool, I pushed my plate aside and reached for the check.

"Bradley..." Mom's tone told me that, under no circumstance, would she allow me to treat.

"I have a job," I reminded her, though at the rate I was going, I would never get paid again if I kept calling in sick.

"You need to save your money, honey," Mom said, slipping the bill from my hand. "For school."

Nina began giggling hysterically. "You said 'money, honey,'" she told Mom, thinking the rhyme the most hilarious joke she'd heard in her life.

She really was still like a child, her emotional development stunted somewhere around age ten or twelve. I perished the thought of what would happen someday when Nina was older and Mom wasn't around to care for her any longer. No doubt the dreaded responsibility would fall on me, her big brother, and I had no idea how I would possibly manage. Especially if I were off living in New York City, the way I planned to be, working on Broadway with Jack's boyfriend, Kirk Bailey.

"Well, thank you," I told Mom, giving in as I ultimately

often did.

Outside in the mall parking lot, hugs were doled out all around. Once we finished, I hopped into my Valiant and headed back to Dad's house. He wasn't home.

Chances are he was up in Lake Orion visiting Grandpa and Grandma Dayton. They'd be packing up soon and driving down to Florida, where they spent their winters. I hadn't yet seen my paternal grandparents since returning from living with Richie in Ann Arbor. As much as it pained me, the less contact I had with Seamus and Cecily, the less I had to avoid discussing anything important that may have been going on, particularly in my romantic life. I was only twenty-two, but Grandpa and Grandma had happily married when they were both right out of high school, as did their eldest granddaughter, Janelle. When was only grandson Bradley going to get serious and settle down? That was a question I'd been asking myself more and more with each passing moment.

Taking advantage of having Dad's house to myself, I decided to get comfortable and make a few phone calls. Try as I might, I couldn't stop thinking about Brad Woodward, gosh dang it!

"Hello?"

"Sarah, it's Bradley Dayton."

"Oh, hi, Bradley! How are you feeling after last night?"

"Pretty good." My morning hangover had been mild, if even existent. "Thanks again for taking me out."

"No problem. What's up?"

I gave her the quick recap of my day thus far. Then I decided to broach a more serious subject. "I wanted to ask you a question..."

"Uh-oh."

"What?"

"Nothing. Go on."

"It's about Brad. The other Brad. Brad Woodward."

"It does get confusing," said Sarah, chuckling. "I'm glad

you're Bradley and he's plain Brad. He's a great guy, huh?"

A great *gay* guy. And great in bed. But I couldn't begin with that intro.

"Well," I said, not wanting to just blurt it out. "He doesn't have a girlfriend, does he? I mean, you're pretty good friends with him, right?"

"As far as I'm aware," she answered, "he hasn't dated anyone since Rain. You know about them being an item, don't you?"

"I kinda had a feeling," I said. "But I'm not exactly sure what the story is."

"Oh, my God!" Sarah groaned. "Talk about a story, indeed."

"Can you tell me?" I asked, boiling over with inquisitiveness.

"How much time do you have?" She said it as a joke, but I could tell that Sarah had some serious business she could discuss, concerning the tumultuous courtship of Brad Woodward and Rain DuBois.

The former couple was first introduced when cast opposite as Cornelius Hackl and Irene Molloy in *Hello, Dolly!*, making the duo the first freshmen to land leading roles on the Bonstelle stage since Avery S. Thaddeus had in *Sarcophagus.* From the moment of their meeting, their chemistry was undeniable, both onstage and off. Once the show closed, they continued seeing each other, in class at Old Main and outside of The Department. They bonded strongly over their similar socio-economic upbringings: Rain, a Catholic school girl; Brad, a private school boy. Rain, growing up in Rochester; Brad, living in the Bloomfield Hills lap of luxury. The fact that both had ended up studying at Wayne State came as total serendipity and was merely another of their many similarities. When Rain was sixteen, her mother was diagnosed with stage four ovarian cancer and passed away within a matter of months. Brad's mom also died tragically, after committing su-

icide when Brad was just twelve. As a result of their both losing the central female figures in their lives, both Rain and
Brad had become estranged from their fathers, yet another
one of the many coincidences that had brought them so closely together.

"So why did they ever break up?" I asked, once Sarah had
finished telling me her tale.

"I honestly don't know," she confided, confounded.

This news I was stunned to hear. I'd been under the impression that Sarah was both Rain and Brad's best friend. I
expected her, of all people, to possess certain knowledge
about the pair, particularly when it pertained to them as a
single unit.

"All I know is, one minute they're hot and heavy. The
next, Rain comes home early from Spring Break last year.
She stops by Brad's studio to surprise him... Then they're
broken up, and she's—" Sarah paused to carefully select her
choice of word. "*Dating* Colm Feore."

This factoid I found fascinating. Not the one where Rain
had slept with some Shakespearean actor; the one that indicated there had been trouble in paradise long before Mr.
Feore and his Canadian codpiece had crossed the border.

"What do you think happened when she went over to
Brad's apartment?" I asked suspiciously.

"I don't know!" answered Sarah, as if she, too, had been
frustrated and dying to find out.

"She didn't catch Brad in bed with another girl, did she?" I
offered. "Or another *boy*, maybe."

"Now that much I'm certain," said Sarah with great confidence. "Brad's not gay."

"How can you be so positive? I'm gay."

"Oh, I know," said Sarah, like she'd never even called my
sexuality into question. Or maybe Rain had finally clued her
in? Either way, I didn't care. "But the whole time Brad and
Rain were together, every once in a while he'd spend the
night over here. And since Rain's room and my room share a

wall... Well, you can imagine the noises I heard."

"That's okay," I said. "I'd rather not."

"I don't blame you," Sarah said squeamishly. "Like that scene with the cats in *Streetcar*, it was."

"Stop!" I had no need to picture Brad and Rain, locked in the throes of passion. And yet, as I allowed my mind to wander, my body began having its own physical reaction. I couldn't believe I was actually getting turned on thinking about another guy having sex with a *girl* and not with me.

"Oh, no!" Sarah gasped suddenly. "You don't have a crush on Brad, do you?"

I did my best to force a laugh. "No, not at all! I mean, so what if I did?"

"Oh, Bradley..."

I took Sarah's reply to say that she pitied me, a poor sweet fool, falling for a man I could never possibly have, like so many other homos throughout history. But what about that kiss—and the action that immediately followed? Admittedly I'd been guilty of having an overactive imagination. But there was no mistaking that, last night, Brad Woodward and I had gotten to know each other a whole lot better.

11

THESE ARE DAYS

◆   ◆   ◆

The coming Monday was Labor Day, which meant an additional day off from class, which just about killed me. I was dying to see Brad Woodward after what had happened between us on Saturday night. Sunday evening, I met Miss Peter for cocktails down at Menjo's, conveniently located within stumbling blocks of her new Palmer Park palace. The majority of cute guys had all gone back to U of M, MSU, or CMU now that "Back to School" season had official kicked off. It was fine by me since I really wasn't looking to meet anybody anyway. I spent most of the two hours sitting in the piano bar area sipping a Blue Motorcycle, listening to Miss Peter babble on about the upcoming Presidential election and her crush on the Democratic hopeful, Bill Clinton.

"What is *that?*" she asked, disgusted by the neon sight of my new favorite drink.

I told her, adding, "They're all the rage in Canada."

"So is Céline Dion. But you don't see me rushing out to buy any of her crappy records. Every time I hear that *Beauty and the Beast* bullshit... Give me Jessica Fletcher any day."

"They're called CDs now," I said dryly. "And I love Céline. She's like a French-Canadian Whitney Houston."

Miss Peter scoffed, downing her Captain Morgan and Diet. "Don't even get me started on that girl. I still can't believe she married that kid from New Edition."

"I hear you," I said, envisioning Bobby Brown's chubby face with his gap-toothed grin and lopsided hairdo. He was not an attractive boy, I had to agree.

"He ain't nothing but trouble," Miss Peter ranted, on a roll. "Mark my words... That is one marriage that ain't going nowhere. That girl will be lucky if she don't end up dead from a drug overdose someday, just like poor Judy."

Good old Miss Peter! How I loved to listen to her pontificate. Especially when she'd been hitting the sauce.

Back at 95 West Hancock, it was business as usual on Tuesday morning. Brad Woodward bounced out of the bathroom, his usual bundle of energy, and into Costuming class, where he acted as if nothing out of the ordinary had occurred over the weekend. I contemplated calling him out about what had actually gone down, but then Marian Stockholm, our instructor, made a special announcement.

"Put your books away, people... We're going on a field trip!"

I did as instructed, packing up my watercolors in their neat little cardboard case, along with the cute plastic palette that accompanied the set. I turned to Rain, who seemed as if she was already knowledgeable of what was on the agenda.

"She didn't tell you last night when you talked?" she said.

"Who?"

"Sarah."

She hadn't. But I was more surprised by the fact that Rain was aware I'd been on the phone with her roommate.

"Strange Bedfellows are playing over at the Stupid Center," she explained. "I talked Marian into letting us skip, so we could all go."

"Awesome!"

Outside, it was yet another gorgeous day, and far too beautiful and sunny to be stuck inside some windowless drafting room working on costume renderings. Rain and I strolled leisurely across campus, smoking while walking and talking.

"Sorry about Saturday," she apologized, brushing her hair

back behind an ear. The wind had picked up, whipping open the flaps of the trenchcoat Rain wore over a long blouse, buttoned up to the collar, dark denim skirt, black tights and flats. It was the first time I'd seen her in a heel less than three inches high. For once she actually appeared shorter than me.

"What are you sorry about?" I asked. "You took me out for my birthday. We had fun."

"A little too much fun. I'm still mortified I got sick all over the Ambassador Bridge."

I couldn't help laughing at the image. "It was hilarious when the woman at customs was like, 'Citizenship? You in the back with your head out the window.'"

"Stop!" she wailed, whacking me on the shoulder. "I told Sarah to make sure I didn't drink too much."

I had a fuzzy memory of Sarah informing Rain that she'd been cut off at some point on Saturday evening. But Rain, of course, hadn't been willing to comply. Not with all the alcohol in her system doing the thinking.

We crossed West Warren, almost getting run down by a speeding Saturn whose driver decided not to yield at the yellow light.

"I'm glad you guys are still talking," I told Rain as we continued up Cass, unscathed.

"Me and Sarah?" she said. "Why wouldn't we be? We're best friends."

"I know," I answered, unsure as to whether I should even bring up the topic. I'd been surprised to see them acting so amiably toward each other at the end of last week and then again at Changez in Windsor. "After what happened with *Chicago* auditions, I thought..."

"I'd hate her for stealing my role?" said Rain, finishing my sentence. "It's not Sarah's fault Will Bilson's a total ass-face. I can't believe I ever slept with that man."

The news that Rain DuBois and Brad Woodward had once been an item had arrived as enough of a shock. To hear Rain reveal, so cavalierly, that she'd also had an affair with the director of the musical we were about to start rehearsing that very evening—on top of the fact that the guy was *married*—just about floored me. I almost fell down right there on the sidewalk in front of State Hall.

By the time we'd arrived at the Student Center, Strange Bedfellows had already started playing their first song. Sarah looked super cute up onstage outfitted in a black cardigan sweater, buttoned only at the top, worn over a white blouse, and a navy and green Scotch plaid skirt paired with dark tights. The whole ensemble appeared very Catholic school girl, making me wonder if she'd borrowed it from Rain, who immediately rushed down front, pulling me along behind her.

We elbowed our way through the decent-sized crowd that had gathered to hear some late morning music by an up-and-coming local Indie band. All around me, I noticed a variety of brown-colored kids: Iranians, Saudis, Peruvians, Kuwaitis, Guatemalans, Indians, Chaldeans, and of course African-Americans. A whole contingent of students existed that I knew nothing about. Primarily they'd come to Wayne State to study Medicine and Law, with WSU's Med School being the university's oldest college, the nation's largest single-campus medical school, and the only in the city of Detroit. As part of The Department, we spent all our time either studying in Old Main or at Ninety-Five, with the occasional class down in the Hilberry Studio. It was easy to forget Wayne State was a major university comprised of kids from all over the world, not just Michigan.

"I love this one!" Rain totally started rocking out, bopping her head up and down and flinging her dark hair around.

I, personally, didn't recognize the tune, so I wasn't as easily able to enjoy it. But Sarah was singing the hell out of the number (whatever it was), her voice unlike anything I'd ever heard from her, which had only been the one time at *Chicago* auditions. Before, her sound was pure Musical Theatre. The woman up onstage, playing guitar and thrashing her body about like that guy from Nirvana, sang with an intensity and rawness that totally reminded me of Janis Joplin.

The rest of the crew consisted of a cute Rick Astley/ Howdy Doody-type on bass, another more dark and brooding dude on drums, and a girl who seemed way too plain and boring, in my humble opinion, to be playing keyboards and singing backup in a rock band. They performed a short set of five or six numbers, none of which I knew. There was one called "Stones," another named "Someday Son," and my favorite had to be the one titled "Lilly of the Valley." I had no idea where they'd gotten their material, and I later learned the songs were originals that Sarah had written herself. Strange Bedfellows were like a real-live rock group, on their way to a successful music career—not just some wannabe cover band, like so many others I'd heard at many a boring wedding.

"We're gonna slow things down," Sarah told the crowd, soft and sultry, the mic held tightly between her two hands. "This is 'Star is Mine.'"

> *And I said Baby, close your eyes*
> *I'm gonna make you a wish tonight*
> *'Cause if there ain't no star that's yours*
> *You know there's gotta, gotta be a star that's mine*

About halfway through the ballad, a haunting poem about different folks all down on their luck, saving their pennies for something better to come, I caught a glimpse of a photographer mixed in among the audience. He held a professional caliber camera up to his eye, so I couldn't quite see his face. But I could tell he was black, dark-skinned and well-built, and he nicely filled out his army green fatigues.

On his head, he wore a military issue hat, the visor pulled low about his brow. Of course I wondered who he was, and what he was doing there, and why the hell he was taking pictures. Once Sarah and the rest of the Bedfellows had sung their last note and taken their final bows, I received my answer.

"Baby!" The African-American guy in the army garb leapt onto the stage, threw his massive arms around Sarah and spun her in circles, like a sailor on shore leave greeting his special lady. He wore dark-framed glasses, à la Clark Kent.

Sarah squealed. "Baby! You made it." She giggled like a school girl as the big man squeezed her tightly. "Okay, you can put me down. Columbus!"

From where Rain and I stood, waiting for our turn to congratulate the star on a splendid performance, I couldn't help but overhear the lovers' conversation. So this was the infamous Columbus? Due to my vantage point, I still couldn't totally take him in until he set Sarah down, allowing me ample opportunity to feast my eyes on his handsome—and all too familiar—face.

Sexy Sid!

I couldn't believe what I was seeing. Again I almost fell to the floor, right in the middle of the Stupid Center, when I made the connection: Sarah Schwartz's boyfriend, Columbus Howard, was none other than the hot stripper from Club Riviera who, just four nights prior, had planted a sloppy kiss directly on my mouth after I'd paid him a mere twenty dollars. I thought for sure I was going to throw up.

"Rain! Bradley!" Sarah greeted us both with a great big happy hug.

"Awesome show," said Rain. "Love the new number."

"Thanks," said Sarah, clinging to Columbus, who simply stared at me, grinning. "We just added it to the set list. Oh, my God! Bradley, I want you to meet Columbus."

I wasn't sure what I should do or what I should say. I could acknowledge that Columbus and I had already made each other's acquaintance and just not admit where. Or I could pretend we'd never laid eyes (or lips) on each other. I felt totally sick to my stomach, and I just wanted to flee.

"Hey, Red," said Columbus, offering me his callused

hand.

"Hey..."

We shook and nothing more was said, though I did won-der what had happened to his distinctly urban accent. Grow-ing up in Hazeltucky, like with the Jews, one rarely encountered anyone of the non-Caucasian persuasion unless they were Arab or perhaps Asian. In fact, during my three years attending Hazel Park High, only one black kid ever si-multaneously walked those same hallowed halls: a boy by the name of Donny White. Two years older than me, a senior when I was a sophomore, Donny was tall, obviously dark, and quite handsome, with a tight afro and perfect Chiclet teeth. To my and everyone else's surprise, Donny received the honor of being voted one of the "Top 5" boys to be cho-sen as Homecoming Court. The thing about Donny, and I'd never forget when my sister, Janelle, his classmate, said this after learning of Donny's victory: "He might be black... *But he's nice.*" Because in Hazel Park, this had always been the prevailing attitude among white people for as long as I'd lived in the area. If someone is African-American, they must be two specific things: mean and poor.

After the show, the Strange Bedfellows disbanded, and the rest of us went along on our separate ways. Fortunately for my sake, Columbus informed Sarah that he had to attend a meeting with a Realtor about renting a gallery. For the longest time, his goal had been to open up an art space where he could display his photographs and Sarah would have a place to perform, along with other local Detroit artists, be they musicians, singers, actors, poets, dancers—whomever. It turned out that down on Woodward Avenue, just past the Bonstelle and next to the Sassy Cat adult film theatre ("Home of Detroit's Finest Movies"), an old deserted store-front had recently been gutted and renovated and was now readily available.

"Good luck, baby," Sarah said, kissing Columbus good-bye.

As her lips touched his, I thought about his lips touching mine and, again, I felt like I could vomit. "*Oh! what a tangled web we weave...*"

Sarah invited me and Rain to grab coffee before Acting began in half an hour. Rain regretted that she had to rush off for a meeting with Will Bilson, to get feedback on her *Chicago* audition. I wasn't sure if this was such a good idea, considering their sexual history. But it was none of my business to question Rain's actions. I blinked and Brad Woodward had disappeared. Sarah said that he'd said he enjoyed the concert, but he needed to find a payphone to call his agent at Affiliated. And yet, on the way back toward Ninety-Five, I saw him hanging around outside Old Main, chatting with the African-American boy I'd seen on the first day of school down by the library; the one the hot Detroit cop had arrested for dealing drugs. I said nothing to Sarah. From where we were on the opposite side of the street, she couldn't see Brad with the black guy, and I didn't want to worry her. But more and more, I sadly suspected my new boyfriend for a drug addict.

The Ice Cream Company was a cute little coffee shop right on West Warren, in a strip-like complex along with the Marwil Bookstore, Johnny's Diner, the University Copy Center, and an Ethiopian restaurant named Epicurus. The place was lemon yellow, from the walls to the ceiling, to the tiny circular tables that barely sat two people and were clumsily crammed together between the windows and the walk-up counter.

I was looking forward to some one-on-one time with Sarah and having the chance to get to know her better. More importantly, I was dying to find out how she couldn't possibly have any idea that her totally hot (and presumably totally straight) hunk of man-love had been spending his late nights working professionally as a go-go boy/stripper in a sleazy 7 Mile gay bar.

"What's good here?" I glanced up at the menu board, marveling at the plethora of baked potato and egg noodle platters. Mozzarella cheese and garlic butter sounded tasty, though lunchtime wasn't for another few hours. Perhaps I would wait and return after Dina's class for a sample?

"They have these chocolate chunk muffins that are to die for!" Sarah said, peering into the glass display case in search of one.

We ordered a single muffin to share and two cups of coffee. The older woman working behind the register nodded and smiled cheerfully. "Hi, Sarah. It's Sue."

She reminded me of Mokey Fraggle, with big eyes and blue hair, and her flowered apron smock made me think of my Grandma Victor, bless her heart!

"Oh, hi, Sue," Sarah said. "I thought it was you."

"How are your eyes today?" asked Sue, concerned.

"Still the same." Sarah shot me a glance, and I could tell she wished she'd never mentioned her lack of sight to the woman, no matter how kind she came off.

We fixed our coffees. Or I fixed mine—milk and two sugars; Sarah took hers black. "Like my men," she teased, quoting the old bit from *Airplane!*, though in her case, she was serious.

"So how long have you and Columbus been together?" Since she'd at last brought him into our conversation, I thought it safe to finally inquire.

"Let's see..." Sarah pulled off a hunk of chocolate muffin top and popped it hungrily into her mouth. "We met second semester of my freshman year," she said from behind a napkin as she chatted and chewed. "So what is that? Not quite two years. He was just about to graduate from CCS."

The Center for Creative Studies-College of Art and Design had its origins in 1906 with the founding of the Society of Arts and Crafts. In 1926, the society became one of the premiere Arts and Crafts organizations in the US to offer an educational program. In 1962, the school officially became a college when the Michigan Department of Education authorized the granting of a Bachelor of Fine Arts degree in Industrial Design and in 1975, it assumed the CCS name.

Sarah went on to elaborate how she and the Bedfellows had been invited to their first major gig back in February '91, at a lounge over on Caniff in Hamtramck called Paycheck's. Coincidentally Columbus happened to be there, taking pictures for a freelance assignment on the Alt/Rock music scene in Detroit for the *Metro Times*. After their set, Columbus had approached Sarah, singing his praises for her songwriting and awesome vocal skills. The couple got to talking, and they totally hit it off. But when they bumped into each other weeks later at a Lili's 21 gig, Columbus accused Sarah of ignoring him, as he hadn't realized she had a visual impairment. Sarah's bringing up the topic offered me the opportunity to finally question her handicap.

"They call it *stargardts*," she explained. "But the technical name is *fundus flavimaculatus*. It's a form of juvenile macular degeneration." She could sense I was sitting there listening, totally lost. "Basically it means I have a blind spot in my central vision."

"You mean like a dark spot?"

"Actually it's all the colors of the rainbow. And it dances."

A dancing, rainbow-colored blind spot?

"How long have you had it?"

"Um..." Silently she counted back the years. "Since I was about thirteen, maybe fourteen. I started having trouble reading the chalkboard at school. Then I came home with an F on my math assignment, and my mother just about had a fit. 'Oh, my God! You got an F?'" said Sarah, impersonating her mother's high-pitched squeal. "I explained that it wasn't for lack of trying. But maybe it had something to do with the fact that when I looked at her, her nose disappeared."

There was no known cure for the condition. Because of it, she wasn't able to drive a car, or read from a book, or do just about anything in terms of a career, other than sing-er/songwriter/actor. And even that had been a challenge, one that required obtaining audition sides weeks in advance and having someone record the dialogue onto mini-cassette tape so that she could memorize it. Practically every single direc-tor or casting person whom she'd met would panic, worrying she'd fall off the stage if they dared give her a part.

"Can you see me?" I asked, hoping I didn't sound too self-centered. "Sitting here, can you tell what I look like?"

"Oh, sure. As long as whatever I'm looking at isn't too far off, I just push the multi-colored blind spot away, sorta look past it, and I can see whatever's on the other side."

"Wow!" I said, trying to envision her daily ordeal. "So is Columbus cool with everything?" From the little bit of inter-action I'd witness between them, post-concert, he seemed like he was clearly into her.

"Oh, yeah. He's totally cool. He helps me with my lines. He chauffeurs me around town. He reads to me in bed. Sid's a great guy; no matter what my mom and dad may think."

"You call him Sid?"

Sarah blushed. "He's my Seeing Eye Dude."

"Gotcha..." I didn't bother pointing out that *eye* started with an E—and not an I (as in S-I-D). But that at least ex-plained Columbus's *nom de plume* at Club Riviera.

"It's not that my folks don't like Columbus," Sarah con-tinued. "They're just both old school Jews from Oak Park. They're not Orthodox or anything, but they might as well be. And marrying a *goy*, particularly a *schvartzer*, is strictly frowned upon."

I didn't understand a lick of Yiddish, except for what I'd learned from *Fiddler on the Roof*, along with the word *fagela* from when Jodie Dallas, aka Billy Crystal on *Soap*, was in the hospital for a sex change operation, and he got stuck with an old Jewish guy as a roommate.

"So did you go to Oak Park High?"

"Berkley. My parents live north of Ten Mile, by the zoo."

This was like our living in Ferndale but going to school in Hazel Park, since our house was located east of Hilton.

"And what year did you graduate?" I wondered.

"1990. Same as you, right? Rain said you went to Seaholm."

The trouble with lying, other than it being a sin, was that one must commit his alternate history to memory.

"Yep," I said, affirming falsely. "Wait! 1990? I saw *Little Shop of Horrors* at Berkley High in '88, I think. Were you in that production?"

"I was. Sophomore year. I played Audrey."

"Now I know why I recognized you...When I picked you up at The Thelma for *Chicago* auditions, I thought you looked familiar."

"You came to our little show?" she asked in awe. "Why?"

"It's one of my all-time favorites," I said. "We did it my junior year at Haz—Seaholm." Luckily I caught my slip before I stumbled any further. "I played Seymour."

Sarah cooed, "Ooh, I bet you made a cute nerd." Then she reached out and playfully pinched my cheek.

"So where did Columbus grow up?" I asked, hoping to at last put all the pieces of this puzzle in place.

"Detroit. He went to Cass Tech."

Technically known as Cass Technical, CTHS was a four-year preparatory magnet school located in an historic building downtown on Second Avenue. Much like we'd done in college, students chose a major area of study, with subjects ranging from architecture, graphic arts, music, business, and science.

"Isn't that where Diana Ross went?" I asked, impressed.

"Diana Ross," said Sarah, nodding. "Ellen Burstyn, Lily Tomlin..."

"I love Lily Tomlin!" I howled. "Have you seen *The Incredible Shrinking Woman*, with her whore of a housekeeper Concepcion?"

"I have not," said Sarah sadly. "I don't watch much TV. You know, she went to Wayne State, Lily Tomlin? But she never graduated."

This fact I found baffling. "How come?"

"According to the story going round The Department, one of the directors—Dr. Gill, most likely—told her she couldn't act. So she said 'screw you' and dropped out."

"Good for her!"

"And then there was Carole Anne-Marie Gist," Sarah said, the name leaving a bitter taste in her mouth.

"Who's she?"

"Oh, nobody," she answered nonchalantly before adding, "Only the first African-American Miss USA ever."

"Right!" I said, knowing the woman sounded familiar.

Growing up, I'd always been a big fan of beauty pageants. Religiously I would watch glued to our tiny television, pad and pen in hand, keeping tally of each contestant's scores throughout the competition. One of my fondest memories occurred on the night of the Miss USA pageant 1981, when I surprisingly discovered that our very own Miss Michigan, Karen Eidson, just so happened to hail from Hazel Park. Sadly she mustn't have made much of an impression in the judge's minds. The poor thing didn't even make the Top 10 finalists.

"Carole and Columbus used to go together back at Cass Tech," Sarah went on with her tirade.

Clearly I could tell the subject of her current boyfriend's ex-girlfriend was a sore one for Sarah, and I swiftly let it drop.

So Columbus Howard, gay-for-pay go-go dancer, dated a former beauty queen? The guy kept getting more and interesting.

12

INFORMER

♦   ♦   ♦

While I felt terrible about Sarah being disabled, I was fascinated by how well-adjusted she seemed in spite of it all, and I was curious to know how she ended up at Wayne State.

"Well..." She sipped her coffee for the first time since I'd forced her into having this conversation. "The summer before I started, I took a class with Dina. That's how I met Rain. She studied privately with her all through high school. When her dad wouldn't let her go to Juilliard, Dina suggested she come to Wayne State. Dina went to the Hilberry, you know?"

"Brad mentioned it," I said. "So wait... Rain got into Juilliard?" Boy, was I jealous!

"And Carnegie Mellon," said Sarah, envious. "And NYU. But her dad didn't want her going away, I guess. Not after her mom died. Anyway, I heard about this summer acting class on WDET, over at the Attic. I signed up, and on the very first day, I was a total bitch to Dina."

"You were?" I couldn't imagine Sarah Schwartz being a bitch to anybody, let alone Dina French. "Why?"

"We were working on cold readings, and she assigned me the Laura/Gentleman Caller scene from *The Glass Menagerie*." She gazed off into the distance, observing the action as it had played out on that particular day. "So I looked at Dina, and I said, 'I'm not doing it. I can't. And besides, I don't even know if I'm gonna stay in this class.' Or something totally mature like that."

"Oh, no," I said, giggling like Sarah and I were two long-lost girlfriends catching up after not seeing each other in forever. "What did Dina say?"

"She pulled me aside, very politely, and told me to cut the shit. Just get up there and do it. She wasn't giving me a refund."

"God, I love her!" I cried, clapping my hands together in approval.

"She even helped me write out my lines with a Sharpie and gave me extra time to memorize them."

"She did?"

Sarah nodded, swallowing the last chunk of chocolate muffin. "She was totally cool. I wouldn't be where I am right now without her."

"Playing a lead role in *Chicago*," I said, in case she needed the reminder.

"I don't know how that happened," Sarah said sincerely. "I didn't even audition for the part. I don't know what Will was thinking."

"He must think you're good. Have a little confidence."

"Oh, I've got confidence. That's not the problem... I worry maybe Will only cast me as Velma to get back at Rain."

We had at last come to the bridge I'd been hoping to cross since first witnessing the tension between the former lovers on the first night of auditions.

"Why would he do that?" I asked innocently, not wanting to appear as if I was one to relish in gossip. Even if I totally was—and I was—Rain DuBois was my friend.

According to Sarah, last spring, after Rain had suddenly broken up with Brad Woodward and she'd had her two week fling with Canadian heartthrob, Colm Feore, Rain got wind that Will Bilson and his wife had recently separated. She'd also heard that he would be directing the fall musical, *Chicago*, as a third year Hilberry MFA candidate. Vying for the role of Velma Kelly, Rain strolled up to Third's one night, where she conveniently bumped into Will, struck up an innocent conversation, and allowed the 33-year-old to ply her with alcoholic beverages. Poor Sarah had been lucky enough to pay witness to the sexual antics that occurred in Rain's bedroom that night and would continue for the next few weeks, only ceasing once Will's wife learned she was pregnant and decided she should reconcile with her cheating husband. Of course Will went crawling back, and he proceeded to call it quits with Rain. But only after she'd called him up in a drunken stupor and begged him to see her one final time, at which point Rain proceeded to stab Will with a six-inch kitchen knife.

Fortunately the resulting wound was only superficial. A quick trip over to Detroit Receiving for a few small stitches and Will soon made a speedy recovery. He agreed not to press any charges, out of fear that the 19-year-old girl would retaliate and inform authorities of his encouraging of underage drinking. But Will also warned Rain to keep her distance and promised he'd think twice before casting her in a show that he was directing. Especially not in a starring role.

"Well, that wasn't very nice," I said, once Sarah had concluded her sordid story.

"She stabbed him, Bradley," Sarah said seriously.

"I mean Will casting you as Velma and pitting you two against each other."

"I suppose. But it's like Dina says... It ain't show friends, it's show *business*." She held her watch up close to her face, its numbers twice the size of a usual timepiece. "Oh, my God!" she gasped. "It's five after eleven."

We had ten minutes to hustle on over to Two Forty-Five or else we'd be sitting out in the hallway listening to today's lecture on Practical Aesthetics, the method developed by the Atlantic Theater Company in New York, from beyond the double doors. Thankfully we made it to Acting with sixty seconds to spare.

The highlight of Dina's class that day came when Sage

Ang got up to work on a scene with Ann Marie Tyson from some British farce called *Dirty Linen* by a playwright named Tom Stoppard. I couldn't tell what the story was exactly, based on the text alone; something to do with the House of Parliament over in England, maybe, and a sex scandal that had made headlines in a tabloid exposé. Ann Marie played Miss Gotobed, and Sage's character, Cocklebury-Smythe, kept calling out whatever he was thinking, sexually speaking, despite trying to cover, and stammering all the way. Dina, as she had done after every pair of actors, gave Sage and Ann Marie an adjustment before having them repeat the scene. The second time through, she made Torrance Andrews leave the acting studio and go down to the bathroom to grab a fresh roll of toilet paper. When he returned to Two Forty-Five, she had Sage wad up several pieces of the tissue, shove them deep inside his mouth, and ordered him to begin the scene again.

With his cheeks all puffed out, like a chipmunk squirreling away a stash of nuts for the coming winter, Sage opened his lips as best as he could, considering. The moment he spoke, the sound that sprang forth from his throat registered two octaves deeper than the nasally voice we had all thought natural.

The concept for the Bonstelle Theatre's production of *Chicago*, according to its director and choreographer, was that of a musical-within-a-musical. As we, the actors, were performing the story of Roxie Hart and Velma Kelly, accused of murdering their husbands in 1920's Chicago, it was as if we were actual actors performing the story of Roxie Hart and Velma Kelly, as if the actual events had already taken place, and they were now being told onstage by the real Roxie and Velma after they'd already occurred in real life. Being my first mainstage show at a major university, after taking the last four years off from acting altogether, I couldn't wait to start the read-through.

"Actors!" Amelia jumped right in with playing the role of angst-ridden, Birkenstock-wearing stage manager. "We need everybody onstage, please. And bring a seat. Sarah, you need a hand?"

"No, thanks," she politely refused. Lifting a metal folding chair off the rack and carrying it center, Sarah asked, "Where should I sit?"

"Somewhere in the middle maybe," Amelia mused. "You are the star of the show."

Sarah smirked. "Well..." She sat beside Brad Woodward—who still hadn't said a word to me—along with Wanda Freeman who was playing Roxie, Ann Marie Tyson, aka Matron Mama Morton, and Sage Ang as Mary Sunshine.

"Okay," said Will Bilson, welcoming us once we'd assembled in a semi-circle with our official Samuel French play scripts. "Let's get this party started, shall we? Amelia, would you mind reading stage directions?"

Amelia nodded nervously, clearing her throat. "That's what I'm here for."

Will turned his attention toward Rain. "As Sarah's understudy, can I trouble you to read for her tonight?"

The tension in the air was cut-it-with-a-knife thick. Everybody in the theatre knew how hard Rain DuBois had fought to win the role of Velma Kelly and how betrayed she now felt—no matter what she said—at her best friend's usurping of the part. But Rain remained the consummate professional.

Biting her lower lip, she sat up straight and tall, glaring only slightly as she replied, "Certainly, William."

"Oh, that's all right," Sarah said lightly. "I've already memorized my script. Thank you, Rain," she told her roommate. "I won't be needing any help."

"Well," said Will, finding himself at a loss for words. "I'm impressed."

As was I. With all the plays I'd appeared in, I still hated

learning my lines. For whatever reason, I had the most diffi-
cult time cramming the words into my brain and making
them stick. In most instances, I'd be lucky to be off book by
Opening Night. The fact that Sarah couldn't even read her
dialogue off the page, and yet she somehow managed to
commit it to memory in a matter of days, was just another
example, I felt, of the diligence and dedication she'd shown in
her pursuit of a career as a performer.

Rain disagreed and, in no uncertain terms, made her feelings known. "I don't believe you," she hissed at Sarah once
we'd stopped for a break between acts. "You planned this entire charade."

She pronounced it cha-*rahd.*

"I did?" asked Sarah sincerely. She and I had just entered
the backstage Green Room, its mint green walls decorated
with faded black-and-white Bonstelle production stills from
days gone by, when Rain launched into her rant.

"What's up?" I wondered, making myself comfortable on
one of several vinyl-covered, verdant-colored cushions that
lined a built-in wooden bench seat.

Rain snapped, "Bradley, stay out of this," her jaw
clenched. "This is between me and Sarah."

When I'd asked her the other day, she'd insisted she felt
no animosity against Sarah and blamed the casting of her
roommate as Velma Kelly on our director. I especially
thought things were copasetic, since we'd all gone out dancing over the weekend. There seemed to be no bad blood between the girls during our Royal Canadian adventure.
Suddenly Rain acted as if she had a chip on her shoulder the
size of Castle Rock, across the Mackinac Bridge in St.
Ignace.

"I honestly don't know what's wrong," Sarah admitted.

Rain laughed, one perfect ha.

"Please tell me," Sarah pleaded. "I'll gladly apologize."

"You know precisely what's wrong. You wanted to play
Velma from day one."

"I didn't. You were at auditions. I never even read for the role."

"Then why have you already memorized all the lines? Obviously you've been working on it for quite some time now."

"Only since Sunday," Sarah insisted. "I knew last week we were having this read-through tonight, so I spent all day yesterday and the day before working on my script."

"Are you sure?" Rain accused. "You know what Dina says... 'Compete or die.'"

"How long have we been best friends? I would never let some part in a play come between us, Rain."

Hearing this exchange called to mind something my junior high Band teacher, Jessica Clark Putnam, once informed Jack and me: "Friends hold you back." Her advice had come in reference to Jack's not wanting to spend the summer after 7th grade alone at Blue Lake Fine Arts Camp, when my mom and dad were unable to afford the three hundred dollar tuition to send me along. At the time, I refused to believe her. But the older I became, the more I began to subscribe to JCP's theory. When the day rolled round for me to leave Michigan, in pursuit of my intended profession, I couldn't let anyone stop me. Not my parents or my sisters; not my best friend; and certainly not some guy like Brad Woodward.

That weekend after our Saturday noon rehearsal, in which we focused almost the entire four hours on learning the choreography to "Razzle Dazzle," I found myself back at Roy Sparks' Country Boy Restaurant. I hadn't worked a single day the entire week due to my evenings being devoted to the world that was 1920s Chicago. It felt odd to once again be wearing my soup-stained white Oxford and faded black slacks, the pad and pen I never used to take orders tucked tightly in my front shirt pocket. Monday through Friday, I was Bradley Dayton of Birmingham, studying Theatre by day and preparing for my Detroit stage debut at night. While

I found the regular patrons at Country Boy to be sweet as pie, the conversations we shared as I refilled their coffee cups ("How 'bout them Tigers?") didn't amount to a hill of beans compared to the topics me and my college-educated friends would discuss ("Ross Perot for President?") over grilled cheese on Greek bread at Johnny's Diner.

After the early evening dinner rush had declined, I stopped to take a breather. Standing stooped over behind the counter, I stared blankly across the dining room at the TV mounted in the corner up near the ceiling. The weathered face of legendary newsman Bill Bonds (and his freshly-washed and styled toupee), filled the screen as the channel 7 six o'clock news began. The volume on mute, I waited patiently for the closed-captions to kick in.

"WE BEGIN TONIGHT WITH SOME SAD NEWS OUT OF HOLLYWOOD. ACTOR ANTHONY PERKINS IS DEAD AT THE AGE OF SIXTY."

A black-and-white photo of the handsome, dark-haired star appeared in a tiny box, the dates 1932-1992 beneath it.

"PERKINS FIRST APPEARED ONSCREEN IN 1957's *THE ACTRESS* WITH JEAN SIMMONS AND SPENCER TRACY AND WOULD GO ON TO BECOME FAMOUS FOR HIS ROLE AS MOTEL OWNER NORMAN BATES IN THE 1960 HITCHCOCK THRILLER *PSYCHO*."

I felt my heart sink at Bill Bonds' next words, spelled out for me once again on the screen below his image.

"PERKINS' DEATH COMES AS A RESULT OF AIDS-RELATED COMPLICATIONS."

I never even knew Anthony Perkins was gay, let alone HIV-positive. I also hadn't realized what an extensive career he'd had. According to old Bill Bonds, Tony Perkins had also taken over the role of Tom in *Tea and Sympathy* on Broadway, a play first brought to my attention by Mr. Dell'Olio during senior year of high school. Leave it to Dell to suggest I work on a monologue about a guy who everybody thinks is gay. But I'm glad he did. Never in my life had I connected to a piece more, and felt like I was acting less, when it came to that one.

Not that I was a big Anthony Perkins fan or anything, but it saddened me to hear of his demise under such tragic circumstances. Especially since the report also announced that he left behind a wife and two children. This made me wonder why he'd gotten married in the first place and, more importantly, how he'd physically managed to father those kids. I assumed it had required his having sex with a *woman*, something I couldn't imagine myself ever being able to do—at least not up until recently.

That afternoon at rehearsal, we were going over what we in the ensemble had come to call the Group Grope, which was basically an intricately choreographed orgy, live onstage. As per some cosmic coincidence, I'd found myself once again partnered with Rain DuBois. Soon we were writhing around on the floor, bumping and grinding together in a simulated sexual situation, albeit on a PG-13 level. Leave it to me, but I totally became aroused as I began pretend-fucking this beautiful girl. I tried telling myself that since we were doing it doggy-style, she could've just as easily been a guy. But even I could sense when I'd been lying to myself.

What the hell did this mean?!

All my life I'd been gay. It was something I'd felt deep down in my soul, since I'd first set eyes on Shaun Cassidy as Joe Hardy on *The Hardy Boys* when I was like 6 years old. Probably even long before that. I had the biggest crush on Speed Racer, which I would watch religiously when I was all of three, along with Jethro from *The Beverly Hillbillies*, the Professor from *Gilligan's Island*, Keith Partridge, and both Greg and Peter Brady. There was also Robbie Douglas from *My Three Sons*, Major Nelson from *I Dream of Jeannie*, *Eight is Enough*'s Tommy Bradford, and Albert from *Little House on the Prairie*. And let's not forget Lexie Winston's father Marcus from *Ice Castles*, Wayne State alum Tom Skerritt; and this was just my pre-pubescent list of potential true loves. Still, all my crushes throughout my entire lifetime had one single, solitary thing in common: a penis between their legs.

I lit up a cigarette, inhaled deeply and exhaled slowly, stopping to mull over my dilemma. Perhaps my feelings for Rain, if that's what they indeed were, stemmed from the fact that growing up, whenever a girl had expressed the slightest romantic interest in me, she hadn't exactly been the prettiest or the skinniest of the bunch, and maybe that was the reason I hadn't felt the least bit of mutual attraction? But ask anyone around, Rain DuBois was gorgeous. Every straight guy in The Department—they were few and far between, but they did exist, and they all wanted to sleep with the girl. Hell, even our Acting teacher lusted after Rain, and she was also female!

Maybe I wasn't actually a homo after all? Maybe I just hadn't met the right woman, as Rain herself had indicated on the night we first hung out together at Third's, when she first tried putting the moves on me? Maybe Rain DuBois was my one last chance at living a (quote-unquote) normal life?

Thoughts of my sexual salvation were abruptly interrupted by the roar of an enormous Harley 1500cc pulling into the parking lot and rattling the windows of the restaurant.

"Would you's get a load of that?" Barb shouted over the noise, sticking an index finger inside each one of her ears.

The biker wore a black leather jacket, black leather pants, black leather boots and gloves, and a black helmet with the dark visor pulled down. In one fell swoop, he hopped off the machine without cutting the engine and forcefully flung open the front door, jingling its bells. He wasn't a big man, not in terms of his height. But he had a solid build and, even without seeing his face, I could totally tell he had to be hot. Usually the motorcycle-riding customers we got at Country Boy would take a seat in one of the corner booths, order a cup of coffee or maybe a burger and fries; usually they shut off their bikes and took off their helmets, and they didn't lurk at the counter like Evil Incarnate.

I looked at Barb over by the cash register, which she gingerly shut closed—just in case—before turning to confront the man. "May I help you?"

"Yeah," said the biker. But he just stood there without saying anything else.

I could tell by the sound of his voice that he was black. Not that it meant anything, but I wasn't surprised due to Hazel Park's close proximity to the Detroit border.

"You left your motorcycle on," I said, in case maybe he hadn't noticed.

"Yeah," he said a second time.

"May I help you?" I repeated, attempting to sound unafraid when, in actuality, I feared for my own mortality.

"I'm here to pick up an order."

"Okay... And what would it be?"

"A son of a cop, with a side of homo." He grinned, big teeth. "Le's go."

For a split second, my mind went blank. Then I felt even more freaked out. At first, I'd thought maybe the guy was going to rob the place, steal all our money, and leave without saying another word. But now that he was ordering me out of the building with him, I couldn't help but think he knew exactly who I was, and he had some beef to settle with my policeman dad by taking it out on his kid.

I decided to do whatever the guy said. No use putting Barb or the lives of the few remaining customers at risk. I didn't see a gun anywhere, but I didn't have time to give the scenario much more consideration. I simply surrendered.

"Just don't hurt me, okay?" I begged.

"What's going on, Bradley?" asked Barb from across the floor.

"I need to punch out early," I told her, bypassing the time clock as the biker pulled me from behind the counter and dragged me outside. I glanced back into the restaurant and saw Barb rushing across the room to pick up the payphone.

"Git on," the guy ordered.

Mounting the huge black saddle, I trembled as I clutched the aptly named sissy bar behind me. I pictured the biker driving us to some deserted building somewhere, beating the living shit out of me, and leaving me for dead. My dad and his fellow officers would have to drag the Detroit River in search of my mangled corpse. Sarah Gibson would play guitar and sing "Everywhere I Go" by Amy Grant at my funeral.

We peeled out onto 9 Mile and headed in the direction of the setting sun. One of the advantages of growing up in the Great Lakes State was that it sat so far westward in the Eastern time zone, providing almost an additional added hour of daylight each evening. During the height of summer, it didn't get dark until almost 10:00 p.m., lengthening the life of twilight games of "Hit the Deck" and "Ghost in the Graveyard."

When we hit the first red at John R, the mysterious biker reached around behind his back to shake my hand.

"What's up, Red?" he asked, in an accent I would no longer describe as ghetto. He flipped up his visor, revealing a handsome face I immediately recognized—and was rather relieved at the sight of.

"Columbus!"

He laughed, the light turned green, and we headed south.

13

MAKE IT MINE

◆ ◆ ◆

We didn't drive the usual route. Instead of hopping on the freeway, we continued cruising down John R, zooming past the familiar haunts from my childhood: the red, barn-like roof of the Dairy Park, the Salem Market strip mall, Kado's Party Store where, in 8th grade, I bought my first pack of cigarettes. I forgot how desolate this area of Hazel Park was, with its windowless, one-story brick buildings lining the street, most of which I had no idea to whom they belonged or what sort of business went on inside.

At 8 Mile, we crossed the border into Detroit, and all at once the four-lane road shrank to half the size. While the scenery didn't alter much, the letters painted on the liquor stores we passed morphed from solid, blocky English to flowing, swirly Arabic.

"Where are we going?" I called out to Columbus, my hands gripping his slim hips. It felt oddly intimate to be touching him this way after having had his tongue inside my mouth. I tried my best not to dwell on this memory.

Either he couldn't hear the question over the roar of the pavement whizzing by, or he was saving our destination as a surprise.

"Hold on!" he advised as we made our bumpy way over a set of rusty railroad tracks. Gravel spun and spat and we almost wiped out taking the right turn onto a street called Oakland.

We had at last come to a part of town that resembled a proper neighborhood, with historic Craftsman houses dating back to the 1920s, complete with covered front porches perfect for sitting on a warm night such as this one. I felt a tinge of remorse in knowing these beautiful homes still existed, and yet they were tucked away, surrounded by areas where no one in their right minds would want to reside.

At Caniff, Columbus took us even further eastward. We made another right onto Russell and continued south, through a section best described as industrial. Semi trucks sat parked alongside the road and in the parking lots of the fenced-in, gated factories. This was the moment when we could finally see, off in the distance just to our left, the blinking beacon.

"Where are you taking me?" I shouted, anxious and also excited by our approach.

Down the desolate highway, the Harley twisted and turned, my body melding into Columbus's as we balanced adroitly on the bike. On either side of us, more forsaken factories and wide open fields whirred by in a blur of lights and darkness, along with the steady rush of wind. On the next corner, we encountered a six-story abandoned building jutting up from the curb. Opposite, a red brick wall ran the length of the road, behind which loomed, like a citadel protecting a primitive people, The Cloud Maker.

"I know this place," I informed Columbus, though in reality, I'd only ever seen it from the confines of my car.

He said nothing, choosing to remain silent for the next half-mile. Eventually we came to an opening in the form of a gated driveway that led into whatever this place actually was; another factory of sorts, I assumed. Suddenly Columbus stopped the motorcycle.

"We're heeere!" he sang, lifting the visor of his helmet to reveal his Clark Kents.

"Where's here?" I glanced around for some sign of a security guard who would, no doubt, order us to get back on our bike and be off.

Again Columbus went radio silent. He marched up to the padlocked fence protecting The Cloud Maker, put his leather-gloved fingers through the diamond-shaped holes, and gazed up at the lofty tower. I stood beside him, but I focused on his face and not the billowy white steam evaporating into the night sky, except for what I could see reflecting in the clear lenses of his glasses. He was freshly showered and smelled of soap, his afro well-coifed despite having been smashed beneath his biker's helmet. Even though he appeared the picture of perfection, something about the look in his light brown eyes, the expression on his handsome face, made me think he felt forlorn. Still, he smiled up at the misty clouds and gave the gate a shake.

"Easy," I told him. "You might break it."

"No need." Producing a small silver key from his pocket, he swiftly inserted it into the metal lock, allowing us access to the secret world beyond. "My pops owns the place."

This revelation certainly came as a shock. Columbus could tell by the way I reacted, saying nary a word as he led the way inside.

The Cloud Maker was nothing more than a glorified garbage incinerator, first opened in 1986 as the Greater Detroit Resource Recovery Facility. Its purpose was to burn trash in order to produce steam that would in turn generate electricity for a cash-strapped metropolis, making it one of the most controversial buildings in all of Motown. During the 1970s, when the United States found itself faced with a severe energy crisis, a new emphasis was put on coming up with alternate sources other than gas and oil. Engineers had suggested that cities like Detroit could effectively burn their garbage and create electricity that could then be sold, instead of paying to transport waste to a landfill somewhere. At first, this seemed an excellent solution to both the energy crisis and the task of getting rid of urban waste. Detroit could greatly cut the cost of disposing its trash while also generating energy.

The idea, however, was not well-received. Environmentalists emphasized the pollutants that the giant furnace would produce, and politicians understood the woes involved in finding a neighborhood that would welcome an incinerator, along with the accompanying odors that would emerge as city garbage trucks visited the facility daily. Threatened by the tremendous financial difficulties of the time, Detroit mayor Coleman Young consented to construct the country's grandest garbage incinerator exclusively designed to produce electricity. The city issued bonds to the sum of $440 million to build the facility, making it the largest municipal solid waste incinerator in the nation. But first, two major setbacks had to be tackled.

Health officials and environmental experts in southeast Michigan and south-western Ontario, Canada, vehemently opposed constructing the incinerator. They believed that millions of tons of toxins would be emitted into the air annually, thus increasing already rising morbidity rates among inner city children. Especially blacks. Upper- and middle-class areas had the strength to block its construction, and there had been lengthy litigation seeking to do so. The Province of Ontario sued, as prevailing winds meant that the effluents coming from the incinerator's smokestacks would quickly reach Canada upon leaving the US. Typical in Detroit at this time, the issue of race regularly impacted the discussion. Opponents of the incinerator argued that the foreseeable consequence was far worse health for those residing closest to the facility.

"Don't you see?" said Columbus, clearly fueled by frustration. "This place is killing people. Kids with asthma, they're getting sicker and sicker. It took five years, but the state finally accepted what everybody else was saying all along. They refused to renew the operating permits unless something was done to make it safe. But that was costly, of course. So what does Coleman A. Young, mayor, go and do? Sells it to the highest bidder."

"Your father?"

"Pops was well aware of all the bullshit," Columbus spat, "when he took it over from the city last year. To the tune of one hundred and fifty-seven *million* in bonds needed for the new equipment. Money Detroit's gonna be paying out till 2009."

"Why are you telling me all this?" I asked, not quite making the connection to the information Columbus had just bestowed upon me.

"This place," he answered softly. "This place is where I come to do my work. It's just one of many parts of our fair city no one wants to see or believe exists." He pulled out his Canon EOS 5 and began snapping off shots of The Cloud Maker and its surrounding environs.

I knew nothing of photography, but I could tell that the camera had cost Columbus a pretty penny, and clearly he was a professional.

"I'm here to remind people," he went on. "So they won't ever forget."

Next he took me to see the former Michigan Theatre—now a parking structure—situated on the corner of Bagley and Grand River, just south-west of Grand Circus Park. Once a part of the historic, thirteen-floor Michigan Building, the theatre opened in 1926 on the very plot of land where Henry Ford had built his first "quadracycle" machine. Unlike most urban locations that had fallen into major disarray and, therefore, had become a destination to local urban explorers, who risked not only their lives but also imprisonment, all we had to do was pay a paltry sum for an admittance ticket, and into the structure we were permitted.

"It cost five million dollars," Columbus informed me once we'd stopped to park his Harley and take a better look around. "That's like fifty mill today. Look up there..." He reached inside his jacket pocket and jerked out a flashlight.

With his leather-clad sleeve, he directed the beam to a darkened spot high overhead. "See that? A ten-foot crystal chandelier used to hang right there. And those pillars, made of pure marble. Where we're standing, this was the lobby."

In its day, the Michigan Theatre boasted over 4,000 seats, making the concert hall/movie palace the biggest in the state. In addition to the screening of films, the theatre hosted band concerts led by Benny Goodman, John Philip Sousa, and Jimmy Dorsey, and live performances by The Marx Brothers, Bob Hope, and Betty Grable.

"So what happened?" I asked, saddened and simultaneously ashamed.

"Back in the seventies, they turned it into a nightclub." He snapped off a dozen photographs as he filled me in with more details. "When the club closed, the tenants in the office building next door started bitching they didn't have enough space nearby for parking. The plan was to demolish the theatre altogether. Till they realized the entire building would come down with it. So they gutted it instead."

"That's terrible," I said, angered by the lack of respect for such an historic building (and the Arts in general) in our modern day society.

"It sucks, don't it?" he said. "You're an actor. One less place in the city of Detroit for you to work. Too bad nobody gives a flying fuck."

"Obviously *somebody* does."

"Sure, I do," he agreed. "Why do you think I'm taking all these pictures? The incinerator, this theatre, the train station..."

"What train station?"

Columbus lowered his camera. Even in the dark, I could see the disbelief in his light brown eyes as he stared back at me. "*Dude!*"

Michigan Central Station became Detroit's premiere passenger rail depot after its predecessor burned down on the day after Christmas 1913. Located at 2405 West Vernor High-way, behind Roosevelt Park in the city's Corktown district, at the time of construction the Beaux-Arts building was the tallest train station in the world, boasting eighteen stories and a roof two hundred thirty feet high, with office space and plans for a hotel that would never materialize.

Because of its close proximity to the Ambassador Bridge and the country of Canada, the new Michigan Central Station was part of a planned project that included the Michigan Central Railway Tunnel beneath the Detroit River, used to transport both freight and passengers across the international border. Travel by automobile was not yet prevalent in 1912 when construction began and is apparent in the design of the depot. The remote location was said to have been selected in hopes that the train station would serve as an anchor for the development that would surely follow in the area.

In the 1920s, Henry Ford began buying up land near the station and making plans for additional construction. But the Great Depression soon put a damper on Ford's (and many other) developmental efforts. Further complications arose for Michigan Central's future as the original design included no facility for parking. When the streetcars stopped offering service less than two decades later, MCS became too isolated for a large part of the Metro Detroit population to access.

Still, the start of the first World War saw rail travel peaking in the United States, with more than two hundred trains departing the station daily. By 1940, more than four thousand passengers used the station each day, along with another three thousand employees working in the adjoining office tower. Prominent travelers to arrive at Michigan Central Station included Presidents Franklin D. Roosevelt, Harry S. Truman, and Herbert Hoover, the inventor Thomas Edison, and silent film star Charlie Chaplin. Even with fewer ways to get to and from the depot, passenger volume did not immediately decrease.

During World War II, the station witnessed heavy military use, though once the war ceased, volume started to decline again. In the 1950s, use of the station became so infrequent that the building's owners tried to sell for a meager five million, one-third of the original 1913 cost. There were no takers then or in 1963, when a second attempt at selling was put forth. In 1967, due to increasing costs in maintenance, the restaurant, shops, and main entrance were shut down, along with much of the main waiting area, leaving only two remaining ticket windows to serve the public.

In 1975, the National Register of Historic Places added Michigan Central Station to its roster. That same year, after Amtrak took over the country's passenger rail service, the main waiting room and entrance were reopened and a $1.25 million renovation project followed in 1978. But six years later, the building was at last sold, and on January 6, 1988, the final train pulled away. Amtrak service continued, however, from a platform erected near the former depot with tickets available for purchase inside an adjacent trailer.

"You're kidding?" I cried. My anguished voice echoed off the seventy-foot-high vaulted ceiling of the main floor waiting area, where I stood inside the station with Columbus, taking in the scene. "A fucking double-wide?"

Unlike the theatre-turned-parking structure we'd just visited, gaining access to the uninhabited train station required more careful navigation. I'd heard about the closing of the building from my dad, who often times drove by to check on the site as part of his DPD police officer duties, and he'd warned me to stay away. He was well aware of my admiration for all things ancient, but I'd not bothered to venture down to MCS so much as to take a peek. I'd never been much of a rule breaker, so helping Columbus hide his Harley in the shadows and sneaking inside a clearly labeled NO TRESPASSING zone went against most everything I'd stood for. Sure, I had a fake ID back in high school I used to buy booze in bars, but that was a whole 'nother story.

"They modeled it after a Roman bathhouse," said Columbus, titling his head back, camera poised and ready to snap another picture.

"Did they?" I asked, having never been to Italy or a bathhouse for that matter. I wondered if either smelled of musty, moldy mildew. It certainly felt like a sauna, the lack of any sort of breeze blowing in through the dozen or so broken windows.

With his flashlight, Columbus gave me a guided tour of the old ghost; first the grand hall, accommodating the ticket office and arcade with its classic Doric columns.

"They remind me of the ones holding up the Hilberry." I watched the smoke from the cigarette I'd just lit waft toward the water-damaged ceiling, chalky with efflorescence.

"Except the pillars at the Hilberry are Ionic," Columbus corrected, though I didn't comprehend the difference.

Beyond the shops lay the concourse, comprised of dusty brick walls and a dirty copper skylight. Columbus pointed out the route that passengers would travel, walking down a winding ramp to the departing train platforms, eleven tracks in total.

"Below, there's an area for baggage, mail handling, and additional office space."

"How do you know so much?" I asked him in awe.

"Me and Sheila," he answered, holding aloft his camera. "We've seen it all."

"And why, exactly, are you interested in all this...old stuff?" I said, carefully selecting my words. I mean, I enjoyed it, too. To quote the adage, "They don't make 'em like they used to." But I wasn't about to go on any *illegal* exploring expeditions, just to see a bunch of condemned structures that might come crashing down on me. I had way too much to live for, and I wasn't about to jeopardize my future.

"Like I said," he said. "The plan is to open up my own gallery. Host my own exhibit; show the people of Detroit these images; how they're sitting by, letting it all go to shit."

"Sounds like an awesome idea," I told him. "When's it gonna open?"

"Soon as I secure myself a space."

"Didn't you go look at a gallery just the other day?" I asked, remembering how Columbus couldn't join me and Sarah for coffee at the Ice Cream Company after Strange Bedfellows had played the Student Center.

"Fell through," he answered, painfully disappointed. "Dude wants ten grand more than I got."

"You'll come up with the money, I'm sure," I said, trying my best to be supportive. "Shit, with what you're making—" Intentionally I stopped myself short, not wanting to acknowledge the elephant in the room that was Club Riviera.

"I'm more than just a stripper," Columbus informed me proudly. "You think I wanna work at that place? You think I want a bunch of nasty old gay guys pawing me all night?"

I took no offense, nor did I remind him of the way in which we'd recently met. "So how come you do it?"

"My pops cut me off," he explained, "when I opted to go to CCS, instead of taking the full-ride to Michigan." He sneered. "Not that I needed a scholarship with all the cash he's got stashed away."

Never mind his father. More and more I was impressed with the man who was Columbus Howard. "You got a full-ride to U of M—for what?"

"Football. Led the team to back-to-back victories for three straight seasons," he humbly bragged. "Starting quarterback."

"Hot."

"You like that?" In the dark of the deserted train station, he grinned at me with his glowing pearly whites. "Perv."

"What can I say?" I said. "I'm a nasty old gay guy."

Clearly he could tell I was calling him out on his earlier comment. Still, he acted as if he didn't care. "Shut up."

"So you played football," I said as we moved toward the exit in which we'd entered. "At Cass Tech?" Columbus eyed me suspiciously, so I added, "Sarah told me that's where you went to high school."

"Brother Rice," he corrected, waving an imaginary pennant, cheering with mock enthusiasm. "Go Warriors!"

"In Bloomfield Hills? I thought—"

"Sarah *thinks* I went to Cass Tech," he confessed. "She believes I'm an inner-city boy, through and through."

Only slightly was I disappointed. "So you never dated Miss USA?"

He blushed. "Carole Gist? No, that part's true. Our dads are best buds from back in the day. Hooked us up when we were kids. Long before the whole Miss USA thing went down."

It felt good to know that not everything about Columbus Howard had been a total lie.

"Don't tell Sarah, okay?" he asked. "She doesn't know I come from money."

As someone who grew up dirt poor, I couldn't imagine ever finding shame in being wealthy. "Okay," I promised. "But why don't you want her to know?"

"Her folks live in Oak Park. They're lower-middle class. Sarah wouldn't feel the same way about me if she knew my dad's loaded."

I noticed he'd made no mention of his mother. And I didn't ask. Instead I said, "You really think Sarah's like that? She'd be more upset if she knew you lied to her."

"You lied to her, too," Columbus accused. "Telling her you went to Seaholm. You ain't from no Birmingham, boy. You went to Hillbilly High, and we both know it."

"And how do you know, by the way?" I wondered. "When you came and got me... Who told you where I was?"

"Dude," he said dryly. "You really *were* wasted last weekend when we met, huh? Back in The Champagne Room, once you started flapping your gums... On and on, all about how you went to Hazel Park, but you grew up in Ferndale.

Now you live with your dad over in White Trash Warren. Work up at Roy Sharples' Country Boy. Yada-yada-yada... Couldn't get you to shut up."

"Roy Sparks," I said. "You're thinking Mel Sharples from *Alice*." I started singing the theme song; the one from the first season that started "Early to rise, early to bed..." Not the "I used to be sad, I used to be shy..." variation.

"You really *are* gay, aren't you?" asked Columbus, glancing at me sideways.

"*You* kissed me," I reminded him, unable to resist now that we'd found a certain level of comfort in our unique circumstance.

"About that... I won't tell Sarah you're from Hazeltucky, if you don't tell her where I've been spending my Saturday nights. Deal?"

We shook on it.

"Speaking of..." I said. "Aren't you working tonight?"

Columbus sighed. "Don't remind me. Say cheese." He held up the camera with one hand and clicked it in my face, briefly blinding me.

Looking away, I observed the optical blobs of light as they morphed across the marbled walls of the abandoned train station. How I wished for the arrival of a long gone locomotive to transport me to another place and time.

14

NO ORDINARY LOVE

♦ ♦ ♦

It seemed that Barb, my boss, hadn't been the least bit thrilled with my leaving Country Boy in the middle of my shift, even after I'd explained that the helmet-wearing, Harley-riding thug who'd abducted me was actually one of my Delta Chi frat brothers—thank you, Max Wilson's brother Timmy for helping me pull that bit of Greek out of my ass!—and that he'd been pissed at finding me making out with his girlfriend at our last kegger.

While this larger than usual little white lie may have scored me brownie points with the cooks in the kitchen, Barb Foeman was not amused. Apparently she'd gotten extremely worried after I'd been unwillingly whisked away, and she called the Hazel Park PD to report me missing. She'd sworn she loved me, but poor Barb had no other choice than to hand me my walking papers upon my return to the restaurant two hours later.

Totally freaked out over my sudden, unexpected unemployment status, I stormed outside into the parking lot, practically tearing my cigarette pack apart to pilfer my last smoke. I sucked the thing down so desperately, as if my very life depended on refueling the nicotine flowing through my bloodstream, I didn't even enjoy it. Normally I liked to stand in front of the windows alongside the building and discretely observe myself puffing away, à la *Pete's Dragon*. I wasn't a narcissist, like my ex-boyfriend, Richie; I'd just always likened the act to eating while talking on the telephone. After I'd finish, I was still hungry; same with smoking. If I couldn't see myself doing it, I felt as if I hadn't really done it. What fun was that?

Once my nerves had somewhat subsided, I hopped into my car and headed post-haste to find the one person I could think of who could possibly help me out of my present conundrum: none other than the guy who'd gotten me into it.

Arriving at 7 Mile and Conant in record speed, I paid the attendant to valet Val the Valiant and forked over my five bucks to Bea Arthur at the front door. It was still early, not even ten o'clock, so the joint was far from jumping. Sexy Sid, aka Columbus Howard, wouldn't take to his see-through shower for at least a good hour. I had no idea where he'd be at that instant, unable to imagine a backstage dressing room in the kind of club that was The Riviera. But the boys did have to prepare for their paying audience somewhere.

Following a dimly lit corridor, I located a door marked MEN, thinking I might find my new friend undressing for his upcoming performance. Instead I discovered the room completely empty. Well, at least the area in front of the sinks and urinals. Beneath the stall door, six sneaker-clad feet, sans socks and/or slacks, could be seen fidgeting, accompanied by the sounds of hushed voices and distinct snorting. And yet no one halted whatever illegal action he may have been in the midst of, just because I'd entered. Thankfully none of the bare legs was black. I couldn't stand the thought of Columbus also being a drug user, along with my new boyfriend, Brad Woodward.

"Who's that?" someone asked suspiciously from beyond the black-painted stall, between lines.

"Um..." Realizing the guy wouldn't know me even if I'd given him my name, I replied, "I'm looking for...Sexy Sid."

"Who wants him?"

"My name's Bradley."

The stall door slowly cracked open. The skinny hustler

who'd offered me his company on my very first visit to the club stepped out, Thumper the bunny on full display beneath the fluorescents. A wisp of white powdered his upper lip, and his eyes were glassy as all get out. I could tell by the way he regarded me, he couldn't recall ever having seen me before. I wasn't going to be rude and remind him.

"Sid ain't here," the guy answered flatly. "Probably he's in back, getting his dick sucked off by some grody old geezer."

I turned to go. The guy grabbed my arm.

"You ain't grody and old," he flirted. "Wanna play?"

"Sorry," I politely refused, sensing by the sound of the kid's voice that, like Columbus, he wasn't even gay. "I need to find Sid."

Thankfully when I did catch up with him, he was still wearing his earlier all black ensemble. I didn't know what I would've done had I found Columbus in the midst of conducting business with a client.

"Oh, my God!" I gasped, strolling up to where he was sitting at the front bar, sipping a bottle of water. "I need to talk to you."

Columbus did a double take, not expecting to see me again so soon. "Back for more, Red? Champagne Room ain't open till eleven."

"Funny," I replied, not finding his humor the least bit.

"How come you're not up at Country Boy? You're gonna get yourself fired, you keep skipping out."

"That's why I'm here," I told him. "I did get fired, all thanks to you."

He signaled to the shirtless bartender. "Lemme by you a beer."

While I didn't appreciate his flippant attitude toward my present predicament, I desperately needed to get drunk. Especially if I was going to go through with asking Columbus for his help.

"You really wanna work here?" he questioned after I'd

made my query.

"Not really," I replied, "but I need money—bad."

"We all need money," he said, offering me a piss warm bottle of Bud Light. "You willing to do whatever it takes to get it?"

Unfortunately I didn't have a choice. I had the matter of next semester's tuition to cover, and I'd yet to pay the current statement. Now that I was finally fitting in with my new friends down at Wayne State, I had no desire to drop out. Surely I'd never see Sarah, Rain and, more importantly, Brad Woodward again if I were to do so. Something had to be did and darn quick!

Sunday morning meant church, followed by lunch at Olga's with Mom and the girls. Normally I'd be happy to see them, even if it meant having to suffer through another sermon condemning the homosexuals, liberals, and almost everything else for which I stood. But after the turn of events that had transpired the evening before, I was less concerned with waking up at the butt crack of dawn than at needing to confess I'd been fired from my job. In the end, I chose not to say a word to Mom, knowing she wouldn't understand why I'd opted to go riding around on a motorcycle with some guy I barely knew—never mind the part about exploring the relics of downtown Detroit.

After saying goodbye to Mom and the girls in the Oakland Mall parking lot late afternoon, I got in my car and drove north up to Big Beaver, aka 16 Mile, which became Quarton Road just west of Woodward Avenue. Seeing that damn street sign, every time, made me think of Brad. I wondered what he'd say if he knew where I was heading and, worse yet, what I was about to do once I arrived at my destination.

Immediately I recognized the affluent area on the border of Bloomfield Hills and Birmingham. In high school, Jack and I would drive out this way with our lesbian friend, Lu-

anne, and the girl of her dreams, Alyssa Resnick, who awk-
wardly enough had dated Jack before he'd concluded he was
gay, upon falling in love with his ex-friend, Joey Palladino.
The four of us would ride around, a bunch of poor kids from
Hazel Park, pretending we went to Seaholm, and that we
lived in one of the many four thousand-plus square foot
houses that were commonplace in the neighborhood, home to
the likes of Christine Lahti, Academy Award-nominee for
Swing Shift, comedian-turned-actor Tim Allen from TV's
Home Improvement, and renowned sculptor Marshall Fredericks of *The Sprit of Detroit* fame.

Born of Scandinavian heritage in Rock Island, Illinois on
January 31, 1908, Fredericks grew up in Cleveland, Ohio, after briefly residing with his family in Florida. In 1930, he
graduated from the Cleveland School of Art and began studying abroad in Sweden on a fellowship with Carl Milles. Later, Fredericks trained in other academies and private studios
in Denmark, France, Germany, and Italy prior to traveling
extensively in Europe and North Africa. In 1936, he won a
competition to create the Barbour Memorial Fountain on
Belle Isle, the first of many public monuments for which he
would take credit. After World War II, the sculptor worked
non-stop on numerous commissions, including the Cleveland
War Memorial Fountain, *Freedom of the Human Spirit*
(originally sculpted for the 1964 World's Fair held in New
York), and *The Spirit of Detroit*, for which Fredericks refused to accept the payment of $58,000 as his fee, believing
its creation part of his civic responsibility.

In its left hand, a large bronze figure sits holding a gilt
bronze sphere, emanating rays to symbolize God. The people
in the figure's right hand represent a family group. The
sculpture also includes the seals of the city of Detroit and the
county of Wayne. A plaque in front bears the inscription:
"The artist expresses the concept that God, through the spirit
of man is manifested in the family, the noblest human rela-

tionship." The recipient of many American and foreign awards and decorations for his artistic and humanitarian achievements, Fredericks' work has been exhibited nationally and internationally. Many of his pieces have found their way into national, civic, and private collections. Of the 26-foot-tall statue known as *The Spirit of Detroit*, the largest cast in bronze since the Renaissance at its installation, Fredericks has publicly stated that he never named the monument prominently displayed at the entrance to the City-County building. Instead he took the theme from 2 Corinthians 3:17: "Now the Lord is that Spirit, and where the Spirit of the Lord is, there is liberty."

It was nearly three o'clock by the time I entered the grounds of Cranbrook Gardens, the expansive estate owned by the present proprietor of Club Riviera. As promised, Columbus had made a phone call and arranged for a meeting between me and the rumored mob boss at his magnificent mansion.

The house itself lay on over an acre of perfectly manicured land, complete with guest cottage, Olympic-sized swimming pool, and an opulent topiary collection. A wedge of Swans swam among a parade of pachyderms, while a solo Chinese dragon snaked up and down the west lawn. At first sight of the sprawling mid-century white brick and wood-sided colonial, I couldn't help but call to mind the South Fork ranch from *Dallas*. Two stories tall; multiple peaked rooftops; meticulously trimmed hedges lining the perimeter. A chimney at least twenty feet high adorned the façade, situated between a pair of black shuttered windows. I could only imagine the immense cost of heating and/or keeping the place cool, dependent upon the season. Had I grown up in such a home, surely I would've gotten side-tracked on my middle-of-the-night trips to the bathroom.

I parked in the stone-paved driveway, behind a pair of luxury automobiles: one, a 1960s periwinkle blue classic Corvette convertible; the other, a brand new Lamborghini

Diablo in bright orange. Hanging my head in embarrassment as I stepped out of my beat up Valiant, I clipped up the stone sidewalk and raised my fist to rap lightly on the dark wood door.

"I'm Red," I told the older man who answered, calling myself by my new Columbus-inspired go-go boy name—should I be given the gig.

"You sure are," replied Mr. Lombardi, looking me up and down. He stood in the doorway, smiling softly, an indicator that he liked what he saw, I hoped. "Come on in. I gave my bodyguard the night off. Don't want nobody bothering us."

Nervously I entered a foyer the size of the room I slept in at my father's. "Thank you for having me."

"Well, I haven't had you yet," Lombardi teased, his demeanor far more casual than I'd originally anticipated.

I'd never met a millionaire before. As I drove the fifteen minutes from the mall to his manor, I imagined how the man would act and, especially, how he'd appear. Columbus had described him as being mid-fifties, which made me think of my father and had totally turned me off. He'd also called him a nice enough guy. But he did not, at any point in his description, use the word gorgeous.

In his two thousand dollar Giorgio Armani suit, Salvatore Lombardi stood well above six feet. Tailored to a tee, the silk garment hugged every contour of his sculpted body. Clearly he hadn't given up his morning regimen of physical activity in his middle-age. His hair remained thick and dark with just a trace of silver sprouting at the temples. His olive skin, fairly wrinkle-free, reflected a summer spent on South Beach with his personal *paisano*, Gianni Versace.

"Can I offer you a beverage?" Lombardi asked. "I've got beer, wine, bourbon. Or would you prefer we get down to business?"

"I'll leave that up to you," I answered, trying to be as agreeable as possible.

"I know what I want." With a large hand, the Italian-American reached for my belt buckle. Licking his cherry lips, he began unzipping my pants.

One of several stipulations to my being allowed to meet with Sal Lombardi was that I agree to an audition, in private, at which I would dance for Big Sal, and then we would sleep together—and not necessarily in that order, depending on how horny he was feeling. Another condition to his considering me for employment was that I pack a minimum of seven inches in my pants, which Lombardi himself would personally verify.

"Nice," the man sighed, exposing me to the open air. "All you straight boys are so damn beautiful."

This was the last of the required rules for all the guys Lombardi hired to go-go, Columbus Howard included. Only males of the heterosexual persuasion were allowed to work at Club Riviera, in any capacity. Lombardi believed it kept the men from fooling around with each other behind the scenes and focused exclusively on the clientele. When Columbus had first laid down these laws, I wasn't sure if I'd be able to comply. As much as I enjoyed having sex, I'd never been intimate with a man who was more than a few years older than me. I also had my own rules when it came to who would give and who would receive in the game of gay *$25,000 Pyramid.* Clearly I'd broken this commandment when I gave myself up for Brad Woodward, two years my junior. But in Brad's eyes, he was my elder and, therefore, had every right to do with me what he did. And, in retrospect, I realized I'd wanted him to.

Pushing thoughts of my Prince Charming aside, I turned my attention to the Italian Stallion nimbly dropping to his knees in front of me. What other choice did I have but to lean back against the archway and allow the hunky daddy to have his way with me? Judging by my physical response to his actions, there was no denying I found Salvatore Lombardi attractive. Perhaps my attempt at landing a position in his employ wouldn't be as painful as I'd expected?

* • •

We did it everywhere. Beginning in the entryway on the cushioned window seat, Big Sal proceeded to pleasure me in the broad light of day. At first, I worried for the neighbors, witnessing our sexual shenanigans—until I remembered there were none for miles around. Next we moved into the dining room, with its crystal chandelier dangling over a solid oak table with seating for twelve, over which I bent myself while Lombardi kissed his way up my thighs and in between.

We took our game of father-son into the first floor library, lined wall to wall with walnut bookcases, shelving nothing but signed first edition hardcovers penned by the top bestselling writers of our time: Stephen King, John Grisham, and local area author Elmore Leonard. Big Sal, which he insisted I call him (and he was!), slowly disrobed, like one of the boys he so gainfully employed. What his action lacked in originality, he more than made up for in the fact that he had a beautiful body. Watching him reveal it, part by part, totally turned me on. I found myself getting more and more aroused with each new flash of flesh; first an Achilles as he slid off a sock; the curve of his hamstring once he'd slipped out of his slacks. His legs were long and lean, but well-formed, from his bulbous calves to his meaty quads, right up to his plump posterior. He wore black cotton briefs by Calvin Klein, though not for long. Turning toward me, he put one thick thumb between his wide waistband and the flat of his abdomen, pulling downward.

"Come and get it," he ordered.

Happily I obliged.

Maybe it was the performer in me, but it didn't matter that I'd arrived pretending I was someone else. I was enjoying playing the part of a guy so desperate that he'd give up his true nature to do something he might otherwise deem disgusting. I hadn't been as excited, sexually speaking, since the time Jack and I were 12 years old and we would routinely call the phone sex party line, acting like we were girls, trying to get guys off.

After I'd crawled across the ornate Oriental carpet, like a panther in search of prey, Big Sal looked down at me lustfully. "You haven't done this before, have you?"

"No, sir," I lied, mumbling with my mouth full of him.

"You like?"

"Yes, sir."

He moaned. "Good little straight boy. Make daddy feel good."

It was a sick and twisted game, but somebody had to play it. I didn't believe I was the first. How could every single guy who go-go danced for Sal Lombardi be one hundred percent straight? Of course there was the case of Columbus Howard, whose heterosexuality I hadn't questioned. I trusted him when he said he loved Sarah; that he only did what he'd done so he could make enough money to take care of her and kick-start both their careers. Still, he had to have found himself in the exact same position as I, at some point, down on his knees, sexually servicing another man.

Whatever it takes, I recalled Columbus telling me. Guess this was what he'd meant. At least I was enjoying myself.

Through it all, Lombardi managed to hold off on achieving any sort of climax. Plenty of times he'd come close to the edge of pleasure but hadn't a problem backing off. Me, I'd always been easy, able to blow at the passing breeze.

Finally our activity progressed into the second floor master suite.

"You like?" asked Lombardi, this time in reference to the room's décor.

I wasn't particularly fond of the cream-colored walls or the seafoam taffeta curtains flanking the floor-to-ceiling windows. But I couldn't tell the man that. Not if I wanted him to hire me for a job.

"I love," I answered, forgetting my faux straightness a second. Butching it up, I added, "Your old lady do this?"

"Before she died, yes." A hint of melancholy crept into Lombardi's tone. "Let's not talk about her, okay? Let's screw."

An odd choice of word; outdated, in fact. But the man knew what he wanted, and I commended him for having the balls to be so blunt.

"Show me that ass," I said gruffly, playing my part as straight boy, soon-to-be stripper stud.

Lombardi laid facedown on the king-sized Queen Anne bed, baring himself, ripe for the taking. "You want this?"

"Yes, sir."

"Come and get it," he ordered once more.

Once again I happily obliged.

For a moment, I worried I'd be the one giving it up a second time. In all honesty, I felt relieved that Lombardi preferred playing the passive role. As silly as it might sound, I was hoping to save that part of myself for Brad Woodward, providing there'd be another opportunity to give myself to him.

It was over in a matter of minutes. Lombardi begged me not to finish, defied me not to lose control of myself, but nothing could I do to hinder the natural sexual progression. We'd been going at it for hours and I was ready to erupt. Thankfully the man sensed my imminent arrival and took it upon himself to join me at the finish line. We exploded within seconds of each other then collapsed in an exhausted heap, wrapped up in the softest Egyptian cotton sheets I'd ever had the pleasure of soiling.

Big Sal retrieved a cigarette from a square white box he'd kept on the bedside table. I recognized the label as the Canadian brand Brad had so enjoyed when we were out at that bar, Changez, with the girls.

"Are those Players?" I asked, hoping he'd hear my subliminal message and make me an offer.

"They are," Lombardi replied, reaching into his pack for a

pair. He lit both and handed me one. "Got 'em in Windsor. I own a casino, right on the river."

We lay together, smoking in silence. I'd often felt the post-sex experience to be somewhat awkward, particularly with a stranger. During the act, I tended to be rather vocal, a technique I'd picked up from watching my fair share of Jeff Stryker gay porn videos. Truth be told, I enjoyed the dirty talk, and I took pride in my talent. I found that it not only aided in my performance, it excited most of my partners, Salvatore Lombardi included. But with the Italian Mafioso, I felt none of the usual post-coital discomfort. Even my most recent encounter with Brad Woodward had ended quite clumsily, with him kicking me out of his apartment and not speaking to me since.

"So what's your real name, Red?" asked Lombardi, tousling my curly locks. Sensing my hesitancy, he added, "You don't have to tell me. But I like you, kid."

"I like you, too."

"You just saying that 'cause you want the work?"

"No," I told him. "I couldn't do what we just did if I didn't." Now that I was getting older, I was over the whole one night stand concept, which upset me even more regarding what had happened with Brad. I would never have slept with him had I thought our relationship wasn't progressing to a deeper level.

"Too bad you ain't a fag," said Big Sal, mentally jolting me back into the bedroom beside him. "I could take real good care of you, boy."

Shit!

I'd almost forgotten the strictest of rules that had brought me there in the first place. Here was my chance to finally snag me a rich man—a real-live millionaire—and he needed to believe I was straight.

"You're about my son's age," Lombardi told me, a far off look in his dark eyes. "Sal Junior."

I'd also totally forgotten the man's former family. There

were no traces of his now dead wife, no memories of a child who'd been raised in the beautiful home. I'd heard tell that he'd had one, but I hadn't been made aware whether he was a boy or she was a girl. At last I'd known the answer.

"Where is he?" I asked, only because I got the impression Lombardi wanted me to.

"Off at school," he answered softly. "We sorta got into it after his mother died. I haven't seen him since he went away to college."

"Does he know you're gay?"

"He does." Lombardi slid out of the big bed and slipped a plush white robe around his broad bronzed shoulders. "And it's the reason he hates me."

Fearing I'd overstayed my welcome, I said, "I can go... Unless you want me to dance for you."

"Won't be necessary." He no longer looked me in the eye when he spoke, clearly still concerned with his long-lost off-spring. "You start on Saturday."

"I do?"

A wave of relief washed over me like a river. As elated as I was to receive the offer, it frightened me to death thinking that, in a matter of days, I'd be up on a sleazy nightclub stage, half-naked, in front of a bunch of horny homos.

15

INTO THE FIRE

♦ ♦ ♦

An entire week passed before I spoke to Brad. Yes, we'd seen each other in class every single day and in the evenings at rehearsal. But he'd somehow conveniently managed to avoid me and, in turn, avoided having to discuss what had gone down between us on the night we'd all gone over to Windsor. I wasn't expecting him to be my boyfriend. I just wanted him to be my friend.

It killed me to see him so close by but feel him so far away. Every time I'd try talking to the guy, he'd come up with some bogus excuse. Either he needed to work on creating his character, or he had to meet with his vocal coach to go over his solos, or he simply needed to rest. Of all people, I knew playing the lead role in a musical was grueling work. At least he hadn't lied to me, insisting he wasn't gay, the way I'd done to Richie Tyler when he first started pursuing me in high school and I wasn't ready for a relationship. This was the only thing that gave me any hope that Brad Woodward and I might someday be together.

Monday evening, we had our first understudy rehearsal. Pia had given the ensemble the evening off so that Rain, Hannah Weiss, and I could sit in the Bonstelle auditorium and observe Sarah, Wanda Freeman, and Brad as they went through their blocking as Velma, Roxie, and Billy respectively.

"What are we supposed to do exactly?" I asked Rain as we

settled into our seats, waiting for the first scene to start.

"Beats the hell out of me," she answered bitterly. "I've never been an understudy."

Neither had I. In high school, I'd always played a principal role. We also never had standbys for any of the plays we put on. If an actor got sick, he or she just sucked it up and performed their part.

Hannah Weiss whispered, "We just watch and take notes." Eagerly she held her script, with a number two pencil poised to jot down Wanda's every onstage movement.

"This is nothing but a frivolous formality," Rain decided. "We'll never go on."

"Maybe someone will get sick?" said Hannah, hopeful.

"I seriously doubt it," replied Rain, dismissing the sophomore.

"There's a first time for everything," I told the girls cheerfully.

"I've known Brad for over two years now," Rain reminded us. "The boy would have to be lying in a hospital, on his death bed, before he missed a performance."

Even if Rain was correct, I took pride in knowing Will Bilson had selected me, out of all the other guys in the ensemble, to understudy Brad Woodward as Billy Flynn. I also realized that if he, or Sarah, or Wanda were to actually take a night off, we'd be in even more trouble since neither Rain, nor Hannah, nor I had understudies of our own. Who would cover for us in the event that we had to cover for one of the leads?

"That's a ten!" Amelia the stage manager called out, once it was time for our first official break. Apparently we'd been rehearsing for eighty minutes already and, as per Actors' Equity union guidelines, were entitled to a time out.

Stretching, I got up from my seat, contemplating what I needed more: a fix of nicotine or to relieve my minuscule bladder.

"Are you popping out for a smoke?" Rain inquired, reaching into her clock-purse for her cloves.

Up onstage, Brad Woodward skipped down the stairs leading into the house, quadriceps rippling with each step. He looked particularly sexy in red cut-off sweatpants, paired with an old Pretenders T-shirt and leg warmers worn low about his ankles. His meaty calves flexed as he raced up the aisle toward the restrooms, totally distracting me.

"I'll meet you outside," I promised Rain. "First I need to make a pit stop."

She looked at me suspiciously, as if she knew my true intention for heading into the bowels of the Bonstelle. "Don't get lost."

Truthfully I didn't know what I was doing or why. Brad had made it perfectly clear he wanted nothing more to do with me. Hadn't he? Still, I followed after him like a lost puppy in search of his master.

Downstairs, all was quiet. When I entered the men's bathroom, I expected to find Brad, his back to me, standing at the urinal. Instead I caught a glimpse of his Capezio-clad feet beneath the stall door, standing in front of the toilet bowl. Once again, I smelled the scent of burning plastic, and I knew exactly what he was up to. The boy had a serious problem, and I seriously needed to turn myself around and get myself out of there. Nothing good could come from trying to force this Love Connection. And yet I couldn't just abandon him, leaving him to the mercy of his vice.

"Brad?" I said tentatively, hoping he'd quit what he was doing before I actually caught sight of it and had to report him to someone. Off all things, I was certain Amelia Morganti, stage manager extraordinaire, wouldn't appreciate an actor getting high in the middle of rehearsal.

There came the sound of a toilet flush, and Brad soon appeared, wide-eyed and raring to go. "Hey, Bradley! What's up?"

"Taking a break," I answered. "What's up with you?"

"*Nada.*"

Not since I'd known Brad Woodward had I heard him speak Spanish.

Stepping up to the toilet, I undid my zipper. But with Brad nearby, checking out his flawless reflection in the mirror above the sinks, I knew I'd never be able to complete my task.

"Pee shy?" he asked, eyeing me playfully.

"Maybe a little," I answered, only slightly embarrassed.

Suddenly Brad sidled up behind me and slipped his hand around my waist. "Want me to hold it for you?"

Instinctively I flinched. My cheeks flushed and my neck reddened. "No!"

"Somebody's got a hard-on," he sang. Then he stunned me by saying, "Lemme see it."

Tucking my flaccid self into my briefs, I was totally taken aback. "Now you're interested?"

If my words had stung, I couldn't tell by the way Brad continued behaving. Whatever drugs he'd taken had set his pulse skyrocketing. In the middle of the Bonstelle men's bathroom, he broke out into a tap routine, blocking my exit.

"Excuse me," I said, attempting to ignore his antics and pass him by.

"Where you going?" he asked, performing a pair of perfectly executed wings, flapping his long arms like a windmill.

"Um... Back to rehearsal."

"We've still got five minutes," he figured, halting his dance break on a dime. "Bet I can get you off." Without warning, Brad lunged at me, trying his best to drag me into the empty stall.

"What is wrong with you?" I demanded, putting up a fight and prying myself free. "Why are you acting like this?"

"Acting like what?" he asked innocently.

"Oh, I don't know..." My tone dripped pure sarcasm. "One minute you're inviting me up to your apartment, the next you're throwing me out in the street. You haven't said a single word to me since. Now, totally out of the blue, you're offering to blow me in the Bonstelle men's bathroom."

"Would you rather blow me?" He reached for his fly with one hand and grabbed hold of my shoulder, forcing me to my knees with the other.

"Stop!" I insisted, rising to my feet. "God, I need a cigarette!" My nerves were just about shot from my run in with Brad Woodward, and I realized Rain would be wondering what was keeping me.

"Good idea," he agreed, not giving up his play for my attention. "I'll go with you."

I considered informing Brad that I didn't want him following after me, but I knew my words wouldn't stop him. Plus, despite my feigning disinterest, it felt nice to feel his attention directed my way.

We climbed the stairs to the lobby, Brad continuing the conversation. "We should hang out sometime," he said, as if he'd forgotten how our last outing had ended. "You free on Saturday? We could hit Changez again in Windsor."

"I don't think so," I declined.

"Why not?" he asked at the top of his voice, upon reentering the auditorium.

Amelia hissed at us over her shoulder. "*Shhh!*" Like we were children running amok in a library.

Onstage, Sarah was still working on some new bit of choreography with Pia. I could tell we wouldn't be reconvening rehearsal any time soon. Holding two fingers to my lips, I took a pretend puff, signaling to Amelia that we were stepping out to smoke. She shooed us away with a flick of her wrist, eyes focused on Sarah's every dance step.

I followed Brad outside into the parking lot where, thankfully, Rain was nowhere to be seen beneath the street lamps. With the Autumnal Equinox a week away, the evening air had turned quite chilly. Most likely, she tired of waiting for me and retreated inside to rest in the warmth of the mint green Green Room.

"So why can't you hang out on Saturday?" asked Brad, refusing to relinquish the subject.

"Other than the obvious?" I said. And then I remembered: my new gig. Just the thought of it caused an enormous ache in the pit of my stomach. Thankfully Columbus had promised to show me the ropes, since we were both on the schedule for that particular evening. "I'm starting a new job on Saturday."

Brad looked at me sideways, as someone who hadn't worked a day in his existence. "What for?"

"Oh, you know," I said easily. "Never hurts to have extra money. It's just part-time."

"Where are you working?"

"With Columbus, actually."

Brad's jaw dropped. "At a tittie bar?" he asked, implying my being gay meant I couldn't gain employment at a straight establishment.

"Why is that so hard to believe?" I inquired, insulted.

He grinned. "No reason. What about Friday?"

"Friday I can't, either," I said regretfully, removing my lighter from my pocket.

Brad reached out and snatched the Zippo, using it to first spark his own cigarette then mine. "Why not?" He looked into my eyes for the briefest of moments and, once again, I found myself smitten.

"I'm going out with my best friend and his boyfriend on Friday," I answered, quickly turning away in an attempt to resist Brad's charms. The last thing I needed was for him to suck me back in and make me fall in love with him all over, even though I don't think I'd ever fallen out.

"I could go with you guys," he suggested. "Unless you don't want me to meet your friends."

On the contrary, I'd been dying to introduce him to Jack and Kirk. But I knew Brad wouldn't be up for the idea of tagging along, not once I shared our plans with him.

"It's not that..." I hesitated. "We're going to Menjo's."

"Oh," he said, sounding disappointed. "I don't go to fag bars."

"Because you're not a fag."

Whatever. I'd heard it all before, and I wasn't buying it.

It took a certain type of man to be a male stripper, particularly if he performed in a gay club and, presumably, he was heterosexual. Columbus assured me that all the men I'd meet on my first night of work were, like him, one hundred percent straight. Even if they turned the odd trick, which they did often, their physical actions stemmed from a burning desire for one thing only—and it wasn't S-E-X. In the mind of the gay-for-pay guy, the object that mattered most was the almighty American dollar. And at Club Riviera on a Saturday night, there was many a bill to be made.

"We get changed in here," said Columbus, leading me into a dank smelling storage closet similar to the one that served as The Champagne Room, only smaller.

Inside, three other men were slipping out of their street clothes and into their so-called costumes. They were all tall and lean, and totally hot, in a white trashy sort of way. And totally hairless.

"Better grab a razor, bud," the first guy said, sizing me up as I took off my shirt. He was overly tan with long dark hair pulled back into a ponytail and five o'clock shadow at 10:00 p.m. A barbwire tattoo wrapped itself around his bulging bicep as he scraped a Bic disposable across the stubbly mounds of his meaty pecs.

"Seriously?" While I wouldn't call myself hirsute, I did have my fair share of body hair, mostly on my legs but also a bit on my torso. Luckily it was light in color, more like the fuzz on a peach. I hadn't even pondered the possibility of my having to remove it.

"House rules," Columbus informed me. "There's a supply

in the back closet. And some Barbasol."

I wasn't sure if I was supposed to just drop trou right then and there, though all the other guys had done so, including Columbus. Instinctively I averted my eyes the instant he took off his fatigues and let his underwear fall to the concrete floor. As curious as I was, I couldn't bring myself to gawk at my friend. I hadn't felt that nervous being around of bunch of naked men since I'd last been in the locker room at Hazel Park High. Then I remembered, they were all *straight*—and as far as the others knew, so was I! It was okay to look because these guys all assumed I wasn't interested in what they were showing off down below.

Fortunately I had previous experience with shaving my legs. Back in high school, I'd done it—twice. The first, for my 17th birthday, I went with a group of Drama Queers out to Lakeside Mall to see *Rocky Horror* and I dressed up as Columbia. The second was later that year when I entered the amateur drag contest at Gigi's. This time, in the so-called dressing room of Club Riviera, I only nicked myself once, behind my left knee, which hurt like a total bitch.

"Don't worry about it," another of my fellow dancers assured me. "Dudes like it when we're all banged up." He sported a small set of facial bruises, as if he'd recently been in a fight, and one of his two front teeth was visibly chipped.

"Nice duds," Columbus complimented after I'd slipped on my cherry red jockstrap.

"Dunham's on Woodward and Thirteen Mile," I said, proudly modeling the new purchase. "On sale."

"You should check out International Male," the third guy in the group insisted. He was pale-skinned and blond-haired and out of the bunch, he looked the most like a redneck. "Got 'em outta their catalogue." He held up a skimpy pair of tiger-striped bikini bottoms that I couldn't imagine any gay man ever wearing, which could only mean he was hetero.

And yet, when he put them on and they clung to his bub-

ble butt, I almost got a boner; a serious drawback to my secretly being a homo. Immediately my mind went to the dark
place: somehow these guys would find out I'm a fag, get
pissed off, and then take their anger out on my ass—literally.
Maybe I'd been watching too much gay porn? I was more
aroused than anxious by this idea.

At last Columbus made the round of introductions. "This
is Blackie," he said, gesturing to the guy with the pulled-back
ponytail and scruffy beard.

"Red," I said, consciously pitching my voice lower so not
to come off as sounding queer.

Blackie reached out for a shake. "What's poppin'?"

"Rocky," the second guy, with the busted up face and
broken tooth, told me. This explained why he was sporting
silk boxer shorts, I assumed.

"Tiger," the third guy greeted, which also made clear his
wardrobe selection.

They all seemed nice, if not the brightest of boys. I figured they were around my age; at least over eighteen but no
more than twenty-five. I was curious to learn all about them:
how they came into this line of work; did any of them have
girlfriends; and if so, did the women know what they did for
a living? Talk about a fascinating character study for an actor.

Columbus clapped a paw on my shoulder. "You ready to
kick it, Red?"

"No," I replied, trying to remind myself that this was just
another performance.

"You ain't never done this before?" Tiger asked as the five
of us, like a posse, headed out into the main bar area. His use
of the double negative made me wonder if he came from an
even humbler educational upbringing than I did.

"Not professionally," I said, though I don't know why. It
wasn't like I'd ever taken my clothes off in public as an amateur.

"Watch the hands," Rocky warned. "Them guys out there
will grab you in places you wouldn't even let a woman touch.

One of 'em tried sticking his thumb up my ass, right when I was dancing on the bar."

"Really?" I replied, thinking it might not be so bad, depending to whom the digit belonged. "What did you do?"

"Took him in The Champagne Room, charged him fifty bucks, then I let him finger me." He chuckled in spite of himself. "There's a time and place for everything. And a price."

That price, it turned out, was a dollar per customer every time I passed them by as I made my way around the bar top.

At first, I had no idea what I was supposed to do. I just kept my eye on the others and followed their lead. If Columbus bent over and stuck his ass in some old queen's face, I did the same on my side, my bare bottom exposed for all to feast eyes on. If Rocky reached up and grabbed hold of one of the light fixtures, guns flexing, I mimicked the gesture. When Tiger dropped down to his knees and started touching himself, I fondled the pouch of my jock strap; and when Blackie whipped out his dick and began beating off in some middle-aged truck driver's face, I picked the first dude with a fiver and played me some public pocket pool.

Never had I done anything so scandalous and for once in my life, it felt sooo good to be sooo bad.

Just before midnight, I was up on the bar, bouncing to an oldie but goodie by Bronsky Beat and having a total flashback to being 15 years old, out with Jack at our very first gay bar, Heaven, right across town. At the sight of some old man waving a dollar in my direction, I was brought back to the present moment. Glancing down at him, I grinned and graciously accepted his offering. As I looked up again, I caught a glimpse of a couple cute guys, waiting in line to pay Bea Arthur their cover, across the room.

With their twin blond heads, they could've easily been brothers. Both were similarly dressed, in tight black T-shirts tucked into dark blue jeans, worn with wide black belts and

Doc Martens. The one was just a hair taller than the other, but besides this tiny detail, they looked almost identical. By far, they were the best looking boys in the entire bar and, more than anything, I wanted them to notice me.

Showing off my best Bob Fosse dance moves, as taught by Pia Mullins during *Chicago* rehearsals, I swiveled my hips sexually. I popped my pelvis and slowly circled my shoulders. Head titled down, eyes wide, with the utmost intensity, I directed all my energy toward my intended subjects. For an instant, they got lost in the crowd. But I wasn't about to let them go.

Like a hungry spider, I waited eagerly; patiently. These young men were my prey, and I had every intention of eating them up and gulping them down.

A second later, the pair reappeared. Holding hands, the taller of the two led the way through the drunken sea of lustful men. My heart sank a little at the terrified expression the shorter boy wore. Clearly he'd never been in such a den of debauchery. Through the smoky haze, I couldn't clearly see his face, but I could sense he was a cutie. And oh, how I wanted to corrupt him! Then I realized I already had.

It seemed that Blond Boy #2 was none other than my former boyfriend, Richie Tyler.

Immediately I panicked. Had I been wearing a T-shirt, I would've totally pitted out. I couldn't allow Richie to see me in such a state of undress, dancing about on top of a bar at a gay strip club. Plus he could've totally blown my heterosexual cover in front of my co-workers.

"And now..."

Thankfully, at the precise moment Richie and his hot friend started walking my way, the room went black.

"Put your hands together, boys..." The boom of the DJ broke through the thick fog. "And get your dollars ready."

The special blue spotlight came up on the far side of the bar where Columbus, in his *Sexy Sid* swimsuit, had just stepped into his Plexiglas shower.

Like Wonder Woman, I leapt down from my perch and bolted for the back storage room to locate my clothes. Miraculously I'd dodged a bullet. The next time, I might not be so lucky.

16

CONSTANT CRAVING

♦   ♦   ♦

By mid-September, my life had fallen into a repetitive rut. Mornings I would wake up at 7:00 a.m., shit, shower, and shave. Around seven-thirty, I'd sit down with my cup of coffee, which I'd drink in silence, reading the newspaper. At eight-fifteen, give or take a few, I'd gather my belongings, head out the front door, and climb into my car.

Providing there were no accidents or other traffic-related hold ups, I'd arrive on campus no later than eight-forty, allowing me ample time to get over to Old Main for whatever class I had that day at nine o'clock. Along the way, without fail, I would peer out my window, longing to catch sight of The Cloud Maker, welcoming me home to Wayne State with its magnificence.

Class, lunch, class. Dinner, rehearsal. This was my week.

It wasn't that I minded the routine. My life, up until this point, had been in desperate need of some sort of structure. From the time I'd been 4 years old, when I'd entered pre-school, up through my graduation from Hazel Park High, I'd known exactly what I was going to do with myself, day in and day out. The past two years, since I'd dropped out of OCC, I spent walking about in limbo, feeling like I hadn't accomplished much, if anything. Now that I was back ensconced in the world of the Theatre, my life finally had a purpose. For the first time in a good long while, I looked forward to each sunrise.

The good news was: Brad Woodward and I were now

speaking on a regular basis. Starting with that evening at understudy rehearsal, when he chatted me up in the Bonstelle men's bathroom, our communication continued well into the next week. As curious as I was over his sudden change of heart—as far as I could tell, he still wasn't a fag—I wasn't about to knock it. I suspected it might have something to do with Dina French pairing me with Torrance Andrews, the super sexy dancer in my *Chicago* cast, to work on a project for Acting.

We'd chosen an obscure two-hander we'd found in the stacks of the DPL, *Some Things You Need to Know Before the World Ends* by Larry Larson and Levi Lee, that premiered at the Humana Festival in Louisville, KY. In the scene, I played a washed up preacher named Reverend Eddie, pontificating on how "Life is Like a Basketball Game," while Torrance was a hunchbacked monk called Brother Lawrence, obsessed with a space lady who'd appeared to him in a vision, wearing a gold lamé jumpsuit and speaking in a soft, beautiful voice with a slight trace of a Spanish accent. Suffice to say, it was hilarious.

Torrance and I had been spending the better part of our free time hanging out, running lines, and rehearsing. He lived in the A-B-C building, a trio of apartments located on Second Avenue between Forest and Prentis, along with another girl in our class, Chrissy Weston, who was also in the *Chicago* ensemble. Torrance and Chrissy had gone to high school together, Down River in Trenton. Chrissy was a blond bombshell and a total triple threat. She could act, sing, and dance with the best of them at WSU, probably in NYC even. Apparently she'd been cast in the only female role of a mainstage drama called *Mister Roberts* during her freshman year, and she'd since appeared in almost every Bonstelle production, ranging from musical comedy to Shakespearean tragedy.

Once Brad Woodward had gotten wind that Torrance and I were becoming the best of buds, he took it upon himself to work his way back into my world.

"So what are you and Rance doing tomorrow?" he asked casually.

We were finishing up our cigarette break during rehearsal the following Friday night, which was about the only time Torrance and I weren't joined at the hip, as he was about the only person in The Department who didn't smoke and/or drink.

"Nothing, actually," I answered, not that it was any of Brad's business. "Columbus invited me up to his family cabin."

The whole idea had come about the night before when, much to our surprise, Columbus and I had both gotten calls from Gary, the manager up at The Riviera, informing us we now had the weekend free from work, due to an unfortunate incident that had occurred earlier in the week. It seemed that a small fire had broken out in The Champagne Room, after some drunken customers had decided to get kinky with candles and hot wax, so the club was temporarily being shut down. And since Pia had also given the guys' ensemble Saturday off from rehearsal, in order to work with the girls on the poker game section, I was without obligation for a full forty-eight hours.

"Awesome," said Brad. He took a long drag on his cigarette, staring off into space.

"Yeah," I agreed, as if it were no big deal. "We're leaving as soon as we're done here."

As if Torrance Andrews wasn't enough, I could tell Brad was also feeling threatened by my newfound friendship with Columbus Howard. After all, he'd met Columbus first. I imagined there'd been a history of double dates between him and Rain, and Columbus and Sarah; nights spent dining on Mexican at Xochimilco or pizza at Nikki's in Greektown, followed by drinking and dancing at The Shelter or City Club. Now that Brad and Rain had broken up, who knew how much time he and Columbus spent together? I got the impression it was minimal at best.

"You're not taking the bike, are you?" Brad flicked his still-lit cigarette butt into the parking lot. It hit the pavement in a burst of embers before finally fizzling out.

"God, no! I couldn't ride all the way up to Harbor Beach on the back of that thing," I said, perishing the thought. "We're taking my car."

Brad gave me a look of stern seriousness. "Are you sure it'll make it?" he asked, ever the smart ass. "I could always go with you guys. We can take my Mercedes."

Shrugging, I said, "I'll have to ask Columbus. It's his place."

"I'm sure he won't care," said Brad confidently. "There's plenty of room." Then he added cautiously, "The girls aren't coming, are they?"

I reminded him of their conflicting rehearsal schedule. He let out a sigh of relief and expressed his gratitude at escaping a weekend get-away spent in the company of Rain DuBois.

"You're the one who dated her," I said.

"True," he answered.

Of course Columbus didn't care if Brad tagged along. Rain, on the other hand, threw a hissy fit of sorts after finding out—from Brad—that we were off together for our Guys Only adventure.

"You didn't tell me *he* was going with you," she whined, teary-eyed as we said our goodbyes in the Bonstelle backstage stairwell.

"I didn't know *he* was," I admitted, mimicking her tone for comic effect.

Rain refused to see the humor in the situation. "So he just invited himself?"

"Yes. He did."

"That is so like Brad Woodward," she pouted. "He's only doing this because he doesn't like me."

"Brad likes you," I insisted, even if I wasn't so certain.

"He likes you, too," retorted Rain suggestively.

"I would hope so. He's my friend."

"But you'd like him to be more, wouldn't you?"

I didn't want to lie. But I couldn't bring myself to tell Rain the total truth. I knew what her question implied: she was jealous of Brad and the time we'd be spending together, because of her feelings for me.

"Brad Woodward isn't gay," I said, despite my own personal opinion of the matter.

Rain leaned back against the banister and stared down at the dirty floor mat, making no reply.

"Hey..." Like something I'd seen on some soap opera, I took hold of her chin and titled her head up toward me. "Even if he was, it's not like we're going away alone. Columbus will be there."

"He hates me, too."

"Nobody hates you, Rain. It's just gonna be us guys, sitting around, drinking beer, stinking up the place with our farts, probably. You know, gross guy stuff."

She scowled. I realized I was being too dismissive, and I felt badly for it. But more than anything, I wanted to spend the time with Brad, far away from the outside forces that kept him from being true to his true self. Among these were anything associated with The Department. Specifically Rain DuBois.

Forty minutes later, after swinging by Studio Four so Brad could pack a bag and I could drop off my car, we stopped by The Thelma to pick up Columbus. In the light of the open doorway, I watched Sarah as she hugged her boyfriend good-bye, worried that Rain had rushed home from rehearsal and was now drowning her sorrows down at Third's.

Due to my limited night vision, coupled with the fact that I had no idea where we were going, I hopped in back and allowed Columbus to sit shotgun and play navigator. I was also exhausted from the week of rehearsals and wanted nothing more than to stretch myself across the cool leather seat for the next two hours with my feet out the window, while the purr of the engine lulled me to sleep. Too bad my mission was thwarted by Columbus and Brad, who kept themselves busy singing along to an old Echo & the Bunnymen album Brad had recently picked up on CD. Even though I wasn't paying the least bit of attention, Columbus took it upon himself to point out the various truck stops, rest areas, and other places of interest along the way where gay men, such as yours truly, had been known to congregate in search of sexual satisfaction.

Finally, after forty-five minutes of tossing and turning, trying to tune them out, I sat up and joined in on the fun. I sang "Bring On the Dancing Horses" from the *Pretty in Pink* soundtrack, a film that had meant more to me during my formative years than any other I could remember. All at once, a melancholy crept over me. Thinking about Jack, in particular, and the separate paths our lives were taking, I felt the sting of tears coming on. He was—and would always be—my best friend. I couldn't imagine using those two words to describe anyone else during the extent of my lifetime. And yet, here I was, off to spend a wonderful weekend with two people I barely knew (but was totally crazy about) while Jack, I imagined, was somewhere with his one true love, Kirk.

"How long has your family had this cabin?" I shouted at Columbus over the instrumental break.

"Since before I was born," he replied, tapping against the dashboard to the music.

"That's a long time," said Brad, smiling sarcastically.

Columbus refused to take the bait. "At least I can purchase alcohol in a bar in my own country. And not one my daddy owns over in Canada."

"Wait a minute!" I leaned forward against Brad's seat to speak to him. "Your father owns that bar we went to in Windsor?"

"Along with a half-dozen others," added Columbus, bopping in place to the beat.

Brad pleaded, "Let's not ruin this trip talking about my dad, please," his eyes on the road.

I needed to say no more but found it intriguing that Columbus knew such personal information pertaining to Brad's father. Obviously they were more than casual acquaintances.

We pulled off the highway well after midnight. The road became bumpy and narrow as it wound its way through the back woods, which grew thicker and fuller the deeper we drove into the dark. I couldn't see a thing outside and, once again, my mind went to the scary place: some psychopathic mass murderer was surely lurking somewhere, waiting to leap out and kill us the minute we stopped the car.

"Are we there yet?" I groaned, becoming a pre-pubescent child in my behavior.

"Hold your water!" cried Brad, quoting what I instantly recognized as the famous line spoken by Sally Field's crazy mother in the made-for-TV movie *Sybil.*

Columbus shook his head in amusement. "You gay guys and your witty quips..."

I paid particularly close attention to Brad's reaction to this comment, expecting him to defend himself by denying he wasn't of the homosexual persuasion. But he said nothing, at last giving me an inkling of hope. My expectations grew even higher upon our arrival at the Howard family cabin, which first merits a description.

For starters, the place was much more modest than I'd expected after the recent revelation of Columbus's father's riches. It really was just a rustic cabin in the woods, though not one made of logs held together by mud. With its gently sloping roof and wide, well-supported eaves, one might call it a chalet of the Swiss Miss variety. Two floors, comprised of fifteen hundred square feet, featured three small bedrooms, two tiny baths, a breakfast nook, kitchen, and an outdoor deck with gas grill.

When I entered the dark cedar-smelling house, Columbus stood facing the stone fireplace. My mind wandered to the image of Brad and me lying lazily in front of it, making love on the carpeted floor.

"Oh, my God! This is so nice," I sighed, dropping my bag at my feet.

Columbus, lost in thought, looked longingly at a framed photograph hanging over the mantel. I came up beside him and took a peek for myself, hoping I wasn't intruding on his private moment. It was a picture of himself, 15 or 16 years old, a devilish grin on his dark face, his light eyes wide, hair long with dreadlocks. I almost didn't recognize him, slight of build, before he'd started regularly working out with weights and wearing his signature spectacles. Next to him in the photo was a white woman with strawberry-colored curls. Happily she smiled for the camera, her pale freckled arm draped around Columbus's shoulder, proudly. At first glance, I thought she was Sarah. But given a closer look, I could tell exactly who she was.

"That's your mom," I said, ashamed of the fact that I'd never stopped to consider he was of mixed race. "She's beautiful."

"Now she's just dead," he said sadly. He placed a finger to his lips and gently touched it to the glass.

The screen door creaked open and Brad appeared. "I'm beat." He flopped himself down onto an old sofa, fresh out of the 1970s, weary from the long drive.

"Bitch!" Columbus teased, his usual cheery self as he turned to confront Brad on the couch. "You knows where yo' room is. Git-cho lazy ass up an' git-cho self-ta bed."

"Where should I sleep?" I wondered aloud.

Columbus grinned. "Wherever." He looked at both me and Brad, as if he knew something we didn't. Then he turned back to the photograph and touched it one more time, saying, "Goodnight."

I wasn't sure if he'd been talking to us or the picture of his mother. He was long gone before I could ask him, disappearing into the kitchen.

"There's two rooms upstairs," Brad sighed, heaving himself up. "I'll show you." Languidly he climbed the carpeted staircase to the second floor and I followed. "I usually take this one," he said, referring to the room on the right side of the hallway.

Below the slanted ceiling, a handmade patchwork quilt blanketed a double bed. Against one wall sat a short chest of drawers with a swivel mirror made of leaden glass. It was far from antique (but definitely ancient), dating back to the early part of the century. Along the bottom, the wood looked as if it had been gnawed at, most likely by a squirrel or some other small mammal that had found its way down the chimney during the frigid winter months. Brad stepped inside and opened a door, opposite the bed, allowing a cool breeze to enter the warm room. I peeked out the screen to see a charming balcony overlooking the front yard and the lake, off in the distance.

"I can sleep in the other one, no problem," I told Brad sincerely.

Across the hall, a pair of twin beds filled the small room, where I assumed the children would sleep, side by side, while on summer vacations. Though, come to think of it, I wasn't even certain if Columbus had any siblings.

"Are you sure?" asked Brad, concerned for my well-being. "I'd hate for you to be uncomfortable."

"Well, I wouldn't wanna kick you outta your room."

"I don't mind sharing it," he said, smiling devilishly.

From somewhere inside the house, a clock struck one. I yawned, partly because I was sleepy and partly because I didn't know how else to respond to Brad's offer. Did I want to share a bed with him? Yes. Should I share a bed with him? Probably not.

• • •

In the morning, I woke to the smell of something sweet and cinnamony. The bed beside me was empty, the sheets wrinkled and strewn halfway onto the floor. I flashed back to the memory of what Brad and I had done together the night before, before falling fast asleep safe in each other's arms. I couldn't believe we'd been so bold, having wild, raucous sex in Columbus's family cabin. I prayed that he couldn't possibly have heard us all the way on the other side of the house.

I crept downstairs, wondering where Brad had disappeared to, and discovered Columbus standing shirtless at the stove.

"Good morning," I beamed brightly. "Has anyone told you, you have a ridiculous body?"

Spatula in hand, he grumbled, "Ain't getting me nowhere."

I could tell he'd been daydreaming about his gallery which, last I'd heard, he still hadn't saved up enough money to make the down payment.

"It smells like heaven in here," I said, hoping to lighten the mood by complimenting his culinary skills. "Where's Mr. Woodward?"

"Fool went for a jog," Columbus answered, tending to six fat pieces of golden French toast. "Round the lake."

"At this hour?" I took a seat at the breakfast table, already set for three.

It couldn't have been much later than nine, and it was way too early for any sort of activity—other than morning sex, maybe, which Brad and I had already had just before sunrise. My fear was that, even this far north, he'd managed to score himself a local hookup, and he was out and about somewhere getting his drug on.

Columbus poured me a cup of freshly percolated coffee, from a glass pot he took directly from the stovetop, and slid two pieces of *pain grillé* onto my plate.

"Shouldn't we wait for Mr. Woodward?" I asked, minding my manners the way my mother had taught me.

"Fuck him," said Columbus flippantly. He sat down with me at the table and dove right in. "He can eat his cold."

Brad eventually returned, his body beaded with perspiration. I couldn't be sure if his sweaty state had been brought on by physical exertion, or it was the result of an illegal substance now racing through his bloodstream. Still, he looked totally hot, as per usual, and the sight of him made me want to head back upstairs and spend the rest of the morning boffing our brains out. I realized I'd told myself I wouldn't have sex with the guy as long as he insisted he wasn't gay. But it no longer mattered. If Brad Woodward was able to get it up, which clearly he could (and on multiple occasions), what difference did it make?

After breakfast, Brad showered, and the three of us went for a walk. With October right around the corner, the air outside had turned cool and crisp. The colored leaves had already begun falling, and the earthy scent they left behind reminded me of being at Yates cider mill, enjoying a jug of cold apple juice and a dozen warm donuts. Columbus found a faded old Frisbee out back in the tool shed. We took it down to the water's edge, but the lake was far too frigid to even sink a toe in, let alone contemplate a swim. Brad and Columbus tossed the plastic disc back and forth for a while, and I watched with the warm sun on my face and not a care in the world—until I started thinking of Rain, off at rehearsal.

I hadn't thought I would, but I missed her. I realized it was ridiculous; we hardly knew each other; we weren't dating; she was a woman. Hours ago, I was having sex with a totally hot man, something I'd been dreaming about for as long as I could remember. Why hadn't it made me happy?

Between us we drank a twelve pack of beer. There was nothing I enjoyed more than being buzzed in the middle of the afternoon. But soon my stomach felt bloated, and my head morphed from giddily dizzy to achy and awful. Leaving

my companions, I stumbled back to the cabin where I proceeded to pass out on one of the tiny twin beds, unable to
bear the thought of sleeping alone in the bigger double across
the hall.

When I rose, after what felt like weeks, the sun had started to set. According to the alarm clock on the nightstand, it
was almost 6:00 p.m. I felt all hot and sticky, having forgotten to open a window.

Admiring my hangover in the mirror, I worried how I'd
ever be able to fall back to sleep when bedtime rolled round.
Earlier, we'd discussed heading into town to see a movie. *The
Last of the Mohicans* had just opened, and I'd been a big fan
of Daniel Day-Lewis since first seeing *My Left Foot* at the
Detroit Film Theatre at the Institute of Arts. But I couldn't
imagine, in my present condition, being able to sit and con-
centrate for very long.

Either my mind had started playing tricks on me, or I
heard shouting coming from below, followed by a familiar
female voice. I traipsed downstairs to have myself a look-see,
afraid of what—or who—I might find.

Just inside the front door stood Rain and Brad, like two
prize fighters ready to duke it out. Sarah kept her distance in
the corner, wearing her official BONSTELLE THEATRE
PRESENTS: CHICAGO shirt that she must've picked up at
rehearsal on that afternoon.

Rain, of course, was dressed to the nines in the same
slinky black dress she'd worn on the day we'd first bumped
into each other in the lobby of Ninety-Five. She looked ready
to hit a dance club, not go on a weekend trip to a cabin in the
woods.

"I never said you couldn't," Brad was saying. "You had rehearsal."

"Well, if I hadn't," drawled Rain, "don't pretend you
would've invited me along."

"You're right, I wouldn't. It's not my house."

"Rain, Sarah," I tentatively interjected. "What are you la-dies doing in Harbor Beach?"

"Oh, hey, Bradley," Sarah said, having not seen me make my entrance. "We got out of rehearsal early..." Her voice trailed off, leaving it up to Rain to finish her sentence.

But it was Brad who added viciously, "And Rain couldn't bear the thought of us having any fun without her."

"No!" Rain rushed over to me, like a lost child clinging to its mother. "I just wanted to see you," she cooed. Her breath reeked of alcohol, and I feared she'd been drinking and driv-ing. This would explain her angry outburst.

"You and Sarah didn't have to come all the way up here," I declared.

"But we wanted to," Rain swore. "Right, Sarah? You wanted to see Columbus."

Sarah stood silent, placing the onus upon her roommate.

"Speaking of..." Piping up, my hope was to alleviate any tension from the air. "Where is Sid anyway?"

"He drove into town to pick up a pizza," answered Sarah.

"Guess we should've ordered two," decided Brad.

"Didn't your mother ever tell you," snapped Rain, "if you can't say something nice, don't say anything at all?"

"Not when it comes to calling a bitch a bitch."

Calmly, Rain turned from me. She marched back over to where she'd left Brad standing by the door. Then she smacked him clean across the face. He touched a hand to his stinging cheek, more in shock than in pain, and gazed at Rain with a burning hatred. But the tempest in the teapot that was Rain DuBois was far from finished brewing.

"You fucking queer," she said, slow and deliberate. "You only came to this cabin because you know how I feel about Bradley. You just couldn't resist putting the moves on him first."

Brad stood idly by, not denying the blatant accusation.

"Go on! Tell our friends the real reason we broke up," Rain badgered. "Get this..." She smiled cruelly at Sarah and me. "I come home from Spring Break this past year, and who do I find him in bed with? Not another *girl*, that's for damn sure."

The revelation of Brad Woodward's secret misadventures with another man didn't startle me nearly as much as it did Sarah. Still, she didn't judge him—at least not based on his hidden homosexuality. For Sarah Schwartz, as I'd suspected, lying to a friend was a far worse sin.

17

IF YOU ASKED ME TO

♦   ♦   ♦

The evening was spent around the dining room table, playing "the hilarious bluffing game" Balderdash. Thankfully I fancied myself rather skillful when it came to making up fake definitions for words most people had never heard of. Sarah and Columbus busied themselves between rounds of witty word play with their own game of kissy-face. Brad pretended his former girlfriend, sitting directly across from him, hadn't swooped in and dropped a bomb by declaring his same-sex infidelity. Rain acted as if she'd done nothing wrong, while I attempted not to take anyone's side or show signs of favoritism, feeling like a fifth wheel the entire night.

At eleven-thirty, we gathered around the twenty-four-inch TV to watch Nicholas Cage host the season premiere of *Saturday Night Live*. I was thrilled to see both Jan Hooks and Cage's *Moonstruck* costar, Cher, make cameo appearances, and I was looking forward even more to the following week's musical guest. I could only imagine what kind of crazy stunt Sinéad O'Connor would pull during her performance. As of late, it seemed the Irish songstress had it in, politically, for one person or another, particularly the Pope. Halfway through the show, Sarah and Columbus got up from the couch, bid us all a goodnight, and retreated to the first floor master bedroom.

"Keep it down in there!" called Brad as the couple disappeared down the darkened hallway.

For a moment, I feared Columbus might make a witty retort, regarding any noise he'd heard coming from the room Brad and I had shared the night before. Luckily for our sake, he kept silent. I could only imagine Rain's reaction at knowing her accusations against Brad were indeed fact-based, and that he'd once again succeeded in seducing me.

Like a gentleman, Brad offered Rain the comfy double bed, but she flat out refused in favor of taking one of the tiny twins across the way. As much as I craved crawling between the sheets with him for another fun-filled romp, I knew I couldn't up and abandon Rain. Not in her fragile state. It was one thing for Brad and me to be engaging in sexual conduct with Columbus nearby. I couldn't allow myself to do that to Rain, sleeping fifteen feet away from us.

"Goodnight," I whispered as we tucked ourselves into our separate beds, on our separate sides of the small room.

She rolled over, facing the wall, saying not a word.

Tossing and turning, I couldn't get comfortable. For the next hour, I stared up at the slanted ceiling no more than three feet from my head, worrying I'd wind up with a concussion if I were to wake too quickly. The house was far too quiet. At home, I always slept with some sort of white noise maker: a humidifier or fan running on high. I'd had three glasses of Merlot with dinner, hoping to drink myself into a stupor, but the wine had turned to sugar in my system, and it coursed through my bloodstream, countering any sleep-inducing effect the alcohol might have had.

Or maybe I was just feeling guilty that I'd slept with Brad a second (and third) time, and now here was Rain, fast asleep on the other side of the room, betrayed by what I'd done?

Like a spotlight, the moon shone silver through the window, softly lighting her where she lay. The most skillful of stage designers couldn't have created a more romantic setting. Rising from the bed, I crossed to sit beside her, Romeo to her Juliet. With my callused hand, I reached out to caress her smooth shoulder. Gently I pulled back the cover, exposing her completely in her nakedness. She did not wake but sighed lightly, her bare bosom rising and falling with each heavy breath. Tentatively I ran my fingers through her dark hair, so lush and long. Leaning down, I couldn't help myself but kiss her; first on the eyelids, followed by the lips.

Her mouth opened, drawing my tongue inside. Eyes still shut, she moaned my name. "Bradley..."

Breathing in the scent of her rapidly beating pulse, I nuzzled her neck, working downward to her breasts. Never had I been this near to a woman. Never had I the slightest desire to take on the task I now found myself compelled to perform. Something deep inside me stirred, struggling to break loose. How I longed to lose myself, to disappear into the sweetness that was Rain DuBois, to fill her up with my—

Oh, my God!

I awoke with a start, gasping for breath, relieved to discover myself safe and secure in my own twin bed, well across the room from where Rain continued to sleep soundly. It had only been a nightmare.

Careful not to rouse her, I tiptoed to the bathroom. When I got there, I happened upon—much to my horror—a sticky wetness in my underpants, something I'd not experienced since self-abuse had become a part of my daily ritual.

In the morning, Rain was gone. None of us had heard her leave the house or the roar of the Eldorado's engine when she revved it and rode away. As per usual, she was playing her part as resident drama queen. Neither Sarah, nor Columbus, nor Brad felt any bit of remorse and agreed it best to leave her to herself. We had one last day of freedom before returning to the real world of Wayne State. There was no use letting Rain DuBois ruin it.

So Sarah was with us now, and while I missed the masculine camaraderie, I did fancy the feminine perspective she'd brought to our little excursion. Maybe it was because I'd grown up in a household full of them, but I never felt quite comfortable without having at least one woman around.

After breakfast, to my surprise, Sarah asked me to go for a walk. Columbus grinned stiffly and raised his glass of OJ; evidently she'd told him she needed to speak to me, one on one.

"What's up?" I asked, slowly putting on my tennis shoes, wishing to delay the inevitable.

Over our morning banana-walnut pancakes, whipped together by Columbus of course, I got the feeling something was amiss. Sarah was concerned. She'd heard about Columbus, maybe, with regards to what he was really doing for a living? Brad came downstairs, holding a script by John Guare, *Six Degrees of Separation*, which failed to take home the Tony Award for Best Play last season, beaten out by Neil Simon's newest, *Lost in Yonkers*. Brad was always up-to-date on the latest Broadway offering, and he was consistently seeking out fresh audition material.

"Where are you guys off to?" he asked, sending a look at the carefree Columbus.

"Town," answered Sarah. "Want us to pick up anything?"

"I could use a pack of cigs," he said. "I'll come with you."

"You need to stay and keep Columbus company."

"I don't mind if he tags along," I said, thinking there was safety in numbers.

Brad looked at Columbus again. "It's okay. I've got some reading to do."

Sarah moved to the front door. I hesitated a moment longer, embarrassed at her singling me out, and was suddenly scared to be alone with her. But once we stepped outdoors into the crisp autumn air, the Sunday in full bloom, I was able to relax. The sun glistened off the lake, and there was barely a cloud in the bright blue sky. All seemed right with the world.

"It's nice here, huh?" said Sarah. "The cabin belongs to Columbus's mom."

"Did you ever meet her?"

"No," she replied somberly. "He won't introduce me to his parents."

This statement shocked me, and it made me realize that Sarah had no idea Mrs. Howard was deceased.

"I'm going to miss coming here," she continued off my silence, "once I'm living in New York."

"You're moving to Manhattan?" I asked, never having stopped to consider that any of my actor friends would also leave Michigan. As far as I'd been concerned, I was the only one of my classmates who would ever attempt to make it big in the Big Apple.

"I have to," she answered. "I've got no other choice. I can't live just anywhere. Not with my eyes."

"How do you mean?"

"It's not like I can drive myself to an audition," she elaborated. "I need to be someplace with a decent public transportation system. They don't call Detroit the *Motor* City for nothing."

We walked down the dirt road toward the highway leading into town. But instead of following alongside, we crossed over and took the train tracks.

"It's more fun," Sarah insisted. "Bet I can make it all the way without falling off."

"Bet you can't," I said, doubting her ability to pull it off, given her limited sense of sight.

We each hopped up onto one of the rusty rails and stuck our arms out. Like tightrope walkers, we sought to sustain our balance as we began, one foot in front of the other, à la Kris Kringle and the Winter Warlock in *Santa Claus is Comin' to Town.* Within seconds I fell over sideways, skinning the palms of my hands on the gravel as I caught myself.

"Are you hurt?" asked Sarah, alarmed.

"Only my pride," I replied, dusting myself off. It was silly, really, and I was still laughing at my own stupidity when she took hold of my hand, tears welling. I was trapped. And I knew what was coming next.

"I know you know," she said seriously. "Tell me what Columbus is doing."

"Doing how?" I asked, playing dumb.

"I bumped into this bimbo, Bunny..."

"There are girls named Bunny?"

"Evidently," said Sarah with disgust. "She used to date Columbus. Briefly."

"What did Bunny say?"

She refused to cry. Wiping her eyes, she shook off her anguish and started walking again. "It's not what Bunny said," said Sarah. "It's what she didn't say."

"Okay... What didn't she say?"

"I always joked she should be a stripper. Well, guess what she's doing now? And guess where she's doing it?"

"At the Booby Trap?" I asked in disbelief.

"Where else? I'm surprised you don't know her. Tall, leggy blond. Dark roots. Tits out to here," added Sarah, gesturing a good foot in front of her.

"None of the dancers use their real names," I explained, a fact I'd picked up, based on my own personal experience now working in the biz.

"Well, I had a nice, long chat with Miss Bunny. And not once did she mention Columbus."

"That's good... Isn't it?"

"Not at all."

"It's not?"

"Think about it. If Bunny the bimbo works at Booby Trap with my boyfriend, why didn't she bring it up?"

"Talk about a tongue twister," I teased.

"I need you to tell me the truth," Sarah begged. "Is Columbus really working at the Booby Trap or not?"

"What else would he be doing?" I said, purposely evading her question.

"That's what I'm trying to find out."

I didn't know how exactly to respond. The last thing I wanted to do was blow Columbus's cover. And my own.

"I was just at work the other night," I said. "And when I walked in, there he was." As far as I was concerned, Sarah didn't need to know that the strip joint I was referring to hadn't been the same one as she had.

"Are you sure he's just working as a bouncer?" she asked next. "He's not doing anything else?"

"Anything else like what?"

"Anything *illegal.*" She'd obviously thought this over, long and hard. "Like dealing drugs, maybe?"

"Definitely not," I declared, happy for the chance to finally tell the truth. "Why would you think Columbus is a drug dealer?"

"Because," she sighed, exasperated. "All he keeps talking about is how he needs more money to buy this gallery. I keep telling him it's not important. We'll get it when we get it."

"Well, I know he's not doing anything like that."

Sarah appeared to accept what I was saying, although I could tell she was still anxious. "What about sex? Is Columbus having sex with Bunny? Or anybody else?"

"Could you define sex?" I wasn't sure if the actions he and I both performed behind the closed doors of Club Riviera would count in Sarah's opinion.

"Bradley..." From the way she said my name, I could tell she wasn't in the mood for my antics.

"Not to my knowledge," I told her, crossing my fingers behind my back.

She stepped toward me, to inspect my expression up close. "Do you promise?"

"I promise."

Sarah scrutinized me carefully. She may have been legally blind, but she could clearly see I'd lied to her. And while she acted as if she believed me, she never quite trusted me again after that.

When we returned to the cabin, Columbus and Brad were

packing up the car. Our weekend get-away was sadly over. The time had come, at last, to head back to life.

The end of the month brought the beginning of a new sticky situation. On Tuesday the 29th of September, Dina French gathered the junior class of actors together in Two Forty-Five, and she paired us up for our next set of scenes.

"Mr. Andrews," she began from her perch upon the battered desk. "You will be working on..."

Torrance remained quiet in the corner. Eyes cast down, his long hair fell across his handsome face as he anxiously awaited his sentence.

"*Of Mice and Men*," continued Dina, "along with... Mr. Woodward."

At the mention of his name, Brad sat up in his seat. He beamed brightly, as if he couldn't have been happier to be paired with Torrance, the better to keep his eye on the boy.

"Whatever you do," Dina warned, "do *not* go and see the new movie. John Malkovich is a phenomenal actor, but I don't want either of you copying him or Gary Sinise. Got it?"

Brad and Torrance both bobbed their heads in nervous agreement.

Smiling her dimpled smile, Dina returned her attention to the pad of legal paper she held upon her lap. She looked particularly stylish on this particular morning in a pair of billowy black Palazzo pants worn with a puffy white pirate shirt.

"Speaking of Malkovich..." Dina glanced up and scanned the room in search of her next victim: yours truly. "Mr. Dayton, your scene is from *Les Liaisons Dangereuses*." The French title rolled trippingly off her tongue, as if she'd spoken the foreign language fluently. "The Vicomte de Valmont and Madame de Tourvel. You, of course, will be taking on the role of the conniving count. And the object of your seduction will be... Miss DuBois."

Rain nodded, accepting her assignment with conviction.

In spite of how beautiful she appeared that afternoon, like a young Liz Taylor in her *Cleopatra*-inspired ensemble complete with stark eye makeup, I couldn't bring myself to meet her gaze. Not after what she'd done to ruin my relationship with Brad Woodward.

As a result of the incident up at Columbus's cabin, Brad decided he still wasn't ready to fling open wide his closet door. Being out to his closest friends was one thing; coming clean to the rest of The Department, especially the heterosexual (and possibly homophobic) directors like Will Bilson, who held the fate of his future casting in their hands, was not a challenge Brad was up to tackling. And I cared about him far too much to see him put through the public ringer, had the rumor of Rain's recent revelation made the rounds. This was my sole reason for finally accepting that Brad and I call it quits.

On Wednesday afternoon following Voice, Rain and I made the trek down Cass to the DPL to look for a copy of the *Les Liaisons* script. I'd seen the movie, starring the aforementioned John Malkovich, the legendary Glenn Close, and the lovely Michelle Pfeiffer, aka Stephanie Zinone from one of my all-time favorite movies, *Grease 2*. But I wasn't familiar with the stage play. Apparently neither was Rain.

"Who's the playwright again?" she asked, having failed to write it down after Dina had specifically told us.

"Christopher Hampton," I said, rolling my eyes the way I'd seen Rain do many a time.

She fumbled through the bottom of her clock-purse. Frustrated, she stopped abruptly when she couldn't find what she was searching for. "May I bum a cigarette?"

I offered her a Marlboro. My hand visibly trembled as I lifted the flame to light it and our eyes locked. I hadn't looked into those pools of blue in what felt like forever, and their coolness soothed the burning fire that had been seething in my belly all morning.

"You're not upset with me?" she asked, realizing it was

time we addressed the issue.

I made no reply, snapping the silver Zippo shut.

"Please say you're not upset with me," she pleaded. "I couldn't bear the thought."

"Rain, did you...? Why did you...?"

"What?"

"Never mind. Forget it."

We resumed our walking up the block. But I couldn't continue pretending that nothing was wrong.

"What about Brad Woodward?" she said, not more than two seconds later.

"I just—I love him, Rain—"

"Ooh, don't."

"Don't. See, that's what I mean. I don't get it. We need to talk about this, okay? I love him, and I love him because I *want* to love him. And I honestly believe he loves me, too. But he wants nothing to do with me now, and it's pretty much your fault."

"I'm sorry."

"That's what you say," I said. "But I don't know if I can believe you."

A long silence fell between us, which led us to the other side of Cass and up the sloping drive of the library. In the distance, I could hear the hum of leaf blowers and the voices of students across the street on the mall, enjoying what might have been the last warm day to sit outside during their lunch break.

"I never thought you'd like him," she said at last. "At least not in that way."

"How could you not? He's gorgeous. I mean, *you* went out with him."

At a loss for words, Rain hung her head. "I know you love Brad. I did, too—once. But then he hurt me, more than any man has ever hurt me. I couldn't stand by and allow him to do the same thing to you, Bradley. I just couldn't. I hope you'll forgive me."

She touched an apologetic hand to my cheek then pulled it away with regret. While I felt filled with sadness with the sincere way she'd revealed herself, I couldn't help but laugh at her histrionics.

"Rain," I said, "you are such a drama queen."

With the fine finesse of an old time movie star, she let her cigarette cascade to the ground and crushed it out with her high heel. Carefully considering the label I'd conferred upon her, I think she rather appreciated my calling her out.

"What can I say?" she finally said. "My mama made me this way."

Deep down, I understood that Rain had only done what she did to spare me the same pain she'd suffered. In my heart, I recognized I couldn't remain involved with a man who refused to acknowledge me as the love of his life.

Back at The Thelma, Rain and I began our rehearsal by reading through the scene that Dina had selected for us from act 1, scene 2.

In the *salon* of a country *château*, the Vicomte de Valmont is concluding a conversation with his *valet de chambre* when they are interrupted by the arrival of Valmont's elderly aunt, Madame de Rosemonde, and the handsome (but happily married) Madame de Tourvel. In an earlier exchange, the equally manipulative Madame Merteuil challenged Valmont with the chore of seducing Tourvel and making her fall in love with him. Back in late 18th century France, a wife cheating on her husband was cause for great scandal, and clearly Merteuil had it in for the lovely (and much younger) woman.

Therefore, my goal in this particular predicament, as determined by the method employed at the Atlantic Theater Company, was "to get someone on my side"—a task often easier determined than executed.

"Maybe we should have a drink?" Rain suggested. "Wouldn't he give her a glass of wine at least? To help loosen her up."

I agreed with her logic, but it was scarcely four o'clock in the afternoon. I hardly thought it wise for us to get all looped when we had to be coherent later that evening for *Chicago* rehearsal. But before I could decline, Rain had returned from the kitchen with an open bottle of Merlot and two metal goblets. She handed me one and splashed some of the crimson liquor into my cup.

"These are lovely," I said, holding aloft the silver chalice. Alongside the beaker, a medieval knight strode high about his horse, wielding both shield and sword. On the stem of the trumpet-belled bottom, a single cobalt stone sparkled, catching the light of the crystal chandelier.

"You like?" Rain replied. "We used them in *Merchant* last season."

"...*of Venice?*"

"Is there any other?" she smiled, taking a sip. "I played Portia."

"Of course."

"The minute I saw them, I just fell in love. I had to have them for my collection. So I slept with the props designer, *et voilà!*"

While I wouldn't put it past Rain to trade sexual favors for a pair of pewter wine glasses, I couldn't completely tell if she was being sincere or just playing me for a fool. Regardless, I became suddenly aware of our solitude behind the closed door of her bedroom.

"Shall we get down to business?" I asked, swiftly changing the subject. "Before Sarah and Columbus come home." Only God knew where they'd gone off to, and as I leaned against the antique vanity dressing table waiting for Rain to speak her first line, I silently prayed for the couple's impending arrival.

We read through the entire scene—twice—polishing off an equal number of tumblers of Merlot, and soon my brain

felt pickled. Across the room, Rain rested herself on the chenille bedspread, her cheeks rosy with a wine-induced blush.
Delicately she patted the spot beside her, beckoning me with
a come-hither attitude the polar opposite of the chaste character she'd been ordered to play.

I realized what was about to happen, but under the influence of the alcohol, I did not pause to consider, only to consider that I understood what was about to occur.

She reached for my hand. Our fingers intertwined. I
pulled her toward me with the force of the 18th century
French aristocrat whom I'd been entrusted to embody. Her
taut hips pressed firmly against my own, and I put my mouth
to hers.

We kissed for a long moment, then she drew back to take
me in. "I can't tell you how long I've been waiting for that."

Whether it was me, or the wine, or the Vicomte de Valmont doing the talking, I was uncertain. But I put a silencing
hand lightly against her lips before sweeping her into my
arms and placing her gently on the bed. We kissed again with
an intensity to rival any I'd ever felt with a man. Always had I
assumed that intimacy with a woman would never quite sat-
isfy my animal instinct; that it would somehow be too deli-
cate, too tender, too passion-free. With Rain DuBois, I was
about to find, sex was none of these things.

"Can we go slow?" I pleaded.

"No," replied Rain.

And she was right.

We did it very swiftly, going from toothy kisses through
each familiar, yet foreign, passage on the good old route to
sexual relations. Suddenly I was overcome with a sense that
our destiny had been written in stone. My heart was filled
with optimistic joy and unbridled sadness. I was totally spent,
and I loved every minute of it.

18

STAY

♦   ♦   ♦

We slept together, that afternoon and for the next five evenings that followed. Mornings we would wake up at The Thelma, where I'd all but moved in, and rush off to class after hitting the snooze button on Rain's alarm clock one too many times.

Since the day of our first dangerous liaison, we hadn't spoken a word of it to anyone. The week that followed was much like any other: days spent in class, evening at rehearsals, and weekends strutting about half naked in front of a bunch of dirty old men. Had Sarah been aware of the clandestine corner my relationship with Rain had suddenly turned, surely I would've gotten an earful from Columbus backstage at Club Riviera. But how could either of them not know? I'd become the fourth roommate residing in the tiny two bedroom apartment. As Sarah had learned from past experience, the walls of the building were paper thin, and Rain DuBois was not one to hold back when reveling in a state of pleasure, which is where we found ourselves as often as possible each night after we returned home.

I didn't consider myself to be straight. In general, I didn't consider myself much at this point. But the entire day, from the instant I opened my eyes until the time I shut them at night, fully aware of Rain's falling breath against my chest, I could think of nothing but her and how she made me feel (dare I say?) more like a man. Never had I been ashamed of being gay, but being with Rain—being seen with her—gave me a sense of masculinity and self-confidence that was stronger than any I'd ever experienced. To have other men look at me as she and I walked down the street, Rain's hand in mine, and to register the undeniable sign of envy in their eyes, all because this beautiful woman had chosen to be with me... For the first instance in my life, I felt what it was like to be hated for being straight.

The sex, itself, was some of the best I'd ever had.

Yes, I missed the firm touch of a man's hands about my body. But whenever I was making love to Rain, I found myself taking on an entirely different role than the one I'd played since I first started having intimate relations. With the other guys I'd been with, no matter their preferred position, there was always an air of competition. Especially the first time, before the clothes came off and we inevitably answered the question on both our minds: *who's bigger?* (Usually I won the contest—not that it mattered, even though it totally did.) With Rain, and any other woman I'd imagine, there was none of that potential, pent up insecurity. The only thing I had to do, as her lover, was make her feel good which, judging by the claw marks dug into my back, I'd succeeded in doing.

About this time, Miss Peter took a weekend trip to the District of Columbia to view the AIDS Memorial Quilt, laid out on the National Mall in full display. She'd already seen it, along with half a million other folks, when it was first unveiled on October 11, 1987, during the National March on Washington for Lesbian and Gay Rights.

Still grieving over the death of Freddy Mercury less than a year prior, it had been Miss Peter's sole purpose to save enough money so that she could pay her proper respects to the former King of Queen by attaching her own handmade panel bearing his name to the enormous blanket. With the wealth she'd recently inherited, she found herself more than capable of making the return trip to our nation's capital, followed by a week's stay in sunny Cozumel.

To show her appreciation for my years of devoted friendship, and because she didn't trust leaving her Frank Lloyd Wright house unattended, Miss Peter offered me the use of her 4,300 square foot Palmer Woods home in her absence.

Named after Thomas Witherell Palmer, one of the most significant figures in 19th century Detroit, Palmer's estate rested on both sides of Woodward Avenue, extending from 6 Mile Road north to 8 Mile. It was a portion of this land that the US Senator donated to establish the city's one hundred and forty acre Palmer Park, as well as the Michigan State Fairgrounds. Two years after Palmer's death in 1913, Detroit real estate developer Charles W. Burton purchased the section of Palmer's property that would later encompass the Palmer Woods Historic District. Burton envisioned an exclusive neighborhood catering to Detroit's wealthiest citizens, comprised of a subdivision with curved, elm-lined streets and nonexistent curbs that capitalized on the natural beauty of the area and created a park-like atmosphere.

The many brick and stone Tudor and Colonial Revival-style homes, constructed circa 1917-1929, were elegant and spacious in size. Each lot had its own unique design with plenty of room for trees and a good amount of grass. So impressed was the Michigan Horticultural Society that the organization awarded Palmer Woods its Award of Merit as the finest platted subdivision of 1938 in the state. The home of artists, business owners, executives, physicians, politicians, and their families, the neighborhood attracted some of Detroit's most prominent citizens, including brothers Alfred and William Fisher of automobile coachbuilder Fisher Body. At 35,000 square feet, William Fisher's house, located on Wellesley, was one of the largest in the entire city.

Almost every dwelling in Palmer Woods was designed with its own unique architectural features, but a number were exceptionally significant. Noted theatre architect C. Howard Crane, whose best designs included Detroit's Fox

Theatre, Capitol Theatre, and Orchestra Hall, designed the home of John H. Kunsky, founder of United Artists theatres, and incorporated many theatrical elements into the dwelling. At the southern edge of the neighborhood, renowned American architect Frank Lloyd Wright built his only house in all of Detroit.

Known as the Dorothy Turkel House, after its original owner, the two-story, concrete block structure was first commissioned by Mrs. Turkel in 1954. The daughter of a man who'd made his fortune constructing parking lots when automobiles were first becoming the fashion, Dorothy Turkel and her physician husband, Henry, had been residing in the historic Boston-Edison district. Fond of contemporary style, Dorothy wrote to Wright after reading his book *The Natural House* and asked him to design a home especially for her family. One of sixty middle-income homes created by FLW, the Turkel House featured a living room (dubbed by Wright as the "music" room), Mrs. Turkel's study, the master bedroom and four other bedrooms, three bathrooms, dining, laundry, utility, and playroom, plus an exterior terrace and interior balcony with peek-a-boo cut-outs overlooking the lower level.

Six months into the planning, Mrs. Turkel wrote again to Wright stating that she required an additional bedroom, so an L-shape was added to the design and shortened to make the house two stories high. The main level was also extended into an L, with the playroom on the lower level and a bedroom and maid's room on the second floor. Mrs. Turkel finally took up residence with her four children in February 1958. Now a divorced woman, her former husband never lived at the 7 Mile address and was said to have never approved its construction. Dorothy remained in the house for two decades, until 1978 when it was purchased by Loretta Benbow. Credited with helping to designate the Turkel-Benbow Historic District, Mrs. Benbow also placed the home on the state and local historic registers.

After Benbow, the Turkel House changed hands several more times throughout the years and soon fell on hardship, going through periods of deferred maintenance and long vacancies. Former owner Tom Monaghan was an avid fan of Frank Lloyd Wright, but the Domino's Pizza millionaire never inhabited the property and was more than willing, in 1992, to turn it over to a hairdresser from Eastpointe, Peter Little, for the bargain price of five hundred thousand dollars.

Once Rain got word that I'd be shut up for ten days with an entire mansion to myself, she extended the offer to keep me company. She reasoned that her vacating The Thelma would provide Sarah and Columbus with some much-needed alone time. But I could strongly sense her generosity stemming from something more. A desire to play husband and wife, perhaps?

"This is going to be so much fun," Rain gushed as she arrived on Sunday afternoon, luggage in tow. "Don't you agree, Bradley darling?"

While I expected the next few nights to be filled with intense sexual pleasures, since living alone at my dad's, I hadn't the need to concern myself with such domestic duties as keeping the bathroom clean, or remembering to put the cap back on the toothpaste, or lowering the toilet lid. All the trivial things women were always complaining about in the pages of *Cosmopolitan* with regards to their men.

"Sure," I said, forcing a smile. "Can I take that?"

Gladly she obliged. "Aren't you a gentleman?"

Her suitcase was one of those old, retro leather types with tarnished brass hinges and stickers stuck to the outside, labeled with exotic locales like Morocco and Timbuktu. Places the weary voyager who owned it had at one time vacationed.

"Right this way," I said leading her through the front door and into the living room at the far end of the house. "Welcome to my humble abode."

Rain peered up at the soaring two-story, all white ceiling.

"Humble my foot," she marveled. "Look at these windows!"

Two hundred panes of pierced, light-admitting glass squares surrounded the room on two sides, each one sixteen inches in size. A trio of built-in bookshelves ran the length of the opposite wall, fabricated from the same light-colored wood, on which Miss Peter had displayed her collection of Frank Lloyd Wright-inspired reading materials.

"Check out the fireplace," I told Rain, pointing to the hearth, tucked away below the interior balcony.

"I can't believe your friend lives here," she said, "alone."

"Crazy, huh? I keep telling her she needs to have a party."

"Oh, my God! We should throw the *Chicago* cast soirée here," Rain cried. "Wouldn't that be brilliant?"

"Totally."

"When does your friend return?"

"Not till next Sunday."

"Perfect! Let's do it after opening on Friday night."

From the glimmer in her eye, I could tell she was serious, so I stopped to reconsider. "I don't know... If anything happens to Miss Peter's half a million dollar house, she'll cut off my balls."

"Well, we wouldn't want that," said Rain, reaching out to fondle them affectionately through my pants. "Now where are we sleeping?"

The idea that I hadn't shared a living space with a female since moving out of Mom's house had given me slight pause when Rain first suggested joining me for my Turkel House sojourn. My other apprehension came from this very question. I had to keep reminding myself that just because I'd had sex with Rain DuBois (several times, in fact) it certainly didn't make us boyfriend-girlfriend. Or did it?

With gay guys, most of the time they would just meet somewhere, at a bar usually, knock back a few drinks, then go off and have sex. After all was said and done, they might become friends. More often than not they wouldn't speak again—until the next time they were feeling horny and looking to hook up. But it didn't mean they were committed to each other. Because I'd never done with another woman what I did with Rain, I wasn't sure how I should behave. Being heterosexual, I was beginning to discover, was hard.

"I thought we would share the master bedroom," I told her as we took the tiny elevator to the second floor. "It's at the end of the hall, with our own private bathroom."

"Sounds lovely." She sighed and held onto my arm, resting her dark head against mine. "I don't suppose there's a tub."

"A whirlpool tub," I answered, having tried it out myself the night before, after a long evening's work of dancing at The Riviera. "Would you like me to show you?"

We sank into the ceramic bath and soaked together in steamy bliss, till the hot water turned tepid, and we both became prunes.

When Miss Peter's phone rang that evening just after five, I knew it had to be my father calling to remind me of our dinner plans. We hadn't seen each other in days. Dad had been busy working on a case, attempting to bust a local drug lord, while I'd found myself preoccupied with classes, rehearsal, and now Rain.

Trying my best not to wake her from her post-coital nap, I slipped quietly from Miss Peter's king-sized bed and padded down the heated floor to the kitchen downstairs. Peter had made it a point to preserve the Turkel House's aesthetic once he'd taken it over by filling it with authentic mid-century décor and period furniture. The Frigidaire refrigerator and chrome Formica dinette set were something straight out of the *Sally, Dick, and Jane* books we used to read in grade school during the '70s.

"Son?" said Dad after I'd answered his call. "Just making sure we're still on for tonight. Six-thirty."

I glanced at the sunburst clock hanging above the sink. With a little over an hour to get ready, I knew I wouldn't have any trouble making it up to Hazel Park on time. We'd planned to meet at Dad's favorite Italian restaurant, Loui's, a Hazeltucky institution known for their thick crust pizza.

"I'll be there," I told him before hanging up and returning to Miss Peter's bedroom to put on some clothes.

I would leave a note for Rain, explaining to her I had to step out for a bit, but she should make herself comfortable when she woke—and feel free to order some take-out. Or so this was my plan. As I was stepping into a clean pair of pants, I heard a sleepy voice address me.

"And where do you think you're off to, mister?" Rain yawned and stretched, arching her back gracefully. She propped herself up on the mound of pillows lining the lavish headboard and watched my every move.

"Sorry, my dad called. I forgot I have to meet him for dinner," I half-lied.

"How wonderful! Just let me get dressed and I'll join you." She hopped out of bed and began scurrying about, flinging open her overnight bags in search of the perfect outfit. "What should I wear?"

"Um," I said, unsure how I'd escape this one.

She stopped to stare at me. "You want me to come with you, don't you?"

"Sure, maybe."

Arms akimbo, she thrust out her chin in defiance. "Either you do, or you don't."

I imagined the surprised reaction on my father's face the moment I entered the pizzeria with a woman on my arm. And then I realized, maybe it was just the thing I needed? Of course I couldn't tell him we were shacking up, living in sin together at Miss Peter's house or, God forbid, that we'd been having premarital sex. But something made me think that, in this instance, he might not mind. Never had Jim Dayton known his only son to be dating a girl, let alone one as beautiful as Rain DuBois.

"Please try to hurry," I said, saying a silent prayer that

Dad would at last be proud.

Sunday night, the roads were relatively empty as Rain and I drove north on Woodward Avenue. She looked amazing sitting beside me on the bench seat, her dark hair piled high atop her head, pale skin powdered to perfection, lips painted crimson. She'd chosen a vintage black satin cocktail dress she'd picked up at Value Village, accompanied by a matching pillbox hat, complete with French net veil that just barely covered her blue eyes. I hadn't the heart to tell her we weren't dining at a fancy restaurant. But she'd indeed fit right in with the old-fashioned feel that was Loui's.

Me, I wore my standard issue Sunday-dinner-with-Dad ensemble: khaki pants and a ubiquitous denim shirt. Once I realized just how chilly it was getting, I threw on a scratchy acrylic cardigan I'd borrowed from Jack back in high school (but had conveniently failed to return) that originally belonged to his Uncle Roy, a local comic who'd opened up for both Judy Tenuta and Ellen DeGeneres, as seen on the HBO comedy special *Women of the Night* back in the late '80s.

Pulling into the side parking lot, we were fortunate enough to snag the last free space. Val coughed and sputtered as I shut off her motor. Rain made no remark, but I sensed she questioned my continuing to drive such a clunker. Surely a man of my supposed-wealth could afford an upgrade to a more classic model of a classic car.

Climbing out, I rushed around to the opposite side and opened the door for my passenger, something I'd never done on any of my dates with other men. With Rain, it just seemed right, as if by performing this small gesture I was helping to keep alive the custom of chivalry.

"Bradley," she said, taking me by the arm as she often did. "What's your father like?"

We headed toward the one-story brick building with its bright neon sign advertising DINNERS, LUNCHEONS, and Cocktail LOUNGE.

"How do you mean?"

"I've never met a police officer. Is he strict?"

I considered her question before answering. "He was, growing up, I guess. He wasn't around for long."

Rain would be the first friend of mine who'd met my father since Miss Peter, back in high school, and that had only happened by default after they both showed up on the exact same night to see my production of *A Christmas Carol*. I'd never forget Dad's reaction as Miss Peter came sashaying up to me at the end of the performance, wrapped in a full-length fox fur, hair wilder than ever. Even though he averted his eyes, pretending not to notice anything wrong with the person who was clearly my acquaintance, I could totally tell Dad was silently judging her.

We arrived only three minutes late and entered with a sigh as the scent of fresh garlic enveloped us.

"Isn't this quaint?" Rain cried, taking in the collection of framed autographed photos decorating the wood paneling alongside the take-out window. Notable past Loui's patrons included local Detroit TV personalities John Kelly and Marilyn Turner of *Kelly & Company* fame and Hollywood stars Mel Gibson and Dom DeLuise.

I spotted my dad at our favorite booth in the far corner, beside the mirrored wall and beneath the sparkly, rose-colored recessed ceiling from which hung a hundred straw-covered Chianti bottles, all signed by the patrons who'd emptied them over the past fifteen years.

Dad looked like his handsome old self, freshly shaved save for his mustache and dressed in his Sunday best. He had on a beige button-down shirt with a decade-old tan knit tie and brown blazer. Surely he'd spent the morning (and a good part of the afternoon) at church. I had a feeling that Rain would find him attractive. He stood for her and offered his hand.

"Rain DuBois," she said demurely. "Your son has told me so much about you." A polite lie, perhaps, but it didn't surprise me to hear her utter it. Again I felt she must've had a

Southern upbringing somewhere in her background.

"Jim Dayton," Dad replied. "Glad you could join us."

If he'd been unhappy at my bringing an uninvited guest to dinner, his face did not betray him. Never in public would my father make a scene. He complimented Rain on her veiled hat, and he smiled a charming, fatherly smile. Of course none of his pleasantries meant a thing. I wouldn't be made aware of his true opinion until long after she'd left us.

"Rain and I are in the same class at Wayne State," I stated as we took our seats, side by side on the opposite bench of the booth.

"Is that right?" asked Dad stoically.

We picked up our menus, and I scanned the list of pastas and pizza toppings that I'd already memorized long ago in my youth. Half-listening to the conversation flowing back and forth, I prayed neither party would say anything to embarrass me or get me in further trouble.

"This is such a charming restaurant," said Rain, glancing around at the glass-topped tables with their red-and-white checked tablecloths. "I've never been to Hazel Park before."

"Oh, no?" said Dad. "Bradley's mother and I started coming here back in the late seventies, when we first moved to—"

I could tell he was on the verge of revealing the city in which I actually grew up, so quickly I cut him off. "Dad, are we getting our usual?"

"Unless Rain objects to pepperoni." He turned to her, raising his bushy brow. "You're not vegetarian, are you?"

"Heavens no!" she answered, aghast. "I'm a voracious carnivore." She let out a playful growl that my dad, I was sure, didn't find the least bit amusing, judging by his reddening ears.

We settled on a large pie and a small antipasto salad.

Rain licked her lips in a show of approval. "Sounds delicious. Shall we order some wine?"

My father frowned.

"Dad doesn't drink," I explained.

"No," he interjected. "Feel free to have some, if you'd like."

The waitress came over to take our order. She resembled nothing close to what a stereotypical woman working in an Italian restaurant might look like. She wasn't dark-haired or olive-skinned, nor was she the slightest bit plump from a diet rich in semolina pasta. In fact, she was the total opposite: gray, fair, and thin. Her so-called uniform consisted of a Willie Nelson concert tee from Pine Knob worn with pleated Lee jeans. She wore no name tag, but from our years as frequent customers, we knew her as Theresa.

"What can I get you, hon?" she asked, laying an exuberant hand upon my father's shoulder.

I let Dad do the talking, hoping the waitress wouldn't ask to see either Rain's or my ID, since we were sitting there dining with a man who was clearly my parent. As far as Rain was concerned, I was also under age, and I think she took this tactic as my being sneaky, which I totally was.

Over the salad, Rain proceeded to gulp down an entire glass of Chianti. Taking full advantage of her captive audience, she turned the talk to my childhood: What was Bradley like as a baby? What kind of toys did he play with? Did he get good grades in school? Since my father and I had never been close during my formative years, he was hardly able to answer. I could tell he felt put on the spot, and I did my best to reply to Rain's questions, which grew more and more personal the more wine she imbibed.

"What did you think the first time you saw him onstage?" she asked Dad, her azure eyes glossing over. An entire piece of pepperoni sat untouched upon her plate, and yet the bottle we shared between the two of us was now less than half full—and I'd only had a few sips. She was clearly drunk, for lack of food, and continued to become more so with each drop she drained from her glass.

The waitress returned to check on us, and Dad requested

that she bring the bill. Rain asked if she could be excused to powder her nose, with a downcast look of humility that suggested we should feel free to discuss her in her absence.

Again, my father rose, and he directed Rain to the far end of the aisle. She stood, clinging tightly to the table, and practically fell on top of me.

"Isn't he the cutest thing?" she slurred, stroking my head like a pet. "You should be proud, Mr. Dayton. The things this boy can do..."

With the determination of an inebriated driver walking a straight line along the roadside, Rain staggered toward the restroom. While I worried what my dad would say once she was gone, I didn't expect him to go all out and pass judgment until much later, when we were truly alone.

"She's nice, huh?" I said, breaking the deafening silence.

Dad looked at me, twisting his wiry upper lip in scorn. The chords of his neck tightened, and he slowly shook his balding head.

Feeling like I was 5 years old, I shrank down in my seat before he uttered a single word.

19

ONLY LOVE CAN BREAK
YOUR HEART

♦　　　　　　　　♦　　　　　　　　♦

Father or not, I wasn't about to sit by and listen to my dad
bad-mouth my girlfriend. Politely I thanked him for the
meal, got up from the table, and met Rain outside the ladies'
room.

"We're leaving," I informed her, then I took her firmly by
the arm and escorted her to the parking lot.

"Bradley," she said sternly. "We can't just go without saying goodbye to your dad. It's rude."

Not compared to the things he'd said about her.

First he questioned what I was doing with such a girl; a
girl who wears too much makeup and drinks too much wine.
How shocked would he (and his Baptist upbringing) have
been to discover Rain DuBois was not only a borderline alcoholic but also a lapsed Catholic? His other complaints
hinged on her pursuing a career as an actress, of all profes-
sions, coupled with the fact that she originally hailed from
Rochester Hills.

This, I was certain, was the crux of Dad's criticisms. His
dislike of Rain, a woman whom he'd only just met, stemmed
not from her nasty habits or overt sexual expression, but
from her future inheritance. As far as James Bradley Dayton
was concerned, boys who grew up in Ferndale and attended
school in Hazel Park did not wed rich women. There was no

upward mobility when it came to climbing the ladder of so-cio-economic advancement. Dad was a poor man who'd made a meager living working as a police officer. If I was lucky, I'd find a woman from a similar background somewhere, and we'd settle down, perhaps raising a couple kids, like he and Mom had done. What Dad didn't seem to understand was that, up until the past week, his boy had been a card carrying homo who hadn't considered the state of holy matrimony be-cause, up until the past week, it had never been an option.

Outside, the smell of burning leaves overpowered the air. I unlocked the passenger door for Rain as she pouted like a spoiled little girl at our evening being prematurely cut short. Walking around the front of my car, I noticed something tucked beneath the left-hand windshield wiper.

"Shit!" I hissed, fearing I'd been given a ticket for violating God only knows what law. As far as I could tell, parking was always free in the Loui's lot. This wasn't Royal Oak where one had to mandatorily feed the meter. Furiously I yanked the slip of pink paper, pulling it free.

"What's it say?" asked Rain as I climbed inside the car.

Fortunately it was only a flyer of some sort:

family

October 4, 1992

10 P.M. – 4 A.M.

Hosted by Super-Scenster Endolphin

featuring DJs

Juan Atkins, Bileebob, Kenny Larkin, Bone

$10 advance*

$15 door

* for checkpoint location: 313-555-7757

"Let's go!" Rain's red-rimmed eyes sparkled with excitement. No longer did she look exhausted and on the verge of a wicked hangover, but as if she could boogie the night away.

"What is it?" I asked, uncertain.

"Don't tell me you've never been to a rave."

"Okay, I won't... But I haven't."

"That's it. We're going," she decided. "We just need to make a quick call."

"For what?"

"You dial the number on the flyer and listen to the recording, and it tells you what to do next." She giggled with glee at the adventure ahead of us.

"You really wanna go to a rave?" I hadn't figured Rain DuBois for the type of girl who listened to House or Techno music; whatever they called it—whoever *they* happened to be.

"They're so much fun," she assured me. "I used to go all the time with—" She may have stopped herself, but I knew exactly who she was talking about. "Come on! We'll get drunk, we'll do some drugs, and we'll dance till we drop."

"What kinda drugs?" I asked, both wary and disturbed.

"Silly boy," she said, giving me a light love tap. "We won't know until we get there, now will we?"

I realized I'd only known Rain for a little more than a month, but it felt like much longer. I never suspected she'd be into anything of this nature. It wasn't that I was a prude. I'd smoked my fair share of pot with Bobby Russell back in junior high and high school. But something about the idea of attending an underground dance party, where we'd be afforded the opportunity to partake in the imbibing of mind altering (and totally illegal) substances, didn't sit right with me. My dad, whom she'd just spent the last hour dining with, was a Detroit cop. God forbid he should get wind of this event about to go down in the depths of the city... Rain should've easily understood my perpetual paranoia.

Still, I wanted to be a good boyfriend. "There's a phone booth up the block," I said, putting the car in gear and pulling out into the two-way traffic.

On the south-west corner of 9 Mile, high atop the local landmark, a laughing donkey rose up on its hind legs, wielding an oversized hamburger. Brayz was a tiny little White Castle-type restaurant, with a white-tiled exterior and a sign out front that proclaimed: BREAKFAST ANYTIME. Through a wall of windows, we could see a sad-looking old man sitting at the stainless steel counter, slumped over a ceramic cup of coffee, his satin baseball jacket both faded and one size too small. He looked as if he'd been a permanent fixture in the place since the Tigers won the World Series. Not the Roar of '84 but way back in '68.

"So what am I supposed to do?" I asked, still unsure as to how we should go about conducting this so-called secret business.

Rain rolled her eyes and sighed, a gesture I was becoming quite familiar with, as it seemed to be her go-to whenever she was feeling frustrated, which seemed quite often.

"Give me that," she playfully demanded, snatching the flyer clean from my grasp.

She got out of the car, taking along her clock-purse, and tottered over to the phone booth, heels ticking against the blacktop. The seams of her stockings, lining the backs of her legs like two lightning bolts, gave my libido a momentary jolt.

Watching her pull back the glass louver door before shutting herself inside, I found myself fascinated by the forceful way she'd taken command of the situation. From her pocketbook, she withdrew a quarter, dropped it into the coin slot, and dialed. Wedging the receiver in the crook of her neck, she listened carefully, jotting down whatever she was hearing on back of the pink piece of paper. When her call had been completed, she hung up the phone and habitually checked the coin return. She zipped up her clock-purse, opened up the sliding door, and scurried back to my car looking ever so excited.

"Zoot's Coffee!" she cried, climbing in and buckling her seatbelt.

"Isn't it a little late?" I asked, even though I personally could consume caffeine at all hours and still be able to sleep at night.

"No, silly," she said, shaking her head. "We need to stop by Space Nineteen, below Zoot's Coffee, to buy tickets and pick up a map."

"Now there's a map involved?"

Couldn't they just tell us where the party was, so that we could simply show up? Evidently things were done differently in the underground world, as I would soon discover.

It turned out that Space Nineteen and its upstairs neighbor, Zoot's Coffee, were both downtown on the Wayne State campus, around the corner from The Thelma and across the street from the A-B-C building, on Second Avenue and Prentis.

Upon our arrival, Rain and I entered the cramped storefront to find a variety of shirts, sweatshirts, and baseball caps branded with names like Digital Laundre, Q Ambient, and Fresh Drive. On a display rack, a magazine called *Urb* was for sale, along with an assortment of mix-tapes by artists I'd never heard of with names like D.Wynn, Mike Huckaby, and Sarena Tyler.

"Dude!" From behind the counter, a black guy around our age greeted us. Dressed rather funky, he sported a pair of denim overalls with a baggy T-shirt beneath. On his head he wore a cute little wool cap, reminding me of those boys in the Disney movie-musical that had come out earlier that spring, *Newsies*.

"Hi," I said, trying to instill myself with some confidence, pretending I'd done what we were now doing a hundred times.

"What's up?" asked the guy in the overalls, eyeing us suspiciously, like we didn't belong there.

"We're here to buy some tickets," I told him.

"For the party," added Rain coolly, the real expert.

"What party would that be?"

"Um..."

Rain pulled the flyer from her purse and showed it to Mr. Overalls. "This one."

"Gotcha." He seemed rather surprised we were privy to such top secret information. "You don't wanna waste your time at that party."

"Oh, really?" I replied, hoping to avoid confrontation at all cost. Obviously Mr. Overalls was attempting to sway us from attending, without being overly overt.

"Because we're rich and white?" asked Rain, taking on a tone that clearly stated she wasn't going to be talked down to. Not by some lowly store clerk at a college souvenir shop.

"You calling me a racist?" the guy asked us, offended.

"Not at all," I said amiably. "My girlfriend didn't mean to imply—"

"Your girlfriend?" he repeated, regarding me like he could tell that, up until recently, I preferred the romantic company of my own kind.

"Yes, his girlfriend," said Rain, practically climbing on top of me to prove we were in fact an item. "And I'd like to know why you have the gall to think we won't fit in at this rave."

The black boy in the blue overalls answered, "It ain't 'cause you're white, girl. I just don't think it's your scene, okay?" He glanced down at the penny loafers on my feet, coupled with my khaki pants and cardigan, all of which gave me the appearance of a total square.

I was well aware I couldn't go to a top secret, underground rave party looking like a *Mr. Rogers' Neighborhood* reject. But even back at Miss Peter's, I hadn't brought anything to change into that would make me look any less nebbish. And after the earlier incident with my dad at dinner, I had no desire to drive all the way up to Warren to pick up new wardrobe, nor could I with Rain in tow.

"For your information," she continued snappishly. "I've been to several of these parties with someone you very well may have heard of: Brad Woodward."

Mr. Overalls cracked a smile, showing us a mouthful of straight white chompers. "You know Brad? Brad's my boy." Then a light of recognition dawned in his deep brown eyes. "Wait a minute! You're Rain Doo-boys? I 'member you."

Rain regarded the guy with the blankest of gazes. "Funny," she said frigidly. "I can't say I recall our meeting."

"Please give us two tickets," I pleaded. "And I'll take one of those T-shirts over there."

Reaching into my wallet, I pulled out a pair of twenties and, because money had the reputation for making the world go round, the black boy in the blue overalls magically granted my request.

According to the map that accompanied our admission, we were to take I-75 north to I-94 east, right on Mount Elliot, left on Grand Boulevard. Where that would put us, I had no idea. But once we'd returned to my car and resumed driving, I realized the desolate area was but a few miles from the one I'd recently been brought to by Columbus.

"Isn't that amazing?" I marveled when we passed by The Cloud Maker, off to our right as we approached the entrance to the Edsel Ford Freeway.

Rain gazed out the passenger window. "Isn't what amazing?" she asked, as if she couldn't possibly tell to what I was alluding.

I told her I was speaking of the incinerator.

She scoffed. "It's a monstrous, toxic chimney."

It pained me that she failed to see the splendor in something I'd come to cherish. Yes, the Greater Detroit Resource Recovery Facility may have been killing us all. But The Cloud Maker was a thing of beauty, pumping out its white, puffy dreams, day in and day out, a symbol of the industrial ingenuity forever rooted in the Motor City.

"Over there," said Rain, pointing to a desolate area where she was insisting that we park.

"Looks like a cemetery," I said, once I'd realized the upright rocks dotting the landscape resembled a series of gravestones.

"That's because it is," Rain replied. "Just pull in and pick a spot."

The last time I'd entered a graveyard was during my junior year of high school. Every Friday night after the Varsity football games, me and my friends, the Band Fags, would pile into someone's car (usually Luanne the lesbian's) and we'd drive all the way out Rochester Road, at least thirty miles, to an area called Oxford, just so we could wander around an ancient burial ground, equipped with a stone crypt built into the hillside, that we affectionately called The Tombs.

"Are you sure it's safe?" I said, silencing the engine and shutting off the lights. Sure, there were a good fifty or so other vehicles lining the unofficial lot. But it didn't mean that nothing would happen to poor Val if I were to up and abandon her here unprotected.

"No disrespect, darling," said Rain as we stepped into the darkness. "I'm sure no one's going to steal your car."

While her comment did sting, I made no attempt to defend myself or my property. Rain was right. My automobile was a total hunk of junk and I knew it. Had I truly been a wealthy, respectable young man from Birmingham, I wouldn't have been caught dead driving around in anything less than a BMW or at least a Mercedes, the very which we passed on our jaunt across the grassy knoll of death. An uneasy feeling made itself present in the pit of my stomach, out of fear that the luxury sedan belonged to Brad Woodward. But when Rain somehow missed seeing it, I decided not to make mention, in favor of not wanting to ruin her night.

"Why did we need to park all the way out here?" I asked,

because Enquiring Minds always want to know.

"In case some lovely police officers, like your daddy, come looking to break up an illegal party."

Once again, the presence of my father and his proximity to the law reminded me that what I was about to do, I should've known better. How many times this school year had I tempted fate and escaped the wrath of Dad the Detroit Cop? One day soon my luck would surely run out.

Still not knowing where we were going exactly, I allowed Rain to continue leading us.

"Now that's an amazing sight," she sighed as we made our approach.

Ahead an abandoned warehouse, much like many others found throughout the burned out Motor City, towered upward. Only this one was colossal. Five stories high in places, the structure loomed before us, spanning the length of the football field at the Pontiac Silverdome. A water tower straight out of *Animaniacs* sat atop, an inky silhouette against the evening sky. Row after row of poked out windows called to mind my favorite game from childhood, "Don't Break the Ice."

"Dude!" I said, employing an epithet I rarely ever uttered. "What is it?"

"That would be the Packard Plant," answered Rain in awe.

A former manufacturing factory where magnificent automobiles were made by the Packard Motor Car Company, the 3,500,000 square foot plant was designed by Albert Kahn, the esteemed Architect of Detroit. The Prussian-born son of a rabbi, other noted works in the Kahn cannon included the 28-story art deco Fisher Building, the Belle Isle Conservatory, and Wayne State's very own Bonstelle Theatre.

Located on over forty acres of land, the Packard Plant was the first industrial structure in all of Detroit to use reinforced concrete for its construction. Opened in 1903, the plant was once considered the most modern auto manufacturing facility in the world. Fifty-five years later, the complex officially closed in 1958, although other businesses continued to operate on the premises and use the plant for storage well into the late '80s and early 1990s.

Stepping up to the marble-framed door, the name PACKARD peered down on us, etched in stone. Around, all seemed silent, with the exception of a couple skater-types hanging out front smoking.

"Shall we?" I said, escorting Rain across the quiet threshold and into the darkened void.

We headed into a short hallway, completely crammed with impatient people waiting to gain admittance. Out of all the clubs I'd ever been to—gay, straight, or strip—none had ever been this run-down and gritty. I seriously worried that if somebody coughed, the entire building would collapse.

After standing in line for at least fifteen minutes, we presented our IDs to the beefy doorman and were permitted to enter the abyss. Next we stopped at an eight-foot card table, covered in postcards advertising other upcoming parties at various venues like 1515 Broadway and Majestic. There we presented a cute boy in a MADE IN DETROIT shirt with the tickets we'd recently purchased at Space Nineteen.

"Have fun." The guy grinned at me, a gesture that didn't go unnoticed by my date.

Rain took hold of my hand. "This way, Bradley darling," she said, taking me toward yet another door. This one was covered by a curtain and had a slit running up the center.

"Ladies first," I told Rain, parting the plastic folds for her.

We entered the large room from the rear. In the middle, the dance floor could be found, filled with a few hundred bodies all moving to the drum and bass beat. High above the crowd on an elevated platform, a DJ stood spinning records on a pair of turntables. Two enormous stacks of speakers, along with another set situated in each of the four the corners, created a complete wall of sound. Instantly I covered my ears, but the racket didn't seem to bother Rain. She threw her head back, extended her arms, and began twirling round and round, ecstatic.

Once she'd come to a stop, I shouted, "Can I get you a cocktail?"

She put an arm around me and leaned in closer. "Sure! The Smart Bar is up front."

Breathing in her fruity, woody fragrance, I replied, "What's the Smart Bar?"

"It's where you get the Smart Drinks."

"Oh."

I had no idea what a Smart Drink was, nor did I inquire. It was bad enough I'd never been to a rave before. I didn't want to appear even more like a square by asking too many stupid questions. I soon discovered that a Smart Drink was a non-alcoholic beverage, full of vitamins and minerals and all sorts of other yummy and good-for-you ingredients, according to the girl who sold me one—for a whopping five dollars—so, in theory, you could dance the night away and not wind up totally dehydrated. Apparently underground parties and alcohol consumption didn't mix well, and there wasn't a lick of booze on hand. So a Smart Drink became my only option for whetting my whistle, the flavor *du jour* being Orange Rave-tastic, which tasted exactly like Tang once I worked up the courage to take a sip.

Returning to Rain, I discovered her off to one side of the dance floor area, speaking with a guy who appeared vaguely familiar. She didn't bother introducing me to the black boy in the brightly colored clothing, right out of *In Living Color*. But I noticed him discretely slip her something, after which she reached into her purse and returned the gesture. It bothered me I couldn't remember where I'd seen the African-American young man. But the obsessive thoughts that filled my brain were soon replaced by other happier reflections.

"Open your mouth and close your eyes," Rain sang like a

child, "and you will get a sweet surprise." She held out a little blue candy, imprinted with a little yellow butterfly. I could've sworn I smelled black licorice, but the pill itself looked more like a Swee-Tart or a Smartie.

Without really thinking, I did as Rain had instructed. As she placed the pill on my tongue, I felt the bitterest sensation, as if Satan himself had taken a piss inside my mouth.

"Do not spit it out," she warned. "I paid ten dollars apiece for these." She popped her own little blue button and washed it down with a sip of Smart Drink, an action I immediately mimicked.

"What was that?!" I wailed, working my lips frantically in a vain attempt to remove any trace of the chemical taste.

"That, dear heart, was your first hit of E."

Talk about a punch in the gut. I couldn't believe I'd voluntarily allowed Rain DuBois to get me high—on Ecstasy. Sure, it wasn't as if she didn't mention there'd be drugs involved in our Sunday night outing, but... I'd been planning to pull a Nancy Reagan and "Just Say No" when the time had come to partake in whatever it was we were going to ingest.

"Now what?" I wondered, starting to feel a tad bit fearful.

"We dance!" Again Rain took my hand, and she led me through the sea of bodies to the center of the room.

I couldn't remember the last time I'd been under the influence of anything stronger than alcohol. Probably high school. And even back then, whenever I'd smoke pot with Bobby Russell, it would totally freak me out. My heart would start racing, and I'd worry I was going to drop dead for sure. More than once I had to call up Jack in the middle of the night and beg him to talk me down from the proverbial ledge. Being the most persnickety-persnick I'd ever met, he never let me hear the end of it. If Jack had known where I was, and what I'd just done... I didn't even want to think about the what-for he would've given me.

At first, nothing out of the ordinary occurred. Rain and I

wedged ourselves into an open pocket, near a quintet of girls who looked fresh from a United Colors of Benneton ad. They wore the exact same extra-extra large polo shirt, but in five different shades: red, green, gray, yellow, and blue. On their heads, they sported athletic visors, and their jeans were the baggiest I'd ever seen worn by a person. Dancing with wild abandon, they each waved a plastic stick, smearing day-glow streaks across the dark. Soon after, a tingling sensation crept into my lower limbs, like the butterflies I'd get in my belly before an important audition. But only from the waist down. Checking out the crowd around me, I realized that every person—man or woman, tall or short, thin or fat—looked super, super sexy. I couldn't exactly see anyone since my vision had begun to grow blurry, but... Nothing could stop me from strutting my stuff.

Suddenly my face started to stretch until I thought the skin would snap. But it didn't hurt. I felt sooo happy, I couldn't stop smiling; happier than I could ever remember being at any point—ever. *Joy, love, inner peace?* I didn't know how to label it. It was like basking in the presence of the Father almighty and feeling a love unconditional unlike no other. My mind raced back to a time when I was a little boy, when my mother was the most important person in my world, and simply having her in my life made me both safe and secure. I turned to Rain and she was smiling too, radiating a halo all around her. We were totally alive, totally in the moment, sharing it with these other totally beautiful people, without hesitation or worry or fear. And I wanted them all.

Whirling myself around, I focused on the first figure in my direct line of vision: another man, tall with thick dark hair. He had his shirt off. His torso glistened under the lights and the lasers cutting through the fog that had started to roll in. His back to me, I couldn't see his front, and I couldn't care less. I could totally tell he was totally hot, and I wanted him, more than I'd ever wanted anyone. Under normal circum-stances, I would've just stood there, willing him to turn around so he could watch me watching him. I would've waited for him to decide if he was interested. But the drug that raced through me was a wicked lady, and she ripped off the shackles that would typically prohibit me from fulfilling my fantasies.

I danced over to the sweaty, shirtless guy—not even stopping to worry what Rain might say—and I whipped him around, staring up into his deep brown eyes.

He gazed down at me and grinned, saying not a single word. With his big strong arms, he reached out and took hold of my face in his big strong hands, and he pressed his mouth to mine. His touch was electric, like a thousand tiny needles pricking me with pleasure. My lips parted, and I took in his tongue, biting and sucking and chewing hungrily. In my pants, I felt the most intense pleasure, as if I could climax from the simple pressing together of our pelvises. When he began kissing my neck and nuzzling my ear, I could no longer stand the sensation. I tossed my head back, screaming:

"*Oh, Brad!*"

For it was he, Brad Woodward, who had found me in a sea of strangers and who had reawakened the burning desire I'd been feeling, for as long as I could remember, for members of my own gender.

When I'd all but had an orgasm, puffing and panting, on the verge of hyperventilation, he said, "Let's go somewhere and fuck our brains out."

I took hold of his hand, about to escort him to the exit when I remembered: "What about Rain?"

Brad looked at me, lost.

I turned to the spot where I'd left her across the room, not five minutes ago.

She was gone.

20

EVERYBODY HURTS

♦　　　　　　　　♦　　　　　　　　♦

Rain, as it turned out, was the first one to hit the wall.

Evidently the shock of witnessing her current boyfriend making out with her ex was more than she could handle after taking a hit of an illegal substance. So she fled. All evening I agonized, riding out the devil-may-care effects of the E, over how I would apologize—if I could ever find her. Brad did his best to keep me from freaking out. In the heat of it, I honestly didn't care that Rain had caught Brad and I cramming our tongues down each other's throats, or that she'd stomped off into the dark recesses of a deserted building down in the ghetto, hopped up on drugs herself. Lord only knew the kind of trouble she'd find or who she'd hook up with. That E was some powerful shit, for damn sure!

One moment, I looked at my watch and it was just before midnight; the next it was well after three o'clock in the a.m. I'd spent the past few hours dancing my ass off, jumping up and down, acting like a jerk. I flitted about the floor on fire, talking to anyone who would listen and touching everyone who would let me. I had the most profound conversation with a kid in a plush *Cat in the Hat* hat whom I'd never set eyes on, centering on the impact Donkey Kong cereal had made on our childhoods. Meanwhile, I'd never even known there was such a thing, nor would my mother have allowed me or my sisters to eat the sugary stuff.

Ultimately being around Brad Woodward while I was, as he put it, *tripping* was about the worst idea ever. Not only did we end up mashing in the middle of the dance floor in front of Rain, once she'd disappeared, we found ourselves a quiet corner where we proceeded to rip each other's clothes off and have unadulterated, unbridled and, I'm ashamed to admit, unprotected sex. I realized I was playing a game of Russian Roulette by allowing Brad to fuck me without a condom. But the entire time he was, it felt so good I didn't want him to stop. I was invincible. I could conquer anything, so long as Brad and I were connected.

But the come down... Talk about being knocked on one's ass and thrown for a loop. Nobody had warned me of the adverse affects I would face once the effects of the drug began to fade. Suddenly I was totally exhausted. The slightest annoyance irritated me. My entire body ached, and I became totally depressed over what had happened with Rain, and with Brad, and with the fact that I'd allowed them both to so easily seduce me into doing so many different things I'd been adamantly opposed to up until this point. By the time the rave was over, I just wanted to be the hell out of that goddamn Packard Plant and safe at home, warm in Miss Peter's bed. Only I couldn't possibly drive back to Palmer Park—I mean Palmer *Woods*—by myself.

"Easy," Brad told me when I started ranting about how angry I was over the events that had transpired. "You're dehydrated. Drink some water."

"I don't want any damn water," I insisted, and yet I tore the plastic bottle from his grasp and glugged it down. "Why did you do this to me?"

"I didn't do a thing. You have your *girlfriend* to thank for scoring the E."

Holding my head in my hands, I slumped down to the floor and curled up in a ball—what my mother called the fetal position—and cried like a baby.

Brad crouched down beside me and rubbed my back. I don't know how he'd escaped feeling shitty like I did. Guess he'd gotten used to taking drugs and knew what kinds of preventative cautions he should employ.

"You're a mess," he said, running his fingers through my curly locks.

"That feels nice," I replied sleepily. And then I made yet another major mistake by telling him, "Take me home." There was no way I'd make it to school in the morning.

I don't know how the hell I even made it out to Brad's car; he may have very well carried me. And I have no memory whatsoever of the ride back to his studio on West Hancock. The next clear image I could recall was waking up on Monday afternoon, alone on Brad's futon, with my entire body throbbing in pain from all the dancing I'd done. I'd missed every one of my classes and, once again, I'd let Rain down by skipping out on our final *Les Liaisons* rehearsal, which we were presenting in front of Dina French and our classmates the following morning. Dragging myself out of bed, I picked up Brad's telephone and dialed Rain's number. I got the machine.

"Hey, guys," I said, hoping I didn't still sound high. "It's Bradley. Sorry about last night, Rain. And for missing our scene rehearsal. I'll be around campus later, if you wanna meet up before we go down to the Bonstelle tonight."

Of course I couldn't ask her to call me back, since I wasn't home at Miss Peter's house. And I couldn't let her know I'd stayed the night at Brad's apartment, so she should ring me there. For all I knew, he'd already run into her over at Old Main and rubbed it in her face. Just because Brad Woodward and I spent almost an entire night naked together, it didn't mean we were a couple again. Or did it?

That evening at *Chicago* rehearsal, I was given a reprieve. Rain never showed up and, according to Sarah, she didn't return to The Thelma on Sunday either, after our little trip to the Packard Plant. She also hadn't attended classes that morning and no one, in fact, had seen her. Immediately I panicked, fearing she'd accepted a ride home from the rave, and she'd been viciously raped and murdered and was now lying in a river or ditch someplace. Luckily we later realized she'd gone to her father's in Rochester, though none of us could figure out how she'd gotten all the way over there on her own, having been wasted and without transportation.

Tuesday, I woke up early, having returned to Miss Peter's in Palmer Woods, and gave Rain another ring. Secretly I hoped she wouldn't answer; that I'd either get a recording or Sarah or Columbus would pick up.

Columbus! I hadn't spoken to him since we last worked together at The Riviera the previous weekend. He'd been in a foul mood on Saturday, after being stiffed by a supposed-sugar daddy whom he liquored up, dragged into The Champagne Room and got a free blowjob from, before the guy took off without bothering to leave a tip. As fate would have it, unfortunately, I got exactly what I did not wish for.

"Hello?" said Rain coldly, as if she'd been expecting my call.

"Oh, hello!"

"Oh, it's you."

"Hey. I was hoping we could meet up this morning."

"Whatever for?" She acted like she had no idea why I was so desperate to see her, which actually had nothing to do with her, I'm sorry to say, and everything with our upcoming project.

"I thought we could rehearse before Dina's class."

"Rehearsal was yesterday. Somebody missed it."

"Did you not get my message? I left it on the machine."

"No, I got it."

"I said I was sorry."

"And I don't give a shit."

A plump gray squirrel scampered onto the ledge outside one of the glass, block-shaped windows surrounding Miss Peter's enormous living room. The rodent peered inside, scrutinizing me as I sat on the phone listening to the silence.

In its tiny hands, the furry creature held a tiny acorn that I imagined it had intended on squandering away for the upcoming winter. I wondered if by springtime the animal would even still be alive.

"I really don't wanna fight," I told Rain truthfully. "How are you?"

"Pissed."

"Don't be," I begged.

"*Where* are you?" she wanted to know.

"I'm at Peter's. In Palmer Park."

Palmer Woods!

"So you're not at Brad's?"

"No... Why would I be?"

"I don't know. You tell me."

Another awkward silence.

"I can be at Old Main in twenty minutes," I said. "We can run through our lines at least."

"No," she said softly. "I'd rather not see you just yet." Her tone was chilly. "Why don't you ask Brad to run lines with you?"

"Rain... Fine, I will."

"No, Bradley," she said suddenly. "Come to The Thelma!"

"No, I'm going to call Brad, like you suggested." There was a slight pause. I looked back at the window ledge. The stout squirrel had skipped away toward certain doom.

"Fine," she said.

I sighed. "Oh, Rain. I'll be right over."

"Forget it. I'm too vexed to see you right now."

Having never heard her use this word to describe her state, I teased, "Vexed?"

"Don't be cruel."

But I couldn't resist. "Don't quote Elvis."

She let out an exasperated huff. "I'll see you in class. Goodbye, Bradley."

Things were spinning out of control. I couldn't be sure if I wanted Rain to call things off, or if I'd wanted us to salvage the last remaining shards of our so-called relationship. "I'm leaving right now."

"Don't bother," she said. "I'm hanging up."

And she did.

When I called her back, the line was busy. So I dialed Brad's number, waking him.

"You do realize what time it is?" he asked rhetorically.

I told him what had just happened and asked if he could meet me for breakfast at Johnny's. He said that he would, gladly, except that he and Torrance Andrews were getting together to run through their scene from *Of Mice and Men*, which they were also presenting that very same morning.

"*Ça suffit*," I said, accepting the fact that, as the Vicomte de Valmont, I was going to have to wing it.

And wing it I did.

Granted, the assignment didn't end up being a total disaster, despite Rain's refusing to rehearse beforehand. But when it came time for Valmont to sweep Tourvel off her feet, flop her down on the *chaise* lounge, and deflower her, I completely lost my confidence. One of the most significant aspects of Acting we'd had drilled into us by Dina was the importance of concentration. Without it, an actor was at his weakest. Upon entering the room or the rehearsal hall (and especially the stage), we'd been taught to leave all baggage behind. Nothing from our personal lives was to enter the sacred space. All thoughts and feelings belonging to Bradley James Dayton were to be banished from my mind, for it was mine no longer; it belonged to the character I'd created. And on today, of all days, I just couldn't commit.

I'd gotten all the lines right, played the beats with the actions I'd chosen, but there had been nothing of substance behind anything I'd done during those brief ten minutes. I even broke the cardinal rule the moment we'd ended by breaking the fourth wall and stating "scene," which was something one might get away with as a freshman but not in your junior year.

"What are you doing?" Dina demanded, staring at me in confusion. "Mr. Dayton, are you feeling all right?"

"I'm fine," I lied.

"Well, this scene certainly is suffering. Shall we try it again from the top?"

Rain and I began over, and it didn't get any better. She wouldn't even look me in the eye this go-round. When it came time for us to kiss, forget it! Her lips may have been firmly pressed against mine, but there wasn't an ounce of passion between us.

"Stop!" Dina shouted, jumping to her feet and joining us in the playing space. "This is eighteenth century France. You're rich and wealthy and totally horny, okay? You, Bradley, are the biggest stud in all of Paris, and you, my dear Rain, are the most beautiful and sought after woman in the City of Lights. And in this moment, you're finally alone...and all you wanna do is fuck. Do you hear me?"

Rain and I both nodded. It seemed silly that we'd recently spent an entire week together, naked, and no matter how hard we tried, we couldn't capture that same intensity onstage. When I was making love to Rain in Miss Peter's bed—and on the living room floor, and in the upstairs bathtub, and on the kitchen table—I gave that girl the ride of her life.

This time, when I forced myself upon her, Dina threw her arms up and screamed out in absolute frustration. "Is that how you touch a woman?" Once again, she leapt up from her perch and lumbered over to us. "This is how you touch a woman!" Snatching Rain by the waist, she pulled her into a heated embrace. "You don't just put your hand on her thigh and leave it there," she continued, demonstrating as she straddled Rain and forcefully fondled her upper leg. "And when you kiss her, you *really* kiss her—no tongues." Quickly she turned her dark head toward the rest of the class. "If you're ever doing a kissing scene and somebody sticks their tongue in your mouth, you bite it off. Do you hear me?"

The peanut gallery giggled gleefully and jotted down the note.

Turning back to Rain, whom she still held suspended in her arms, Dina leaned down and laid the sloppiest kiss upon the girl's lips. From where I stood, watching in absolute awe, it looked to me like the ladies' tongues were totally entwined. But who was I to remind Dina French of her own rule?

The next night on the break at *Chicago* rehearsal, instead of using the toilet, I decided to be adventurous and ventured next door to the Sassy Cat with Ann Marie Tyson.

"I need to pick something up, real quick," she confessed as we hurried along, passing a cigarette back and forth between us. "From the gift shop."

I didn't dare ask what, exactly, she was looking for. But to be honest, I'd been wanting to take a peek inside the window of the gallery/performance space next door; the one Columbus had his heart set on purchasing for himself and Sarah.

When we arrived, we were greeted by a middle-aged bald man wearing a dirty wife-beater who worked the door. By the look of it, he'd had split pea soup for dinner, maybe lunch?

"Welcome to the Sassy Cat," he sang, his voice gravelly as if he'd swallowed broken glass, "where you can cold wax da booty!"

At first, he wasn't going to allow us inside unless we each forked over three dollars for what he called a (quote-unquote) browsing fee.

We told him to forget it, so he said, "Well, you two look like nice folks..." And he let us in free of charge, adding, "How's about a tour of the place?" I think he thought we were a couple.

Ann Marie turned to me, and I'm sure she could see I was totally terrified. I tried giving her the signal that we should get the hell out by shaking my head. But she persevered.

Before we knew what we were getting into, the bald guy in the stained wife-beater brought us inside through what I believe was the employee's entrance. Things were very dark. Off to the right, we could see the movie theatre. Well, we could see the seats and a movie playing onscreen, but I refused to look too close for fear of what we might witness. There may have also been one or two silhouettes belonging to the men who were actually watching the film. Since it was still early in the evening, the place wasn't exactly packed.

Directing us to the left, the bald guy said, "This here's our couple's room... C'mon in." He opened the door, taking it upon himself to point out that it locked from inside. He told us, "That's 'cause alotta folks out here would like to get in on the action... If you know what I mean."

Another porn movie played on a small screen hanging on one of the grimy walls. Several built-in benches lined the perimeter, but no other furniture existed inside the room, leading me to assume this was where all the actual so-called action actually took place.

Eeeewwww!

The bald guy also explained that a lot of couples like to come into that particular room to watch the movies, "And then they like to switch things up."

Thank God there was no one else in there at the time! I don't know what the hell we would've done. As much as I loved Ann Marie Tyson, I wasn't going to have sex with her. At this point, I felt super uncomfortable and wanted to leave. But Ann Marie seemed to find the whole experience hilarious. And the best part of the story? When the guy informed us we could stay and hang out in the couple's room—free of charge. We, of course, declined the offer.

By the time we got back to the Bonstelle, Amelia Morganti had already called places. The entire cast was now up onstage doing the Honey Rag, save for Ann Marie Tyson and me; and Hannah Weiss and Sarah Schwartz, who were both absent from rehearsal due to the Jewish holiday. As I'd

not known a single Semite up until I started at Wayne State
(with the exception of my 5th grade teacher, Mrs. Goldfeder), I hadn't yet understood the significance of Yom Kip-
pur, aka the Day of Atonement. Nor was I aware that, as the
holiest day of the year on the Jewish calendar, it featured a
twenty-five hour period of fasting, along with intense, all day
prayer. Basically both Sarah and Hannah got to skip classes
so they could spend the entire day in synagogue, where they
would repent for their sins and beg God for forgiveness,
while not eating a single morsel as they were doing it. I had
no idea how they both would survive without adequate nour-
ishment.

Because Sarah was away, Brad turned to me in his hour of
need. We'd not spent any real time together since our recent
rendez-vous on Sunday. I chalked his indifference toward me
up to my own against him. Did I still love him? Maybe. Was
I still attracted to him? Definitely. Still, I thought it best we
keep our distance. But when I discovered him emerging from
the Bonstelle lobby phone booth, red-faced and angry, I could
tell Brad was in trouble.

"Are you okay?" I asked, saying the only thing I could
think of.

"Oh, my God, Bradley!" he exclaimed, rushing to my side,
a sweaty mess. "I need a favor."

He was also in awful need of a fix, I figured.

"I wouldn't ask you," he went on, "but Sarah's not here,
and I want somebody to go with me."

"Go with you where?"

"I've gotta pick up some cash. Unless you can loan me
some."

"How much?"

"Two hundred, maybe? Two-fifty, if you can spare it."

I understood that, since he'd met me, Brad had been under
the impression I, too, had grown up wealthy. But even if I'd
had *one* hundred bucks—which I didn't—I couldn't have just

given it to him.

"Sorry, I'm flat broke," I apologized, adding, "till I get paid on Friday. What about asking your father?"

He scoffed, confessing, "I haven't spoken to him in years, the son of a bitch." Then, like a ray of hope, he wondered, "What about *your* parents?"

Oh, how I wished I could just call them up and ask for a handout! Poor Laura was poorer than I was, and there was no way on God's green earth that Jim Dayton would part with so much as a penny. Especially if he knew it was for his formerly gay son's former gay lover.

"Then will you come with me? Please," he pleaded.

How could I resist those beautiful brown eyes and that sexy smile with those luscious lips? Still, he hadn't yet revealed where, exactly, we were off to. Soon enough I'd find out.

Brad pulled his keys from his pocket to unlock his car. I could see his hands were visibly trembling. In fact, I'd noticed earlier when he and the girls were onstage rehearsing "All I Care About (Is Love)" that he looked a little jittery. My guess was he'd run out of drugs, but he'd also run out of money to buy more. Now he was experiencing early symptoms of withdrawal. As both a nicotine and caffeine addict, I couldn't imagine what life would be like if I couldn't smoke or drink coffee whenever I wanted.

"You can't drive," I told him. "Let me." I'd never been behind the wheel of a Mercedes-Benz. Compared to the piece of shit I'd been driving since 1987, it felt like pure heaven. "Where am I taking us?"

Brad slouched down into the genuine leather seat cushion. "Bloomfield Hills."

Heading up Woodward Avenue, we took a right on West Warren, passing by yet another Detroit institution I'd never once visited: the Science Center with its red-tiled, rounded exterior.

"Should I take the expressway?" I asked, assuming so.

Brad didn't answer, staring obliviously out the window into the dark toward Eastern Market.

After almost twenty miles, I figured we were getting close. But I still wasn't privy to our final destination. Glancing over at Brad in the bucket seat beside me, I could see that he did not look well. With his arms wrapped around himself, he sat rocking back and forth and muttering incoherently, clearly anxious about where we were heading.

"Do you need me to take you to a hospital?" I worried, not sure I could even find one. We'd missed the exit for Royal Oak Beaumont a few miles before.

"Just get me to my dad's, okay?" he begged. "He's got some money in the safe."

"Where does your dad live?" I asked, growing impatient. Other than the fact that Brad and his dad were estranged, I knew nothing about the man who had given life to the man I now loved. "Brad! You gotta give me some direction here. I'm not a mind reader."

Had I been, I would've immediately turned the Mercedes around and returned to Wayne State, where I would've tucked Brad into bed and crawled in beside him. The information about to reveal itself would forever change my life and drastically affect any chance that Brad and I might have for a happy future.

"Quarton and Woodward," he said, coming around.

From my recent expedition out to meet my new employer, Mr. Lombardi, I remembered that Quarton Road became 16 Mile, aka Big Beaver, in Troy, the suburb we'd been currently driving through.

"Wait, I thought you said Bloomfield Hills," I said, ten minutes later when we were crossing his family's namesake boulevard, Woodward Avenue, into Birmingham.

"This is the Bloomfield-Birmingham border," Brad confirmed, pointing out the windshield. "Take a left up here."

Without question, I obeyed his orders. But when we

came upon the placard announcing our arrival at the exquisite suburban estate, right then and there, I almost shat my pants.

Welcome to Cranbrook Gardens

There it was: two stories tall, white brick and wood-sided with peaked rooftops and meticulously trimmed hedges; the imposing chimney out front, at least twenty feet high and perfectly placed between the pair of black shuttered windows. Somewhere, on the impeccably manicured grounds, a quaint little guest cottage lay quietly, along with a luxurious swimming pool and a collection of exotic topiary. Perhaps I'd been wrong in my remembrance? But down to the tiniest detail, something told me the one thing I'd already realized, deep within... I'd been there before.

What gave it away, what caused it to be completely crystal? The set of luxury automobiles parked in the stone-paved driveway, one behind the other: a periwinkle classic Corvette and the brand new, bright orange Lamborghini.

At least this time I'm arriving in style, I sadly told myself.

"Your dad isn't home, is he?" I said, hoping the darkened house meant that Mr. Woodward was away on business. Or should I say, Mr. *Lombardi*?

For it was he, the proprietor of the seedy Detroit nightclub where I currently worked as a gay-for-pay go-go-dancer, who was also the owner of the lavish house I was about to enter for the second time in just over four weeks—the very home where the handsome man had had his way with me, sexually speaking, in almost every single room.

He was also the man whom Brad Woodward, born Salvatore Bradley Lombardi, had once called father.

21

WE GOT A LOVE THANG

◆　　　　　　　◆　　　　　　　◆

The fact that his dad was a closeted homosexual, coupled with the fact that his mom had taken her own life upon her learning of this fact, had fueled Brad's hatred for his father for almost a decade. It was also the reason, I'd come to realize, why Brad had been so ashamed to accept his own sexuality, and why he'd made it a point never to frequent gay bars, lest his father should find out. More than anything, he wanted to have nothing in common with Salvatore Lombardi, hence the decision to re-christen himself by his middle and mother's maiden names.

He borrowed five hundred dollars from his dad's safety deposit box, along with a nickel-plated cigarette lighter originally belonging to his grandpa.

"I'm keeping this," he told me, pocketing the antique trinket. "*Nonno* promised I could have it when I grew up."

It felt surreal being back inside Big Sal's mansion, seeing the various locations where Brad's father and I had had sexual relations. Of course I couldn't mention this discovery, though I almost gave myself away while Brad was digging through Lombardi's dresser and I excused myself to the bathroom without first asking where I might find it.

After Brad had finished collecting what he'd come for, we climbed back into his car and returned downtown. But we didn't head directly back to Studio Four on West Hancock. Instead he bade me to drive him to the city's southwest side to meet up with his drug dealer—the very same African-

American boy I'd seen being arrested out front of the library at the beginning of the school year, then again talking to Brad outside Old Main on the day I'd gone to the Ice Cream Company for coffee with Sarah, and then offering Ecstasy to Rain at the Packard Plant rave.

The house in which he resided, with its red brick exterior, expansive front porch, and detached garage, could've easily been considered a castle back in the glory days of early 20th century Detroit. But decades of economic downturn, coupled with a rising crime rate, had caused the home to fall into serious disrepair. Now almost all its window panes were broken and boarded, and the stately columns that once held up the awning had been replaced by rotting two-by-fours.

The drug dealer unlocked the door to greet us. Inside, I could see a brood of children sleeping on the bare floor. He couldn't have been more than twenty, but still I suspected these were his own kids and not his siblings.

"Who's the chump?" he asked, obviously annoyed that I'd been brought along.

Brad answered flatly, "A friend."

"I done told-ju befo', don't be bringin' nobody 'round here. How I know he ain't no cop?" He sized me up and down nervously, as if he were memorizing my face so he could find me if he needed to, to rub me out.

"I'm not a cop," I told him, failing to mention that my dad was, and that he and his fellow police offers might appreciate the tip-off I could give them, now that I knew where Brad's supplier lived.

"You gots da bills?" the drug boy demanded.

Brad pulled the cash from his pocket and counted it out.

"Not here!" the black boy cried. "Git yo' ass inside, mutha-fuckers."

No way in hell was I about to go willingly into the den off a known drug lord. "Just give him the money," I ordered Brad. "And give us what we've come for," I told the African-American young man, "so we can get the hell outta here."

"Wait," said the boy, and he slammed the door on us.

Brad and I stood beneath the broken porch light, shivering silently in the dark. While he didn't say it, I could tell he wasn't only tired, but he was also ashamed at my seeing him in such a desperate state. It pained me to watch him waste good money on throwing his life away, though I understood he had a serious problem. I wanted to help; to put my arm around his shoulder; to hold him close. But this was one of the most dangerous parts of Detroit, and we were two white guys. We'd be lucky somebody didn't shoot us just for being here, let alone touching each other.

The black boy returned. He presented Brad with a plastic baggie containing a few chunks of off-white-colored rocks resembling soap. Brad slipped the boy some money (I don't know how much), and we got back into the Mercedes Benz. Not a solitary word was said as I drove us back to the Bonstelle to pick up my car.

The following evening, we had our *Chicago* final dress before an invited audience culled from faculty and students of The Department. As excited as I should've been, I found myself simply going through the motions the entire performance. Fortunately everything went smoothly—at least until after we'd finished running through the show.

"May I speak with you, Bradley?" Rain popped her head into the second floor dressing room I shared with Torrance Andrews and Sage Ang.

I'd just finished hanging up my wardrobe and replacing my belongings in my muslin ditty bag. Marian Stockholm, who had designed our costumes, could be quite anal when it came to we student actors taking proper care of our personal props.

"Sure," I said, wondering what Rain could possibly have to say to me. It had been two days since we'd last talked, since our disaster of a *Les Liaisons Dangereuses* scene had been presented in Dina's class.

"Do you guys want us to leave?" asked Torrance, well aware that something odd had been going on between Rain and me all week.

"You're fine, Rance. Bradley, I'll meet you in the Bonstelle room," answered Rain. And like magic, she disappeared.

"God, I need a drink!" Sage groaned, throwing his head back dramatically.

"You and me both," I whole-heartedly concurred.

"Are you guys coming to Third's?" asked Torrance, as he and Sage started out.

"I would think so," I told them, though I wasn't sure what Rain DuBois had in store for me—or for us.

Since we'd taken to holding rehearsals onstage, I hadn't been up to the small room with its slick, polished wood floor and low-hanging ceiling. In less than twenty-four hours, the walls would be buzzing with season subscribers enjoying their Opening Night pre-show soft drinks and cocktails. But for now, the Bonstelle Room sat completely bare.

"Rain!" I called out as I entered and couldn't find her.

"Up here," came a reply from somewhere far off, yet still close by.

"Everybody went out for a drink. They're waiting for us."

"First I need to show you something."

"Where are you?"

"Follow the bread crumbs, Bradley."

Sure enough, when I glanced down at the ground, an actual trail of croutons dotted the floor, leading from the spot where I was standing over to a set of stairs I'd never noticed. Not sure what exactly I was getting myself into, I climbed the creaky steps.

At the top, I came upon a dim rectangular room with dusty wooden floorboards matching those of the mezzanine lobby, one level below. Due to the architectural structure of the theatre, the ceilings were unusually high. Dark moldings with gold detail trimmed the doorways, and a series of small arched windows rose up a good foot off the ground. All around, there were boxes and boxes filled with a sundry of miscellaneous theatrical odds and ends.

I reached for the old-fashioned light switch, about to push one of the two circular buttons, when Rain halted me with her voice. "Leave them off."

My eyes having finally adjusted, I could see her standing in the center of the room, dressed in her thrift store trench-coat. "What is this place?"

"Jessie Bonstelle's apartment," Rain replied.

I stepped further inside, asking in a state of astonishment, "You're kidding?"

"This is where she lived, the legend herself. If you look down there, you can see the stage." She indicated a small window, out which an antique spotlight had once been point-ed. "This was where she watched the plays she produced."

"How did you know about it?"

"Everyone knows." She gestured to her feet, where a lumpy, old mattress lay flat.

"Don't tell me..." I could only imagine the actions that went on in this secret room, along with the folks who'd per-formed them—and that Jessie's ghost had witnessed.

"Why do you think we're here?" She let the dark coat fall to the filthy floor, and she stood in front of me, wearing nothing but her birthday suit.

"Rain," I sighed, drawing closer to her. "We can't do this."

"Who's going to stop us?" She reached out to unbuckle my belt and unzip my pants, like a little girl unwrapping a special gift. They dropped to the ground around my loafers. "Ah," she said, thrilled at the outline of my erection in my underpants. "There he is."

Playfully she pushed me onto the mattress. I fell hard against my back, but it didn't hurt badly. With two hands, she tugged at the waistband of my BVDs, pulled them down past my hips, and mounted me.

"That's nice," she said, settling herself into position, wriggling a bit to get the fit just right.

I shook my head softly, unable to believe what was happening. Essentially I was being raped. But the softness of her skin against mine, the warmth as she wrapped herself tightly around me, was far too overwhelming, and it felt too goddamn good to ask her to stop.

In less than two minutes, it all came to a crashing conclusion—and it had started all over.

When we climbed back into Miss Peter's bed that night, again she was the one to initiate intimacy. Again she led, and I followed. But this time, I soon found myself on my hands and knees with Rain behind me—the way Brad Woodward had recently been. Contorting my body, I buried my face in the feather pillow. She said, in a strange, distinct voice that cut through the dark, she wanted to fuck me—the way Brad Woodward had done. Something primal stirred inside my being as she made this wish. I flipped over, breathing hard, and our love making came to an abrupt halt. Rain started to cry, and I wondered if she was sobbing because the thing she wanted had scared her, or because she would never be able to accomplish it. Or if it was because she realized she would never truly know me—the way Brad Woodward had.

"Another op'nin', another show..."

Since I'd begun doing Theatre during my sophomore year of high school, this classic lyric from the classic *Kiss Me, Kate* would consistently pop into my head on the night of every first performance.

Thankfully our *Chicago* opening went off without a hitch. As far as I could tell, no one had made any major mistakes, and both Will and Pia seemed pleased once we'd exited the stage after our final curtain call.

"Don't forget... Soirée *chez* Bradley's!" Traipsing around to each and every cast member's dressing room, Rain made sure they'd all seen the posted memo announcing the party she and I were throwing at Miss Peter's in Palmer Woods. It seemed that, again, we were an official item, and that she'd forgiven my momentary lapse into the world of gay sex at the groin of Brad Woodward. But considering he and I had barely been in contact since the night I helped him break into this father's house, steal an exorbitant amount of money, then drove him to score his drugs, I didn't suspect we'd be getting back together anytime soon. Part of me thought this entire situation totally sucked; another just wanted it to be all over. But what, exactly, did that entail?

The theme for the Turkel House soirée, as chosen by Rain DuBois, was a classic one: leather and lace. She appeared from the master bedroom, where she'd slept peacefully the previous evening after our sexual escapade in Jessie Bonstelle's apartment, poured into a black one-piece bodysuit. While it wasn't leather, the shiny spandex clung to her silhouette, suggesting an S & M dominatrix about to strike.

"Where did you pick that up?" I asked after I'd picked up my jaw.

"You like? It's an exact replica of the one Catwoman wears in *Batman Returns*."

I hadn't seen the box office blockbuster earlier that summer, but I was more than familiar with the outfit. "All you need now is the little black mask and cat ears," I teased.

She pulled them out from behind her back, put them on, and gave me a sultry *meow*.

For my ensemble, I wore a black leather motorcycle jacket I borrowed from Jack, sans shirt, and around my neck, a lacy *cravat* I'd gotten from the costume shop. Marian Stockholm made it a point not to loan items from her collection to students. But since I was one of her favorites, she willingly made an exception.

Our guests began arriving around eleven. Everyone looked super sexy in their various degrees of lace and/or leather. I don't think I'd ever seen so many men wearing women's lingerie and not been at a drag show. Sarah just about shocked me by appearing in the doorway of the Turkel House kitchen dressed in Rain's rubber bustier; the one I'd seen displayed on the dressing dummy the first time I'd entered her boudoir. Technically it didn't qualify as leather either, but the girl looked damned fine.

"Columbus would kill me if he saw me right now," she blushed, spinning around in a circle to show off the goods.

"Well, it's a lucky thing he's not here," I agreed.

Unfortunately Columbus couldn't get the night off from Club Riviera since I'd already requested it due to the *Chicago* opening. Honestly I couldn't afford to take time off myself, but I wasn't about to miss my first Bonstelle show cast party. Especially since I'd been elected to play co-host.

One of the evening's highlights included the passing around of a massive Blue Motorcycle cocktail. Rain's creation, she concocted the beverage in a giant brandy snifter that, I believe, was actually meant to hold a potted plant. The drink contained an entire fifth of vodka and at least as much blue curaçao. Later on, it was quite easy to tell who'd been partaking in the exotic libation by the color of their stained lips and tongues. I didn't even want to think about the morning when it came time to sit down on the toilet.

The other event of epic proportion involved our castmate Brett Pearson, the excellent tap dancer with the rubber ankles, dragging out the Sex Tree, which had been entrusted to him by his former roommate, Avery S. Thaddeus. A diagram, more or less, the infamous document had been handed down from one senior class to another and was an ancestral record of sorts, mapping out who in The Department had slept with whom over the course of the semesters.

"Lemme see that thing!" Rain barged into the kitchen, where a small group had gathered, and snatched the Sex Tree from Brett's hot little hands. Clearly she was worried (yet curious) to discover whether her own name would appear on one of the many crooked branches—and to whom she would find herself connected.

Peeking over her shoulder, I caught a glimpse of the chart and located the bough labeled RAIN DUBOIS. Linked to it, I read the obvious BRAD WOODWARD and WILL BILSON. But there were several other names I didn't recognize (STAN COSTELLO, DARREN STOKEY, SHANE SWENSON), and I soon realized that Rain's sexual history had been an even longer one than I'd initially anticipated.

Suddenly she screeched, "I never had sex with Dina French!"

Brett Pearson, busting out of the pale pink camisole belonging to his girlfriend, Wanda Freeman, calmly defended this bit of information. "That's not what we heard."

"Who's we?" snapped Rain, about to scratch Brett's beady eyes out with her Catwoman claws. At first, I thought she was just playing along but, beneath her mask, her face grew beet red, and it wasn't from the abundance of alcohol she'd been imbibing.

"I'm not at liberty to answer," answered Brett. "But the Sex Tree don't lie."

In tears, Rain stomped off into the living room, which had been designated as the official party dance floor. Somebody had been playing "Personal Jesus" on a loop for the past forty-five minutes, and it was starting to grate on my drunken nerves.

I contemplated going after her, but I decided to confront Brett first. "What was that all about?"

"I shouldn't say anything," he said, "but I'm hammered." He took a sip of his Jack and Coke, bicep bulging as he raised the rocks glass. "Rumor has it Rain DuBois only got into the Theatre program on account of she and Dina French were bumping nasties."

"When?" I wondered, having never heard tell of anything so salacious.

"Back when Rain was in high school, I guess," Brett shrugged. "She took private acting lessons with Dina."

"Sarah told me," I said. "So?"

"So, you know how them lesbians get. When they got carpet to munch..."

I didn't know what Brett was talking about, and I don't think he did either. Like he said, he was totally wasted. No one in their right mind believed any of the rumors that were tossed around The Department, like headlines out of the *Weekly World News.* Sure, it was fun to gossip about people behind their backs. But everybody knew gossip was just gossip. Wasn't it?

Taking another peek at the limbs of the Sex Tree, I noticed my name was nowhere to be located. Either Brett Pearson hadn't yet gotten wind of my intimate involvement with both Brad Woodward and Rain DuBois, or it would just be a matter of time until I'd had my own branch.

Later, well into the ever darker and deafening evening, I took a wrong turn at the top of the staircase, and I chanced upon the individual I was most hoping to avoid—and yet, most wanting to find.

"Brad?"

He was lying on top of Miss Peter's bed, shirtless and sound asleep. A pair of tight black leather pants hugged his meaty thighs, and my eye couldn't help but drift to the contour of his bulge beneath. A hardcover copy of a steamy Danielle Steele romance lay beside him. Perhaps he'd taken time out from a happening party to curl up with a trashy bestselling novel? I seriously doubted it.

I noticed a dusting of white powder on the book jacket and dabbed at it lightly. Touching fingertip to tongue, it tasted medicinal and metallic. It could've been cocaine or crack, but whatever it was, I realized immediately the reason why I hadn't seen Brad all night. He'd been up here in Miss Peter's bedroom getting high, and now he'd passed out. As angry as I was that he'd dare to bring drugs into the Turkel House (what if some neighbor filed a complaint over the noise level and the cops arrived?), he looked so innocent, so like an angel, sleeping. Reaching down, I couldn't resist touching the dark stubble on his olive cheek.

"What's he doing in here?" Startled, I turned to see Rain slouched against the doorjamb, so drunk she could barely stand in her high-heeled Catwoman boots. She'd removed her costume's mask, but the pointy ears still rested crookedly upon her covered head. "This is *my* room," she slurred, her volume louder than required for the short distance between us. "I want him the fuck out of here, Bradley. Now!"

I rushed to the door and slipped my arm around her, holding her up. "Brad's asleep," I said softly.

"I can see he's asleep," she said in full voice. "And I want him the fuck outta my house."

"This isn't The Thelma," I reminded her. "This is my friend Peter's place, remember? We're having a party."

"No, we're not," she said. "I told everybody to leave."

The music of Depeche Mode still blared from downstairs but, apparently, the Turkel House had indeed been vacated by this point.

"You kicked our guests out?" I asked angrily. "This soirée was your idea, Rain."

"I know," she said, suddenly trying to seduce me by stroking my bare chest and purring in my ear. "But I'm horny." She kissed my cheek with her blue curaçao lips. "Do nasty things to me, Bradley."

"I can't," I said, gripping her wrist, in no mood to play. "Brad's sleeping."

"So wake him up. Tell him to go home."

"He's unconscious, Rain. I just hope he hasn't OD'd."

Thankfully he hadn't. But Brad wasn't going anywhere. Not in his current condition. When I told her this, Rain was not the least bit pleased.

22

JUST ANOTHER DAY

♦   ♦   ♦

"Opie." Darkness. "Opie." Light. "Opie."

"Hello. Huh. Oh."

Filling the bedroom doorway in a flurry of stark sunlight, the silhouette of a slight man, arms akimbo, materialized. He lifted one black hand, and the bright rays whirred around it like the blades of a blender.

"God." I blinked my eyes and sat up on my elbow. My head felt as if it had been bashed in with a ball-peen hammer. "Good morning."

"Try afternoon," scoffed Miss Peter. "It's almost one o'clock." He nodded his head of big hair. "Who's your trick, and what's he doing in my bed?"

Glancing down at the pillow beside me, I smiled at a still-sleeping Brad Woodward. "I'll tell you downstairs," I whispered, not wanting to rouse him.

Lighting a cigarette, I put on a pot of coffee. Miss Peter joined me at the kitchen counter, and I filled her in on the past week's events—leaving out the part where I'd invited a girl to join me as my house guest; and also how I'd slept with said girl, multiple times. As far as gay men go, Peter Little was pure old school. Had I told him that after almost five years of accepting myself as a total fag, I'd changed my tune and now I liked women, he would've totally freaked out. And it wasn't as if I'd completely converted. At that very moment, the most gorgeous man I'd ever met was upstairs, sound asleep in the same bed I'd shared with said female.

Of course nothing sexual happened between Brad and me after Rain stormed out of the room and left us alone. I could've (and probably should've) crawled into one of the other beds in one of the other bedrooms, but... I'd told myself I didn't want to dirty another set of sheets when, in all honesty, I was just worried about Brad, and I wanted to keep my eye on him, just in case.

"So you had a hot date?" droned Miss Peter, pouring herself a hot cup of Folgers once it had finished brewing.

"Not exactly. It was Opening Night of our show, *Chicago*. I invited a few folks from the cast over. Hope you don't mind."

"You had a party here?" Miss Peter asked, astonished but not the least bit angry.

"I wouldn't call it a party," I lied. "More like a soirée."

"Well, I certainly wouldn't have known. The place is cleaner than a nun's knickers."

This statement I was surprised to hear. Not the one about the nun; Miss Peter was full of off-colored aphorisms. But I'd expected to come down in the morning and find the Turkel House in shambles, with empty beer bottles strewn about in each and every nook and cranny. Alas, the mess had somehow been straightened up and the home scoured from top to bottom. Nowhere were there any indications that anything debaucherous had transpired on the premises.

There was also no sign of Miss Rain DuBois when I went looking for her.

Brad woke around two o'clock. We had five hours until we were called for that evening's performance. I'd considered confronting him about the drugs he'd taken the night before. But with Miss Peter in the house, I decided it best not to bring it up. We showered and got dressed then drove to Royal Oak for lunch and to do some light shopping. The day was rather gray, and the smell of impending rain hung heavy in the atmosphere. Popping into Repeat the Beat on Washington, I discovered one of my favorite bands, The Sundays, had recently released a new CD. The dark brown cover featured the close-up face of a creepy kewpie doll, and I quickly snagged myself a copy and took it up to the front counter.

"Have you heard this yet?" the black guy working the register inquired, referring to my purchase. His name tag read ROGER. He was slightly chubby but charming, with a little goatee and tiny braids wound tightly all over. "It's really awesome."

"Is it?" I said, making polite conversation as I suspected he, too, was like me—a homo.

"Totally. Did you see them in concert?"

"No, I must've missed it. Where'd they play?"

"Nectarine."

Yep, he was totally gay. No straight man would be caught dead in the Ann Arbor nightspot. We bantered back and forth for a bit, me and Roger, until Brad had finished his used record browsing. He picked up a *Metro Times* from the rack by the door and showed me an ad for a movie that was playing at the Detroit Film Theatre called *The Crying Game.*

"Never heard of it," I confessed. "Who's in the cast?"

"Stephen Rea, Miranda Richardson, Forest Whitaker," read Brad. "I caught an interview with the director, Neil Jordan, on NPR. Supposedly it's got some shocking twist, he wouldn't say what."

Because I trusted Brad's opinion, I suggested, "We should go and see it."

"What about tomorrow after the matinée?"

As much as I fancied the concept of sitting alone in the dark beside Brad Woodward for two hours, I was going to have to pass. "My dad's coming to the show. We're having dinner."

"Well, that sucks!" he groaned, and I couldn't have agreed more.

I was almost positive Dad wouldn't approve of the production. Singing and dancing he'd always enjoyed, and classic musical comedies like *Oklahoma!* and *Hello, Dolly!* were among his all-time favorites. But back in high school when I played Doody in *Grease* during my senior year, he absolutely abhorred it and dubbed it far too anti-Christian. I could only imagine what he'd think of a show like *Chicago*, with its overt sexual themes and the racy costumes most of us in the cast wore throughout.

"Some other time?" said Brad, harkening back to the subject of the movie.

"Definitely."

On our return to the structure where we'd parked Brad's car, the sky decided to open and drop buckets of rain down upon us. Totally drenched, we had to drive all the way back to Detroit a soaking mess. We arrived at Brad's studio with less than an hour to both bathe and get over to the Bonstelle for our 7:00 p.m. call time. If we were even one second tardy, Amelia Morganti would be sure to make note of it in her handy stage manager's Bible. She'd also give us a lecture on how things worked in the theatrical real world, as if spending a summer at the Fort Peck Theatre in Fort Peck, Montana had taught her everything she'd ever need to know.

Brad took off his damp sweatshirt and slipped out of his soggy jeans. "I'll just be a sec." His wet hair hung across his dark eyes, making him look even sexier than he did when dry. "Unless you wanna save time and join me?"

I couldn't help but think it not the best idea to get naked around Brad Woodward, let alone share a shower with the boy, which is why I declined his generous offer. "I can wait."

But if that was the case, then how come the minute he stepped into the bathroom and closed the door behind him, I wished I wouldn't have been so wise?

After the Sunday matinée, as planned, I had dinner with my dad at a cute little café on Canfield called Traffic Jam & Snug. I especially enjoyed the hand-crafted beer I'd ordered to go with my fish and chips. But the highlight of the meal, by far, had to be dessert: double chocolate cheesecake, wrapped in coffee ice cream, coated with bittersweet hot fudge and sprinkled with ground espresso. Dubbed the Carlotta Chocolatta, as the menu declared, "Be still my beating heart!"

Dad hated *Chicago*, and for all the reasons I'd expected. He found all the performers talented—his son included—but he couldn't understand the incessant talk of sex or the need for so much bare skin. And during the onstage orgy, aka the Group Grope, Dad complained that he'd felt so uncomfortable, he had to cover his eyes. Talk about a tough crowd.

Monday morning, it was back to class, business as usual. With the musical now up and running, my schedule finally freed up a bit. For the first time in over a month, I had my evenings all to myself. I had no idea what I'd do to pass the time. I'd never been big on watching TV. Growing up, we rarely owned a set that worked; we certainly never had cable. But on Wednesday of that week, I got together with Jack and Kirk at Kirk's parents' house to check out a new show they'd been raving about, *Melrose Place*. Personally I couldn't see what all the fuss was. Sure, there were some hot guys on the program, particularly Grant Show who played bad boy Jake. But the one gay character, Matt, might as well have been a eunuch he was so asexual.

Thursday evening, we were called for a re-dress down at the Bonstelle. Both Will and Pia warned us that the president of the university, David Adamany, would be in attendance at tomorrow's performance, so we should strive to take rehearsal seriously. But without an audience, something seemed missing. Admittedly my mind had been elsewhere the entire run through. While Brad and I were once again copasetic, Rain still hadn't spoken to me since the Opening Night party, when Brad had passed out in what had been hers and my bed. I was beginning to grow tired of her games, and yet I didn't appreciate seeing her so upset.

Post-show on Friday night, after President Adamany dropped by backstage to sing his praises, again Brad invited me to hang out with him. Sadly I had to pass—again.

"I'm starting to think you don't like me," he pouted.

"I'm sorry," I said sincerely. "Duty calls."

It had been almost two weeks since I'd stepped inside the sleazy Club Riviera, and also since I'd seen my long-lost pal, Columbus. But when I arrived for my shift, I was surprisingly informed by my fellow dancers that Sexy Sid was no longer part of our pack.

"He didn't get fired, did he?" I feared.

"Hardly, Red," answered Rocky, slipping into his silk boxers. "He quit."

"You're kidding?" Last I'd heard, Columbus had been dead set on securing the final funding for his gallery space. In fact, he'd sworn he was willing to do anything in order to get it. There had to be more to the story, but who could I question?

"Maybe try Big Sal," Blackie suggested, pulling back his long dark hair into its signature pony tail. "I seen him talking to Sid last night. Looked pretty serious."

Of course I couldn't ask Mr. Lombardi. Never again would I be able to stare the man in the eye after what he and I had done together, now that I'd known he was Brad Woodward's dad. It appeared as if I'd have to wait and learn it from the source himself—if only I'd known where to find Columbus Howard.

"And now..." The booming voice of the DJ cut through the sweet-smelling fog as I climbed inside the see-through shower. With Sexy Sid out for good, it was up to Racy Red to get all wet and wild. "Put your hands together and get your dollars ready. Club Riviera presents our dirty boy of the evening..."

Stepping into the cool spot of blue, I began soaping myself up behind the clear Plexiglas. Thankfully I'd seen Columbus's routine on enough occasions that I could replicate it, move for move. Granted, I wasn't nearly as beefy, and I didn't have as much going on down below. But I was young and cute, and I could shake my booty with the best of 'em, so I had no problem pleasing my audience. Bending forward, I grabbed my ankles and offered my bubble to the mass of men alongside the stage. Slowly I slid down my swim trunks, revealing the skimpy red Speedo I wore underneath. From the dark, a firm hand reached out to fondle my right cheek before slipping a dollar into my waistband.

Standing upright, I turned forward to face my admirers, smiling slyly as I reached for the fluffy white towel hanging nearby. Appearing from the shower, I began drying myself, muscles flexing with each slow motion. Wrapping the wet terrycloth tightly around my hips, I scanned the room in search of the perfect victim to drag up onstage for a little rub-a-dub-dub rubdown—the way Sexy Sid had done to yours truly on the night we'd first met, eons ago.

And this was the instant I saw him, buried deep within (but towering well above) the rest of the throng.

Brad?

Right off, I could totally tell he was totally flying, from the glazed over gaze in his glassy brown eyes with their wide-open pupils, to the fact that when I approached and started speaking to him, he acted all edgy and angry.

"What are you doing here?" I shouted over the driving dance music that I was supposed to still be dancing to.

"I stopped by the Booby Trap. You weren't there..."

"That's because—"

He gave my bare shoulder a shove. "What the fuck, Bradley? You're a fucking stripper!"

"Let's go someplace and talk," I pleaded, trying to guide him toward the exit. But he wouldn't budge. He was far too coked up or cracked out to even listen to a word I was saying.

"I'm not stupid," he insisted, jerking away from my grasp. The force of his forearm as he yanked it back sent me flying into the mob of men, who acted as if they actually expected me to finish my performance. "I know what you did to get this job. And I know *who*."

Before I could get to my feet, before I could fully explain myself, Brad had disappeared, lost in the crowd.

Making a mad dash for the backstage dressing area, ignoring a slew of drunk guys attempting to cram their hard-earned cash down my Speedo, I quickly changed into my street clothes. As I sprinted across the club and out the side door, I heard Gary the bar manager bellow, "Red, you're fired!" But I couldn't be bothered to care about losing some stupid job. Yes, it was my only source of income, and I had no clue how I'd paid for college without it, but... My boyfriend needed me. He was totally pissed and totally high, and I didn't know where he was going. Or what he might possibly do once he finally got there.

He wasn't home when I arrived at Studio Four. He didn't answer when I called, hours later, and again first thing in the morning. He also never showed up at the Bonstelle for our Saturday evening performance of *Chicago*. No one had heard hide nor hair from him. Not Amelia the stage manager; not Will the director or Pia our choreographer; not even Sarah, his closest friend. She'd been staying with her family out in Oak Park in celebration of yet another Jewish holiday called Sukkot. I'd wanted to ask if she also knew what had happened to Columbus, and why he was no longer working at Club Riviera. Of course I could not.

Unfortunately I had more problems on my hands as a result of Brad Woodward going AWOL.

"You need to head upstairs and see Marian Stockholm," Amelia informed me as soon as I arrived at the theatre. "She's got all of Brad's costumes. She's taking them in for you."

"I'm playing Billy Flynn?" I asked, having almost totally forgotten I was the understudy.

Amelia patted me on the shoulder. "It's up to you to save the show. No pressure."

Under any other circumstances, it would've been the greatest moment of my acting career. Like Anne Baxter in *All About Eve*, I'd been dreaming of this since day one of rehearsal. But how could I bask in the glory when I was far too worried over what had happened to the poor guy I was replacing?

"Hold still," Marian muttered, pins in her mouth, as she measured my inseam. "If you ever wanna father children..."

Talk about a nightmare. All Brad's pants were at least six inches too long, and his shirts two sizes too big. I looked like a little boy playing dress up in his daddy's closet. Thankfully once Marian had finished working her magic, I appeared somewhat passable as a big time singing and dancing Chicago lawyer. Hopefully I'd be able to remember all Billy Flynn's lines, blocking, and choreography.

Sarah took hold of my hand before we went onstage and gave it a hard squeeze. "Break a leg!"

Waiting in the wings wearing Brad's white tuxedo, I could faintly smell his cool scent, still clinging to the costume. My eyes burned, and I closed them tightly to ward off any tears. Saying a silent prayer, I pleaded for God to get me through this—and for Him to keep Brad safe until I could hold him again in my arms.

The next two hours and twenty minutes whizzed by in a musical whirlwind. From the second I stepped into the spotlight and sang my first note, there was no turning back. Scene after scene, song after song, I acted my little heart out, and I danced up a hurricane. So what if my Chicago accent sounded more like Staten Island? Everyone knew I was the understudy; nobody stormed the box office demanding their money back. I'd been given the opportunity to prove my talents, and my future on the Bonstelle stage looked rosy and bright.

I had to find Brad so I could thank him.

Once I'd walked off the stage after taking my final bow, I picked up the nearest phone and dialed Brad's apartment. But still there was no answer. I contemplated calling Mr. Lombardi out in Bloomfield Hills, but I knew I'd need to explain how I'd known Brad was his son, Sal Junior. Desperate, I tried paging Columbus. Recently he'd gotten one of those silly beeper thingamabobs. I wasn't sure, exactly, how they operated. But I did what he'd told me and called his number then waited for the beep before punching in the number I was calling from. Hanging up, I waited for the phone to immediately ring, the way it had when I'd last "beeped" him. Only this time, nothing happened.

Digging into my pocket for another quarter, I dropped the coin in the slot and dialed my dad at home in Warren.

"Sorry to call so late," I apologized. "I'm down at the Bonstelle."

"Is everything all right, son?" asked Dad, alarmed. He sounded as if he'd been sleeping, even though it was barely eleven o'clock on a Saturday.

"Everything's fine," I lied. "I just wanted to tell you, tonight I went on as Billy Flynn. You know, the lead in the show? The lawyer."

"That's terrific, son."

"Thanks," I said. "Unfortunately I only got to 'cause the guy who usually plays the part never showed up at the theatre."

Suddenly my dad grew silent. "About that, son," he said. "I'm afraid I've got some bad news concerning your pal."

My heart sank to the pit of my stomach. I thought I was going to throw up. I'd imagined, maybe, with Dad being a cop, if anything bad had indeed happened to Brad, he would've known all about it. But when I'd made the call, I kept my fingers crossed I was just being paranoid.

It turned out I had every reason to be anxious.

According to Dad, a boy in his early twenties had been

discovered that evening, holed up at seedy motel on 8 Mile. For the previous twenty-four hours, he'd been smoking crack cocaine and drinking himself into oblivion. When the motel manager received complaints of loud music playing from inside one of the rooms, he went to check on the registered guest. There had been no answer, though the blaring noise continued. Concerned, the concierge let himself in with his passkey and found the boy alone. By the time Dad had arrived on the scene in his squad car, the boy was being taken away, unconscious, in an ambulance. Although he possessed no proper identification on his person, Dad instantly recognized the young man as the singing and dancing lawyer from his son's most recent school musical.

"Oh, my God!" I gasped, struggling to catch my breath as Dad relayed this information. "Where'd they take him?"

"Detroit Receiving. Down by Wayne State."

I knew right where the hospital was, around the corner and up the block from the Bonstelle. "I need to go and see Brad. Now."

"I'm afraid you can't, son," Dad told me. "Not till morning."

"But he's my—"

In as much pain as I was feeling, I couldn't bring myself to say the word boyfriend. Not with my Baptist, police officer father listening on the other end of the line.

23

END OF THE ROAD

◆   ◆   ◆

At the front desk of the trauma center, I gave the receptionist my name. I told her I was a classmate, a close friend, and I was very concerned. The fact that I'd even made an appearance was proof positive. I hated hospitals. They reminded me of sickness and death—and of the sick and the dying.

According to the tiny Asian woman sipping her Sunday morning cup of hot tea, Mr. Woodward was not accepting visitors. Not family; not friends; no one. Politely, as my mother had taught me, I thanked the woman, and I left. At two o'clock that afternoon, we had our final performance of *Chicago*. Again I'd be playing the part of Billy Flynn, providing I could keep my act together onstage. Once more I'd let down someone important. First Rain, now Brad.

Arriving at the Bonstelle, I bumped into Sarah inside the mint green Green Room. "Have you heard what happened?" I said softly, before sharing with her the entire story, the way I'd heard it directly from my dad.

Upstairs, I ran into Rain on the stairwell, just outside the makeup room. She looked amazing dressed in her opening number costume: a gold sequined, flapper-style skirt, complete with slinky fringe that barely covered her beautiful bare body beneath. A shiny red garter circled her shapely thigh, and a string of black pearls wrapped themselves around her lovely, long neck. For an instant, I flashed back to the last night we'd made love. It had only been a little over a week, but with all that had happened in the past ten days, it felt like a lifetime.

"Did you hear about Brad?" I asked, taking a seat beside her at the mirrored table.

"No," she replied, speaking more to her reflection than to me. "And I truthfully don't care to." Seeing her come off so callous was more than I could handle.

"He almost died last night," I informed Rain emphatically. And then I repeated the tragic story for the second time in less than twenty minutes. But it would definitely be the last I spoke of it on that Sunday afternoon. The details of what had happened to Brad Woodward (and of his horrible addiction) were nobody's business. The sole reason I'd revealed the information to both Sarah and Rain was because, like me, they both loved the guy.

After the few days I'd been subjected to, I needed a cigarette—bad. Taking a deep breath, I reminded myself of the Closing Night party being thrown later. There'd be plenty of opportunities to drown my sorrows in alcohol and tobacco.

"Maybe we should cancel," Sarah worried once I'd arrived at The Thelma, ready to drink up.

"Why should everybody else suffer," I decided, "just 'cause Brad did something stupid?" Pouring myself a stiff vodka-soda, I noticed someone missing from our usual entourage. "Where's Sid? I feel like I haven't seen him in like years."

"Me neither," Sarah sighed, sipping a neat Scotch. "He's been working extra hours at that bloody Booby Trap."

This was news to me, and it made me wonder how he'd actually been occupying his time. I still hadn't learned the real reason why Columbus had left The Riviera, or what kind of work he'd taken on in place of taking his clothes off for a bunch of horned-up gay guys. Soon enough I would find out the answer. And, like my uncovering the true identity of Brad Woodward's father, it would forever change my life.

It was just after supper on the 17th of October that Columbus Howard first considered the compromise. Until the offer had presented itself, not once had he contemplated the notion. Yes, on many occasions he'd had intimate encounters with other men, entertaining them at the club in exchange for their cold hard cash. But, deep within, he was an All-American, red-blooded, heterosexual male. He enjoyed the company of women, and most of all, he loved his lady, Sarah Gibson, née Schwartz. Still, he knew in his heart what must be done, if he were ever to truly make her happy.

Two nights prior, Columbus had made an appearance at Club Riviera, where he begged a meeting with his boss—in private. Being his favorite of all the dancer boys, Big Sal Lombardi extended the invitation for dinner and quiet conversation at his Bloomfield Hills estate on Saturday night. It had been years since Columbus set foot on the grounds of Cranbrook Gardens, yet he recalled clearly the distant summer evening on which he'd first come to feel the touch of another man. While he feared reliving the remembrance, he'd also accepted the fact: there was only one way to get what he really desired.

The millionaire, Lombardi, pledged the much-needed sum of ten thousand dollars to help fulfill the handsome photographer's dream—under the proviso that the millionaire be permitted to venture where no man had ever before, sexually speaking. It was a small price to pay, turning the other cheek, Columbus had decided when, following dessert, the proposition had been laid bare upon the table. After all, it was just fucking. Gay guys did it all the time, so surely there must've been some pleasure involved with the act. In a mere fifteen minutes, all would be finished. Lombardi would get exactly what he wanted, and so would he: his gallery and performance space.

When the men were through, he'd found himself in more pain than he'd ever imagined possible. Physically, he hadn't suffered. His pride and his principles had been bruised, but not his body. Columbus Howard was a strong man, and he took the beating Sal Lombardi had given him—along with the brown paper lunch bag containing a hundred pieces of crisp green paper, all bearing the image of our country's founding father Benjamin Franklin. But come the next morning, his conscience couldn't forgive what he'd allowed himself to do; what he'd allowed to be done to him; the pent up wrath he'd been carrying around could no longer be contained.

Sunday evening, he returned uninvited to the Bloomfield Hills mansion, under the pretense of looking for more money and, therefore, more action. Happy to oblige the handsome young stallion, Lombardi set his bodyguard free, the second time in two evenings, and prepared himself; only to be caught off-guard once his defenses (and his pants) were down, at which point Columbus proceeded to beat the man to death before escaping into the dark.

It took only a matter of minutes for word to get round of the Cranbrook Gardens killing; a security alarm tripped; a video tape reviewed of a muscular African-American male fleeing. Through the woods he crashed, having concealed his motorbike, envisioning the scene back at the estate: the shock of the policemen who'd discovered the bloody corpse, its features (and its genitals) mangled beyond recognition. Hitting the hard surface of the highway, he revved up his cycle and tore off in a blaze of black leather.

As he merged onto the boulevard, habitually swerving south, he became acutely aware that he had no concept of where he was heading. To muster up his courage, he'd drunk far too much liquor. The alcohol had abandoned him on his jaunt through the forest, but now the woozy feeling was back, and with all its bitterness. He contemplated pulling to the side of the road, but he realized that perhaps more than just the cops might be hot on his tail. Salvatore Lombardi was a well-made Mafioso. He possessed a posse comprised of the most dangerous men in all of Metro Detroit. If Columbus were to have any chance of survival after the crime he'd committed, he'd need to secure his own form of protection. This was when he thought of his friend, Bradley Dayton.

For some reason, Columbus came up with the crazy idea that I could do something to help him; that I might say something to someone (my policeman father, perhaps?) to take off some of the pressure. Then he remembered Sarah and that safe world they shared and wondered if he should take his chances and return to her at The Thelma. He raced past two cop cars cruising in the opposite direction, heard the far-away screech of tires as they retreated. The paper sack full of money still in his possession, he crossed the Rouge River, intent on shaking his hunters. Fifteen minutes later, he parked his Harley in an empty lot down in Berkley, behind a strip mall that hid him from the main drag. In the days of his youth, he would wait with his dad on a similar corner, watching the Dream Cruise cruise by down Woodward Avenue. He picked up the nearby payphone, pulled the last drop from his silver flask then fished a quarter from his jacket pocket.

"Columbus!"

"Red," he said, "you're just the dude I'm looking for."

I'd taken it upon myself to pick up the line when I'd heard it ringing off the hook in the background of the *Chicago* cast party. A drunken game of Celebrity had just gotten underway, and I couldn't bring myself to rack my brain and come up with a clever trio of famous names to add to the mix. Coincidentally I'd been thinking of Columbus and wondering if I'd ever see him again.

"What are you doing?" I said. "Where are you?"

"How quick can you get to Old Main?"

"Ten minutes... Five if I speed-walk. What's up?"

"I need protection," he said wryly.

"You're wasted," I worried. "You shouldn't be driving."

"Shit, Red, just get your ass over there. Pretend this is a movie and you're the star. It's your big scene."

"Are you in trouble?"

A nasally, pre-recorded voice cut through our conversation, indicating Columbus's time was running out.

"I'm coming to pick you—" There was a scratchy sound and a loud clunk, and we were disconnected.

I explained to Sarah, Rain, and the rest of the cast that I needed to step out momentarily, for some fresh air and a fresh pack of cigarettes. Arriving at Cass and West Warren, I waited a full ten minutes, alone on the corner, until Columbus finally appeared on his motorcycle.

"Good to see you," he said, raising the visor on his helmet. He grinned for all of a second behind his dark-framed glasses. "Get on."

I did as ordered, wrapped my arms around him and held on for dear life, all the while wondering about the brown paper bag he'd tucked inside his leather.

The roar of the engine, and the speed of the bike, and the desolation all around us were more thrilling, more genuine and personal than anything I'd sensed that autumn with either Brad or Rain. There was no reciprocal attraction to tarnish or intensify it. Only howling terror and my hands about Columbus's waist. We were just friends.

"Lombardi is dead," he declared, like it was no big deal. Then he informed me, shouting over his shoulder, of what exactly he'd been up to for the past twenty-four hours.

"You killed him?"

"In self defense."

I couldn't believe what I was hearing. My friend was a murderer; my boyfriend's father, his victim.

We arrived at The Cloud Maker, faint in the light of the streetlamps, and were on the verge of driving by when Columbus veered into the shadows alongside a shut up factory and turned off the motor. Ahead, we spotted an unmarked black sedan fresh out of *The Untouchables.*

"Let's just sit here a sec," he said, his attention focused on the mysterious car as it crept past us. The figure behind the wheel appeared both harmless and disinterested. Still, Columbus reached inside his jacket to check on the brown paper sack.

"What's with the lunch bag?" I wondered.

He gave it a shake. "You ever seen ten grand?"

I may have visibly blanched I was in such a state of shock. "Did you steal that from Big Sal?"

"I most certainly did not," he swore. "Guy gave it to me."

"And now he's dead."

"Good point." Hopping off the Harley, Columbus moved cautiously toward The Cloud Maker, blood money in tow. He unlocked the gate with his key, disappeared into the dark, then magically reappeared.

"What did you just do?"

"Relax, Red," he replied, a bit out of breath. "May The Cloud Maker watch over my future. Now listen up. I need you to make an important phone call." With one hand, he hoisted me off the back of the bike. With the other, he dug deep into his pocket and retrieved a couple quarters. "Take these," he told me. "Call your daddy, the Detroit cop, and tell him your friend needs a favor. He's been a bad boy. But he's willing to save his own ass by spilling the dirt on a certain Seven Mile gay strip club."

"What's my dad supposed to do?" I said, skeptical of this so-called plan. "It's not like he's Chief of Police."

"But he knows people." Columbus climbed back on the bike and jumped hard on the starter. The cycle sputtered and stalled.

"Where are you going?"

"To see Sarah," he answered, giving it another shot. This time, the engine roared to life and he rode away.

I made the mistake of trusting my father. After walking a good half a mile to find the nearest payphone, I finally got a hold of him. Relaying what I'd been ordered, I pleaded with him to please help my pal. Being a good Christian (as well as an officer of the law), Dad felt it his obligation to turn Columbus in. And so he made a call himself.

A couple of his Detroit cop buddies were on duty patrolling the Wayne State campus. In five minutes, they would arrive at The Thelma to pick up Columbus and bring him to the nearest DPD station. But when the police officers showed (the same pair I'd seen on my first trip to the DPL: the burly one with the mustache and the hunk with the meaty forearms), handcuffs ready to cart the culprit away, they'd not anticipated his resisting arrest or fleeing yet another scene, again on his Harley. In hot pursuit, they trailed after the muscular African-American man, a blur of black leather and chrome-plated silver, purely judging his guilt by the color of his skin. Through the streets of the Cultural District he led them, past the bronze replica of Rodin's *The Thinker* pensively perched on the steps of the DIA, in the direction of the one place where he knew he'd find sanctuary, all wrapped up in a brown paper lunch bag.

As I slowly strolled back, I heard the distant howl of sirens. For a split second, I thought I saw Columbus on his motorcycle racing toward The Cloud Maker. But by the time I'd reached the gated driveway, he was gone. Only the Harley remained, lying in a heap. In his haste, he must've dumped it and scaled the cyclone fence, disappearing into the dark of the opposite side. A pair of cop cars pulled up out front of the Greater Detroit Resource Recovery Facility, following after.

Crouching behind the red brick wall running the length of the road, I crossed my fingers that they wouldn't find him— or me, the not-so-innocent bystander.

"Somebody, please..." I whispered, my prayer drowned out by what sounded like the beating of an enormous flock of birds' wings. "Help."

Out of nowhere, the helicopter swept in and hovered, a shaft of light shining down from the cockpit like a sunbeam. A quick swing to the left located its target: Columbus Howard, a wanted man, sought after for premeditated murder.

From above, a metallic sounding voice called out an unintelligible order. Columbus stopped in his tracks, most likely from the horror of seeing the chopper hanging mid-air. Then he darted over to The Cloud Maker, still hunted by the haunting ray. I sprinted from my hiding place to assist him.

"Stay away!" warned the voice from on high.

Attempting to leap the fence, I was quickly apprehended by the hot cop with the nondescript hillbilly face; the one I'd fantasized about on more than one occasion since classes had started in September. With his meaty forearms, he took me into his custody and, had it not been that my new best friend was in some serious shit, I would've been thankful for the stud's attention.

Me and my cop continued observing the action at a distance. The spotlight captured Columbus climbing the concrete smokestack. Hand over hand, he gripped the iron rails, the brown paper bag still wedged in the crook of his arm.

I screamed out, "Get down!" But he kept on rising higher, like Icarus toward the scorching sun, each move bathed in a single beam, until he could ascend no further.

"Quiet," said the hot cop. "You think he can hear you?"

Columbus's captors had already hopped the fence and were right behind him when he reached The Cloud Maker's cap. I could see him, legs spread wide, his left hand blocking his eyes from the blinding light, while the right resolutely clutched the brown paper lunch sack.

A shot rang out. In the short flash before he lost his footing and came tumbling down, the searchlight caught him peculiarly. Casting a colossal silhouette against the flawless clouds, for a tiny instant, Columbus Howard flew higher than the wind-machine that taunted him. He emerged over the great furnace, over his good friend, and over the grand city of auto manufacturing. And the brown paper bag burst open, spewing forth a hundred pieces of crisp green paper, all bearing the image of our country's founding father Benjamin

Franklin, fluttering down like confetti.

As William Shakespeare once said, "Friendship is constant in all other things/Save in the office and affairs of love." I've often thought I loved both Columbus and Rain because they taught me something about myself. I know that behind Rain DuBois lies my ability to appreciate the beauty of a woman: her scent, her softness, her sex. From Columbus Howard, I take my ability to perform without fear, to command a stage with the utmost confidence. Alas, I see no sign of Brad Woodward in me. No manner, no maxim, no custom, or expression and, for a while, I questioned whether I ever truly loved him, or was it just plain infatuation? But as I've discovered over the years since leaving Detroit, as often as I might fall head over heels for a woman (love, cherish, send flowers), I've also learned the mark a man leaves—that Brad left—and it is far more satisfying to my soul. The last I heard, he'd checked himself out of the hospital and into a rehabilitation facility in Pontiac, after dropping out of the Acting program at Wayne State. I never saw him again, and he, Rain, and Sarah never learned my true identity. To them I would forever remain Bradley Dayton of Birmingham.

Columbus's funeral, I've been told, was an elegant and formal affair, attended by a flock of Michigan's finest, all friends of his entrepreneur father. Sarah, as expected, had been shocked to learn her lover's secret: that he'd come from one of the wealthiest and most connected families in all the Motor City. Former President Gerald Ford was among the celebrities to give speeches in honor of the deceased, along with Aretha Franklin, a distant cousin. Former Miss USA, Carole Anne-Marie Gist, unfortunately had to send her regrets, as did I. Like hospitals, I hated funerals even more, which is too bad really. I never got the chance to say goodbye.

For a while we continued to see each other, Rain, Sarah, and me. But without Brad or Columbus around to connect us, we sadly drifted apart. In retrospect, I think none of us knew what to say to the other, for words would not bring back either of our lost loved ones.

On a cool day in the fall of 1994, Sarah Gibson boarded a Greyhound bus and headed east to the Big Apple, with its bright lights of Broadway and twenty-four hour public transit system. In New York City, she continued pursuing her career as a professional performer and has since worked extensively in Theatre, Film, and TV as the go-to blind girl.

As a senior, Rain DuBois took to the Bonstelle stage in the title roles of both *Peter Pan* and *Cinderella*, along with Beatrice in the commedia del arte *Servant of Two Masters* at the Hilberry Studio. Post-WSU, she shot a low-budget horror film, featuring a 1970's B-movie star, called *Skeeters!* To my knowledge, she gave up acting soon thereafter and went on to find full-time employment as a product specialist for the Auto Show circuit.

My dad, I will never speak to again. He may not have fired the shot that killed my friend, but he made the call to the men who did. It also turned out that Dad had been one of the Detroit PD members who'd been kept in the back pocket of Salvatore Lombardi. His connection to Columbus's death was more than coincidental; it was payback for what Columbus had done in taking out the notorious mob boss. Once I learned this, how could I ever forgive my father?

When I think of that autumn—that tedious, silly, divine, grim autumn—it's as if in those short six weeks, I breathed, felt the touch of another, perceived the sounds around me, with greater passion and optimism. And I desired with greater conviction, trusted with a greater lack of restraint. The friends I'd made were superstars, besieged by a world full of gossip and slander; the spots where we played were soundstages and shrines. Without a doubt, none of these recollections are based in reality. They are the product of an overactive imagination that remembers the past, not as it truly unfolded, but how one wishes it would have.

ACKNOWLEDGMENTS

Sincere thanks to the following friends and fellow Detroiters, without whom this story would never have been told: Thad Avery, Craig Bentley, Mary Copenhagen, Grat Dalton, Andrew Fitch, Thomas Fitzpatrick, Donald Robert Fox, Kim Fox, Rhonda Furman, Suede Garret-Alan, Missy Gibson, Andrew Glaszek, Stephen Hurley, Sean Allan Krill, Wayne Laakko, Denise Lilly, Rachel Loiselle, Dinah Lynch, Scott Peerbolte, Nira Pullin, Amy Ricketts, Bonnie Russell, Pamela Sabaugh, Jan and Tony Schmitt, Michael Serapiglia, Wendy Shapero, Patrick Sharpe, Norman Silk, Kimberly Sparkle Stewart, Michael Swanson, Ed Teer, Adriel Thornton, Mary Ann Tighe-Redhage, Holly Walgreave-Gaverick, Kenneth M. Walsh, Christy Watson, and Bill Wilson.

ABOUT THE AUTHOR

♦   ♦   ♦

Frank Anthony Polito was born in Detroit. He received his BFA in Theatre from Wayne State University and his MFA in Dramatic Writing from Carnegie Mellon. He lives in Pleasant Ridge, Michigan, with his partner, Craig Bentley.

Made in United States
North Haven, CT
01 April 2023

34881823R00166